DANGEROUS CARGO

Paul Selkirk was used to carrying dangerous cargo on *The Eleanor*. Guns. Diamonds. Any goods that offered extra profit for peril. But Lady Caroline Watchbury represented a different form of danger.

Brutally he confronted her in her cabin.

"I've watched you rubbing up against my son, Charley, teasing him, making him wild with wanting you. Now I'm telling you, either give him what he's wanting, or stay away from him. The lad has never had a woman, and I won't have you playing cruel games with him."

Suddenly Lady Caroline began to laugh. When she caught her breath, she said, "You're a little late, Captain. I've just come from his cabin."

And this intoxicatingly sensual creature looked directly into Paul Selkirk's eyes, as if challenging him to see what she remembered—this woman who was still warm from his son's fiercely burning body and now so close to his own. . . .

THE SELKIRKS

Sensational SIGNET Bestsellers

The Selkirks

BY
EDEN HUGHES

A SIGNET BOOK
NEW AMERICAN LIBRARY
TIMES MIRROR

PUBLISHER'S NOTE

This novel is a work of fiction. Names, characters, places, and incidents are either the product of the author's imagination or are used fictitiously, and any resemblance to actual persons, living or dead, events, or locales is entirely coincidental.

COPYRIGHT © 1982 BY WILLIAM E. BUTTERWORTH

All rights reserved

SIGNET TRADEMARK REG. U.S. PAT. OFF. AND FOREIGN COUNTRIES
REGISTERED TRADEMARK—MARCA REGISTRADA
HECHO EN CHICAGO, U.S.A.

SIGNET, SIGNET CLASSICS, MENTOR, PLUME, MERIDIAN AND NAL BOOKS *are published by The New American Library, Inc., 1633 Broadway, New York, New York 10019*

FIRST PRINTING, MAY, 1982

1 2 3 4 5 6 7 8 9

PRINTED IN THE UNITED STATES OF AMERICA

Chapter One

1

Kolbe, Hesse-Kassel
May 7, 1769

The carriage bearing the Honorable Edgar Watchbury, a major in the Household Cavalry, and his wife, Lady Caroline, down the Post Road along the Lahn River was preceded by two horseman. One was Viscount Malvern, a seventeen-year-old lieutenant who had just joined the Household Cavalry and had been assigned, as part of his military education, to accompany Major Watchbury on this official visit to the Landgrave of Hesse-Kassel's Regiment of Light Foot. The other was Hauptmann Ritter Ernst von Kolbe, age thirty-eight, commander of the Cavalry Squadron of the Hessian Regiment of Light Foot.

The carriage was trailed by two more horsemen, Trooper Thomas Wood, age twenty-five, of the Household Cavalry, who was Major Watchbury's batman, and a trooper of the Cavalry Squadron who was serving as the Ritter von Kolbe's servant. He was also his son, although the ritter had not seen fit to identify him to Major Watchbury's party. Wilhelm Karl Philip von Kolbe was, at sixteen, six months younger than Lieutenant Viscount Malvern, and about that much older than Trooper William Harris, the viscount's batman, who was perched precariously and uncomfortably atop the carriage, between the luggage of the others.

Major Watchbury was thirty-eight, sixteen years older than his wife of six years. He was pudgy, but not quite stout. His legs drew the material of his tight cavalryman's breeches tighter still, and there was a bulge at his middle that even the built-in and quite uncomfortable girdle of his uniform did not manage to conceal completely. Major Watchbury's mustache, and what was left of his hair, had in recent months turned silver. Actually, there had been traces of silver for some years, but it was only recently that the major had abandoned the practice of coloring his hair and mustache. He was old enough, he had concluded, to be a silver-haired major, very possibly on the threshold of being a silver-haired lieutenant colonel. There had been reason to believe that His Majesty had plans for him not involving the Household Cavalry, that might well include a promotion. It was no longer necessary, in other words, to present to the world in general, and the Court in particular, a picture of youthfulness. Quite the reverse might well be the case. A certain aura of maturity might well be indicated.

Lady Caroline, her blonde hair concealed by a scarf, looked somewhat tired, the major thought. They seemed to have been traveling forever. It was a pity, he thought, that they had no children. If there had been children, it would have been all right to leave her behind in London. But he could not afford, especially right now, the gossip that would inevitably ensue about which young officer was comforting the major's childless young, wife while the major was on the Continent.

It was inevitable that, sooner or later, Caroline would take young officers as her lovers. But she had not done so so far, and the later it happened the better, for appearance's sake.

The Post Road, which paralleled the river, turned a bend, and came to the river. The coachman reined the four horses in near a ferry landing on the river bank. Major Watchbury pushed himself stiffly from the cushions of the carriage and put his head out the window. Then he pulled his head back in and turned to his wife.

"The ferry's on the other side of the river," he said. "Would you like to stretch your legs?"

She nodded and gave him a faint smile, and forced herself away from the corner of the carriage, where she had made herself as comfortable a place with loose pillows as possible. Major Watchbury unlatched the door and pushed it open. Viscount Malvern's batman climbed off the roof of the carriage in time to unfasten the step and lower it into place.

Major Watchbury got stiffly out of the carriage, then turned to offer his young wife his hand. She dabbed at her face with a handkerchief and looked at the handkerchief with distaste.

2

As she suspected, her perspiration had mixed with the dust of the road and formed a sort of mud.

She handed the handkerchief to the viscount's batman and asked him to wet it in the river. When he returned with it, she wrung it dry and mopped her face with it. She felt cleaner, and, more important, cool.

There came the sound of the horses' hooves, several horses, and at the canter. Like the others, Lady Caroline looked up the Post Road, in the direction they had traveled. Eight horsemen, in single file, were coming down the road. The lead horseman was naked to the waist, and Lady Caroline modestly averted her face. She retained, however, a clear mental picture of the half-naked young man. He was large, and swarthy-skinned, and wore his hair long. There hadn't been more than a brief moment to make the judgment, but she had seen that his mount was a good horse, an Arabian stallion, she thought. That was rather extraordinary, a peasant on a mount like that.

Then there was something else extraordinary: Hauptmann Ritter von Kolbe, their escort, spurred his horse into movement, and as the bare-chested rider reached them, touched the brim of his shining steel helmet in salute.

"What have you here, von Kolbe?" the bare-chested young man asked.

"Major Watchbury of the English Household Cavalry, Your Imperial Highness," von Kolbe replied.

Your Imperial Highness?

The bare-chested young man slid easily off the Arabian stallion and walked up to Edgar Watchbury.

"Alexei Androvich," he announced. "Colonel of the Saint Petersburg Regiment of Dragoons."

Major Watchbury, to Caroline's surprise, bowed his head and stood to attention.

"Your Imperial Highness," he said.

The bare-chested young man slapped him on the arm.

"Today, we are both simple cavalrymen," he said. "I heard you were coming. Your name?"

"Watchbury, Your Imperial Highness," Colonel Watchbury said. "May I present my wife? And Lieutenant Viscount Malvern, my aide?"

The viscount bowed, and the bow was acknowledged by another slap on the arm. Then the bare-chested young man

3

looked at Caroline. More specifically, Caroline thought, he looked at her bosom.

"Madame," he said, switching to French, "Je suis enchanté."

Caroline curtsied.

"Your Imperial Highness," she said.

"von Kolbe," the bare-chested young man said. "What are the plans for these people?"

"We are bound for my home, sir," Hauptmann Ritter von Kolbe replied. "Tomorrow Major Watchbury will be received by the landgrave and Colonel von Grieffenburg."

"Not tomorrow," the bare-chested young man said. "The landgrave and the colonel are off in Frankfurt am Main. Tomorrow, the major and the viscount, and you, von Kolbe, if you wish, will hunt with me. And tonight, the major and his lady and the viscount and yourself will dine with me."

"Your Imperial Highness is most gracious," von Kolbe said.

"Not at all," the bare-chested young man said. "I am bored with schoolteachers and tax collectors, and the company of cavalrymen will be pleasing to me." And then he looked down at Caroline's bosom again and added, "Not as pleasing, of course, madame, as your company."

The ferry, propelled by the flow of the stream, had made the near bank. As soon as it touched shore, the bare-chested young man, smiling at Caroline led his Arabian stallion aboard. The others in his party followed him. For the first time, Caroline examined the others closely. There were three other men in open-collared, sweat-stained shirts, whom she knew were not German, and two troopers of the Landgrave's Cavalry Squadron in uniform. On their horses were the carcasses of wild pigs. *Boars,* she corrected herself. The cavalry troopers also carried, somewhat awkwardly, four lances. She put this all together. His Imperial Highness, whoever he was, and his retainers, had been boar hunting.

She felt the bare-chested young man's eyes on her as the ferry moved slowly across the river. She looked at him, and met his eyes, and then looked modestly away. Imperial Highness or not, she thought, he had no manners, and he was actually rather crude and animal-like.

The party on the ferry mounted their horses as the ferry approached the far shore, and rode off the ferry as soon as it

4

touched the bank. The bare-chested young man waved at them and then spurred his stallion into a canter.

Hauptmann Ritter von Kolbe, only then, came to them.

"His Imperial Highness, the Grand Duke Alexei," he explained, "who has been turned over to the landgrave's protection while he is a student at the university in Marburg."

"I had been told he was here," Major Watchbury said, "but not the circumstances."

"If the landgrave were not detained," von Kolbe said drily, "I am sure that he would have planned activities for you, Major, that would have precluded your acceptance of His Imperial Highness's gracious invitation."

"By hunting," Major Watchbury said, "I presume he meant boar, taken with a lance?"

"Yes."

"That might be interesting," Major Watchbury said.

"It is to be hoped," von Kolbe said.

2

The home of Hauptmann Ritter von Kolbe appeared at first sight to be an outlying fortress on the approaches to Marburg an der Lahn. But as they came closer, Caroline saw that a two-story house had been built against the sheer stone block walls, and when they actually reached it, she saw that what had been an outlying fortress had (apparently over many years, as much as a century) been turned into a farm, and stable.

The old fortress itself, and God only knew how long it had been standing there, was now used as a stable and barn. The living quarters used one wall of the fortress for their rear wall; against it had been built comfortable and quite roomy accommodations for the Ritter von Kolbe, the windows of which looked down upon Marburg an der Lahn itself.

Baroness von Kolbe turned out to be a pleasant, simple, gracious woman, who immediately arranged for a bath for Lady Caroline. She came into the room the Watchburys were given on the first floor as Caroline was finishing dressing.

"My husband tells me you have encountered our naughty boy," she said.

"The grand duke?"

5

"It was unavoidable," the baroness said. "One of those things that happen."

"Why do you say 'naughty boy'?" Caroline asked.

"He's nineteen," the baroness said.

"He looks much older," Caroline said.

"He is much older," the baroness said. "The Russians, at least the Imperial family, are different from us."

"How so?"

"For one thing, they are Orthodox, not Protestant," the baroness said, significantly.

"Oh?" Caroline had no idea what she meant, but guessed correctly that it had something to do with morality.

"They believe, since god has made them the defenders of the faith," the baroness went on, "that they have a certain latitude in intercepting the commands of the church. A personal latitude, as it were."

"Meaning what?"

"Don't get too far from your husband, Lady Caroline, at dinner," the baroness warned, nodding her head for emphasis.

"We have gentlemen, *and* nobles, in England," Lady Caroline replied. "Who have certain ambitions a lady must deny. And I have learned how to handle them."

"I'm sure you have," the baroness said. "But on the other hand, as I said, the Russians, and this one in particular, are different."

"Men are men," Lady Caroline said. "I can handle this boy."

"I wish you good luck," the baroness said.

Caroline smiled, but she was honest enough to admit to herself that her virtue was based less on moral considerations than on the fact that she didn't seem to find the pleasure in physical relations with a man that other women professed to.

Lady Caroline, the third daughter of the marquess of Kelden, had of course had no say in her marriage. There had been a pro forma proposal, two weeks after she had turned sixteen, but before it came her father and mother had made it clear that Edgar Watchbury was the best prospect she could expect. He was likely to be named a lieutenant colonel, and possibly even eventually a colonel, and more important, he was a very well-off, if not actually wealthy, landowner. His proposal of marriage was not to be refused by a young woman who had little to bring to a marriage but her name and person.

6

Lady Caroline had gone to her wedding bed a virgin, and she had been a dutiful and faithful wife for six years. No one had told her about the physical side of marriage, and she had quickly come to believe that intercourse between the sexes consisted of the female permitting a sweating, grunting male to spend himself in her.

Edger wanted very little of that. When he did, she dutifully offered herself. It was her duty, and she recognized it as such. But the idea of offering herself to another man seemed rather absurd. If she didn't like it, why in the world should she take the risk it would entail? A relationship like that (and she had had many offers, some blunt and some more veiled) would have been entirely one-sided. The man would have relieved his bodily hungers, and she would not only have had to endure that but run the risk of discovery, scandal, pregnancy, and even disease.

Her attitude toward the whole subject permitted her to think of herself as a lady, and she found that rather nice. She frankly did not understand other women she knew in London, who hopped from bed to bed like so many rabbits.

When Caroline dressed, she selected a gown with a high neck and a rather loose-fitting bodice. The "naughty boy" would be given no enticement, no hint that Lady Caroline Watchbury was anything but a good wife.

She thought Edgar rather foolish to put on a dress uniform. The Grand Duke was liable to greet them dressed as he had been on the road. But Edgar told her that it was his duty, that it was more than a dinner, it was a semiofficial meeting between a senior officer of King George's Household Cavalry and the colonel of Tsar Nicholas's Saint Petersburg Regiment of Dragoons.

"I've been thinking about the protocol," Edgar said. "He wasn't just being polite when he introduced himself as such. It was the only way, colonel to major, so to speak, that a grand duke could have asked us to dinner. They don't recognize the aristocracy, you know, just the nobility."

Grand Duke Alexei and his entourage occupied a wing of the landgrave of Hesse-Kassel's palace in Marburg. As they approached the rather formidable and unattractive building, set against a granite mountain in the center of the small university town, Edgar told her that Marburg had once been an independent landgraviate, subsequently absorbed into the landgraviate of Hesse-Kassel. The landgrave occupied this palace only in name, maintaining his real residence at Kassel. But the palace here was a palace, and thus, according to protocol, suitable accommodation for a grand duke of the Russian Empire while he was attending Philip's University.

When she saw the Grand Duke, Caroline thought that Edgar had been right again, as he usually was. The Grand Duke Alexei was uniformed as Colonel of the Saint Petersburg Regiment of Dragoons, and so were three of his entourage.

He did not, she thought, look any more civilized. Despite the two layers of uniform, a high-collared shirt, and a tunic heavy with gold braid that now covered his chest, Lady Caroline still saw the grand duke as she had first seen him, his muscles rippling under an extraordinary amount of body hair, sweat plastering his hair to his chest and rising from his waistband. When she saw him now, she remembered that she had been able to smell him, the smell of a sweating male mingled with that of a sweating horse. Not unlike, she thought then, and now, as Edgar smelled after he had had his way with her.

The grand duke didn't smell of sweat now. He had probably bathed. From the way he smelled now, it was apparent that he had been drinking. The wine, Caroline was relieved to find, was French. It was, he said, for her and the baroness. Cavalrymen drank hard spirits. The hard spirits were French, too. Cognac, which he quickly pressed on Major Edgar Watchbury, Viscount Malvern, and the Ritter von Kolbe, splashing large amounts of it into heavy silver goblets.

There was, Lady Caroline thought, something very medieval about the dinner party. The room in which the grand duke received them was high-ceilinged, with exposed stone work and a floor of stone slabs on which carpets had been laid. The carcass, split lengthwise, of one of the boar she had seen that afternoon was being roasted in an enormous fireplace on a spit turned by a pair of sweating girls of about ten. Lady Caroline believed that food should be roasted in a kitchen, not in the dining room, but it made an interesting picture, and the aroma of the roasting boar made her mouth water.

She concluded that the roasting was being done for the guests' benefit, as a sort of entertainment, rather than for lack of adequate kitchen facilities. There was no evidence of any other cooking going on in the fireplace.

They were seated, their backs to the wall, on a bench at a long, wide table. The table was covered with a linen cloth, and places had been set for each diner. Each place was set with a china plate with a china bowl on it; a stag-handled knife and matching two-pronged fork; a large, round spoon, suggesting that soup would be on the menu; a gold salt cellar engraved with what Caroline presumed was the Imperial coat of arms; and two silver goblets, in addition to the ones the guests had been handed upon entering the room. There were four eight-candle candelabra, and for further lighting, there was a chandelier with perhaps fifty short, squat candles suspended from the high ceiling, and additional practical, rather than elegant, candle holders on the stone walls. The flickering lights cast interesting shadows on the walls and floor.

When they sat down, the grand duke and Edgar, as the host and guest of honor, sat in the center of the table. Lady Caroline sat next to the grand duke, and Baroness von Kolbe was seated beside Edgar. The Ritter von Kolbe was seated on Lady Caroline's right, and Viscount Malvern sat at the left of the baroness. The other places at the table were filled by Russians. There were no other women.

As soon as they were seated, the entertainment began. Three Russians appeared dressed in what was obviously their native dress: white, loose-fitting, flowing tunics drawn tight at the neck and the wrists, and equally billowing black trousers jammed into the tops of nearly knee-high soft black leather boots. They carried what looked to Lady Caroline like extraordinarily crude guitars. The bodies of the instruments, unlike the smoothly curved guitars with which she was familiar, were triangular. And there were only three strings.

"I hope you like music," the grand duke said to her, in French, as they came across the room.

"I fear, Your Imperial Highness," Lady Caroline replied, "that I don't know the instrument." What she really feared was that she was about to be subjected to an hour or more of wailing native music. She and Edgar had once been invited to an entertainment at the home of the duke of Bedford, and what she had looked forward to as an evening of elegance at the highest level had turned out to be two hours of an incredibly crowded drawing room, listening to the most astonishing, actually painful, sounds by an "orchestra" the duke had brought back from Bengal.

"They're called balalaikas," Grand Duke Alexei told her. "A peasant instrument. I'm very fond of them. I'm very fond of many things our peasants do, their music, their food. I've concluded that I have peasant blood."

She smiled at him, thinking that was an extraordinary thing for a member of the Imperial family to say, even in jest. And she had the even more astonishing feeling that he hadn't said that just to be clever.

As the peasant musicians began to play, Lady Caroline recalled that the serfs in Russia were not like English farm workers, but more like "natives" in their own country, with the Russian nobility and aristocracy and landowners regarding them as the English regarded the natives of India and Africa.

The music was a pleasant surprise. It was alternately sweetly sad and wildly joyous.

She felt a hand squeeze her upper leg and turned in shock to face the grand duke, a look of outrage on her face.

"In a while," he said, "we'll have dancers. I think you'll like that."

She jerked her leg away from the possessive grip of his hand, glowering at him as she did do. The grand duke smiled warmly at her, as if he both had expected her discomfiture and was amused, even pleased, by it.

The meal was served, first a bowl of thick potato soup, accompanied by chunks of nearly black bread, which the grand duke dipped into the soup and ate with obvious relish. He did not, she noticed, even pick up the spoon on the table before him.

His hand didn't reach for her leg again, but (possibly in innocence, she thought) his leg frequently brushed against hers.

The main course of the meal, when it was served, was delicious, despite the charred appearance of the roast boar meat. It was accompanied by roast potatoes, and cooked cabbage flavored with dill. And by a good deal of wine.

While they were eating that, a six-man chorus appeared and, accompanied by the balalaika players, sang doleful Russian folk songs in deep, reverberant voices. The grand duke's leg continued to brush, and sometimes press, Caroline's, although she moved as far away as she dared, fearing that if she moved any further they would encounter those of the Ritter von Kolbe and possibly give him an erroneous impression.

The singers were suddenly replaced by dancers, men and

10

women, who came rushing, leaping into the room, hands on their hips, kicking their legs high in time with the balalaika music, which was now the frenzied sound Lady Caroline associated with gypsies.

One at a time, the men performed an astonishing dance, squatting on their heels and kicking one leg and then the other straight out in front of them. She had just begun to wonder how they could do that without losing their balance when she felt the grand duke's hand on her leg again, six inches above her knee. His fingers, gently, began to stroke the muscles of her leg.

Desperate measures were called for, and Lady Caroline put her hand beneath the linen tablecloth and buried (or tried to) her fingernails in the back of the grand duke's hand. She heard him chuckle pleasantly deep in his throat and was furious that she hadn't been able to cause him pain.

And then he did something even more outrageous and unspeakable: he suddenly shifted his hand from her leg and caught her wrist, and with undeniable strength moved her hand to his middle. She felt faint for a moment; she had just decided that he must be crazy if he thought he could force her to lay her hand on his leg, and formed her fingers into a fist, when he made his real intention apparent. He had, incredibly, opened the fly of his breeches, and freed his erect organ. He pressed her balled fist against it.

She turned to face him, suddenly aware that she would have to deal with this outrage herself. Slapping his face or seeking Edgar's assistance would create a scene.

There was a pleading look on the grand duke's face and in his eyes.

"Please," he said.

Caroline, at once furious and desperate, had a surprising new thought. He was nothing more than a spoiled child. When she thought of that, she thought that there was probably no more-spoiled child in the world than a nineteen-year-old grand duke of the Russian Imperial family.

"If I do," she said, "will you behave?"

"Please," he repeated, as if it caused him pain to speak.

With a conscious will, she slowly opened her fist and then closed her fingers around him.

With enthusiastic shouts, the Russian dancers continued their leaping on the stone floor before the table. Lady Caroline glanced down the table and saw her husband leaning

11

forward over the table, resting his chin on his hand, as he watched in fascination.

She tried to take her hand from the grand duke. He grasped her wrist in his strong fingers and then began to move her hand up and down on him.

Then, suddenly, there was a sobbing groan in his throat, and a spasm passed through his body. It took Lady Margaret a moment to realize what had happened, for the incredibility of it to be overcome by the reality. Her hand was now free of his firm grip and she withdrew it, and wiped it on the linen tablecloth.

Had no one seen what had happened? Or heard his groan? Or had others heard it and pretended not to? Her heart was beating furiously, and she was sure that her face was flushed with what she was convinced was embarrassment.

Before them, the dancers continued their wild leaping. The grand duke leaned back against the wall. When he did so, Lady Caroline caught the movement in the corner of her eye, and stole a look.

The Grand Duke Alexei was smiling fondly, gratefully, at her. She snapped her head back to the front and pretended fascination with the dancers.

What she wanted to do was stand up and flee that moment. But she kept control of herself, and even forced herself to pick up her wine goblet and sip from it.

An animal, that's what he was. He had been right when he said he had peasant blood; his behavior proved that beyond question. The thing for her to do was remember that she was a lady and rise above this humiliating outrage.

She waited not only until the dancers had finally finished, but five minutes longer.

Then she stood up.

"Your Imperial Highness," she said, repeating what she had rehearsed mentally, "you must forgive me, but I fear that our travel has exhausted me."

She got a shocked look from Edgar. She had violated protocol. A party given by a Royal, or an Imperial, was over only when the Royal or the Imperial left the room. In England, her behavior would have been an inexcusable insult.

"Sir," Edgar said, leaning over the table to face the grand duke. "My wife has been ill. May I ask your indulgence that she be excused?"

"My dear Major," the grand duke replied, leaning over the

12

table to face Major Watchbury, "it is your indulgence I must beg. Not only have I held you here far too long, but in the pleasure of yours, and Lady Caroline's company, it quite slipped my mind that we hunt at first light."

Lady Caroline felt something brushing against the skirt of her gown, and almost as soon as she noticed it, she felt the grand duke's fingers on her calf. And then, even as she shifted her legs so that they pressed together, he moved his hand quickly upward, so that his fingers were running over the soft flesh of her upper legs. She wondered if the flush on her face was evident to any of the others.

And then he took his hand away and rose to his feet. He turned and took her hand and kissed it.

"Your presence, madame," he said, "has been a joy."

She made a crude curtsy, and when he had let go of her hand, stepped past the Ritter von Kolbe and walked to the end of the table. Edgar came around the other end of the table and took her hand. He bowed to the grand duke as Caroline curtsied again.

"First light, right, von Kolbe?" the grand duke asked.

"First light, sir," von Kolbe replied.

As soon as they were back in their rooms at the von Kolbe residence, and Edgar had closed the door after him, it all began to spill out of her.

"He's a disgusting animal!" she said, almost a hiss.

He looked at her without speaking.

"That Russian!" she explained.

"I rather enjoyed myself," he said.

"He touched me," Lady Caroline said. "He kept touching me."

"I'm sure," Major Edgar Watchbury said, after a moment, "that you are putting an unfortunate meaning where there is no reason."

Lady Caroline stopped herself just before correcting him with a detailed recitation of what had happened. She realized that if she told him what had happened, he would, as a gentleman, be forced to do something about it. It was absurd that a member of the Russian Imperial family be challenged to a duel by anyone, and even more absurd to consider that Edgar would, in any case, be able to do anything about it but get himself killed. Or humiliated. Nothing could be done about what had happened. It was better simply to put it from her mind. She felt quite proud of that mature decision. She would put the incident behind her and not even think about it. All she would have to do was keep her distance from the grand duke as long as they were here.

Certainly, she thought, she would be able to do that. As bold as he was, she doubted that he would, should they be with him again, chase her around a room. And it was entirely possible that they would not see him again, anyway.

When they were in bed, beneath a huge, billowing, feather-filled cover, she thought about that again. He had gotten what he wanted from her, a moment's masculine pleasure. Why should he want to see her again?

And she thought again that he was an animal, who had done *that* with so little actual contact between them. It proved that he was an animal, little better than a rooster, getting his satisfaction as quickly and with as little meaning.

And then she had a final thought, just before she dropped off to sleep, one that was somehow flattering: it was possible, she thought, that he had been so taken with her as a woman, so excited by her, that the simple touch of her hand had produced the reaction it had. Certainly, he had been on the edge of *that* when he had forced her hand on him. Edgar had never been that hard. Or large.

3

Lady Caroline had been dimly aware that Trooper Wood, Edgar's batman, had knocked at their door very early in the morning, and had helped Edgar dress in the flickering light of a candle, and that they had gone. She had heard, before going back to sleep, the sound of their horses' hooves riding off.

The snorting and whinnying of a horse woke her again, and she sat up in bed, afraid that she had slept much longer than she had intended to sleep, and that Edgar, the hunt over, was already returning. She got out of bed and walked across the chilly stone floor to the window. If Edgar had returned, she would see the horses. If not, in any event, she would be able to estimate the time by the sun.

She unfastened the window latch and peered out.

It was a hunter returned from the hunt all right, but it was not Major Edgar Watchbury. It was His Imperial Highness, the Grand Duke Alexei, dressed much as he had been the first time she had seen him, except that he was now wearing a flowing Russian peasant shirt. And he was alone. And he

14

saw her, and turned his horse with his knee from where he had planned to tie him on the rail before the door, and walked him toward Caroline's window.

She quickly closed it, and latched it, and stepped away from the window, resting her back against the wall beside it, so that if he looked into the room (and, she thought, he was quite capable of that) he would think she had fled.

She knew that he had dismounted and was looking into the window when his body broke the streams of early morning sunlight.

He will see the room is empty, she decided, and go away. Or at least, go into the house proper, where I will have the protection of the baroness and her servants.

There was the sound of shattering glass, and shards flew inward onto the stone. And them the sound of the latch being opened. And then he was in the room.

He looked at her appreciatively, smiling conspiratorially. She put her hands to cover the private parts of her body that might be more visible than she liked through her light cotton gown.

"How dare you?" she asked.

"You knew I was coming," he said. "You knew I had to come."

"I'm a married woman," she said. "Doesn't that mean anything to you?"

"He's old, and we're young," the grand duke said.

Damn him, she thought.

"Please leave," she said, with as much dignity as she could muster.

He chuckled.

"My husband may return any moment," she said.

"I have arranged it so that he won't" the grand duke said.

"I'll shout for the servants," she said.

"Oh, stop it," he said. "I am tiring of you. I no longer find this amusing."

She opened her mouth and began to scream.

He slapped her, as hard as she could ever remember being slapped, with the back of his hand, cutting off the scream.

She took her hand from in front of her bosom and put it to her face and looked at him with loathing. He reached out and grabbed the bodice of her nightgown and ripped it down the front.

"I thought you would have nipples like that," he said.

15

She swung at him. He caught her wrist, and turned her around, and ripped the gown off her. Then he picked her up under the arms and carried her to the bed and threw her down on it, on her back. She covered her mouth with her hand and looked up at him in terror.

He stood looking down at her as he effortlessly pulled off his soft black leather boots, and then dropped his trousers. When he pulled the peasant blouse over his head, she stole a glance at his naked body, and then closed her eyes.

She was going to be raped. There was nothing she could do about it. She decided that it would be no worse than it was with Edgar. She would lie there and he would move on her, and sweat, and groan, and that would be the end of of it. She could only pray that he would not make her with child.

She felt the bed sag, and felt his warm breath on her chest, and stiffened her body in anticipation of the touch of his mouth. She wondered if he would hurt her.

He kissed her eyelids very gently, and told her she was the most beautiful woman he had ever seen.

Startled (Edgar had never kissed her eyelids), she opened her eyes and found him looking down at her. He has beautiful eyes, she thought.

"Please," she said, almost a whisper.

"Ssssh," he said, and kissed her forehead.

"Please, Alexei," she repeated.

And then his hand was on her bosom, very lightly, very gently, caressing it as if he were afraid it would disappear beneath his fingers.

His hand moved from her bosom to her stomach. She had a very strange feeling. She decided that the best thing to do under the circumstances was get this mating over with. Then, certainly, he would leave her alone and she would have time to think it all over, to decide what she must do about it.

"All right," she said. "If you must, go ahead."

He chuckled again deep in his throat, and spread her legs and crawled between them. Then he bent and kissed her nipple.

"If you insist on violating me," Lady Caroline said, "do it and get it over with."

He responded by taking her hand and forcing it between them, and placing it on his organ. She removed her hand as soon as it was free. He shrugged, and resumed nibbling at her nipple.

16

She realized that if he was going to do it, he expected her to be the guide. Damn him, she thought, and reached for him. He was larger and harder, she thought, than a moment before. And larger and harder than Edgar had ever been. And then he was inside her.

And moving. Slowly. *Exquisitely* slowly.

And something was happening to her. Her body seemed to have a mind of its own. She had firmly intended to lie immobile until he had his way with her, but her body was now moving against him.

And then her body began to shudder.

"Oh, my God!" she heard herself saying. And then, "Yes, yes, yes."

And then, before she stopped thinking about anything, she was dimly aware that she was screaming.

4

Major Edgar Watchbury returned to the residence of the Ritter von Kolbe just before noon.

It had been a good hunt, he reported, damned good sport, nothing like it at all in England. But the important news, news that he was sure Caroline would welcome, was that a rider had brought a message from the landgrave of Hesse-Kassel. He and Colonel von Grieffenburg were returning from Frankfurt am Main via Braunfels. There was a detachment of the Cavalry Squadron of the Regiment of Light Foot at Braunfels, and Major Watchbury had been invited to inspect it and see it at its maneuvers.

"There is no point in you going along, Caroline," Edgar said. "I'll only be gone tomorrow or certainly no more than tomorrow and the next day. You'll have that time to rest. There will be an official banquet here when we return. You'll want to look your best for that."

"Will Malvern be going with you?" Caroline asked.

"Yes, of course," Edgar said.

"And the Russian?"

"Oh, no. He sent his regrets."

He knows, Caroline understood surely. He knows and he doesn't care. It is more than that. He knows and is pleased. He has turned me over to the Russian precisely as a Cheapside whoremonger turns his girls over to a client.

The only difference, she thought, is that unlike the Cheapside tarts, I look forward to the assignation. I was very, very afraid that Alexei would be riding off to wherever he's going with him.

I suppose, she thought, that makes me a whore.

So be it. I have never felt that way before, and I have been thinking of nothing but Alexei since he left my bed and crawled back out of the window. And now I will have him all night.

"When are you leaving?" she asked.

"As soon as I change. Wood is changing our mounts."

All afternoon, Lady Caroline thought, *and* all night, and God willing, tomorrow, too.

Chapter Two

1

Tatta, Hyderabad
May 9, 1769

Able Seaman Charles Selkirk stood on the deck of the anchor locker of *The Eleanor*, looking out the hawsehole down at the muddy yellow, waters of the Indus River swirling below. Charley Selkirk was tall and well developed for his nineteen years. He wore his sun-bleached hair gathered behind his neck. He was bare-chested, barefooted, and wearing only a frayed pair of baggy canvas trousers held up by a length of line tied around his waist.

His large, calloused, but still somehow graceful fingers rested on the handle of a large, two-bladed forester's axe, the head of which lay on the deck. Sweat ran down his face and chest and legs.

He heard the command before he should have, that is, before it was bellowed through a speaker horn on the quarterdeck for relay down the main deck to him, and before it was actually relayed to him.

"Let loose the for'd port anchor!" the bosun bellowed.

Charley got a good grip on the axe handle before he started to lift it from the deck.

"Let loose the for'd port anchor!" the order was relayed.

Charley moved to the block of wood across which was stretched the line he would sever, and raised the axe over his head.

"Let loose the for'd anchor!" The order was relayed a final time from the foredeck over him.

Even as he slashed down with all his strength with the axe, he heard the bosun bellow the next, anticipated, command: "Let loose the for'd starboard anchor!"

19

The taut hemp line split under the axe, and the anchor, dragging its chain behind it, dropped like a stone into the yellow waters of the Indus. Charley Selkirk grunted as he freed the axe head from the block of wood. He raised it over his head again, and swung again. The starboard anchor dropped into the Indus.

A moment later, the port anchor chain began to draw taut, as the anchor began to hold *The Eleanor* against the current of the Indus, and a moment after that, the links of the starboard anchor chain aligned themselves and grew rigid.

Looking more than a little pleased with himself, Charley Selkirk tapped the taut chain with the side of his axe, got a satisfying dull metal clunk, then stowed the axe on the bulkhead and hoisted himself through the hatch on the locker overhead.

It had been hotter than Hades in the anchor locker, and even the warm, moist wind coming down the Indus was a welcome relief. He stepped to a sweet-water barrel, drank deeply from a dipper. Then, deciding that since they had made land and limitless sweet water the strict water conservation rules were no longer in force, three times poured a dipper of sweet water over his head.

There was a sharp whistle—as if I'm a dog, Charley thought with the anger that always came—and he located its source, Bosun Theo LaSalle. LaSalle, scowling, jerked his thumb toward the quarterdeck.

"Lively," Bosun LaSalle snarled.

LaSalle believed that only seamen with business on the quarterdeck should be on the quarterdeck, and in Theo LaSalle's black-and-white view of the world, and shipboard discipline, there was no room for an exception, even in the case of an able seaman whose father was the owner and master.

Charley Selkirk trotted down the deck and up the ladder to the quarterdeck. He went to Mr. Porter, *The Eleanor*'s first mate, and knuckled his forehead. Mr. Porter inclined his head toward Captain Paul Selkirk, and Charley went and tugged at his forelock before his father.

When Paul Selkirk had seen his son hoist himself effortlessly and gracefully through the anchor locker hatch onto the deck, and then pour the dippers of drinking water over his sweat-soaked body, a not inconsiderable wave of parental pride had swept through him. Charley was a well-set-up lad, there was no doubt of that, or doubt that by the time he turned twenty, or maybe even before, he would be larger than his father. And he was a seaman, there was no question about that either.

"I don't seem to recall," Paul Selkirk said to his son, "giving permission for sweet-water bathing."

Charley was surprised, his father saw, but not crushed by the accusation, nor afraid of the punishment he felt sure would follow.

"No excuse, sir, Charley said.

"On the other hand, in the absence of orders to the contrary, when at anchor . . ." Captain Selkirk said, reasonably.

"No excuse, sir," Charley interrupted him.

His father looked at him coldly, inwardly pleased that Charley had not leapt at the excuse offered.

"Presume nothing, Charley," Captain Selkirk said. "Not as long as you're in the fo'c'sl."

"Aye, aye, sir."

"We'll let it pass," Captain Selkirk said, and handed Charley his glass. The brass-cased telescope was twelve inches long collapsed, and more than twice that long when extended. "Tatta is over there," Captain Selkirk said.

Charley put the glass to his eye, extended the tube, and examined the Indian town.

"See anything unusual?" Captain Selkirk asked, idly.

"No, sir," Charley confessed.

"Can you make out a building that looks English? Something the English would call 'Government House'?" his father pursued.

Charley picked out the one building, the large, two-storied somehow official-looking structure that could be Government House, and then confirmed his decision when he saw a flag pole before it.

"Yes, sir. A two-floored brick affair."

"You see anything unusual about it?"

Charley studied it a long time before he confessed that he could not.

"You didn't miss King George's flag?" Captain Selkirk asked.

Damn, Charley thought.

"Not until you pointed it out to me, sir," Charley confessed.

21

"What would you guess that means?" Captain Selkirk said.

Charley thought that over before replying.

"There's no British officer in residence?" he asked, finally.

"There *may* be no Englishman here," Captain Selkirk said.
"If there's not, things may go more smoothly than otherwise."

"Yes, sir," Charley said.

"The reason I was concerned with your sweet-water bath,
Charley," Captain Selkirk said, "is that we won't be able to
take on sweet water until we go ashore. And we'll not send
anyone ashore until someone comes out here first. You understand?"

"Yes, sir," Charley said.

"I don't think three dips of sweet water will cause us all to
die of thirst," Captain Selkirk said. "But there's a principle
involved."

"I'm sorry," Charley said.

"Carry a message to the bosun to rig sunshades," Captain
Selkirk ordered.

"Aye, aye, sir," Charley said, tugged at his forelock, and
left the quarterdeck.

Captain Selkirk turned to his first mate.

"I think we'd better keep a couple of riflemen aloft," he
said. "And when it grows dark, I want watches posted all
around us."

"Aye, aye, sir," First Mate Porter said, and picked up the
speaking horn to relay the necessary orders. Captain Selkirk
went to the ladder leading from the quarterdeck directly to
his cabin and went down it.

Paul Selkirk was determined that nothing should go wrong
with his call at Tatta. The probable absence of a British harbormaster was a mixed blessing. Had there been a resident
Englishman, the business of exchanging *The Eleanor*'s cargo
of Pennsylvania ironwork for Indian finished and raw silk
would certainly have gone smoothly and safely. In exchange
for tariff of one form or another, His Majesty's representative would insure the safety of the ship and her crew, and it
could be safely presumed that any Indian merchant a British
official recommended would be as honest as possible.

On the other hand, if there was no British officer, obviously there would be no one to pay tariff to, and that money
would be saved.

But the exchange of plowshares and axe bits and iron
chain and wrought-iron wagon wheels and hinges for silk and

silk products, the ostensible purpose of the voyage, was not all that Captain Selkirk had in mind.

A Jewish diamond merchant he had come to know in Amsterdam had told him that he was always in the market for good stones, and that it was often possible to buy them at far below their actual market value in India. He had told Captain Selkirk that if he would take the time it would require to learn how to judge a good stone (as well as a real stone from a glass or crystal counterfeit) and if Selkirk were willing to invest a little of his own money, it was possible that he could make money.

Paul Selkirk had taken the time to learn about diamonds and emeralds and pearls, surprising the diamond merchant both by his intense interest and the time he was willing to spend. The diamond merchant had in mind the possibility that the sea captain might come up with three or four stones of interest to him, giving the captain a small extra income in addition to whatever share of the profits of the voyage he might get from *The Eleanor*'s owners.

The diamond merchant's misconception of *The Eleanor*'s ownership was understandable. It had been purposely fostered by Captain Selkirk's third-person references to "the owners." *The Eleanor* was, in fact, his. Captain Selkirk believed that less attention was drawn to the activities of a shipmaster in the employ of someone else than to those of an owner-master.

In a wrought-iron-bound case beneath his bunk there was a substantial amount of gold that few people suspected he had at all, and whose worth no one alive had any conception of.

Bosun LaSalle knew about the case. Theo had been with Selkirk when he had taken it from the master's cabin of a Spanish ship in the West Indies. But Theo, like the others, believed that the contents of the case had long ago been divided among the others who had participated in the taking of the Spaniard.

Paul Selkirk did not regard his lopsided division of the booty as unfair. He knew that the master under whom they all sailed (and under whom he had risen to first mate) had habitually taken more of a share than he was entitled to take. That was the way things were done. The booty that Paul Selkirk had distributed among his men was more than they expected to get, and probably twice as much, he believed, as they would have received at the hands of the master had he lived to complete the voyage.

23

The owners' share had been more than they had expected in their wildest dreams to get for what was really a minimal investment in a tired old ship and the supplies necessary for it to sail under letters of marque against the French. Everyone had come out of that voyage richer than they had any reason to think they would.

No one was surprised that Paul Selkirk's share had been enough for him to build *The Eleanor*, and a house for his wife in Philadelphia, and to invest in the iron mine and forge at Durham Furnace. What would have surprised them was how much he still had in the iron-bound case.

It was no one's business but his. Not even his wife knew.

Money made money, he believed, and if the diamond merchant was right (and he had no reason to doubt him) about being able to buy jewels in India and turn them at a profit, that was exactly what he intended to do. Not three or four stones, but ten times, twenty times that many. He could get far more jewels in the iron-bound case than he could get gold coins. And no one would have to know anything at all about it.

What was true, however, about the presence of a British officer in dealing in the ironwork-for-silk trade was doubly true about his intended dealing with the Indians in jewels.

If there was no British officer around, no one would ask questions about his dealings with the Indians. On the other hand, once he made it known that he had sufficient gold on board to make large purchases of jewels, the Indians were likely to interpret the absence of a British official as a license to help themselves to the gold without exchanging diamonds or other precious stones for it.

And quite conceivably, to kill the crew and scuttle *The Eleanor* at sea.

He would have to proceed very carefully, feel his way around. He was not, he thought, a greedy man, and he knew that he was not a foolish one. He was prepared to sail from Tatta without offering to buy a stone, if that seemed the most prudent thing to do.

If he proceeded carefully, however, he thought it likely that he would be able to make some sort of deal in safety. A smaller deal than he would have liked, but a larger deal than the diamond merchant had thought would happen.

The key to success was caution.

24

Deal with the Indians about silk for iron, and then see what happened.

And, he had decided, the way to deal with the Indians was to pretend that if there was not an Englishman ashore that there was a fleet of them just over the horizon. He would anchor in midstream and stay there until the Indians came to him. He would tell them that he had been forbidden to go ashore until the English arrived. They would probably believe that, and then propose that they both deal to their mutual interest, that is to say, with neither of them paying taxes to His Britannic Majesty. He would reluctantly agree, but only so far as dealing, and not so far as going ashore.

Captain Selkirk opened the lock of the iron-bound case beneath his bunk with the key he wore on a thong around his neck. He toyed first with the small eye-magnifying glass he had bought in Amsterdam, and then with the stacks of gold coins.

All it was was yellow metal, he thought, and wondered again what gave it such value. Then he closed and locked the case, and pushed it under his bunk.

Then he pulled off his shoes and lay down on his bunk. It was likely to be a long wait before curiosity got the best of the Indians.

2

There was no sign at all from Tatta that anyone had noticed the arrival of *The Eleanor* all that day. The few small boats, sweep and oar and sail, that plied the river gave her a wide berth, and none pulled out from shore to make for her.

At nightfall, Captain Selkirk ordered lamps mounted on all quarters and personally checked the number and location of watches Theo LaSalle had set around her.

"If a boat appears," he ordered, "wave it off. If it comes closer after you've waved, shoot at it. Miss, but shoot at it."

If there was a shot, he reasoned, he would hear it, and could make what other decisions had to be made when, and if, that happened.

Nothing disturbed his sleep the first night but mosquitoes. They got through his net and seemed immune to the burning oil of camphor that was supposed to drive them away. He thought it really must be bad for Charley, sleeping either on deck, because of the heat, or in the fo'c'sl, where there was a

25

camphor lamp but no netting. He was surprised that the wind sweeping down the Indus didn't blow the mosquitoes away.

The mosquitoes, for reasons he couldn't imagine, were gone with the morning light, and just about as soon as the sun had come up, signal flags went up over Government House, spelling out, "What ship is that?"

He ordered the reply flown: "*Eleanor* of Philadelphia."

While they were spelling that out, he trained his glass on Government House long enough to convince himself there were no English present, despite the message in English. There was still no flag on the pole, and there was not an Englishman alive, he thought, much less an Englishman with an official position, no matter how minor, who could have restrained himself from climbing onto the roof of Government House to supervise the exchange of messages.

"Add 'out of London' to that," Captain Selkirk ordered. He was out of Philadelphia by way of Cape Town, but it was better to let them think that he was straight from the seat of the British Empire.

About noon, a boat put out from the wharf near Government House. It was a squat and ugly boat of shallow draft, and the oarsmen were natives, not English. There was someone in Western clothing aft in it, sitting on a high-backed chair. It looked to be an unsteady perch, and when Captain Paul Selkirk put his glass to his eye, he saw that the man in the chair was hanging onto its arms for dear life.

"Wave it off when it gets close enough to hail," Captain Selkirk ordered.

Theo LaSalle, who had a voice as loud as any Selkirk had ever heard, did as he was ordered. His booming order to "get away, there!" when the boat approached *The Eleanor* served also to wake the crew, many of whom had been dozing in the sun on deck, and who, bored, went to the rail to see who the bosun was shouting at.

A British flag was produced aboard the boat. It had been rolled and lying in the scuppers, Captain Selkirk decided. That proved that the man in Western clothing was not British. An Englishman would have had the flag flying, if he had to hold the flagstaff himself, and no Englishman would lay the Cross of Saint George in the foul water in the bottom of a longboat. For that matter, he concluded, no Englishman would set out on the river in a boat like the one approaching *The Eleanor*.

26

One of the Indians in the boat waved the British flag back and forth, and then the man in Western clothing got out of the chair, and stood aft of it, using it for support.

"Ahoy, *The Eleanor*," he shouted.

"Theo," Captain Selkirk ordered, "tell him to state his business."

Theo parroted the order in a voice so loud Selkirk turned his head away from him.

"Permisson to come aboard," the man shouted.

"Ask him who he is, Theo," Selkirk ordered.

"Sidonio Arriaga," came the reply. "In the service of the maharaja of Hyderabad."

"Sounds Portugee, Captain," First Mate James Porter said at Selkirk's side. He had not heard him come up.

"Yeah," Selkirk said. "Let him wait a full minute, Mr. Porter, and then give him permission. When he comes aboard, him alone, make sure there's riflemen he can see."

"Aye, aye, Captain," Porter said.

Many of *The Eleanor*'s crew were from upriver Pennsylvania, that is to say up the Delaware and then the Lehigh river valleys from Philadelphia. In Easton, at the confluence of the the the Delaware and Lehigh, and elsewhere in the region, gunsmiths had developed firearms to meet the peculiar game-taking requirements of the region. They had built oversized shotguns, so large and heavy they required a mount in the punts hunters used to take ducks and geese on the river marshes, often twenty or more wildfowl at a single shot. And they had developed a hunting firearm far superior for its purpose than the British Brown Bess musket.

The Brown Bess musket had a barrel twenty-four-inches long and fired a ball weighing about an ounce from a barrel nearly three-quarters of an inch in diameter. Although it was powerful enough to kill a deer, or a bear, at one hundred yards or better, it was nearly impossible to hit an animal at that distance. The Easton gunsmiths had developed a weapon with a much smaller bore, and a much longer barrel, which threw a much smaller projectile. It was, however, deadly at one hundred yards, or even, with a first-quality gun in the hands of a skilled marksman, at two hundred yards or more. The secret was thin grooves cut into the inside surface of the barrel. They caught the soft lead of the ball and caused it to spin. Spinning somehow made the projectile fly true.

The grooves, or "rifling," inside the barrels caused these

27

firearms to be known as rifles, and because of the place of their manufacture as Pennsylvania rifles.

They were capable of taking a deer at more than a hundred yards, and the first time Paul Selkirk had seen one he had seen their potential as shipboard weaponry. A man was a larger target than a deer. He purchased rifles for his arms locker and saw to it that those seamen from upriver farms who were skilled in their use passed their skill on to the others. Charley had pleased his father by quickly becoming a "crack shot." A crack shot was someone who not only could hit the foot-square piece of wood used as a seventy-five- or hundred-yard target, but hit a crack in the wood.

When the man in Western clothing climbed the ladder lowered over *The Eleanor*'s side, six of her seamen were gathered in a semi-circle on the deck, rifles in their hands, and a half dozen more were perched on the rails and in the rigging with their weapons trained on the boat.

When the man was aboard, Captain Selkirk came down the ladder from the quarterdeck and walked over to him, trailed by Theo LaSalle.

"Paul Selkirk," he said. "Master."

"I am honored to make your acquaintance, Captain Selkirk," the man said, in heavily accented English. "I am Don Sidonio Arriaga, in the service of the maharaja of Hyderabad."

Selkirk nodded, but said nothing. There was something about Arriaga that made him distrust him, as well as dislike him, at first glance.

"May I ask what brings you to Tatta?" the Portugee asked.

"We expected to find Admiral Taylor and his fleet here," Selkirk replied, picking the name "Taylor" out of the air.

"Obviously, the admiral has not yet made port," Arriaga said.

"Obviously," Selkirk said.

"You are a supply ship for his fleet?" Arriaga asked.

"We are a merchantman under the protection of the admiral," Selkirk replied.

"May I inquire as to your cargo?"

"Ironwork, intended to trade for silk and silk products," Selkirk replied.

"Then you have made the right port, Captain," Arriaga said. "There is silk here at a good price, and there is always a market here for good ironwork. English, you said?"

"From the Pennsylvania colony," Selkirk replied . "As good as any made in the British Isles."

"I will look forward to examining it," Arriaga said. "Among my duties for the maharaja is the inspection of incoming goods."

"And what are your other duties?" Selkirk inquired, bluntly.

"My mission at the moment is to offer you and your officers the hospitality of the maharaja's palace," Arriaga said. "Until Admiral Taylor and the fleet arrive, of course."

"Thank you, no," Selkirk said.

Arriaga looked at him thoughtfully for a moment before replying.

"Forgive me, Captain," he said. "Let me presume to tell you that when one is invited by the maharaja, one accepts. In his own way, here, he is quite as royal as King George. It is a command, as well as an invitation."

Selkirk thought that over before deciding that he really had no choice in the matter.

"Please tell the maharaja," he said, "that I accept his kind offer on behalf of myself and my son. I will be accompanied by a guard of eight men."

"That will pose no problems, I'm sure. Except that I don't have room in the boat for ten men."

"That will be no problem," Selkirk said. "We will come ashore in our longboat. When are we expected?"

"Now, Captain," Arriaga said.

"You may expect us on shore in an hour," Selkirk said. "Thank you, Don Sidonio Arriaga." He bowed, turned on his heel, and walked back up the deck and to the ladder to the quarterdeck. When he was sure that Arriaga was over the side and out of hearing, he motioned for First Mate Porter and Second Mate Peter Dillon to join him.

3

When the eight seamen LaSalle had named to accompany Captain Selkirk to the maharaja's palace were turned out by the ladder, Captain Selkirk was pleased with them, and their appearance. LaSalle had somewhere, on this very short notice, even come up with hats for them. Their dress—white duck trousers, short-sleeved, horizontally striped cotton shirts, and, on most of them, stockings—was similar enough to look

29

like uniforms. The straw hats, with a ribbon around the crown and a foot down the neck, were identical. Selkirk wondered where LaSalle had found them.

Able Seaman Charles Selkirk, however, was something else. He was going ashore as the Captain's son, and thus in civilian clothing. The suit of clothes his father had bought for him just before sailing from Philadelphia was already too small. Charley's broad shoulders strained the coat, and his muscular wrists stuck far too far out of the cuffs, making it impossible to conceal the fact that his wrists were now too thick to permit the lace-trimmed cuffs of his shirt to be buttoned.

The mararaja, Selkirk told himself, would not know the difference. The Americans would be as strange to him as he would be to them.

He gestured with his hand, a signal for the crewmen to go down the ladder and into the waiting longboat. When they were all aboard, he motioned Charley over the side, and finally climbed down the ladder himself.

"The picture we're trying to paint for these fellas," he said, loudly, as soon as he had sat down, "is that we're the kind of sailors who can row one of these things at least as well as an Englishman. Can you fellas manage that?"

There were chuckles and laughter.

"Make believe you're a coxswain, Charley," Captain Selkirk ordered. "Call the stroke."

Charley, who had been sitting beside him, stood up and moved aft, where he stood supporting himself with a hand on the shoulder of the sailor at the rudder.

"Hoist oars," Charley ordered. He sounded, his father noted with pleasure, as if he knew what he was about.

"Oars in the water," Charley went on. "Prepare to stroke. Stroke!"

The longboat of The Eleanor made its way across the muddy yellow Indus River to the Government Pier. As they approached it, Captain Selkirk saw Arriaga waiting for them.

It was more than a mile to the maharaja of Hyderabad's palace. It had not been visible from where The Eleanor was anchored in the river, and Selkirk was impressed with its size, if not its construction or style.

It looked as if it were a city square or more long, and maybe that deep. It was built as a sort of fort, he saw, but it would pose no real resistance to cannon fire. It might be able to defend itself against bow and arrow, or even musket fire,

30

but it could not hold against rifle fire, and certainly not against even the lightest cannon.

That did not reduce what Captain Selkirk saw as the danger. The eight seamen with them were good for show, and nothing else. He hoped their presence might make the maharaja think he was sufficiently important a personage that he always went about with a guard. As a practical matter, the guard would be no more than a hair's width from useless. If anything happened, if the maharaja tried, for example, to take them hostage, their salvation, it there was to be salvation, would be in *The Eleanor*'s cannon. A threat to shell the city, if they were not released, followed by the execution of the threat, and the destruction of these mud-and-flimsy-timber buildings just might save them.

And it just might see the maharaja slit their throats or their bellies for having been responsible for the shelling.

Selkirk had been distinctly uneasy as the procession made its way through the town, and he felt even more uneasy once they had passed through a door and entered the palace itself. They were, and there was no putting a shadow on it, quite helpless.

The maharaja turned out to be an effeminate, obese, short, olive-skinned man of about fifty. Selkirk didn't connect the tall, hawk-nosed young man who stood behind the maharaja's "throne" (actually, an enormous pillow) with him at all until Arriaga identified him as the maharaja's son and heir.

When they had been seated, the maharaja said, through Arriaga, that he would be honored if he could be permitted to see to Captain Selkirk's guards' comfort. What that meant, Selkirk realized, was that he was being separated from his men. But he understood that there was nothing he could do about it.

When the men had been led off, and they were seated on large, silk-covered cushions, the maharaja offered them French wine. Through Arriaga he explained that his religion forbade him to use alcohol.

"Tell him, Don Sidonio," Selkirk said, "that it is the custom of my people to follow the customs of their hosts."

He saw from the maharaja's eyes that Arriaga's translation was unnecessary; the maharaja understood, and possibly even spoke, English.

Instead of wine, Captain Selkirk and Charley drank tea thick with sugar. And then the meal was served. Selkirk had no idea what it was, except that it was in small chunks, mixed with chopped vegetables, and coated with a sauce both cloyingly sweet and hot as Hades. He was proud that Charley not only managed to get it down but actually was able to come up with a smile and a gesture to express his appreciation.

The meal went on in virtual silence for more than an hour, but finally the bowls were cleaned away and servants with bowls of hot water knelt beside them and first washed, then patted dry their hands.

The maharaja said something to Arriaga.

"The maharaja asks that you forgive his bad manners," Arriaga began. "He has, of course, scheduled an entertainment, but he thought he might dare to inquire about the ironwork you have aboard before that starts."

Selkirk gave a brief listing of the ironwork aboard *The Eleanor*. As he spoke, the maharaja kept smiling and bobbing his head. Selkirk wondered if that was simply his idea of good manners, or whether he had abandoned the pretense of not understanding English.

The maharaja patiently sat through Arriaga's translation, and then spoke himself, almost as long.

"He says," Arriaga said, "that he understands you wish silk and silk products." Selkirk nodded. Arriaga went on, "He said that, if you can find the time in the morning, he would be happy to show you what silk is available."

Selkirk looked at the maharaja and smiled his agreement.

"At the same time, if you would permit the prince to examine the iron work aboard your ship . . ."

Here comes the hook, Selkirk thought. He wiped the smile from his face.

"It might be possible for us to complete our business before the arrival of Admiral Taylor, and his fleet, and the king's taxes." The Portugee smiled ingratiatingly.

That seemed like a fair enough proposition, Selkirk thought. He wondered why it bothered him.

"Tell the maharaja to spare the prince the trouble of coming to the ship, with its danger of passing on infection; I will have my crew bring samples of the ironwork ashore at first light," Selkirk said.

The translation was made, and the maharaja responded.

"The maharaja says you are most accommodating," he said. "And further, that if your ironwork if as good as his silk, your plan will make it possible to do our business even more qiuckly."

I've got what I want, Selkirk thought. So why am I uneasy?

The maharaja said something else.

"The maharaja asks if there is anything besides silk in which you might be interested," Arriaga translated.

"Tell him that I have heard much about the fine jewels of India," Selkirk said. "And that I would like, within my humble means, of course, to purchase a jewel for a ring for my wife. Make sure he understands this is a private matter, not the business of the owners of the ship."

The maharaja nodded his understanding long before Arriaga had made the translation. He said something to one of his servants, who got quickly to his feet and left the room. He returned holding a square of black velvet, its four corners tied together to form a bag.

The maharaja spilled the jewels, mixed diamonds and emeralds, on the carpet before him, spread them with his index finger, and finally selected the largest emerald. He wheezed as he bent over and handed it to Captain Selkirk. He said something to Selkirk, which Arriaga translated:

"To the captain's lady, with the maharaja's compliments."

There's the hook, and it's deep in me, and I didn't even see it coming.

"Tell the maharaja that I cannot accept a gift of such value, for I am a poor man and have nothing to give to him in return."

"He doesn't expect anything in return," Arriaga replied.

The hell he doesn't, Captain Selkirk thought. Then: Maybe if there is a goldsmith in this godforsaken place, I could arrange to swap some of the coins for something, a bracelet or something, worth as much as this. In any event, I'm stuck with this.

"Tell the maharaja his generosity overwhelms me," Selkirk said.

The reply to that was: "The maharaja can only hope the captain's lady will be as gracious in describing his small gift."

Selkirk smiled a smile at the maharaja that he hoped would appear grateful and charming.

The maharaja, somewhat shyly, Selkirk thought, said something else to Arriaga, who then produced the surprising translation.

"If the captain just happened to be interested in purchasing other jewels," Arriaga said, "the maharaja would be happy to discuss this."

"I have a few pounds in gold," Selkirk said.

The response to that was that since he had a few stones right here, the maharaja suggested that the captain might look at them.

When he had examined the stones in front of him as well as he could (not as he would have wanted to, through the jeweler's eyeglass—that would have been bad manners, even if he had had it with him), he reached into his waistband and pulled out a leather pouch that contained two dozen Spanish pieces of eight.

"Tell the maharaja I know nothing of the value of stones, and can only place my trust in his hands," Selkirk said. "I would be grateful if he would select what few stones that much money would buy."

The maharaja nodded his understanding and smiled, again before Arriaga had completed the translation. He spent a good five minutes picking out stones, and then telling Selkirk, through Arriaga, that he thought the price fair.

Selkirk was not at all surprised to find out that the maharaja knew almost exactly what his stones would be worth in Amsterdam. He offered them for sale at that price, plus about a fifth. The additional fifth, Selkirk decided, was to insure the maharaja's good will. *That* was the hook. But he didn't mind the hook, now that he knew what it was. What he had done, he knew, was buy life insurance as well as diamonds at more than their worth.

He wondered if he would be offered the same sort of terms the next day, when they bartered for the silk. So far as the maharaja was concerned, it would be just about as profitable as piracy, but carry none of the risks. Selkirk had been robbed with his permission, not at the point of a sword. On the other hand, the swords of the maharaja's men had never left their sheaths, and his and Charley's throats had not been slit.

The maharaja retied the black velvet cloth into a bag and handed it and Selkirk's gold to his servant. He said something to Arriaga.

"The maharaja asks that you now join him for the entertainment he has arranged for you," Arriaga translated. "And asks your understanding for its poor quality. He had so little time to arrange for it."

The maharaja hoisted himself with a wheeze to his feet and led the way out of the room. The prince, who had so far said not a word, followed him, and Arriaga bowed Captain Selkirk and his son into line behind them. They passed through long, narrow, high-ceilinged passages until they came to a gallery overlooking an interior garden.

The gallery was nearly as long as the building, but what surprised and pleased Selkirk was the presence of his guard. They were arranged against a wall, and to judge from the short-legged tables before them, had been fed, and fed well, here. Their Pennsylvania rifles were leaning on the tiled wall behind them. They smiled when they saw the Selkirks, and Selkirk wondered if they had any idea of the trouble they might all be in. It was still possible, if not likely, that now that the maharaja had time both to consider the situation, and possibly to conclude that *The Eleanor* and her crew were about as vulnerable as they could be, that they still might have their throats cut.

The entertainment consisted of first a magician, who was really quite clever, and young dancing girls, wearing very little clothing above or below the waist. Selkirk saw that the maharaja was bored with it, and twice actually dozed off and shook himself awake.

The prince, however, while paying as little attention to all the exposed flesh as his father, had found something that interested him. He had been stealing looks at the rifles. The first thing Captain Selkirk thought when he saw this was that the prince was worried that eight men were still armed, which, had he unpleasant plans for them, could pose problems. But then Selkirk decided that the prince was simply curious. These were probably the first Pennsylvania rifles in Hyderabad.

"Theo," Selkirk called softly to LaSalle. "Pick up a rifle by the muzzle, and hand it butt first to the tall one."

Theo gave him a curious look, but did as he was told.

The prince was somewhat startled, but smiled when he took the rifle in his hands. He looked at Selkirk and bobbed his head in sort of a bow.

"Don Sidonio," Selkirk said, "please tell the prince I would be honored if he and his father would accept Pennsylvania rifles from me as a poor gift." Then he added, to Theo, "Give the maharaja another one, Theo."

The maharaja beamed his thanks, and immediately hoisted himself wheezing to his feet. He ordered that a red clay jar, nearly the size of a man, be set up in the gallery no more than forty paces away. It took Selkirk a minute to understand that the maharaja intended to fire the piece, consequences be damned, in his palace.

"Tell the maharaja," Selkirk said to Arriaga, "that that is an American rifle, which carries two hundred paces to hit a target the size of a man's head."

The maharaja was impressed with that startling announcement, and, with a gesture of his hand, ordered another jar set up in the gallery a hundred paces beyond the first.

Holding the rifle in both his hands, the maharaja carefully counted off two hundred paces, stopped, and directed servants to move the target to conform with Selkirk's announcement of the rifle's capabilities.

Then he came excitedly back down the gallery, smiling from ear to ear in anticipation, Selkirk thought, of making Selkirk out a liar.

Selkirk experienced a sinking feeling when the maharaja raised his rifle to his shoulder, pointed it in the general direction of the jar-target he had ordered set up, and prepared to fire it. Selkirk realized that if the maharaja fired and missed, the capabilities of the rifle wouldn't mean a thing.

He went to the maharaja and took the rifle from him, and tried to hand it to Theo, who was a crack shot and would deliver what was promised. The maharaja pushed Captain Selkirk aside, took the rifle from Theo's hands, and gave it to Charley.

"I am sure that the captain is as proud of his son as I am of mine," the maharaja said through Arriaga. Captain Selkirk had no idea what that was supposed to mean, except perhaps that the maharaja was saying they were both too old to be good marksmen.

"Charley," Selkirk said, "show the prince the sights, and the lockwork, and then blow the top off that jar."

Charley raised his eyebrows but said nothing. He went to the prince and explained the rifle's sights and lockwork to him. The prince smiled and nodded his understanding. Charley turned, glanced at his father, and put the rifle to his shoulder. He took careful aim and fired. The ball struck the jar five inches from its opening, and shattered the top third of it.

Both the prince and the maharaja were now beaming. The maharaja ordered another man-sized jar to be put in place. Long before the servants who put it in the middle of the gallery were safely out of the way, the prince put the rifle to his shoulder, aimed carefully, and fired. His ball struck the red clay jar further down than Charley's had the first jar, and the shattering of the prince's jar was more spectacular.

It was more than enough to awe the maharaja. Selkirk glanced around his men for a third rifle to give to the maharaja. If he kept the maharaja in his debt, he thought, there was a much better chance they could get back to the ship with the overpriced diamonds he had bought, the remaining rifles, and their lives.

The maharaja however, shook his head when a third rifle was produced. Through Arriaga, he said that Captain Selkirk had been more than generous, and he could accept no more from him than the two rifles already so graciously offered.

He then offered Selkirk overnight accommodations, and his choice of any of the dancing girls who had performed to share his bed.

Through Arriaga, Selkirk replied that he could not accept the gracious offer, as it was his duty to the owners of his ship to spend every night aboard.

The maharaja made a movement something like a bow and uttered a brief sentence.

"He says your presence and your generosity have honored his house," Arriaga said. By then, the maharaja and the prince had left the room. Neither, Selkirk saw, had turned their rifles over to a servant.

"I presume," Captain Selkirk said, "that we may now return to our ship?"

"I'll escort you, of course," Don Sidonio Arriaga said. "And I will look forward to seeing you in the morning on the Government House wharf."

They reached *The Eleanor* in midstream without incident. For some reason, however, Selkirk still felt uneasy, and he personally checked the watches on duty and repeated his orders that no small craft be allowed to approach the ship.

4

Through his glass, Captain Selkirk saw Don Sidonio Arriaga on the Government House wharf early the next morning. He sent First Mate Porter ashore with three assorted barrels of plows and wrought-iron wagon tires and hinges.

Porter returned within an hour saying that the Portugee had examined everything carefully and pronounced it of good quality. He had sent samples of the raw and woven silk he wished to trade back with Porter.

The negotiations were Captain Selkirk's responsibility, and somewhat reluctantly, still harboring a premonition that something was going to go wrong, he went ashore.

The terms to which Arriaga finally agreed were fair; there would be a decent profit. It would have been foolish to refuse them.

"I will return to the ship, and we can begin the transfer," he said, and shook Arriaga's hand.

When he returned to the ship, he was trailed by the boat in which Arriaga had first appeared. He ordered the long boat stopped, and signaled to the Indian boatmen to return to shore. The cargo would be off-loaded in *The Eleanor*'s longboat. He did not want Indians aboard, or even beside, *The Eleanor*.

It was a lengthy process, and he knew that the crew was grumbling about having to do the stevedores' labor. It was better to work up a sweat, and more callouses, Selkirk knew, than to be floating dead in the Indus.

About three in the afternoon, while Selkirk was examining, at random, cases of silk to make sure they contained silk and not cotton, or street sweepings, *The Eleanor*'s quartermaster, who was in charge of the watch, came to him and reported that a small boat was approaching.

It was litterally a small boat, and it was sparkling white, and it held, rowed by two oarsmen, just one passenger. The prince.

Selkirk could hardly deny the prince, alone, permission to come aboard. He greeted him at the rail and halfheartedly tried to discourage him from coming aboard by holding his nostrils and pointing at his ship.

"India, Captain Selkirk, is a land of unpleasant smells," the prince said, in perfect English and with a wide smile, exposing his small perfect teeth.

Selkirk smiled back at him, and waved him onto the ladder.

Once aboard, Selkirk led the prince to his cabin, where the prince produced a small leather box containing two emeralds, and handed it to him.

"What's this for?" Selkirk asked.

"A small token of our appreciation for the rifles," the prince said.

"Too large a token for too small a gift," Selkirk said.

"The penalty for arming 'the natives,' " the prince said, "is death. Or didn't you know?"

"I didn't," Selkirk said.

"A small token for a very valuable gift," the prince said.

There was no doubt in Selkirk's mind that the emeralds were genuine, or that they were worth a small fortune.

"Did you ever hear the English expression, 'Hung for a sheep as a lamb'?" Selkirk asked.

"No," the prince said, amused.

Selkirk looked around the deck for a seaman. The first one he spotted was Charley, part of a crew hoisting barrels of plowshares from the hold. For a moment, he was uncomfortable to have the prince see his son working as a seaman. But then he realized the time for pretense had passed.

"Charley," he called, and Charley, who looked uncomfortable himself when he saw the prince, torn between being son and seaman, came over. At the last moment, he opted to be what he was, a seaman. He tugged at his forelock.

"Sir?"

"Get the key for the arms locker from Mr. Porter," Captain Selkirk said. "And pick out the best-looking two rifles you can find. Bring them, and a ball mold, a small bag of flint, and two three-pound kegs of powder here."

"Aye, aye, sir," Charley said, and trotted down the deck to the quarterdeck.

He was back on deck within five minutes.

"I want you to show the prince how to charge, and prime. And how to cast bullets, and how to clean the rifles," Selkirk said.

"Aye, aye, sir."

"Your father and I," the prince said, "are thinking of going into the firearms trade, are we not, Captain Selkirk?"

"That would depend on the price and the profit," Captain Selkirk said.

"We have just established the price," the prince said.

"And how many are you willing to take at that price?" Selkirk asked.

"Let us say an initial order of three hundred rifles, with powder and flints," the prince said. "Delivered safely ashore. After that, we can talk about the price again."

Selkirk met his eyes. Then he nodded.

Chapter Three

1

Two weeks after Major Edgar Watchbury of the Household Cavalry returned from his trip to discuss military affairs with the landgrave of Hesse-Kassel, he was promoted to lieutenant colonel and gazetted military equerry to his Brittanic Majesty, King George III.

Lady Caroline was pleased for him, and for herself, for the appointment meant they had moved one level of society higher. They had previously been at the upper echelon of military society. Their social peers had been the senior officers (and their wives) of the Palace Regiments, the Coldstream Guards, the Life Guards, and of course, the Household Cavalry. Edgar's position had earned them a position at the larger palace affairs, but they had never come close to being considered part of the Court.

Now they would be. With Edgar a lieutenant colonel assigned to the War Office and gazetted to attend the king personally, they would now be considered members of the Court, and their names were now beginning to appear on guest lists that previously had excluded them.

Their new status, however, she pointed out to Edgar, was going to pose a new problem. They would be expected to reciprocate socially, to have to dinner those who had entertained them. It had not been a problem before Edgar's promotion, when a dinner at the Guard's Club had been repayable at the Army and Navy. And it was not yet really a problem, for their apartment at Number 101 King's Way, overlooking Lincoln's Inn Fields, had a dining room

41

large enough to seat twelve people, and the apartment would serve for the time being.

But they were just, as she pointed out, inside the door of the upper levels. At the moment, there was no problem of entertaining, for example, the duke of Leicester, for not only did the duke not expect it, but more than likely would have considered it presumptuous of the lowly Lieutenant Colonel Edgar Watchbury to extend an invitation.

That was *now*, Lady Caroline pointed out. But it was reasonable to presume that other promotions, and possibly even elevation to the knighthood, or one of the other Royal Orders, maybe even as a Knight Companion of the Bath, would follow.

Edgar took her meaning.

"I quite agree that we should look around and see what sort of house comes on the market," he said. "Nothing ostentatious, mind you, we have to be very careful about that, just now in particular. But something more in keeping to the status of someone in His Majesty's personal service."

It wasn't a question of money. Edgar was not being overly frugal. He was concerned, and justifiably, with appearances. He had to appear to the king, and, just as important, to those around the king, as a stable, responsible officer who would never do anything to make the king uncomfortable, much less subject him to embarrassment.

They both understood that Edgar was in a sort of probationary period. Three things could happen to him. He could in some way displease the king, or his own military superiors. In that case, he would be placed on half-pay, and they would be expected to return to Edgar's estates in the country, to spend the rest of their lives among the landed gentry: "Lieutenant Colonel (Retired) and Lady Caroline Watchbury request the pleasure of your company at the annual auction for the benefit of the Orphan's Fund of Saint Matthew's Parish. On the Church Grounds from two past noon May 17."

Or he, professionally, and they together, socially, could prove not quite up to the hopes for them. Not that they would do anything wrong, but that Edgar would not display the outstanding characteristics expected of him, or that she would commit some social gaffe, from spilling tea in the queen's lap to having an affiar with someone become public knowledge.

In that event, Edgar would receive some out-of-London (or perhaps out-of-the-country) posting. Deputy Inspector General of Cavalry for the War Office, with duty station Glasgow, for example. Perhaps even be given command of a battalion, of a staff job calling for a lieutenant colonel, in India or one of the colonies in North America.

Or, and this was what they must work toward, he would prove personally pleasing to the king and professionally satisfactory to those who would judge him in the War Office and in Parliament and the House of Lords. Edgar was a good soldier, Lady Caroline had no doubt about that. Otherwise he would not have been able to purchase a commission in the Household Cavalry.

And she felt that, with her help, he could win the social battle as well. Certainly, he wasn't blind to the importance of that. Since their trip to Germany, she had given a good deal of thought to their relationship, more than a little surprised that she hadn't done so before.

She had come to understand that Edgar had offered her marriage because someone in his position had to be well married. It obviously had nothing to do with love, and neither, she concluded, had it had anything to do with her attractiveness to him physically.

A man in his position, and in the positions to which he aspired, had to have a wife of suitable background, like hers, matching his, they were both younger children of minor noblemen. He could not have married above him, even if his money had been adequate to make such a marriage, and he could not have married beneath him. He needed a suitable wife, and she had been suitable. It was to be hoped that she would produce a male heir, but that had not happened.

She now believed she understood his reaction to the affair with the Grand Duke Alexei. He really wished the whole thing not to have happened, not because of any jealousy, but because it was the sort of thing that could have gotten out of hand, out of hand meaning becoming public knowledge.

If Lady Caroline had insisted on telling him of the unspeakable behavior of the Grand Duke Alexei, Major Watchbury would have considered it his duty as a gentleman to do something about it. What would have been required by social custom would have been to challenge the grand duke to a duel. They would never actually have faced one another with drawn swords, or cocked pistols, for the grand duke was too

43

important to become involved in something like that. Some solution would have been found to keep a British major from killing or wounding or being killed or wounded by a Russian Imperial. What would have happened, finally, she now understood, was that it would have been *Major* rather than *Lieutenant Colonel* and Lady Watchbury who would have been patrons of the charity auction of Saint Matthew's Parish if her relationship with the grand duke had resulted in a confrontation. Edgar would have been put on half-pay and never have come close to becoming a lieutenant colonel, much less an equerry to the king.

Her own reactions to the affair with Alexei had ranged from ecstasy to despair. She had been more than a little ashamed of her own shamelessness, her tartlike behavior, her brazen willingness to take him into her bed again. There was an explanation for that, of course. In the church it was described as the sinful lusts of the flesh.

He had been the first to trigger those lusts. She wasn't sure if that was because she was of an age where those lusts had naturally come to the surface, making her one with the women she previously had not understood, those who willingly shared their beds and their bodies with men not their husbands, or whether it was because Alexei was one of those men the other women had talked about so wonderingly, the magnificent lovers.

Caroline had only Edgar for comparison. All she knew for sure was that Edgar was not much interested in the physical side of marriage, and that Alexei was an animal of a man for whom the act had no more meaning than eating. It was painful for her to admit this to herself, but the truth was that she and Alexei had been like a dog and a bitch in heat. She had no more idea of what was happening to her, what she was willing, even eager to do, than a bitch in heat had.

It was only when she had time, that is to say, when the worst of the despair she had gone through when Alexei hadn't even troubled to say goodbye to her when they left Marburg an der Lahn had diminished so that she could think, that she understood what had happened. It was quite simple, really: she had, for the first time, experienced the "sinful lusts of the flesh" she had been hearing about from Church of England priests all her life. Now she knew what they had been talking about, and now that she did, she felt herself entirely capable of controlling them.

44

She had come to understand that the sinful lusts had overwhelmed her because she had not known what to expect. Where she had started out loathing Edgar for his apparent disinterest (she was ashamed to remember that she had believed he had actually encouraged her relations with Alexei), she was now grateful to him for his understanding. He was a man, and he knew about such things, and he had understood.

She had vowed that now that she knew how the sinful lusts of the flesh could take possession of one's soul and body, she would, with God's help, never again succumb to the Devil's temptation. She had sinned against God, and she acknowledged this, and had begged God's forgiveness, and been absolved by a priest, and she would not repeat her sin. She would pray to God that he would give her Edgar's child, and she would devote the rest of her life to being the wife he wanted her to be.

She knew the Devil was still after her, for she often had dreams of Alexei, dreams so real that they frightened her. Worse, sometimes when she was wide awake, her mind was suddenly full of embarrassingly intimate memories of Alexei and what they had done together. She learned that, when this happened, she could force the imagery from her mind by reciting the Twenty-third Psalm.

There was more: specifically, there was Captain Sir Richard Trentwood. As an equerry to the king, Edgar was himself authorized an aide-de-camp. He told her that he would have liked to have had Young Tom, Lieutenant Thomas William Whitleby, Viscount Malvern, given the post, but it was "recommended" to him, when he made the proposal, that in his new duties, he would require someone with a greater stock of military knowledge than the viscount.

"They're right of course," Edgar had told her. "Tom really wouldn't have been of much help to me, and I would have been doing his career a disservice. What Tom needs is some time with troops, and what I need is an experienced officer."

Captain Sir Richard Trentwood was twenty-nine, and, like most of the other officers of the Palace Regiments, financially independent. Unlike many of them, however, who regarded their military duties with troops as an unwelcome interference in their social lives, Sir Richard took his military duties very seriously.

Lady Caroline had been bored silly on the dozen or more occasions that she had had dinner with Sir Richard. Edgar had almost immediately on Sir Richard's assignment as his aide-de-camp fallen into the habit of bringing him home when his work day at Buckingham Palace was over. They had a cognac or two to relax, and then went over their work load together. Most often, this required Sir Richard to head for the War Office, but sometimes this was not necessary, and then, if he and Caroline had no plans for the evening, Edgar routinely asked him to "pot luck," over which they discussed affairs of which she had neither knowledge or interest.

She could not recall Sir Richard ever having said more than "Good afternoon," "Thank you," "No, thank you," and "Good evening" to her, and he certainly had never even troubled to make a pretense at polite conversation with her at table, proving that he was only dimly aware of her as a female. This, and her own sure knowledge that she certainly had no interest in a taciturn-to-the-point-of-discourtesy, mustachioed cavalry officer, is what made the dreams she had lately been having, in which Sir Richard replaced the Grand Duke Alexei, seem either grotesquely absurd, or, if she permitted herself to dwell on this, even further proof of the temptations of which the Devil was capable.

When she did permit herself to dwell on the idea of Sir Richard appearing in her dreams, his head on Alexei's body, it sometimes seemed less absurd than it should have on its face. It was entirely possible, she thought, that the Devil, aware that she had put the temptation of Alexei out of her mind, was offering her an alternate temptation in Sir Richard.

When she was face to face with him, however, the idea seemed ridiculous. Sir Richard regarded her as nothing more than another servant in his colonel's apartment. She had to be acknowledged with the required greeting, and the required courteous leave-taking remark, but in between, she was useful only to ring for a servant and a fresh bottle, or a plate of cold meat.

Lady Caroline thought of this again at half past two in the afternoon, when Bridget the maid came to the bedroom where Lady Caroline was taking a nap, and announced that Sir Richard was at the door.

Lady Caroline pulled a robe over the thin cotton gown in which she had been napping, made a perfunctory effort to repair the damage her pillow had done to her hairdo, and then went into the drawing room.

Trentwood was sitting with his back to the door on a

couch. When he heard her footsteps, he stood up, his dress uniform helmet under his left arm, his sword bumping into the legs of the couch.

"Sir Richard," Lady Caroline said.

"We're to go to Buckingham Palace," he bluntly announced. "I'm to tell you, and then fetch you by carriage at five."

"By 'we,' I presume you mean my husband and I?"

"All of us," he said.

"And where is the colonel?"

"War Office," he said.

"And he is going directly to Buckingham Palace, without coming by here?"

"I'm to carry you there," he said.

"At five, you said?"

He nodded his head.

"Thank you," she said. "I'll be ready."

He nodded at her and then marched out of the room, putting his helmet on his head as he walked. He presented, she thought, an attractive picture of a fit, trim, and erect cavalry officer. Edgar had not looked so striking when he had been a young captain.

Lady Caroline dispatched Bridget to the livery stable to make sure that Trooper Wood, Edgar's batman, would have the carriage when it was required, and then went into her bedroom and prepared to dress. Trentwood had not offered any information regarding the purpose of the summons to Buckinghan Palace, nor explained the unusual hour at which he would fetch her, and she was annoyed because she didn't know precisely how to dress.

She had recently come into, from an aunt, a truly lovely necklace, a triple string of pearls that held a diamond-and-emerald pendant. She had not yet had the chance to wear it in public at an affair she thought worth it. To display the necklace properly meant wearing a gown with a low-cut bodice. She had such a dress. But if the affair were not formal (and the sudden command suggested it would be rather informal) and the necklace thus inappropriate, the low-cut dress without the necklace would also be a bit daring.

If she wore the wrong thing, Edgar would be coldly disapproving. He should have, she decided angrily, sent clearer word with his taciturn messenger. She somewhat petulantly decided to wear the dress and the necklace.

Despite what Trentwood had said about Edgar's plans to go directly from the War Office to Buckingham Palace, he came home about four-thirty.

"I didn't expect you," she said.

"Trentwood told you about this afternoon, and tonight, did he?"

"Are there two affairs? Afternoon and night?"

"Investiture this afternoon," he said. "Don't even know who. Pin a medal on somebody, or lay a sword on some old duck's shoulder and make him a knight, followed by champagne and whatever. You know the drill. Don't know why they want the women. Then, tonight, dinner and afterward cards for the men. Don't know why I'm invited to that, either, but I am. Trentwood will see you home, if necessary."

He went into their bedroom and got out his dress uniform. While he was dressing, Sir Richard appeared, similarly uniformed. He nodded at her but said not a word.

When Edgar came into the drawing room, she asked him if she looked all right. He examined her as if he were seeing the dress and the necklace for the first time.

"The necklace is a bit much for an afternoon investiture," he said, after a moment.

"Then I should change the dress as well," she said.

"No time for that," he said. "Just get rid of the necklace. You can wear it tonight, if you're of a mind." He went to the full-length mirror in the foyer and examined himself in it, tugging on the waistcoat of his uniform to straighten it.

Lady Caroline, annoyed that she had worn the necklace, put her hands to her bodice to unhook the latch. It wouldn't open.

"Edgar, I can't get the catch open," she said.

"Get your maid to help," he said, still tugging on his waistcoat.

She called for Bridget, who appeared wiping her hands. She had been cleaning pots. Margaret did not want her dirty hands near her dress.

"You'll have to do it, Edgar," Lady Margaret said. "Bridget's hands are soiled."

Edgar turned and gave her an impatient look.

"Trentwood, perhaps you would be good enough to give her a hand?" he said, and turned and resumed the adjustment of his uniform before the mirror.

Trentwood, looking quite as annoyed as Edgar, walked to

her. She was reminded how large he was, compared to Edgar, perhaps even larger than Alexei, when he stood before her. She lifted the diamond-and-enerald pendant from her bosom and showed him the location of the malfunctioning catch.

It wouldn't open for him, either, at first, until he applied the masculine solution, brute force. The catch then burst open in such a manner that his hand thumped her bosom painfully.

"Sorry," he said.

"It didn't hurt," she said.

"I think I broke it," he said, and turned his back on her and walked away.

She pulled the necklace off her neck and examined the catch. He had bent it, not broken it, and she thought she could easily straighten it herself, without having to send it to the jewelers. She went into the bedroom, she and Edgar shared, and put it back into her jewel box.

When she returned, they were both waiting for her impatiently. It was quite clear that, at that moment, both wished Lieutenant Colonel Watchbury were not encumbered by a wife who delayed the schedule.

2

Trooper Wood and the carriage were waiting at the curb. They mounted the carriage according to protocol, Lady Caroline first, then Edgar, and finally Trentwood, who took his place on the rear-facing seat, holding his sword between his knees. Without intending to, Lady Caroline glanced at Sir Richard's skin-tight white whipcord uniform breeches and saw that he parted on the left. Edgar parted on the right. Edgar, the Devil put the thought in her mind, did not have as much to part as did Sir Richard Trentwood. Sir Richard Trentwood apparently had even more to part than did the Grand Duke Alexei.

Lady Caroline forced that entire line of shameful thought from her mind by raising her parasol above her head, and wondering aloud why Trooper Wood had not raised the carriage top against the heat of the afternoon sun.

They came to Buckingham Palace, which Caroline privately thought was an ugly building on the outside, looking more like a manufactory than a palace. Edgar and Richard returned the crisp, foot-stamping present-arms salutes of the Coldstream Guards who had the duty with casual waves of their hands. They rolled through a passageway into an inside courtyard, where servants in white stockings and powdered wigs came out to put a step in place and to open the carriage's door.

When Sir Richard helped her from the carriage, he grabbed her upper arm with a strong, even painful, grip, as if he were prepared to pull her bodily down to the cobblestones if she hesitated. When she glowered up at him, she was taken again with his size. He was enormous. She wondered why she had never particularly noticed this before.

They were led by a servant to the foyer outside a small hall, not the usual audience room. A dozen other people were already gathered there. The chamberlain was there. He shook Edgar's hand and nodded at Lady Caroline and Sir Richard Trentwood. Then he turned and signaled to a servant, who walked toward them carrying a tray of glasses, champagne and sherry. The champagne, she decided, was bound to be warm, and she didn't like warm champagne, so she took a sherry.

She knew none of the others waiting for permission to enter the hall, and neither apparently did Edgar or Richard, for they spoke to no one. They were kept waiting some time, time enough to drink three glasses of sherry. Lady Caroline regretted this, for when a gentleman usher offered her his arm to lead her into the hall, she felt the alcohol. She was a little dizzy.

They were shown to chairs quite close to the chair in which the king would sit, and that told her that this was really an unimportant investiture, for had it been important, there would have been important witnesses, and the chairs they would have been given would have been some distance from the king.

And then the king came in, through a door at the rear of the hall, she could tell from his relatively informal dress that he didn't consider what was about to happen of monumental importance, either.

Four people received official recognition from the king of the British Isles, of Scotland and Ireland, the emperor of the lands beyond the seas, and the defender of the faith.

The first was a mousy-looking little man in an ill-fitting suit of clothes and an even more badly fitting wig who nearly fell over as he knelt on one knee before his sovereign. The king smiled, turned, and took a thin-bladed, silver-chased sword from a retainer.

He laid it on each of the mousy little man's shoulders, and said, in a rather high-pitched voice, "Rise, Sir Allan."

Whoever the mousy little man was, he had done something (no suggestion of what had been offered) for the crown which had earned him a knighthood and the right to be called Sir Allan for the rest of his life.

Three other people, all back from Indian service, were given medals, one at a time. An equerry stood beside the king with the medals on a pillow. The chamberlain read their names aloud, one at a time, and the king picked one of the medals from the pillow, and, each time, said, precisely the same thing.

"It gives us great pleasure to make this award."

That was all he said. He seemed more than a little bored.

Lady Caroline was frankly bored, and decided that they had been commanded to appear at the investiture solely for appearance's sake. There should be some sort of senior officer present, and Edgar was the most junior lieutenant colonel, so that "privilege" had therefore come to him.

The king took a step forward and made a little speech: "It gives us great pleasure to make a promotion in our army at this time," he said. "Acting upon the recommendation of my lords of the Military Council, we name Lieutenant Colonel Edgar Watchbury Colonel of Cavalry on the Imperial Staff."

Lady Caroline was sure that Edgar was as surprised as she was. Edgar literally did not know what to do. He simply stood where he was, at attention.

The king, smiling, made a little impatient gesture with his hand, ordering Edgar to approach him. Edgar marched over to him, and knelt on one knee.

"That will not be necessary, Watchbury," the king said, and Edgar, flushing with embarrassment, got to his feet. Another equerry handed a sheet of rolled parchment about eighteen inches tall and tied with a red ribbon to the king, who handed it to Edgar.

No sooner had Edgar taken it than the chamberlain snatched it away from him, opened the ribbon, unrolled the parchment, and read the commission aloud. Then he rolled it back up, tied it with the ribbon again, and handed it back to Edgar.

51

That, Lady Caroline thought, made it official. She was very pleased, and thought that, if nothing else, it insured that Edgar would now get them a suitable house. As a colonel, especially one who had been promoted so soon after promotion to lieutenant colonel, which indicated even further plans for him, a suitable house became an essential, rather than just something that would be nice.

"And now, Colonel," the king went on, in his high-pitched voice, "would you kneel before your sovereign?"

Edgar knelt, trying unsuccessfully to hide his confusion.

The king again took the thin, silver-chased sword from the equerry who held it, and tapped Edgar's shoulders with it.

"Rise, Sir Edgar," the king said, and when Edgar had regained his feet, departed from protocol. He grasped Edgar's arm. "We were really pleased to do that, Edgar," he said.

Lady Caroline rolled the words in her mind. *Colonel Sir Edgar and Lady Watchbury.* They had a very pleasant sound.

The Chamberlain banged a varnished, gold-embellished staff about seven feet tall on the ground. The king, trailed by several equerries, left the room by the door through which he had entered. The first man to be knighted, the mousy-looking little man in the ill-fitting wig, started a procession out of the room. Since Edgar had been invested last, it would follow that he would be last to leave the room. But when he started to do so, the chamberlain signaled him to remain with a small gesture of his hand.

When the last of the others had left the hall, and the door had been closed after them, the chamberlain led them through the door the king had taken. Beyond it was a small anteroom, and beyond that, Caroline was surprised to find herself in the king's private apartments. She had, of course, heard about those people privileged to associate personally with the king in his private apartments but had thought that she and Edgar were some years away from being included in their number.

The king was standing by a pianoforte, helping himself from a bottle of cognac. When he saw Watchbury, he beamed.

"Surprised you, Edgar, didn't we?" the king said. "We rather like to do that to our friends."

What an astonishingly intimate thing for the king to say to Edgar, Lady Caroline thought.

"Yes, sir," Edgar said, bowing his head. Lady Caroline took his cue and curtsied.

"Surprised you, too, did we, madam?" the king asked, obviously quite pleased with himself.

"Yes, indeed, Your Majesty." Lady Caroline said.

"Your husband deserves everything we gave him," the king said, and then handed her a glass of cognac. "This is for the shock of the surprise."

Then the king motioned to a man Caroline could not remember having seen before.

"We would have a word in private with you two," he said, and took Edgar's arm and led him out of the sitting room, and deeper into the apartment.

"Now what?" Caroline asked Captain Sir Richard Trentwood.

"We wait," the taciturn cavalryman replied. He walked away from her and settled himself on a couch. After a moment, feeling foolish standing there alone, Caroline walked over and sat in a chair facing the couch. Sir Richard Trentwood looked her square in the face for a moment and then looked away.

Trying to converse with him, Lady Caroline decided, would be a futile effort. She sipped her cognac. No sooner had she lowered the glass from her lips than a servant, hovering behind her, filled it half full again, and then leaned over and did the same to Sir Richard's glass.

An hour later, during which no conversation at all had passed between them, and there had been no indication from anyone as to how long they would be required to wait for Edgar to be through with the king, Captain Sir Richard Trentwood leaned forward on the couch and spoke to her directly, in a voice louder than necessary.

"I have been thinking," he announced.

"About what?"

"*I* would appreciate you," he said. *I* wouldn't leave you waiting out here like a bloody batman, king or no king."

"Sir Richard!" she said, the words coming out not quite as coldly reprimanding as she intended.

"Bloody damned pity I didn't meet you before he did," he said.

It took a moment for the significance of what he had said to sink in. What an astonishing thing for him to say, out of the blue!

53

He was drunk, Lady Caroline realized. Edgar would be furious if he found out.

"You there!" Sir Richard Trentwood said loudly to the servant with the bottle. "Give Lady Caroline some more brandy, and point me in the general direction of the officer's latrine."

He was drunk nearly out of his mind, Caroline thought, wondering why the cognac had not affected her.

"You will excuse me," Sir Richard said, getting unsteadily to his feet. "I will return directly."

She nodded her head. He marched out of the room behind one of the servants. She noticed how tight his uniform breeches were over his buttocks. Nearly as tight as they were in front.

3

When Lady Caroline first woke, with memories of a firm masculine body overwhelming hers, she first thought that the Devil had again filled her dreams with the Grand Duke Alexei. Next, she became aware that the chills that had brought her from sleep were because, for reasons she couldn't understand, she had gone to bed without her nightdress. Only then did she become aware that she was sharing her bed with a naked male body that did not belong to her husband.

Horror-stricken, she searched her mind for a reconstruction of the previous evening. She recalled, first, having champagne from a roughly opened bottle erupt over her dress. She remembered Captain Sir Richard Trentwood, laughing, showing her how champagne bottles were opened in the officer's mess, by unwrapping the wire that held the cork in place and then sharply smacking the bottom of the bottle with the heel of his hand. That had opened the bottle, all right: champagne had erupted, soaking the upper half of her dress.

At the palace? Had that happened at the palace?

It had happened here.

She recalled one of the palace servants coming to the sitting room in the king's private apartments with the announcement that Edgar would be delayed, and that Trentwood was to take her home, and return her for dinner at half past eight.

She remembered stumbling as she got into the carriage, and Trentwood catching her and practically shoving her into the carriage.

She remembered Trooper Wood shaking her awake when

54

they arrived at the apartment, and she remembered standing up in the carriage, leaning over Trentwood, shaking him awake.

She remembered coming up the stairs with Trentwood, his arm around her to prevent her from stumbling again, as she had stumbled going up the marble stairs from the street. They had been laughing, she remembered that, because she remembered how his laughter had moved the muscles of his chest.

No one had answered her knock at the apartment door; no servants were in the apartment. She remembered being furious that Bridget had not been there, and that it had been necessary for Trentwood literally to break in. She remembered Trentwood raising his black-booted foot and smashing the lock from the door.

And then she remembered more about the champagne.

Offering him champagne had seemed at the time, to be, simple courtesy.

And she'd found champagne in the pantry, and he'd followed her in there, and shown her how they opened champagne in the mess, and it had gone all over her, and he had been so sweet, mopping at it with a napkin, taking extraordinary care when he came close to the exposed flesh at her neckline.

She remembered going to her bedroom to change. She remembered being angry and surprised and then amused that her chemise, as well as the gown, was wet with champagne, and she remembered the difficulty she had pulling the chemise over her head. Wet, it had stuck to her body.

And when she finally got it over the head, she had looked toward the balcony overlooking Lincoln's Inn Fields and seen Trentwood. He was resting his hands on the railing, his back to her, and she had understood that in innocence he had gone onto the balcony, which ran across the front of the entire apartment, from the drawing room. And then he had turned, and from the look on his face, it had been evident that he was as surprised to see her as she had been to see him.

More surprised, because with the chemise gone, she had been standing there in nothing more than her waist-cincher and the stockings it held up.

And then he'd come into the bedroom.

And staggered up to her, a very strange look on his face, looking down at her.

Had she told him to leave? Had she done nothing but stand there until his hand reached out to touch her face with exquisite tenderness, and then to slide off her face onto her neck, and then down to her breast?

She remembered that he had groaned, and said, "Oh, God, you're so beautiful."

And then, she told herself, almost immediately aware that she was lying, she had fainted.

What about the dinner at Buckingham Palace?

She remembered nothing about returning to the palace. She remembered nothing beyond Richard half pushing, half carrying her to the chaise longue. She had no idea, at first, of how she had gotten into the bed, until the details of that popped painfully into her mind.

They had fallen off the chaise. He had been perfectly willing to continue what they were about on the floor, but the carpet had been rough against her shoulders and back, and she had led him to the bed. She closed her eyes and shuddered at the memory of how she had led him to the bed.

Edgar! Had Edgar come home and found them?

What time was it?

Lady Caroline Watchbury put her hand out and laid the balls of her fingers against Captain Sir Richard Trentwood's naked back. It was firm and without fat and surprisingly warm. When he didn't stir, she pushed harder.

He suddenly stiffened, frightening her, and then, frightening her again, rolled over to face her.

"Good God!" he said, softly.

"What have we done?" Caroline asked.

"Good God!" he repeated, louder this time. Then he rolled away from her and got out of the bed. He stood unsteadily by the side of the bed for a moment, then staggered across the room to the mantlepiece, where one candle of the candelabra had not yet burned itself out. He picked up the whole candelabra and held it before the clock.

"Half past two!" he croaked.

"Richard," she said, almost a wail.

"My God, I'm sorry," he said.

"Richard!" she repeated.

"By God," he said, having considered it. "I am *not* sorry!"

"What about Edgar?" Lady Caroline asked.

"If he'd come home," Captain Sir Richard Trentwood said, with irrefutable logic, "we'd know it."

"Oh, my God, Richard!"

He picked up the candelabra with its one flickering candle and walked around the room, picking up his clothing and his boots where he found them, and then set the candelabra on the floor. He sat on the chaise longue and pulled his shirt over his head.

The candle went out.

"Damn!" his voice came out of the darkness. "Where do you keep your candles?"

"There's a candle here," she said. "On the bedside table."

She tried to sit up to get it for him, but when she did, she felt dizzy, and lay down again. She heard him coming across the room, felt the bed sag as he sat on it, heard him feeling around on the table for the candleholder and matches, and closed her eyes against the flare of the match. When she opened her eyes again, he had the candleholder in his hand and was looking down at her.

"You look like an angel," he said.

"Richard, you have to *leave*," she said.

He touched her face, very gently, and then moved his hand down her body. She caught it.

"Richard, no," she said.

"I can't control myself," he said.

"You have to," she said. "*We* have to."

He moved her hand to his mouth and kissed it. She allowed her fingers to run across his face, feeling the bristling whiskers. This freed his hand, and it moved surely to her breast.

"Oh, Richard," she said, softly, resignedly.

4

Edgar came home thirty minutes after Richard had left.

He came into the bedroom carrying a candleholder.

"What the hell happened to the door?" he asked.

"There were no servants, and I didn't have a key," Lady Caroline said. "Trentwood had to break it down."

"Damn," he said. Caroline sensed that her husband had had quite a bit to drink.

He sat down on the chaise longue with a grunt and started to pull his boots off.

"How was the dinner?" he asked.

57

"I don't know," she said. "I felt ill and didn't go. I sent word with Trentwood. Didn't you get it?"

"No matter," Edgar said. "I wasn't there. And neither was His Majesty."

"Oh?"

"We got tied up with business," Edgar said, a bit smugly.

"I see."

"I'm to be gazetted His Majesty's military inspector to the Royal East India Company," he said. "We were discussing that."

"What did you say?"

"I'm being sent to India," Edgar said. "As H.M. special representative, to come up with a realistic picture of their military requirements. H.M. thinks they don't need half of what they're asking for, and he's probably right."

"How long will you be gone?"

"You'll come with me, of course," he said. "Including travel time, we should be back in six or seven months."

This was not the time to bring it up, she decided, but she was going to have to talk him out of her going to India.

Edgar carried the candleholder to the chest of drawers and took out a nightshirt and pulled it over his head. He came to the bed, got in it, turned his back to his wife and was asleep in sixty seconds.

Chapter Four

1

Aboard The Eleanor
Delaware Bay off Cape May Point
August 2, 1769

There had been a pleasant breeze all day as they had sailed south with the shore of Long Island and then New Jersey off their starboard quarter, but once they had turned Cape May Point into Delaware Bay, the cool northerly wind had died down. Now, at anchor just inside the bay, it was hot and humid.

James Porter, *The Eleanor*'s first mate, had wondered if, considering the heat, Captain Selkirk would go through with the ritual last-night-at-sea dinner he had announced at breakfast.

"Presuming we make Cape May Point in time, Mr. Porter," Captain Selkirk had said, "I would be pleased to have the ship's officers take dinner with me."

What he meant, what Porter understood, was not what he said. The officers of *The Eleanor* habitually took all their meals together in the wardroom. The captain himself seldom missed a meal, using the occasion to direct the ship's business through the officers assembled to eat.

He had the custom, however, on the night before they made port, of making the evening meal a formal occasion. The table in his cabin, normally covered with his personal charts, his clothing, his books, his coffee pot and china mug, his flat-bottomed bottle of brandy, and the battered silver goblet from which he drank his brandy, all of which the cabin boy was at other times forbidden to disturb, was cleared and polished and set with linen and china and crystal and silver. The captain dressed for dinner. He wore a wig and a lace-trimmed shirt, and shoes with silver buckles. The officers were expected to follow his example.

The cook selected what he thought were the plumpest chickens in the chicken house and roasted them. The rest of the chickens, no longer needed for eggs, were stewed and served to the crew. If there were potatoes left in the larder, there were roast potatoes. If there was any flour uninfested with weevils after their time at sea, it was baked into fresh bread.

Cognac was served beforehand (and, if they had it aboard, New Jersey applejack), and wine during the meal, and cognac and applejack, a good deal of both, afterward, straight and mixed with coffee.

It was a ceremonial meal, the purpose of which, James Porter believed, was to mark the successful end of a voyage. Sometimes, he thought it was a pleasant custom, and sometimes, now, when it meant that he would have to take a bath and put on a wig and his uniform and sweat through the evening, he wished that it was not the captain's custom.

He never inquired as to the origin of the captain's custom, and it never entered his mind to suggest, no matter how politely, that under some circumstances, such as a hot and humid night, the custom be passed over.

This morning, he had said, as he always said, "I'm sure the officers would be honored to take dinner with you, Captain. I'll pass the word."

Fifteen minutes before they were due to go down to the captain's cabin, all the officers (the helm of *The Eleanor* at anchor having been entrusted to her quartermaster, Peter O'Keefe), the captain appeared on the quarterdeck, coming through the hatch leading directly from his cabin.

He was dressed for dinner. Porter marveled again how a wig transformed Paul Selkirk. At sea, or for that matter ashore, dressed in simple clothing, Paul Selkirk's profession, or his trade, could not be judged from his appearance, except that from his sun-darkened skin it was obvious that he worked outside. He could have been a farmer, or a seaman, a shipwright, a wagon driver, or any other kind of tradesman whose work required strength and stamina. When he spoke, however, in the deep voice he used softly, someone who knew about men could tell that he was used to giving orders, and that he possessed quiet commonsense and high intelligence.

Dressed as he was now, no one would mistake him for a

farmer or a wagon driver. He was clearly a leader, and successful at what he did. Now he could be a surgeon, or a lawyer, or a banker. Or a shipowner. He didn't look like a master: the wig and the well-fitting, expensive clothing seemed a bit too elegant for a master seaman.

"Good evening, Captain," Porter said to him. Selkirk nodded his head and smiled in reply, and then walked to the aft railing and leaned on it and looked ashore for a minute or two at faint lights visible on the New Jersey shore. Then he returned to where Porter stood by the binnacle.

"I think, Mr. Porter," he said, "that we would be more comfortable in this heat were my table set here on the quarterdeck. Would you see to that, please?"

"Aye, aye, sir," Porter said. "Captain, would you like a canvas rigged too . . . ?" he gestured with his hand to indicate what he meant, to shield the officers from the sight of the crew.

"That would defeat my intention, Mr. Porter," Captain Selkirk said. "The crew have seen us dressed before."

Porter naturally assumed that the "intention" a canvas blind would defeat would be the flow of wind across the quarterdeck. He was wrong. Captain Selkirk had several reasons for ordering the officers' table set on the quarterdeck, and only one of them was to avoid the stifling heat of the cabin.

He went down the ladder to the deck and walked forward until he located Bosun Theo LaSalle.

"Well, we must be near home," LaSalle said, with the ease of an old friend. "We're all fancied up."

"A bath would do you no harm," Captain Selkirk said. "Nor a shave."

"When I'm ready to go ashore," LaSalle said.

"I will require the services of a man to help with the dinner," Selkirk said. "What I have in mind is someone freshly washed and shaved and in a clean shirt, jacket, and trousers."

"I have a man in mind for you, Captain," LaSalle said with a smile. "Would you be pleased with young Selkirk?"

"He'll do," Selkirk said. "Since you didn't volunteer."

"There are some things I don't do," LaSalle said. "And waiting at table is one of them."

"I think you'd make a fine waiter, Theo," Selkirk said. "Don't challenge me."

"You wouldn't do that to me, Captain."

61

"Only because you'd likely spill the soup on my clean trousers," Selkirk said, and nodded and walked further forward to the aft bulkhead of the fo'c'sl, where the cook had set up a stove on the deck. The crew's stewed chicken was about done. Selkirk took a large spoon and tasted the gravy.

"You must be sober for a change," he said to the cook. "That's very nearly edible."

The cook beamed.

"If by some chance a young able seaman with an enormous appetite should appear at the head of your line," Selkirk said, "Arrange for him to eat last, somehow, will you? Not at all, is what I'm saying."

"Aye, aye, Captain. What have you planned for him?"

"He's to come to my table," Selkirk said.

"He's a good lad, Captain," the cook said, pleased. "And I think it's time."

"He may make a sailor yet," Selkirk said, and turned and walked back to the quarterdeck where already a table made from planks and horses was being laid with a linen cloth.

"Set five places," he said to the cabin boy, and then walked to the aft railing again, and put his hands on it, and looked ashore.

Porter was right in his belief that the captain's dinner, their last night at sea, was a ceremony, but he did not understand the depth of its meaning to Captain Selkirk. The meaning of it was especially important to Selkirk right here, where *The Eleanor* lay at anchor. It was important to him elsewhere, no matter where they made port, but it was speical here.

Paul Selkirk had been born in a stone house in the Scottish Highlands, the only son of a scar-faced chieftain who served Bonny Prince Charley with a devotion that touched on the fanatic. To put Bonny Prince Charley on the throne of Scotland, his father waged constant war against the British crown. Selkirk had grown to sixteen knowing nothing but war, and raids, and hatred for the English.

Their dreams of making Bonny Prince Charley king had been shattered once and for all in 1746, at the Battle of Culloden, when English forces under the duke of Cumberland had won a near-total victory over the Scots. Afterward, a price was put on the head of Robert Selkirk, outlaw, and upon the head of his son, Paul, sixteen, who, if he was old enough to wield a sword at Culloden, was old enough to be hanged as a traitor to his rightful king.

It was the first time Paul Selkirk had ever told his father no.

"I will not go," he said, when his father told him he had arranged passage for him on a ship, the *Devon*, bound for the Pennsylvania colony.

"You'll do what I tell you, or be damned. Damned and probably hung."

"I will not go."

"You're thinking of that little girl," his father had said. "You're a lovesick puppy and a fool. She's but fourteen."

"Mock me not. I'll stay and wait until she's old enough."

"You'll stay and the goddamned English will hang you from a tree where she can see your rotting corpse."

"I'll stay," he had said. His father had given him the back of his hand, knocking him to the stone floor of the shepherd's cabin where they were hiding from the English troops.

"You'll not talk back to me, his father said. "You'll stay here until I return, and then you'll go to North America."

His father came back in two days with Mary and Alex MacGregor, and a dominie who had been with them at Culloden, and with Eleanor MacGregor; and with her mother sobbing behind her, Eleanor had married him in the shepherd's cabin.

They left immediately to catch the *Devon* and spent the first night of their marriage huddled together under canvas in the sail locker of a tired merchantman while British soldiers searched the ship for wanted traitors.

They had worked their way across the Atlantic, Selkirk as a sailmaker's boy, Eleanor as serving girl to the officers. Selkirk had gone to the captain on the voyage and told him that if the third officer laid a hand on Eleanor again, he would be obliged to kill him. The captain had had him whipped for daring to threaten an officer, whipped with a knotted, tarred line until his back ran blood.

But the captain kept his eye on the third mate, and the next time he had touched Eleanor, the captain had opened the third mate's cheek with the muzzle of the pistol he kept jammed into his waist and promised to kill him if it happened again.

When the *Devon* reached Delaware, she had anchored overnight where *The Eleanor* was now anchored, waiting to sail to Philadelphia at first light in the morning. And he had had a moment alone with Eleanor, on the fo'c'sl deck, and they had looked at the lights on the Jersey shore, and Eleanor for the first time had broken down and, weeping, confessed her fear for the future.

And he had held her, and told her there was naught to fear, and something astonishing had happened, something he had promised her would not happen until she was ready. They had become, truly, husband and wife, under the canvas of the *Devon*'s longboat.

And at noon the next day, carrying all they owned in two cloth bags slung over their shoulders, with one crown their total wealth, they went ashore from the *Devon* in Philadelphia.

He couldn't get a job at first, but Eleanor had found work washing pots in a kitchen, and that had kept them alive for the first weeks. And then he was taken on as a shipwright's apprentice, and they had found a room they could afford. There had been no bed, only a feather mattress on the floor, but it was their home.

Mrs. Eleanor MacGregor Selkirk and her daughter Mary now lived in a three-story brick house behind a white picket fence at the corner of Arch and Third streets. While her husband, Captain Paul T. Selkirk, owner-master of the ship *Eleanor* was at sea, she occupied her time with religious and intellectual matters. She was a member of both Saint Paul's Presbyterian Church and its Women's Altar Society, and of the Library Company of Philadelphia, founded by Mr. Benjamin Franklin. She was driven to the various meetings by her husband's coachman in a carriage drawn by matched sorrel mares.

Paul and Eleanor Selkirk had come a long way since they had first seen faint lights flickering on the dark shore of New Jersey from the fo'c'sl deck of the *Devon*. Paul Selkirk rather liked to remind himself just how far, with his officers gathered around him at a well-set table, aboard his own ship. He almost invariably held such a dinner wherever *The Eleanor* made port, but it was always sweeter here, as he, now a responsible and respected member of Philadelphia society, could be the host at a captain's dinner not far from the very spot where he, a nearly penniless fugitive, had become a man.

And tonight was going to be even sweeter.

When he turned from the rail, he saw Tony, the cabin boy, at the head of the table with a bottle of brandy and a tray of glasses. And he saw Charley standing nearby, freshly washed and dressed in clean clothes, waiting to be told what to do.

Selkirk snapped his fingers, caught Tony's attention, and gestured the order to bring him a brandy, and to pass glasses to the other officers. Tony nodded his understanding, and came quickly to him with a glass. Charley, who had seen his father's signals, started to help, to pick up the tray and offer brandy to the other officers.

"When I want you to serve drinks," Captain Selkirk said sharply, "I'll let you know."

Charley, flustered, stepped again from the table and stood to attention.

He really, Paul Selkirk thought with pleasure, has no idea what he's doing here.

Getting drinks in hand was the signal to take their places at the table. The officers waited until they saw their captain walk toward the head of the table, and then they moved to take their seats. When they were all seated, Selkirk looked at his son.

"What are you waiting for?" he snapped.

"Sir?" Charley asked, in utter confusion.

"Do me the great honor, sir," Paul Selkirk said, "of sitting when your seniors sit."

Charley acted as if he didn't quite believe what he was hearing.

The way I put it to him, Paul Selkirk remembered, pleased with himself, was, "One day, Charley, after a voyage or two more . . ."

He had said nothing to him, so Charley had naturally assumed that it would happen after the voyage after this one, or the voyage after that.

"Gentlemen," Captain Paul Selkirk said. "May I present to you Mr. Charles Selkirk? Mr. Selkirk will be sailing with us as junior third mate until Mr. Greene leaves us for *The Mary*."

Each of the officers, according to their rank, shook Charley's hand, as if they were meeting him for the first time, and each said exactly the same thing: "How do you do, Mr. Selkirk? Welcome aboard."

First Mate James Porter now understood why the captain had not wanted him to have a canvas screen erected to bar the crew's view of the table. He wanted the crew to see and hear. And they saw and heard and approved. Several of the young seamen who had been berthing with Charley in the fo'c'sl put fingers in their mouths and whistled shrilly.

"I think, Mr. Selkirk," Captain Selkirk said, "that under the circumstances you could tell the bosun to issue another round of rum to the crew."

"Aye, aye, sir," Charley said, and got up and went to the railing overlooking the main deck.

"Bosun!" he called.

Theo LaSalle looked up at him, but said nothing.

"There will be an extra issue of rum, Bosun," he said.

"Aye, aye, Mr. Selkirk, sir," Bosun LaSalle said, very loudly.

That made it official, Captain Selkirk thought, as Charley, flushing, returned to the table and sat down. When LaSalle had called him "Mister Selkirk" and "Sir," that made him an officer of *The Eleanor.*

Captain Selkirk picked up his glass.

"Gentlemen," he said. "The king. May the bastard be boiled in tar."

They sipped their brandy.

"Gentlemen," he said. "I give you the lady without whom most of us, probably, and Mr. Selkirk for certain, would not be here tonight. I give you my good wife."

"Hear, hear," all of his officers said, chuckling, getting to their feet, and raising their glasses.

Damned shame she couldn't be here, Captain Selkirk thought. Eleanor would have liked to see Charley become an officer.

2

They had a hell of a time docking *The Eleanor.* The current seemed determined to frustrate them. It was a long time before they could get close enough to the Water Street wharf to get a line ashore, and it took seemingly forever for them to winch the ship out of the channel.

It wasn't lack of trying on the part of the crew. They pushed the windlass around and were literally soaked in sweat with the effort.

Well, it was no one's fault. Sometimes you could bring a ship into a wharf with no effort at all, and sometimes it was like this.

Finally, *The Eleanor* was in place, and home.

An officer from the harbormaster's office was first aboard. Selkirk did not recognize him.

"Captain Lewis's compliments, Captain," the officer said. Captain Ephraim Lewis and Captain Paul Selkirk were old friends. "He asks that you attend him; he will be here shortly."

"My compliments to Captain Lewis," Selkirk replied. "Will you please tell him that I will be greatly pleased and honored to receive him at my home?"

"He seemed especially anxious that you wait for him here, sir," the officer said.

"And I am especially anxious to get to my home," Selkirk said. He turned to First Mate Porter. "You will, I am sure," he said, "both offer Captain Lewis, when he appears, the hospitality of the ship, and offer my apologies for my not remaining aboard to receive him."

"Aye, aye, sir."

"Mr. Selkirk will accompany me home," Captain Selkirk said, "for the obvious reasons, and then he will shortly return aboard so that you and the other officers can be relieved."

"Aye, aye, sir."

"Come on, Charley," Selkirk said, nodding to the officer from the harbormaster's office. "Let's go home."

"Would you like to use my carriage, sir?" the officer from the harbormaster's office asked.

"We can walk, it's but three blocks, but thank you kindly just the same," Selkirk said, and then he walked down the gangplank onto the wharf. Charley went ashore after him, and they started up the shallow hill from Water Street to Second Street side by side, walking quickly.

When they got to the house, the reason that Captain Ephraim Lewis had been so anxious that they wait for him aboard *The Eleanor* became immediately apparent.

Mary Selkirk, fifteen years old, dressed in black, ran down the brick wall when she saw them coming, and threw herself in her father's arms and, weeping, told him that Mamma was dead.

3

Mistress Ingebord Johnson, a tall, well-muscled woman of thirty-nine, who wore her dull blonde hair parted in the middle and brushed back into a bun, watched out the window

67

of her third-floor room as Captain Paul Selkirk pushed open the gate in the picket fence and walked up to the house. There were two advantages in letting the girl break the news to her father: it would spare her that unpleasantness, and it would give her an opportunity to examine his reaction closely without his being aware of it.

Ingebord Johnson prided herself on being both a Christian, content to put matters in God's hands (never forgetting for a moment, of course, that The Lord Helps Those Who Help Themselves), and a practical woman. When she had ordered the tombstone for her late husband, her thoughts had naturally turned to what would eventually appear on her own. What she decided she wanted for her epitaph was the phrase, "A practical Christian wife and mother."

As a Christian, she believed that Eleanor Selkirk was now in heaven with Jesus. So was Nils Johnson. They had lived good Christian lives, and they had died as baptized Christians, and according to Ingebord's understanding of the Christian faith, that had earned them life eternal in the Lord Jesus Christ.

As a practical matter, they had left this life, and the problem she faced was what to do with the rest of her time on earth. She had concluded within a week of Nils's death that she was going to have to remarry and within two days of learning that Eleanor Selkirk had passed to her eternal reward that the man she should marry was Captain Paul Selkirk.

There were no financial problems, thank the Good Lord. Nils had been a good provider, and Selkirk she knew to be comfortable, and suspected of being even more well-to-do than his somewhat ostentatious style of life suggested.

She had disagreed with Nils about that. Nils had said that Paul Selkirk maintained the big three-story brick house and all that went with it—the servants and the matched sorrel mares to pull his wife's carriage—from vanity, and that he was probably deeply in debt, and constantly on the brink of ruin.

Ingebord agreed that the house and the rest of it fed Paul Selkirk's vanity, but she sensed somehow that Paul Selkirk would walk barefoot before he would borrow money to possess a carriage with a matched pair of sorrel mares to pull it.

She suspected further that the "investors" in the construction and operation of *The Eleanor* and *The Mary* that Captain Paul Selkirk "had to consult" so frequently in his business dealings with Nils were imaginary and that he was the sole owner of everything. His motives in publicly denying his full ownership of his ships, or for that matter, his actual financial status, had nothing to do with modesty. He had practical reasons for wishing to appear only moderately successful, and she thought she knew what they were.

To tell God's truth about it, she didn't like Captain Paul Selkirk, nor, for that matter, his daughter. They were different kinds of people, different in background, temperament, and in practically every way she could think of except business acumen.

Captain Paul Selkirk had met Nils Johnson while looking for a good business deal. Selkirk had been the owner/master of *The Mary*, a small three-masted coastal merchantman named after his daughter. Before Ingebord had actually met Paul Selkirk, Nils had told her something about his background: the Selkirks had come to Pennsylvania from Scotland after Selkirk had gotten himself into some unspecified trouble with the authorities of the crown. It had, Nils had told her, something to with his family having supported Prince Charles Edward, "Bonny Prince Charley," who had aspired to the throne.

She wasn't sure if her husband really believed what Selkirk had told him about his father being a Scottish chieftain and that Paul Selkirk himself had actually been in the Battle of Culloden in 1746 when the duke of Cumberland had settled the business of "The Young Pretender" once and for all. She didn't entirely believe it herself, although it was possible. If Selkirk had actually been there, he would have been little more than a boy. But on the other hand, the Scots were crazy and hardly civilized, and it was possible. What was more likely, she had decided, considering Selkirk's vanity, was that he was simply one more impoverished immigrant to the colonies, who had invented a romantic story so that people would not know him for what he was.

She did believe that Selkirk and his wife had, as he proudly claimed, arrived in Pennsylvania with little more than the clothes on their backs. That was the seed for the respect in which she now held him. Captain Paul Selkirk and his wife had, in their way, done much what she and Nils had done, built a business by hard work and sacrifice. That was commendable, and worthy of her respect.

Nils told her that Selkirk had told him that he had started out as an apprentice shipwright in the Philadelphia shipyards, hired solely because he appeared to be a strong and healthy back who could be trained as a shipwright.

Nils had talked a good deal about Paul Selkirk. Selkirk really impressed Nils, and Ingebord knew why: Nils was a good man, but he was a slight, retiring one who was impressed by, perhaps jealous of, the flamboyant, outgoing sailors with whom he sometimes did business. He often told her about them, taking vicarious pleasure in their exploits at sea and ashore.

He had heard, he had told her with relish, how Captain Paul Selkirk had come to go to sea the first time. He had worked his way up to being a journeyman shipwright, and a foreman, in the shipyards in Philadelphia—both at a very young age and by the traditional method. He had first learned his craft and then earned his promotion and held it with his fists.

"He's not the typical brawler," Nils had told her. "There's no fat on him, and that makes him quick, you see. He just dances around the other fellow, dodging his punches, and landing his own."

Ingebord knew that Nils, in his mind, was dancing around some of the men along the river he didn't like, dodging their punches, landing his own.

Nils, of course, had gone on with the story: the owner of a ship being built and the captain who would sail her when she was completed had been in the shipyard and witnessed a brutal fight between Foreman Selkirk and one of his Irish shipwrights. No-holds-barred fighting between shipyard workers was not only common but provided an opportunity for gentlemen financing ships, and the officers who would sail them, Nils told her, to wager on the outcome.

The shipowner had wagered on Selkirk, against the ship's captain, who bet on the side of age, bulk, and obvious experience, and thus on the Irishman. Selkirk had exhausted the Irishman by staying out of the range of his furious lunges, while simultaneously turning his face into a bloody pulp with a series of accurate punches. When the severely beaten Irishman, who was as game as he was large, had finally been led off, in a daze, by his friends, the ship's captain, after he paid off his lost wager, had gone down from the scaffolding to the ways. He told Selkirk that he was always looking out for someone who knew how to "control men," and that he would be needing a boatswain's mate to keep the crew in line, not only when the ship was in the water and being outfitted, but later, at sea.

It was not important that Selkirk knew nothing about seamanship. He could acquire that knowledge. The captain offered him better wages than he was then earning, and Selkirk went aboard the ship the day it was launched, even after the shipyard offered to raise his wages to keep him.

On the first six-months' voyage to the West Indies and the Home Isles and back again, Bosun Selkirk had become Third Mate Selkirk. He had left his wife for ten months out of the year for the next three years, but at the end of that time it was First Mate Selkirk, more a tribute to his ability to acquire the skills of navigation and seamanship, and apply them, than to his fighting skills.

Then he had gone out, Nils told Ingebord he had heard from people who should have known, for fifteen months, without once returning to Philadelphia, and when he had returned that time, he was the master. The master had been killed in "an encounter with pirates," and First Mate Selkirk had assumed command of the ship, and of the pirate ship, claimed as a prize.

His share of the prize money had provided him with the means to buy an old but well-cared-for schooner, a small coaster that he renamed *The Mary* after his daughter.

Ingebord Johnson privately believed it was far more likely that Selkirk's affluence had come at the expense of some Spanish (or French) shipowner. There was no question in her mind about what they had been up to was either privateering, or smuggling. Or, probably, both. Or, for that matter, outright piracy.

It was after he (and his "gentleman investors") had come into possession of *The Mary*, and he was sailing as her master from Philadelphia as far north as Boston and as far south as Savannah, that he had met Nils. Selkirk had lost three of *The Mary*'s four anchors, one of her two masts, much of her rigging, and most of her canvas during a hurricane off the coast of South Carolina. When he'd made port in Philadelphia, he had been infuriated by the price quoted by the shipyard for replacement anchors and other ironwork.

71

The shipyard complained that they had to pay the merchants, both commission and wholesale, through the nose for the ironwork, and that it wasn't their fault. The most superficial investigation by Captain Selkirk had revealed that the merchants, simply because they had the ironwork in stock, felt justified in charging almost exactly twice what they had paid for it.

So Selkirk had journeyed upstream on the Delaware to the forges at Durham Furnace, twelve miles south of the confluence of the Delaware and the Lehigh at Easton. Most of the forges in the area—in defiance of the law, which forbade the manufacture of most heavy ironwork in the colonies—cast anchors and chain. They quietly sold their forgings to shipowners at prices much lower than the ship chandlers in Philadelphia charged. And sometimes they sold it to shipcaptains, who reported to their owners they had bought the goods from chandlers in Philadelphia, or elsewhere, and then pocketed the difference in price.

In this way, trying to buy anchor and chain and other ship fittings at a decent price, Selkirk had come to meet Nils Johnson. Nils was not above closing his eyes to the fact that the seafarers with whom he dealt were often cheating their employers. He was just careful not to deal with anyone who could prove embarrassing. He had checked out Paul Selkirk before agreeing to sell him more than a few small items.

Nils had not only found that Paul Selkirk was what he said he was, but that the rest of his story was true, too. For his own silly reasons, in Ingebord's opinion, Nils had wanted to make a friend of a man who had become a ship's officer with his fists, and who had been, it was reliably rumored, a privateer.

When Selkirk had returned to pick up the ship's fittings, Nils Johnson had invited him to spend the night at the farm. It would be his pleasure, he told him, and it would spare Captain Selkirk either having to ride on to Easton or spend the night in one of the filthy and disreputable "hotels" along the riverfront.

Ingebord Johnson, seeing Selkirk awkwardly trying to comfort his daughter now, remembered the first time she had seen him. She had, out of simple courtesy, offered him a glass of cider or milk.

"I have applejack," he had replied, taking two bottles of it from his saddlebag and setting them on the table right then and there, "if you have glasses."

And then he'd gotten tiddly, and loud, and gotten Nils drunk. Nils was not used to spirits, but he would not have admitted this to Selkirk nor refused Selkirk's spirits had his life depended on it.

When his tongue was loosened by the spirits, Captain Paul Selkirk said what he thought, and what he thought was that the merchants and ship chandlers in Philadelphia were a "passle of goddamned thieves." Nils had not only agreed with him but let the blasphemy pass. Ordinarily, Nils would not have permitted blasphemy in his house, for he believed that taking the Lord's name in vain was a sin.

Ingebord had seen then that Selkirk was capable, intentionally or otherwise, of influencing Nils, and had set her guard against Nils getting them into trouble, moral or financial.

Nils told Selkirk that he thought there was something less than fair in a system that saw the price of his rough product (pig iron) double in Philadelphia when the merchant to whom he had sold it in turn sold it to the agent of a merchant in New England, and then double again when the New England merchant sold it to a New England forge. The same was true of the finished products of the forge, the scythes and plows and axes and sledges and other ironwork. The ultimate purchaser of the products of Nils Johnson's forge paid three times, sometimes four times, as much for them as Nils had first sold them for.

Full of Selkirk's applejack, Nils had told Selkirk that he was prepared to make him a very special price on three first-quality Admiralty-pattern anchors, warranted as good as anything made in England, and the necessary chain for them, delivered on board Captain Selkirk's *Mary*, if Captain Selkirk agreed to also take aboard, directly from the Durham boats, as much pig iron and finished iron products as his bottom would carry, and transport it directly to Boston without having it pass through the merchants or chandlers in Philadelphia.

Captain Selkirk made a counter-proposal. For a cargo of pig iron and axe heads and plows delivered aboard *The Mary*, he would pay Nils Johnson what a Philadelphia merchant would charge the agent of a New England founder. He said he would not be able to pay Johnson, of course, until he had disposed of the pig iron and the tools in New England, at which time he would also settle for the anchors and chain.

Nils had agreed on the spot. Ingebord could cheerfully have poured boiling water on him. Or if not really boiling water, then hot soup. Or at least a bucket of water, to wake him up. She had to stay up much later than she liked, until the bottles of applejack had been drained, to make sure Paul Selkirk didn't talk her husband out of the farm, as well as the products of the forge. When she finally got him into bed, she told him in no uncertain terms what kind of a fool he had made of himself.

Even if the blasphemous Scot were honest, she had hissed at him, and she had strong doubts about that, since the title to the tools and pig iron would remain with Nils Johnson until it was sold, they would lose everything if his ship were lost at sea. Or if he *said* it had been. He wouldn't be the first sea captain to report the loss of a ship at sea when he had really sold the ship and somebody else's cargo to a Frenchman or a Spaniard. She had told Nils that in the morning he would have to tell Selkirk that he had thought it over and realized that he had been a little hasty, and that he could not, now that he'd thought it over, go through with the deal as originally agreed.

Ingebord realized that it would be more than a little embarrassing for Nils, who prided himself that his word was as good as his bond, but it had to be done. The humiliation would be good for him, the next time he came close to letting spirits do his thinking for him.

Normally, Nils would have listened to her, for he knew that she was a good woman who always made a genuine effort to keep her temper, and lost it only where there was sufficient justification. But he was full of Selkirk's applejack, and the spirits gave him courage,

"I'll get nearly twice what I'm getting now," he had replied. "That's worth the risk. He's an honest man."

"You don't know that!" she argued.

"I'll run my business, thank you, Mistress Johnson," he had said angrily, and she had known that with the applejack in him, there would be no further reasoning with him.

Ingebord had realized that her only hope would come in the morning, when Nils was sober and possessed of his faculties again, and, she hoped, as sick as the spirtis could make him. He might then realize what he had done.

But in the morning, although he was sick, and she knew that he regretted what he had done, his masculine pride took over. He had given his word to Captain Paul Selkirk, brawler and privateer. He could not go back on it now.

Selkirk had ridden off to Philadelphia, and Nils had loaded everything, the anchors and the chain, and the tools and the fifty-five tons of pig iron, onto Durham boats, and gone down the Delaware with them, and supervised their off-loading onto Captain Selkirk's *Mary*.

If the money had not been forthcoming, they would have truly been in bad trouble. Ingebord had had more than a month to consider what fools men generally, and her husband specifically, were. It was absolute insanity to risk the roof over their head simply because he was unwilling to "go back on his word as a gentleman" and admit he had been drunk and not responsible for what he had said.

But just over a month later, a week after Ingebord Johnson, convinced that they were out two year's profit, had for the first time in their marriage called God's damnation down on her husband, Captain Paul Selkirk rode up to the house on the farm on that fancy mare of his and squared all his accounts to the last farthing.

That began their business dealings, and they had grown. Selkirk, Ingebord suspected, was making more money, dealing directly with the foundries in Massachusetts, cutting out the Boston merchants, than he was admitting. But she was honest and fair enough to realize that she and Nils were making a nice profit, too, and that greed had killed the goose which laid the golden eggs.

She had come to have grudging admiration of Paul Selkirk. Despite his drinking and his blasphemy, despite what they said about his past, so far as his dealings with them were concerned, he was an honest man, and a smart one.

Several months after he had made the first settlement of the accounts between them, sitting again at their table with a bottle of applejack before him, Captain Paul Selkirk had announced that he and the "gentlemen investors" who had financed *The Mary* were about to begin constrcution of a large merchantman, near three times the size of *The Mary*. He intended to supervise its construction himself, in a shipyard at Baltimore, on Chesapeake Bay, in the Maryland colony.

He knew something about shipyards and shipbuilding, he announced somewhat smugly, and he had been impressed with both the quality of the work done in Baltimore and with the prices asked there.

And incidentally, Ingebord had thought, if he built a ship in Baltimore, the questions sure to be asked in Philadelphia about where the money for its construction had come from would not be asked.

Selkirk quickly corrected Nils's pleased notion that a larger ship would mean larger cargoes of pig iron and tools per voyage for the New England colonies.

"No, we're still going to need the little coaster," Selkirk said. "We can figure, even with the loss of some voyages during the winter, between twelve and fourteen trips a year with her. And she can be sailed right up the rivers, which means that we save whatever it would cost to unload a bigger vessel and reboard the iron on a smaller bottom. I want the new ship for the African and Indian trade."

"You say 'we' and then you say 'I,'" Ingebord had interrupted. "You don't expect my husband to become involved in this, do you?"

"That would be entirely up to your husband, mistress," Selkirk had replied. Then he turned to face Nils. "What I think would make both of us a little money, Nils," he said, reasonably, "would be to make a separate company with *The Mary*. I've got a mate, who for a goddamned Irisher's not a bad sailor. He can handle *The Mary*, and'll do it well, if we give him part of the profits. And I'll take *The Eleanor* to North and South Africa, and India."

"You're proposing a shipping company?" Ingebord asked, sharply.

"Aye."

"But only with *The Mary*, and not with *The Eleanor*?"

"Unless you," he replied, "and your husband, mistress, should want to share in *The Eleanor*."

"We have no such amount of money," she said, firmly.

"Not for an African/Indian venture," Nils had spoken up. "But perhaps we could invest in a coastal enterprise."

"I thought perhaps you could," Selkirk said.

"Why are you thinking of going as far as India?" Ingebord asked. If he was lost at sea, or even gone for a long time, the coastal business would likely suffer.

"If there is a profitable cargo, I'll go anywhere."

"And pick up slaves in Africa for the West Indies?" she asked.

76

"No," Captain Selkirk said, bluntly.

"I'll have nothing to do with the slave trade," Nils Johnson said. "It's something I want nothing to do with."

"Nor I," Captain Selkirk said. "They stink up a ship."

"My objection is on Christian grounds," Nils said.

"The result is the same," Selkirk replied. "I've never carried slaves, and I never will."

Ingebord had had the idea then that Selkirk, though he wouldn't admit it, was also repelled by the immorality of the slave trade.

"We could, I think, make a small investment in a small shipping company," Ingebord said. "Couldn't we, Nils?"

"I'll have to hear more of the details, of course," he said. "But I can think of no reason we couldn't."

Nils took Ingebord into Philadelphia to meet *The Eleanor* when she arrived there on her maiden voyage. And there, for the first time, she had met Eleanor Selkirk. Mrs. Selkirk had met them in her elegant carriage at the waterfront and carried them to the big house at Third and Arch streets.

Ingebord had at first disliked her, for she was a bit too fancy, but that hadn't lasted long. Eleanor Selkirk was, like herself, a good Christian woman, devoted to her husband and children. The main difference between them, Ingebord decided was that she was burdened with a mouse of a husband who wanted to *be* a lion, and Eleanor Selkirk was burdened with a husband who had to be kept from acting like the lion he was.

She had gone to Philadelphia reluctantly, for she would not have been surprised to find Selkirk married to a sailor's whore and living in rooms over some waterfront tavern. When she found Eleanor Selkirk to be a lady, and the Selkirk house, ostentatious as it was, really comfortable, with a water pump right in the kitchen, and Franklin stoves in practically every room, as well as other expensive modern comforts, she had reconsidered her own position. It was not beyond possibility that they could one day live nearly as well as the Selkirks, presuming she could continue to separate the possible from the fantastic in their business plans.

All her private dreams along those lines had been shattered when Nils had taken a fever and chill and died. As she stood at the graveside with her sons, she had known that she would be lucky to keep what she had, and that things in any event were going to be very difficult.

When word came up river that Eleanor Selkirk had died, apparently of the same fever and chill that had taken Nils to his Eternal Reward, she told herself that with Captain Paul Selkirk and his son off God only knew where in India and the Horn of Africa, it was her Christian duty to go to Philadelphia and see to the girl's welfare..

The boys could handle the simple work of the forge while she was gone, and she planned to be gone no more than five days before returning with Mary Selkirk.

That hadn't worked out. Mary Selkirk had flatly refused to come up river with her. She would stay where she was, she said, until her Pappa returned. Ingebord was tempted to take her up river by force, if necessary, and she made what she thought to be a reasonable presentation of her case to Paul Selkirk's good friend, Captain Ephraim Lewis, the Philadelphia harbormaster.

She could be considered Captain Selkirk's business partner, as well as his friend, she told Captain Lewis, as until her son was old enough to take over the forge, she was now running it. She could offer the girl a good home, and the protection a girl needed, until Captain Selkirk returned home.

Captain Lewis's response had been astonishing. He and Mistress Lewis had offered Mary Selkirk their home, he said, and Mary had refused. Mary had said she would stay in her home until her father returned. There were servants to care for her, and there was no problem of money.

"My good wife looks in on her daily," he said. "And we take her to church with us, and have her to dinner on Sunday. All things considered, the girl's making out all right, the way things are."

Ingebord knew that her plans for Captain Paul Selkirk depended in large measure on her relationship with his daughter. She managed to get Captain Lewis to believe that it was his idea that she, at the considerable sacrifice that meant for Mistress Johnson, stay in the house with the girl and keep an eye on her until Captain Selkirk made port.

And she had really gone out of her way to indulge the girl, whom she privately thought was a strong-willed, ungrateful little bitch who would be the better for a regular whipping.

Chapter Five

1

Philadelphia, Pennsylvania
September 15, 1769

> Captain Paul T. Selkirk, widower, of Philadel-
> phia, and Ingebord Johnson, widow, of Dur-
> ham Furnace, Bucks Country, were joined in
> Holy Matrimony by the Reverend Ingmar
> Sooth at Saint Olaf's Lutheran Church in this
> city on 12 September.
> *The Philadelphia Gazette,* September 15, 1769

It was agreed between Paul Selkirk and Ingebord Johnson
that all property of which they were possessed at the time of
their marriage, that is to say the farm and the mines and the
forge in Bucks County, the property of her late husband, and
The Eleanor, and what other property Paul Selkirk owned,
would not become part of the marriage agreement.

It was his intention, Paul Selkirk told her, to pass his holdings onto his son, less what was required to make a good
dowry for his daughter. Ingebord Johnson replied that it was
her intention to see her late husband's farm and the mines
and the forge divided between her sons, Nils and Luther,
when they reached their majority.

The Mary, which had been jointly owned by Nils Johnson
and Paul Selkirk (Selkirk abandoned the pertense, at least as
far as the Widow Johnson was concerned, of having investors
in his share of the shipping venture), would remain their joint
property. Selkirk would have issued to her a power of attorney to do all things necessary to operate *The Mary* in his absence.

For legal reasons, the attorney they consulted told them, it would be best for Selkirk to assume title to the mines and forge, again issuing her a power of attorney to operate them in his absence, and also to give her a written promise that he would relinquish title to the property to her sons, half as each came into his majority.

The farm, according to the laws concerning widowed farm wives, could remain in her name, pending the coming of age of her sons, the intended heirs.

Selkirk announced that he intended to put the house on the corner of Third and Arch streets, and its contents, on the market, the sale to take place as soon as he put to sea.

"Frankly, mistress," he said to Ingebord, "there would be too many ghosts here for me to continue to live here. I happen to own the building in which the Safe Harbor Tavern is located, and I could easily take the third floor over as a flat for Charles and myself when we are in port."

The truth of the matter was that he owned both the building and the tavern, but he decided, considering Mistress Johnson's feelings about demon rum and sailor's taverns, that it would be best not to tell her the whole story.

"We have been speaking frankly about business matters," Ingebord had replied.

"Aye, we have, and I appreciate it."

"You have said nothing to make me believe that you are in particular need of the money selling the house would give you."

He nodded, agreeing with her observation.

"And I understand your feelings about not wishing to live there, with the house reminding you every day of your loss."

"But?"

"The house will grow in value, because of its location, as time passes."

He nodded again.

"You spoke of a dowry for the girl."

He disliked intensely her manner of referring to Mary as "the girl," but he held his tongue.

"You have a point," he admitted.

"If not as dowry for Mary, then perhaps for the boy. Or my boys."

"*Your* boys?" He noticed that her impersonal reference to offspring at least included her own.

"I'm looking to the future, Captain Selkirk," Ingebord Johnson had told him. "I see it possible that both of my sons would not wish to stay at the farm or the forge. Nils has already shown an interest in moving to the city."

"And the house would be suitable for him? Is that what you're suggesting?"

"I'm suggesting that it would be suitable for any one of them," she said. "If you did not give it as dowry to the girl, or as a gift on the boy's wedding, which will come certainly, and not too far away, I would be willing, very possibly, to buy it for one of my sons. At whatever the market would bring."

"You have a very practical mind, mistress," Paul Selkirk said.

"It could be sold at any time," she went on.

"Aye, it could."

"I am trying to suggest that your grief might make you do something you would not do, had not God taken your Eleanor from you."

"You are saying let the house stand empty?"

"I am saying offer it for lease," she said.

"I could not have strangers in my bed," he said.

"Take those things you wish especially to keep to the flat you talk about," she said. "And sell the others."

"I would give them to you," he said. "You could take them to the country."

"I would buy them," she said.

"No, you would not," he said. "I would not sell things to my wife."

As he spoke, he wondered if Ingebord had known that all along. Probably, he thought, she had. It made no difference, he told himself. He didn't want the furniture any more, and better that she have it. Otherwise, he might find himself buying her furniture.

"The girl's things, in any case, could be taken to the country," Ingebord went on.

"Yes," he said. "She would be pleased."

"Then that is settled?"

"Aye."

They talked (almost, he thought, as man to man) not only of the disposal of the property of his marriage, and not, even, only of the business between them of *The Mary*.

They talked of his intention of breaking the law on a grand scale.

Ingebord Johnson seemed neither shocked nor afraid of the

81

consequences of what he intended to do. Since he had given the idea of talking to her at all about it a great deal of thought before he finally brought the subject up, this came as a great relief to him.

And he was pleased and surprised at her general knowledge of the subject of firearms manufacture, both technical and legal.

"The crown," she told him, "forbids the manufacture of firearms in the colonies. They want to keep the steel-making for Birmingham, and the gun-making for Birmingham and Leeds and London."

"I can walk three blocks from this house, mistress, and buy all the Pennsylvania-manufactured muskets and rifles I want."

"Not in the quantities I believe you have in mind, Captain Selkirk," she said. "One musket, or a dozen rifles, or two dozen, to take aboard a ship is one thing. A three hundred-stand purchase is something else again."

"I know little of this," he confessed. He was aware that he was making a confession to her that he would not have made to most men.

"The constable and the customs look the other way most of the time," she explained, "because they have more important things to do than run down one little gun-maker at a time, and charge him before a court that would more than likely turn him loose."

"I see."

"They pretend that the muskets and rifles are not manufactured," she said, "but *repaired*. They know they can't stop gunsmiths repairing weapons, that the repair of a firearm is as necessary to a colonist as is a blacksmith to shoe his horses. And so long as a gunsmith makes only a few weapons, and of such quality, by that I mean at such a high price, that they will not fall into the hands of the Indians, they look the other way."

"How can they tell how many a gunsmith makes?"

"They keep track of good steel," she said. "They know how much steel is required to make a gun, and if someone starts buying more than they think he should have to repair guns, or make more than five or six a month, they pay him a visit and remind him that the penalty for violating the tariff acts is confiscation of his shop and lands; and that the penalty for arming the Indians is death."

"And what is the penalty for exporting firearms?"

"Confiscation of the vessel on which they are transported, and imprisonment of the smuggler."

"There are always risks," he said, as much to test her reaction as anything.

"Yes," she agreed immediately.

"I have been offered a price for three hundred-stand of arms," he said, "that makes the risk seem worthwhile."

"Worth the risk of forfeiting *The Eleanor*?"

He snorted and shook his head, "No."

"If you throw contraband cotton over the side when you're stopped by H.M. revenue cutters," he said, "it floats, and they can pick it up, and swear before an admiralty court they saw you throw it over. Rifles don't float."

"H.M. Revenue Service has been known to pay informers, and pay them well," she said.

"There are no informers on *The Eleanor*," he said.

"You seem determined to do this."

"I haven't made what I have, mistress," Paul Selkirk said, "without taking a risk here and there. And I haven't kept what I have made by being a fool."

He was not, for example, he thought, fool enough to tell her that the profit he stood to make on the three hundred-stand of rifles for the prince of Hyderabad did in fact justify risking the forfeiture of *The Eleanor* if he were caught.

There were some "ifs," of course. *If* he could get the rifles at a reasonable price; and *if* he could carry them safely to Tatta on the Indus; and *if* the prince of Hyderabad held up his end of the bargain, and paid him for the rifles he brought at the agreed price in jewels; *if*, in other words, the prince was not already making plans to rob him of his rifles, secure in the knowledge that a smuggler of firearms to the natives was in no position to scream "piracy" to the English when he was relieved of the rifles at swordpoint; *then* he could make a good deal of money.

A very great deal of money. He had suspected that the diamonds and emeralds he had received from the prince were very valuable, but it hadn't been until he'd taken them to Amsterdam that he was sure. The diamond merchant in Amsterdam had not been able to keep his excitement from making his eyes bright when Selkirk had laid the stones on the black velvet before him. The profit of the trading in silk for ironwork had not been a fourth of the profit he had realized in trading just four rifles for jewels.

83

On the voyage home from Amsterdam Selkirk had given the whole business a good deal of thought. He had long ago taken stock of his personal weaknesses and knew that high among them were greed (anyone who had been as poor as he and Eleanor had been when they had started out was bound to be greedy, he thought) and hatred for the English. Five years after Paul Selkirk had come to the Pennsylvania colony, he had learned that Robert Selkirk, outlaw, had been captured and, after a year in chains and a ten-minute trial, hanged. His wife had died a year before his son heard of their deaths.

There was no question that both greed and hatred were involved here. He could make an unholy amount of money selling rifles to the prince of Hyderabad, who was willing to pay that much for them not because he liked firearms but because he intended to use them against the English.

That was the sweetest kind of business deal, one so sweet that his eyes might be blinded to the dangers involved. For one thing, even if they couldn't convict him before an admiralty court, once the name of Paul MacTavish Selkirk started cropping up in official crown business, someone might make the connection between Paul MacTavish Selkirk, owner-master of the ship *Eleanor*, and Paul MacTavish Selkirk, outlaw, believed to have fled Scotland.

He was still wanted, after all these years, by the English, and the king's government had a long memory.

He had played the devil's advocate in his mind on the voyages from Tatta to Amsterdam, and from Amsterdam to Philadelphia, and he played it again when he talked to Ingebord Johnson before he married her.

He had concluded that there was nothing wrong in doing the crown ill and at the same time making a lot of money doing it, if you didn't get caught. And the way to keep from getting caught was to keep in mind that you really liked what you were up to, and consequently might be prone not to think everything through clearly.

And to think everything through meant considering what would happen if everything went wrong.

There were two ways in which everything could go wrong:

The prince of Hyderabad might try to kill him and his crew, take the rifles, and scuttle *The Eleanor* at sea. That was a problem he could handle. It was simply a matter of never giving the prince an opportunity to do what he certainly must at least be thinking about doing. So long as they were aboard *The Eleanor*, Selkirk and his crew could handle any assault the prince could think up. All the captain would have to do to deal with the threat of the prince was make sure he always met him on his own ground. That wouldn't be hard to arrange.

The second thing that could go wrong was to be caught by the English with the rifles. That possibility had to be considered. And what would happen then was that he would be taken in chains before an admiralty court, where he would be certain to lose *The Eleanor*, and probably his freedom, and possibly his life, either as a smuggler of arms to the natives or as Paul Selkirk, outlaw, who had escaped hanging by fleeing H.M. justice nearly a quarter of a century before.

That prospect didn't worry him personally, for he had lived with death and the threat of imprisonment all his life. But it would take him from Charley and Mary, and that was a problem.

Under the principle that a master's word was law, ships' officers were not held responsible for anything done under the master's orders, so Charley would lose neither his life nor his freedom. Charley was nearly a man, and between Charley and Mistress Johnson, they could raise Mary to womanhood. If there was money.

Two days before Paul Selkirk went to Saint Olaf's Church to have that cadaverous Swede dominie marry him to Nils Johnson's widow, he went to Captain Ephraim Lewis's home and turned over to him the chest of gold from under his bunk.

"Eph," he had told him, "this is a little something I've put away for Charley and Mary should anything ever happen to me. Enough to keep them for a short while until Charley finds his way, and to keep the girl out of the asylum."

"Wouldn't it be better in a vault at the bank?" Eph Lewis, ever practical and cautious, had replied.

"I don't see any reason why Mistress Johnson should share in this," he had replied, "as she would if the courts got involved. This is money my Eleanor and I made together, and I think that it should go to our children, the law be damned."

"I see your point," Eph had replied. "God forbid that anything should happen to you, Paul, but you can rest assured that if anything does, the children will get this. For themselves."

Eph, Selkirk thought, would have had a heart seizure there in his drawing room if he had had any idea of how much gold was in the chest. It would buy Charley a ship as large as *The Eleanor*, and with more than enough left over for a splendid dowry for Mary.

His plans to protect his children in case the worst possible thing happened having been made, Selkirk proceeded with the preparation for the voyage.

The first thing to do was to get the Pennsylvania rifles he needed to make the three hundred-stand he was going to sell to the prince, and to get them without directing attention to himself. He sought out Theo LaSalle and gave him money and explained what was required. Theo dispatched the crew: one man going alone all over Pennsylvania and New Jersey and Maryland to buy rifles one at a time, if that was what was required to keep from arousing suspicion, three or four if the storekeeper or gunsmith didn't seem to want to ask questions.

It almost immediately became apparent to Selkirk that this was something he could do only once. The authorities would note that there had been a sudden and unusual demand for steel. They might not, probably would not, connect that with Captain Paul Selkirk and *The Eleanor*, but they would be aware that someone was buying large quantities of rifles.

He was back to what Mistress Johnson had explained to him: the crown kept control of things by keeping an eye on the flow of steel.

"Tell me about steel," he said when he went back to her.

"What do you want to know about it?"

"Why, for example, can't it be made at Durham Furnace, where the authorities wouldn't have to know about it?"

"We do make it," she said.

"Then why can't we furnish what is needed to the gunsmiths?"

The explanation was complicated. He learned that there were two ways of making steel; the way that it was made in the colonies, by heating iron ore and ash and some other ingredients in a furnace, not unlike making bricks, and the way it was made in England, by the new crucible-steel method.

"I don't think I understand what you're telling me," he said.

"The authorities know how much steel a furnace like ours

can make. If we were suddenly to start making in large quantities, they would want to know what we were doing with it."

"But there would be a difference with, what did you say, crucible steel?"

"If someone had the ability to make crucible steel," Ingebord Johnson told him, "and was willing to work at night, no one would have any idea how much steel they were making."

"And if the gunsmiths could get all the steel they wanted, without anyone knowing where it came from, they would make as many rifles as someone would be willing to pay a good price for?"

"They're Germans and Swedes, most of them," she said. "Willing to make as much of anything as anyone's willing to buy."

"Then the thing to do, it would seem, mistress, would be to start making crucible steel."

She snorted her contempt for his ignorance.

"Making crucible steel is something that requires an investment in capital, is that what you mean?"

He had the money to build anything within reason, he thought.

"It's a secret process," she said.

"How do you mean, a secret?"

"You need two things to make crucible steel," she said. "For one thing, the crucibles, and then the other equipment."

"And you can't make them?"

"We can make anything out of iron that can be made," she said. "*If* we know how. And *how* is the problem. *How* is the secret."

"Who has the secret?"

"A journeyman steelworker in some English furnace," she said.

"Then the thing to do is get us an English journeyman steelworker," he said.

"That sounds simpler than you'll find the case," she said.

"How so?"

"They're placed under a lifelong contract to the furnace where they're employed," she said. "*Before* they're taught the process. Their contracts are not for sale. At any price. And the penalty for running away from the contract is seven years in prison for the craftsman *and* for his family, *and* for anyone involved in helping him."

Paul Selkirk was neither surprised to hear what she told him about the severity of the penalty for interfering with England's industrial monopoly nor particularly worried about it.

"And the equipment? If you had a crucible-steel maker, could you make the equipment?"

"If he knew about it, he could tell us," she said after thinking that over. "But he may be taught only how to use the equipment, not how it works, or how it's built."

"Then we'd have to have the equipment and the craftsman?"

"If you wanted to make crucible steel, you would," she said. "It doesn't look to me like that risk would be worth the trouble."

"If I had the craftsman, and the equipment, where could I set it up?" he asked.

"Here, I suppose," she said. "There's place here, and they would have no way to know how much ore we were taking from these mines."

"I intend to work on this problem, mistress," he said.

"I would ask you not to tell me any more about it, Captain Selkirk," she said. "I think you're going to find that what you have in mind is not going to be quite as easy as you think it will be."

"I'll not involve you, mistress."

"I have my sons to worry about," she said.

"I'll not involve you or your sons, mistress," Paul Selkirk told her.

2

On the day of his wedding, right after the ceremony, Paul Selkirk sent his son Charley upriver with his daughter Mary, and his wife's two sons, Nils and Luther, who had come down for the wedding.

He didn't want any of them around on his wedding night, and sending Charley to pick up the hundred-stand of arms that had been gathered there from gunsmiths further upriver had solved both problems neatly, if it had not solved the problem of the wedding night itself.

He had all the normal drives of any man, he thought, and probably a share more. And, once he'd done it, once he'd taken her to wife, and thought it over again, he was convinced

88

that he'd done the right thing. Mistress Johnson, now Mistress Selkirk, was an extraordinarily good woman, a Christian woman whose word he trusted, who would be a good mother to Mary, providing a service he could not himself provide.

He had made the right decision, and he was glad that he had married her.

But he was no more attracted to her than he was to the trollops who sat around the tables in the Safe Harbor Tavern. Less, he decided.

He was enormously relieved when he went to his wedding bed after delaying as long as he dared and found his wife asleep. And even more relieved when she woke him in the morning. She was fully dressed, and she explained that the only reason she had disturbed his sleep was to tell him that she was leaving for Durham Furnace and wanted to wish him Godspeed on his voyage.

When he went to the window to watch her go, he was not surprised to see that there were two ox-drawn wagons on Arch Street, loaded with the furniture he had not selected from the house to take to the flat over the Safe Harbor Tavern.

Neither was he surprised to note that not once had she looked back at the house.

As soon as she was out of sight, he got dressed, and went down to *The Eleanor* and ordered Theo LaSalle to hire a wagon and send a crew to the house to move his things to Water Street.

Very privately, he was pleased that he not only had kept his and Eleanor's bed, but that, while his new wife had spent the night in it, nothing had happened between them; and with the bed now being moved to Water Street, nothing ever would.

He told himself again that he had found the best possible solution to the problem.

3

Near Durham Furnace, Pennsylvania
October 1, 1769

Mary Selkirk, who was fifteen, fair-skinned, red-haired, and small for her age, sat against the trunk of a walnut tree on a hill overlooking a sweeping bend of the Delaware River. She was close enough to the river to be able to run to the water's edge in a minute or two, when it was time, and far enough back from it so that it was unlikely that anyone would notice her there, or be able to identify her if they did happen to look exactly her way.

She had been waiting for two hours, and she was prepared to wait another two hours, until the sun was directly overhead at midday.

If no boat came by then, she would give up and go back to the house and take another whipping. And tomorrow, she would run away again.

It was either today or tomorrow, or she would have to think of something else. After tomorrow, it would be too late. Tomorrow, she would not come on foot the four miles from the house to the river. Tomorrow, she would steal Lucy, her father's mare, and ride her to Philadelphia. Riding hard, riding steadily, she could make it to Philadelphia in one day.

She had to be in Philadelphia by tomorrow night. Her father and her brother were sailing for England and then India tomorrow, and unless she could see them and beg them not to, they would leave her behind.

If she had stolen a horse today she could have been in Philadelphia by four o'clock. Or maybe a littler later. But if she stole Lucy, her stepmother would know for sure where she had gone, and one of her stepbrothers, or both, would be set out after her. Neither Nils nor Luther would be able to catch up with her, because there were no other riding horses available, and they would have to take one of the draught animals. But they would know where to look for her, so it wouldn't make any difference if they caught up with her or not.

If she had stolen Lucy today, in other words, they would have known where she was going and they would have caught her tomorrow in Philadelphia. The way it was now, since she hadn't stolen Lucy, her stepmother would more than likely think that she had run off into the woods after the whipping, and that, when she'd had time to consider what a sinful thing she had done, she would come home to face the punishment for that.

When she didn't come home tonight, her stepmother would more than likely figure a night out in the woods would do her a lot of good. Ingebord Johnson Selkirk was smart enough to realize that looking for Mary in the woods at night would be fruitless. Tomorrow morning, at eight or nine o'clock, when Mary hadn't shown up, her stepmother would probably send Nils or Luther looking for her.

When they hadn't found her after, say, an hour or two, her stepmother would probably check with the neighbors. That would take until after lunch, and by then it would be too late.

But it would be much better to go by boat today, if one came down the river, and if she could pay her way aboard with a dozen eggs and two loaves of bread. She would avoid another whipping, and her chances of getting away would be that much better.

An hour later, she saw a Durham boat coming downstream. There was little wind blowing from the north. The Durham boat's square sail hung limply from the single mast. Mary wondered why they didn't rig a lanteen sail, for what they had was of value to them only when the wind obliged by blowing in the direction they wanted to go. Other times, they had to either coast with the current of the river or row the boat.

Her father had told her that the men who operated the Durham boats (which were named after the half-dozen iron furnaces and as many mines around Durham and were designed to carry both ore and products of the foundries on the Delaware) were "riverboatmen" and not sailors. He didn't seem to be suggesting that sailors were better than riverboatmen, just different.

Mary looked down to the bank of the river. There were people standing on it now, two men and a woman. The man was waving something, a shirt, possibly, to attract the attention of the man who stood at the stern of the Durham boat, steering it with a twenty-foot sweep.

When it was apparent that the Durham boat was putting in

to the bank, Mary got to her feet and brushed the leaves and soil from the seat of her dress. Then she picked up her bags. There were three. One of them, the largest, held her clothing. It was large but not heavy, and for balance, she had tied it with the next largest bag, which held a dozen eggs and two loaves of bread, one rye and one white, at one end of the willow sapling. At the other end was the bag holding her treasures.

First among these was the battered Bible given to her parents when they were married. She had no intention of leaving that with the new Mrs. Selkirk. She wasn't even a real Christian at all, but a heathen Lutheran.

The pages immediately behind the frontispiece listed Mary's parents' names, and the name of the priest, whom her parents had called the Dominie, who had married them, according to the rites of the Church of Scotland, just before they had come to Pennsylvania. Then came the name of their first-born, Charles MacGregor Selkirk. Charles after Bonny Prince Charley, MacGregor after her mother's father. And then her name, Mary Elizabeth Selkirk, born the seventh day of April in the Year of Our Lord 1754, in Philadelphia, Pennsylvania colony.

And two more entries, both painful:

> Taken Into The Arms of Jesus the second day of April, 1769 at Philadelphia, Eleanor MacGregor Selkirk, beloved wife of Paul.
> Entered into Holy Matrimony the 12th day of September 1769 at Saint Olaf's Lutheran Church, Phila., by the Reverend Ingmar Sooth, Paul Selkirk, widower, of Philadelphia, and Ingebord Johnson, widow, of Durham Furnace.

There was also, in the small bag, a silhouette of her mother, scissored from black paper by a widow woman who had come to the house in Philadelphia, and now mounted behind glass in a small frame.

There was her mother's prayer book.

There was a scrimshawed walrus tooth, weighing almost a pound, that her father had given her.

Altogether, everything in the treasure bag, the things she had no intention of leaving with her father's wife, balanced out the clothing and food in the other two bags, and carrying them at the ends of the willow sapling as she made her way down the steep slope to the river's edge gave her no trouble.

By the time she got close to the Durham boat, the woman and two men she had seen from the hill were already aboard, and the crew was about to push the boat away from the shore and into the stream.

Mary yelled at them to wait, and after a moment's hesitation, the man at the sweep called to the others to hold off.

"Would you take a dozen eggs and two fresh loaves of bread to ferry me to Philadelphia?" Mary shouted at him, when she was standing on the river's edge.

"I don't want no runaway girl," the man at the sweep called back, but it was obvious to Mary that it was a question, rather than an identification of her status.

"I'm going to Philadelphia to meet my father," Mary called back. "He's a seafaring man and just arriving."

She was furious with herself for lying. All she would have had to say was that she was going to meet her father. She hadn't had to embellish the story.

"The eggs are fresh as can be," she went on. "Still warm from the hen. And the bread came from the oven only last night."

"Give her a hand," the man at the sweep said. "And make sure she really has the eggs and bread."

One of the crewman leaned over the side of the Durham boat and took from her the willow sapling with the three bags hanging from it.

"Careful not to break the eggs," Mary said.

The man opened the bag with the bread and eggs and then, after looking inside, tied it again.

For a moment, Mary was afraid that he was going to take the bread and the eggs and everything else she owned in the world, and push off without her. Riverboatmen were sometimes thieves and pirates. But then he leaned over the side again and offered a thickly calloused hand and pulled her aboard.

Then he, and two other men, pushed their sweeps against the shore. The sweeps bent in the middle, but then they straightened out, and she felt the current of the river begin to swing the boat.

93

4

Ingebord Johnson Selkirk was no fool. She had known that Mary had been planning to run to her father for several days, ever since she had discovered the cache of eggs under a loose board in the hen house. What the girl was doing, had been doing for a week or ten days or more, was setting aside an egg or two from the day's laying. Each day, she would take the eggs she had hidden the day before, bring them into the house, and replace them with that day's eggs, plus one or two more.

She would eventually have a dozen or more.

What she would do then, Ingebord Johnson Selkirk decided, was make her way to the Bethlehem Pike, thirteen miles west of the Johnson Forge, fifteen miles north of the Delaware River, and there use them to barter for a ride into Philadelphia with either a farmer or one of the draymen who moved along the Bethlehem Pike to Philadelphia.

She didn't like the girl, to tell God's truth about it, and she knew that the girl disliked her, quite apart from her resentment at Mistress Selkirk's having taken her mother's place. But her feelings about the girl, she had vowed would not in any way affect her relationship with her. She had the moral obligation to raise the girl as best she could, to turn her into a good Christian young woman, and she intended to meet that obligation.

The girl was just too hardheaded to understand the way things were. She had no intention of taking Eleanor Selkirk's place in Paul Selkirk's life, much less his bed. Theirs was, and the girl should have been smart enough to see this, a marriage of convenience. She had been left, comfortably, to be sure, a widow with two underage sons. She was comfortable because Nils had built a good business with his forge and his furnace and his mines. If the boys had been several years older when Nils died, she would have gone it alone, but it had not turned out that way, and while she knew nearly as much (more, to tell God's truth) about the business as Nils had, she was still a widow woman, and she was old enough and wise enough to know that widow women's property had a way of being separated from them.

Paul Selkirk was, in his way, Ingebord was willing to admit, a good Christian father. He could have put the girl in

94

school, either with the Society of Friends, who operated an asylum for that purpose near Chester, or with the Sisters of Saint Francis of Assisi. Ingebord was also honest enough to admit that the sisters had a better reputation for the rearing of children in Mary's position than the Friends did, even if they were part of the corrupt Church of Rome.

Ingebord knew that Selkirk was pleased with her business sense, but she also knew that he would never have offered marriage for that alone. He had wanted for his daughter a good Christian home, to have her reared, especially since she was about to enter womanhood, by a good Christian mother. He had done what he had done for the girl's benefit, which spoke well of his character, at least in that regard, and for her part, Ingebord had privately vowed to raise the girl as if she were her own flesh and blood.

But the girl was, no surprise, her father's daughter: hot-tempered, rebellious, hardheaded, and bitterly resentful of Ingebord. She had arrogantly announced that if she couldn't stay in the house on Arch Street, she would rather go to the Friends' asylum, or even to the Catholic sisters. She didn't want to go in the country, and she didn't want to live with "that Swedish shrew." Her father had slapped her when she said that, but he hadn't been able to make her apologize, and she hadn't cried.

And now she'd run away. Sneaked away. She had deserved the whipping she'd been given, and she would deserve the whipping she would get when she was found and brought home. It was Ingebord's Christian duty to see that Mary was raised as a clean, God-fearing girl, and she intended to meet her responsibility.

When Mary had turned up missing, Ingebord had known what to do. She'd sent the boys after her on horseback. Nils was sixteen, nearly a man, and as solid and reliable as his father. Luther was fourteen, a year younger than Mary.

If they could catch up with her here before she reached the Bethlehem Pike, they were ordered to being her back, if it was necessary to tie her to a horse to do so. If she somehow managed to elude them, Nils was to make his way to Philadelphia as quickly as he could, on Lucy. For the first time, Ingebord Johnson Selkirk regretted having talked Captain Selkirk into selling the matched carriage sorrels. He had kept Lucy, his saddle mare, but he had given in to her argument that it was a sinful waste of money to maintain four horses, two for his carriage, and two saddle horses, when he was gone for near a year at a time. If they still had the other horses and the carriage, she could have gone after Mary herself, instead of sending the boys after her, one on the mare that her husband had refused to sell and the other on a plow horse. In the event Nils had to go on to Philadelphia, Luther would bring the plow horse back to the farm.

If Mary made it to Philadelphia, her father would have to deal with her. Whip her himself, even if he didn't relish that sort of thing at all, and make her understand that she had no choice in the matter, that she would have to return to the country and behave like a dutiful daughter when she was there.

If *The Eleanor* had sailed by the time Mary got to Philadelphia, Nils was instructed to look for Mary until he found her in the home, somewhere, of her father and mother's friends, probably that of Captain Lewis, whose indulgence toward her had obviously had more than a little to do with her rebellious attitude, and to tell whoever she was found with the situation, and enlist their support to get her back where she belonged.

Ingebord did not dwell on what might happen to her alone in Philadelphia if Mary didn't ask her family's friends for help, but she told Nils that if *The Eleanor* had sailed and he couldn't find her in a day, he was to go to the constable, explain the situation, and offer a reward of ten pounds for her as a runaway.

The alternative to that, for Mary, was too unpleasant to think about: Runaway girls found themselves as kitchen maids, or dairy maids. If they were lucky. Ingebord didn't like to think to what other purpose the sinful and depraved people around the waterfront (which is where she would go) would put Mary if she fell into their hands. Ingebord had heard, and believed, that there were men who would pay for a virgin, and that the women who operated the brothels were constantly on the lookout for young girls to meet the demand.

If that happened to Mary, she didn't know how she would handle Captain Selkirk. He would decide, and with justification, that she had failed her responsibility. The thing to do was pray to God for Mary's safe return, and then give her a

96

whipping (whether or not she got one from her father first) that would make it clear that running away was not one of her future options.

5

"There is no doubt in my mind that she'll show up, probably the moment we make mid-stream," Captain Paul Selkirk said to the people who sat with him in the harbormaster's carriage on the wharf at the foot of Chestnut Street. "For good and obvious reason, she is afraid to face me."

"Of course she will, Paul," Captain Ephraim Lewis, harbormaster of the port of Philadelphia agreed. "For all we know, she's already had second thoughts and is back at your wife's farm this very moment."

"If, by some chance, she made it to Philadelphia," Edward Kells, the high constable of the city of Philadelphia said, "my watch will find her. That is, as you say, if she doesn't present herself at Mistress Lewis's door the moment you head downstream."

"Twenty-five pounds to the watchman who finds her," Captain Selkirk said. "I'll give it to you now, if you like."

"It's not going to be that way at all, Paul," Captain Lewis said. "She'll come to our house, you mark my words."

"And I'll send a watchman with the lad to make sure they all get back safely," the high constable of Philadelphia said.

"If we weren't ready to sail," Captain Selkirk said. "If she had done this two days ago, before we loaded everything, particularly the livestock . . ."

There was no reply for a moment. The harbormaster and the high constable were both thinking the same thing, that it was a shame that a man like Paul Selkirk should be put through something like this by a fifteen-year-old girl, and that what the girl needed was a good beating.

"It would be difficult to delay sailing," the harbormaster finally said.

"Aye," Captain Selkirk said. "And it wouldn't do any good, either." He stood up in the carriage.

"Nils," he said, to Nils Johnson's son, now his stepson, "I want you to be sure to tell your mother, no matter what happens, that I . . . that what Mary's gotten herself into is Mary's fault, and not your mother's."

He didn't believe that at all. It was clearly the damned

woman's fault. If Mary had run away, there was a reason for it. And Ingebord should have seen to it that she wasn't given the chance to run away. Goddamned cold-blooded Swedish bitch!

He put his hand on Nils's shoulder. He liked Nils. Nils was like his father, fortunately, and not like his mother. "You use your own judgment, if Mary doesn't show up in the next couple of days, about going back to Durham Furnace."

"I'll look for her, sir, until I find her," Nils said.

"You let the high constable and his watch look for her," Captain Selkirk said. "The one thing I don't need is to hear from your mother that I sent you prowling along the waterfront."

And then, as if saying that in front of the harbormaster and the high constable embarrassed him, he turned and backed out of the carriage.

"Thank you, gentlemen, for all your courtesies," he said.

"Paul," the high constable said, "everything will be all right."

"Yes, of course it will," Captain Lewis said. Neither of them sounded as confident as they intended.

Captain Selkirk removed his white tricorn from his white wig, and bowed formally.

"A good voyage, Paul," Captain Lewis said. "Go with God."

"Mary's the one who needs God, not me," Selkirk said. Then he put his hat back on, put his hand to the gilded hilt of his dress sword to steady it so that it wouldn't swing between his legs and trip him, and walked purposefully down the wharf and then across the gangplank onto *The Eleanor*.

She was low in the water, but even. He thought again that so far as a cargo that permitted you to balance the ship, there was nothing better than pig iron.

He made his way along the deck, aft, to his cabin. Mr. Dillon, the second mate, was on the deck. He tipped his tricorn to Selkirk, and the dozen or so seamen on deck either removed their caps and held them against their chests as he passed or tugged at their forelocks. He tipped his tricorn back to the second mate, said, "Mister Dillon" to him, and somehow acknowledged, either with a small nod of his head, or a quick smile, or a wink, each of the seamen.

He went into his cabin and undressed. He had dressed formally for his call on the harbormaster and the high constable. He had a good wig, seldom worn, and he'd powdered that and put it on. And the English sword, which he considered useful if one intended to impale a cat, but useless for much else. And silk leggings, and low-cut black shoes with a buckle. He looked the gentleman, he thought, and on purpose. He wanted the high constable to think of him as a gentleman sailor, whose daughter would be a lady, not just a female he had sired.

He dressed in a cotton shirt and duck trousers and sturdy boots, and put a battered, salt- and sweat-stained tricorn on his head. He had designed *The Eleanor,* and one of the innovations was a ladder built against the side of a cabinet in his cabin to a skylight on the quarterdeck, giving him access to and from the quarterdeck without having to make his way through the passageway and then the deck.

He climbed the ladder and pushed the skylight open and emerged on the quarterdeck. Both the chief mate and the third mate were on deck. They tipped their hats to him.

"Make all preparations to take her out to sea, Mr. Porter," Captain Selkirk said.

"Aye, aye, sir," the chief mate said. "Mr. Selkirk, I'll have the gangway taken aboard, and then the lines let loose fore and aft, and then I'll have all hands aloft."

"Aye, aye, sir," the third mate said, and put a leather megaphone to his lips and shouted the necessary orders.

The wind was not being cooperative. It was blowing from the east and could not be used to move *The Eleanor* from the wharf into the stream. It was evident that they were going to have to wait for the current of the Delaware, enforced now by the ebbing tide, to move her into the stream. That was not going to happen quickly. There was time for the master of *The Eleanor* to have a word with her third mate about something unrelated to taking her to sea.

"Your sister has not shown up," he said. "God knows where she is!"

"She'll turn up at Captain Lewis's door the moment she knows we've sailed," Charles MacGregor Selkirk, making his first voyage as an officer, said.

His father did not reply.

"God, if I could get my hands on her," Charley added, "I'd take a tarred line to her bottom. She'd not sit for a month."

Captain Selkirk turned to his first mate. "Mr. Porter," he

said, "do you think before we lose the tide it might be a good idea to fly a lanteen, and then try to turn her in midstream?"

"Mr. Selkirk," the chief mate ordered, "I'll have a lanteen from the foremast."

"Aye, aye, sir," the third mate said, and put the leather megaphone to his lips to shout the order to the bosun.

The current of the river and the ebbing tide had moved the stern of *The Eleanor* further away from the bank than her bow. When the lanteen sail caught the wind, it pushed *The Eleanor* into the stream, where the current moved her so that when she was free of the wharf, she was headed upstream. It was then necessary to turn her in the center of the Delaware, so that she was pointed downstream.

This took a good ten minutes.

"Well done, Mr. Porter," Captain Selkirk said, finally. Then he went down the ladder from the quarterdeck to the main deck. He inspected, again, the ship's rigging, and the fastening of her hatches, and had a look at her crew, to make as sure as he could, one last time, that one of them was not bringing disease aboard. The bosun, keeping one eye on the quarterdeck for orders from the chief mate, joined him.

"I heard about the girl, Captain," he said. "She'll turn up."

"Good God, Theo, I hope so," Captain Selkirk said.

"Everybody in Philadelphia knows who she is, and who you are," the bosun said.

"I expect when we make London, out from Amsterdam, there'll be a letter from Mrs. Selkirk saying she's safe and sound," Captain Selkirk said.

"It'll be there, Captain," Theo LaSalle said confidently.

Captain Selkirk turned on his heel, ending the conversation, and made his way to his cabin, where he first had a drink of applejack and water, and then, after thinking it over for a full minute, got on his knees by his bunk and locked his fingers together.

"God," he said, in a firm, conversational tone of voice, "spare that child from the evil that can come her way."

He stayed there for another two minutes, silently, and then concluded that he had said all that had to be said, and that there was no sense in bothering the Deity by saying it all over again in different words. Then he got to his feet and helped himself to more applejack.

The Eleanor made her way down the Delaware, past the

shipyards, past Little Tinicum and Chester islands, past Wilmington, Delaware City, Port Penn, and into Delaware Bay.

The wind now began to cooperate, and there was room to maneuver. The sails were set, and *The Eleanor* began to pick up speed. Captain Selkirk felt the Atlantic's swells in his legs. He stayed off the quarterdeck. He didn't want to face his son. Should he have stayed and looked for her?

He had decided that he would simply be making a fool of himself if he stayed ashore. The girl would show up, and he would have made a mountain out of a molehill, and it would have cost him a good deal of money.

But now, as the coasts of Maryland and New Jersey receded, as they actually entered the Atlantic, the money it would have cost him and the chance that he would have looked like a fool didn't seem nearly as important as it had before.

If Mary had only been a boy, he could have taken her with him. Charley had gone to sea at twelve for the first time. But she was a girl, and a girl, particularly a girl of her age, needed a woman. Leaving her with Ingebord had seemed, then, to be the wisest thing to do, even if that meant marrying that cold-blooded Bible-quoting Swede. It was, he decided, just another proof that whenever he tried to do the right thing, he got himself in trouble.

He was shamed by that thought, when he realized that he wasn't in trouble, Mary was in trouble, and instead of being with her he was ten miles at sea.

He sent the cabin boy to ask Mr. Porter to take dinner with him. He was very afraid that if he ate alone, he would drink the rest of the bottle of applejack and probably open another and drink that, too.

There was the usual first-night-at-sea wealth of food (a rib of beef, a loin of pork, turkey, duck, and venison, roasted as soon as it had been brought aboard to keep it edible longer), but he didn't have much of an appetite, even with a bottle of wine to encourage his palate.

He talked with Mr. Porter about the crew, about the condition of the sails, about the weather, about everything but what was on his mind.

He decided that if there was no letter waiting for him when they landed at London, outbound for Tatta from Amsterdam, he would then come home, and worry about the rifles, and the jewels, and the crucible-steel maker, and every-

101

thing else, later. That could all wait, no matter how much it cost him. Mary couldn't. For a long moment, he considered ordering *The Eleanor* back to port. He should have done something, if only ordering Charley ashore to find his sister. Why did he think of that only now?

He looked at Porter and saw that he was tired and was having trouble suppressing his yawns, but he did not let him go. He did not wish to be left alone.

And then there came the knock.

"Come!"

"I'm sorry to disturb you, Captain," Third Mate Charles MacGregor Selkirk said. "But I thought you'd want to know about this right away."

"Where did you get that?" Captain Selkirk asked.

"It was in the longboat, Captain."

"How did you get aboard?" Captain Selkirk asked.

"Up the aft hawser, through the starboard anchor port," Mary Selkirk said to her father. "When Charley was busy loading the rifles over her stern."

He wondered if the rifles being "discreetly" loaded had been as evident to people on shore as they had been to Mary.

"You're to be whipped for running away, you understand," Captain Selkirk said.

"Yes," she said. "I figured on that."

"Your brother will give it to you," Captain Selkirk said. "Ten strokes with the tarred end of a line."

She met his eyes unflinchingly.

He looked at his son. "Tanning her bottom with a tarred line was your idea, Mr. Selkirk," he said. "An officer must learn never to say something he doesn't mean. I'm going topside. I expect to hear her howl, Mr. Selkirk."

"Aye, aye, sir," Charley Selkirk said.

"I have kept you too long, Mr. Porter," Captain Selkirk said. "Forgive me."

"Goodnight, Captain," Mr. Porter said.

"Rig a hammock for her in your cabin, Mr. Selkirk," Captain Selkirk said. "And we'll work her as cabin boy and messman until we can arrange to ship her home."

"If you ship me home, I'll run away again," Mary Selkirk said.

"Make that fifteen strokes with the line, Mr. Selkirk. And if she opens her mouth one more time, she'll do without the hammock."

Then he climbed the ladder through the skylight to the quarterdeck. He checked the binnacle and the report of the second mate. Then he went aft, and leaned on the railing, and looked up the at quarter-moon.

"Thank you, God," he said, very distinctly, and then he waited for the sound of his daughter's weeping. He heard nothing but the whistle of the line. Charley was doing what he had been ordered to do. And Mary was taking it. And not crying. She was a Selkirk, all right.

Chapter Six

1

Bombay, India
October 10, 1769

H.M.S. *Indomitable*, forty guns, Captain Peter Fielding, forty-five days out of London, had run into a storm in the Arabian Sea. The storm had caused navigational problems that saw *Indomitable* make Indian landfall at Murud on the forty-seventh day of the voyage. It was Captain Fielding's first voyage to India, but his second officer recognized the bay at Murud, and they were thus able to proceed to Bombay, 120 miles to the north, without having to land at Murud to inquire as to their location.

The seven islands that made up the port of Bombay came into view on the morning of the forty-ninth day of the voyage.

Indomitable carried, jammed tightly in her holds, the 2nd Company of the Hertfordshire Yeomanry, Captain Philip Ward, four-hundred-stand of muskets, with powder and shot, and two field cannon, all sent in response to a request from the governor of the East India Company for additional military forces to insure the safety of the company.

The Hertfordshire Yeomanry, the four hundred muskets, and the two field cannon were not all that the governor had asked for, or hoped to get. He had asked for a battalion of infantry. The king had sent him a company. He had asked for two eight-gun batteries of artillery. The king had sent him two cannon. He had asked for permission to recruit and train a nine-hundred-man regiment of native infantry, and for the British officers necessary to command it, and for the equipment to outfit it. The king had sent him four-hundred-stand

104

of smooth-bore Brown Bess muskets, but neither officers nor equipment.

The king believed that the governor of the East India Company thought he was made of money; that the governor habitually overstated the threat of the natives to British interests in India; and that, in any event, one company of good English yeomanry backed up by four hundred native troops would constitute a significant force. It would, in any event, have to satisfy the governor for the time being.

His Majesty accepted the remote possibility that he could be wrong. *Indomitable* also carried aboard to Bombay Colonel Sir Edgar Watchbury and Lady Caroline. His Majesty trusted Sir Edgar both as a soldier and as a man. Nevertheless, His Majesty had taken pains to make it absolutely clear to Sir Edgar that even if he determined that vast reinforcements of British forces in India were needed, Sir Edgar would not, under any circumstances, be given a command in India.

His Majesty expected to get an accurate appraisal of the military requirements of the East India Company. And, for his part, Colonel Sir Edgar Watchbury, on his first important mission for his sovereign, intended to give it to him.

Sir Edgar and Lady Caroline had been quartered aboard the *Indomitable* in the cabin normally occupied by the chief mate. In relatively calm seas, with the ports open, the wind had swept most, but by no means all, of the dreadful stench from the holds, where 250 sergeants and other ranks were quartered. In rougher seas, when it was necessary to close the ports, the heat, as well as the stench, were very nearly unbearable.

Lady Caroline had passed most of the voyage, that is to say from their passing of the Gates of Hercules at Gibraltar (and into the heat of the African latitudes), on her bunk, wearing only a thin cotton chemise. She tried to sleep most of the day, and to emerge onto the deck at night to take what often was her only meal in the relatively cooler night.

Sir Edgar had felt it incumbent upon him, as a senior officer, to make himself visible. He had spent most of the voyage on the quarterdeck, in uniforms that quickly had become sweat-logged and foul. In order not to disturb Lady Caroline, he had taken to sleeping in a chair on the quarterdeck rather than getting into the narrow bed with her.

He had played a good deal of chess with Captain Philip

Ward of the Hertfordshires, and at Captain Ward's request had frequently given unofficial lectures on military matters to the Hertfordshire's officers and noncommissioned officers. He talked to them about, among other subjects, his official visit to the Hessian Regiment of Light Foot, comparing its organization and tactics to those of the British.

Sir Edgar was aware, of course, that despite his (he thought successful) attempts to conceal it, the voyage, the heat, the food, and the stench had sapped his strength. He was sure, however, that once ashore, he would quickly recover.

He was very glad indeed to see Bombay, the central island of the seven islands that made up the port of that name, appear off the bow. He dressed in his remaining clean Southern Climes uniform and, with Lady Caroline sweat-soaked under a parasol standing beside him, made it through the docking process, through an informal welcome at dockside (during which he informed the representative of the governor of the East India Company that he would be pleased to make an official call upon His Excellency at His Excellency's earliest convenience), and through the carriage ride to the official guest house.

There, he turned to offer his hand and express his gratitude to the representative of the governor for his courtesy to himself and Lady Caroline, and swooned. He saw the polished tile floor tilt, and rise up to meet him, and then he felt absolutely nothing at all.

Both the physician and the surgeon sent to the official guest house by the governor tried to assure Lady Caroline that her husband was in no danger and what had happened to him was by no means unusual.

"It has to do with the thickness of the blood, my lady," the surgeon informed her. "The body will naturally adapt to the climate. In some cases, the adaptation occurs quite quickly, within a matter of weeks. In other cases, it is a rather more lengthy process. In the latter, we often see minor disturbances, such as that Sir Edgar has experienced."

"He's not going to die, is he?" Lady Caroline asked.

"That is a very remote possibility," the surgeon told her. "Very remote, indeed. What Sir Edgar must do is give his body a chance to adjust to the climate, meanwhile not taxing his strength. We will make every effort to reduce his temperature with the appropriate drugs, and at the same time, make every effort to keep him cool."

The drugs administered to Sir Edgar made him groggy to the point of incoherence. They also deprived him of control of his bowels and bladder, and a flock of Indian servants spent a good deal of their time cleaning him and changing the linen on his bed. He was kept cool through all this by means of covering his near-naked body with wet sheets. He was cooled by what the surgeon called evaporation. Sometimes, the sheets steamed from the heat of his body.

He was fed nothing but beef broth and crackers, and Margaret thought that she could almost watch the fat disappear from his body. There was a point when she thought he was going to die, and she was frightened by the prospect of being left all alone, a widow, so far from home, and wondered what would happen to her in that circumstance.

Then she remembered that she was not alone. Edgar was here as the king's personal representative. The king, therefore, would certainly have an obligation to her should anything happen to Edgar. When she got that straight in her mind, and especially after Edgar showed some small signs of getting better, she was ashamed of what else she had thought about: the chances of getting Captain Sir Richard Trentwood, after a suitable period of mourning, to propose marriage to the well-to-do widow of Colonel Sir Edgar Watchbury.

Despite her quite firm determination to have nothing further to do with Sir Richard, they had been together again. Actually, they had been together three more times in the two weeks between the first time and the sailing of the *Indomitable*.

Although Sir Richard had not roused in her the same lusts of the flesh as had Alexei (at least not to the same degree: she had gone quite mad with Alexei), there was no denying that what they had had together was astonishing. She had been unable to refuse to meet him, no matter how solemn her pledge that she would not.

Richard had announced, the second time, that he was in love with her. She didn't believe him; she had heard from the other ladies that that was what men always said. It was cheaper than a brooch, the ladies with more experience than she had jokingly told one another.

Still, it had been pleasant to hear, and it was remotely possible that he meant it. There had been a brooch. An old brooch, to be sure, to keep Sir Edgar from asking her when he had bought that for her, but a brooch. He had asked her to wear it while she was away in India, and to think of him when she did.

She was certainly *fond* of Sir Richard Trentwood, but she was not at all sure that she was in love with him, despite what happened when they were together. She didn't love Edgar, at least not in the way that lovers were supposed, from what she had heard, to feel. Sort of a divine madness. It was possible that she had loved Alexei, although certainly the reverse was not true. Alexei had produced in her emotions she had not previously suspected existed. She could, she realized, have really made a fool of herself over Alexei, quite literally have ruined her life, brought disgrace to her family and humiliation to Edgar. It was really a good thing, she knew, that Alexei had not loved her. The consequences of such an announcement on his part, coupled with a request for her to come to Russia with him, were almost frightening to think about.

Thinking about Sir Richard was not nearly so frightening. When they finally could leave this filthy oven of a country and go home, certainly she would see him again. After passage of that much time, it was entirely likely that he would have found another woman, in which case, she was sure, she was now sophisticated enough to handle the situation with grace.

If he were, so to speak, waiting for her, that would lend credence to his statement that he was in love with her. There was no question of divorce, of course, for as protector of the faith (the Church of England forbade divorce), the king could not have around him anyone who was divorced. But Richard could be her lover. If Edgar had been so willing to overlook her being with Alexei, it was likely that, presuming they were very discreet, he would overlook Sir Richard's relationship with her. For that matter, there was no reason that he had to know about it.

Everybody else, to judge from what she had learned from the other ladies, was straying from the connubial couch. There had been no lightning bolts from an angry God that she knew about. She had begun to consider that there were two kinds of love among people of her class. One was a sort of familial love, as between parents and children, where husband and wife cared for one another in practical matters.

The other was where two people attracted to one another indulged their sinful lusts of the flesh, knowing that was where the relationship began and ended.

It would only be in the event that she was widowed that she could really begin to consider the merits of marrying Sir Richard. And now, with her lawful husband lying drugged beneath wet sheets in Bombay, India, it was really despicable, and very possibly sinful, for her to be thinking at all of such a thing.

She should be, she thought, deeply ashamed of herself. And she was able to convince herself, as Sir Edgar's blood slowly thinned, that she was.

The surgeon and the physician reduced the dosage of laudanum as Edgar's recuperation progressed, substituting bleeding as the treatment. Their idea, they told her, was that the blood that had not thinned as it should have on his movement to the warmer climate was interfering with his health, and the logical thing to do was relieve its harmful effects by bleeding.

The leeches they had available here in India, they told her, were far more powerful than anything available to medical science in England. His recovery should therefore be more rapid than it would be at home.

A dozen or more large, ugly leeches at a time were placed on his back, his neck, and his calves. They filled with blood overnight, and were replaced each night. She could see their effect. The unhealthy ruddy color of Edgar's cheeks and neck faded. He complained to her privately that he felt quite weak but professed to feel "just splendid" to the surgeon and the physician when they came to see him each day.

He was, she understood, embarrassed that he had fallen ill at all. It was not the sort of thing a soldier could be proud of. He was worried further that word of his weakness would get back to King George III and give the monarch cause to consider that he had perhaps made an error of judgment in promoting Lieutenant Colonel Watchbury, knighting him, and sending him off on important business to India.

Long before Lady Caroline thought he was really up to it, Sir Edgar got out of bed, stopped the leeching, and prepared to get about the king's business. The first time he tried to put on his uniform, it became apparent that he had lost so much weight that considerable alteration to his uniform would be required before he could wear it in public.

Lady Caroline, thinking that it would take at least as long in this backward country to have a tailor's alterations performed as it would have in London, was privately relieved. Another three days, or four, of relative rest would do Edgar a lot of good. Particularly if she could use the period to get him eating again. What he needed to regain his strength, she was quite confident, was a hearty English diet. Roast meat, sauce, and potatoes.

Sir Edgar's uniforms were turned over to the head boy at half past five on a Tuesday afternoon, together with instructions from Lady Caroline that while speed in alteration was a consideration, she would not tolerate sloppy workmanship. She felt confident that her firm admonition would add at least a day, and possibly two, to the time needed to perform the necessary alterations.

When the sleeping-chamber boy delivered their breakfast tea the next morning, the head boy came in on his heels, proudly carrying Edgar's dress uniform in his arms. Lady Caroline was unable to find anything wrong with the alterations. If anything, the stitching was of even higher quality than that of Edgar's Bond Street tailor. And the uniform fit Edgar at least as well as it had when he first put it on in London.

With his potbelly (actually it was more of a circle of fat, circling his body at the level of his hips) gone, Edgar really looked quite striking in his uniform. She thought that she hadn't seen him looking so good since the day of their marriage. The problem was that he was as pale as a sheet now. The bloodletting had been necessary, of course, for it had produced his recovery, but it had not been without price.

Edgar refused her suggestion that he rest a day or two longer before calling on the governor of the East India Company.

"Nonsense," he said. "I feel quite fit."

He took off his dress uniform tunic, and sat bare-chested at the desk in their bedroom and wrote a note to the governor, stating that he had, with the assistance of the physician and the surgeon the governor had been so gracious as to make available to him, recovered his health, and that he would be honored to pay a call on the governor at the governor's earliest convenience. He gave the note to the head boy and ordered that he carry it to Goverment House straight away.

2

Aboard The Eleanor *of Philadelphia*
West longitude 4° 10' north latitude 50° 20'

November 3, 1769

Mary Selkirk had frequent occasion on the voyage of *The Eleanor* for England to test what she considered to be her Christian obligation to believe that since God ordained all things, it was meet and just that she had been born a female.

Certainly there was a place in God's scheme for females, otherwise there would be no children. There had been incontestable proof lately that God intended her to be a mother. Her chest, which a year ago had been indistinguishable from a boy's, had finally started to swell, and as if to make up for lost time, had rapidly given her a bosom that looked to her as adequate to nurse children as any she'd seen on full-grown women and mothers.

They actually got in her way, and she didn't like the inconvenience of that, and she frankly didn't like the notion of bearing children.

Four years separated her from her brother. At the moment, he spent his days strutting about the quarterdeck, wearing a clean white shirt, carrying a polished telescope in his hands as a symbol of his authority, and being called sir by the seamen, while she spent her days washing the next day's shirt, searching in the chicken house for eggs, which she would then boil or fry, to accompany the other food she prepared.

Five years from now, it was entirely likely that Charley would strut the quarterdeck of his own ship, Captain Selkirk instead of Mister Selkirk, and she would still be getting eggs out of a chicken house somewhere, when she wasn't washing some other man's shirts, and probably baby's clothes as well.

It might be God's plan, but she didn't like it.

She was at least as smart as Charley, and she knew it, and there was no good reason, except God's plan, that she was going to go through life taking orders with no chance of ever being in a place where she would be able to give some orders.

The chicken house was forward of the mess, in the lee of the fo'c'sl, and when she made her way back and forth to it,

or when she was for some other reason on the deck, the
seamen acknowledged her presence by either getting out of
her way or getting out of her way and simultaneously tugging
at their forelocks. When they spoke to her, they called her
Miss Mary. Not because they thought she was *personally* entitled to respect and formal courtesy, but because she was
Captain Selkirk's daughter, and Mr. Selkirk's sister.

She was complimented, Mary thought, in precisely the way
people said nice things about Lucy, the mare: "That sure is a
fine animal you have there, Captain Selkirk." Lucy and she
were both the property of strong and powerful men; the compliments to her were just about the same thing as the men
tugging their forelocks to her father and brother. The only
difference between Lucy and her was that no one, yet, had
tried to throw a saddle on her back.

"Don't be looking so glum, Mistress Mary," Chief Mate
James Porter said behind her. She turned from the railing,
where she had been watching the water swirl around the rudder, and looked at him. She saw that he was alone on the
quarterdeck, save for the quartermaster and the helmsmen at
the wheel.

"We should be making land any time now," Porter went
on. "We had Land's End off the port a while ago. Soon you'll
be able to go ashore."

She smiled at him. He meant well. He was simply incapable
of believing that while she was as anxious as anyone else
aboard to make land, to see trees and land again, she didn't
mind being aboard any more than any of the men did. He
reasoned that she was female and therefore hated the sea.
That simply wasn't so. Being at sea, even for as long as they
had been, was much better than what her father wanted for
her, living on the farm at Durham Furnace. If it came down
to it, she would wash Charley's and her father's linen, and
iron it, and make their bunks, and cook their food, and all
the rest of it, from now on, without complaint, if she didn't
have to go back to Durham Furnace and live with her
stepmother.

Mary looked to port and then forward. All she could see
was the early morning fog. She wondered how Chief Mate
Porter knew that they were about to make land. Her father
probably knew, too, and Charley, and the brighter of the
seamen. They had their sea legs.

She had not been seasick at all. She had been a little

whoozy once or twice, on the first couple of days out of Philadelphia, but never sick. She had thought that meant she had natural sea legs, but then she came to understand that what "sea legs" really meant was knowing where you were in the fog, or in the dark of night, and being able to climb the rigging as naturally as people ashore went up a flight of stairs.

Mary had given a good deal of thought to the rigging, and she looked up at it now. Tony, the plump, dark-skinned Italian boy who had been her father's cabin boy until she stowed away and who was now, since she had been put to work as her father's and brother's cabin girl, working as sort of a junior apprentice seaman, was in the crow's nest. He was holding onto the mast with one hand, but there was a line around his waist in case he lost his footing.

It was now or never, Mary decided. Really never. If she didn't go aloft now, she would never go aloft. Tony was alone up there. If one of the seamen were aloft, she'd never make it halfway up the shrouds before she was caught.

She smiled at Mr. Porter and the quartermaster and the helmsmen, and then went down the ladder from the quarterdeck to the deck and started forward. She paused at the chicken house as if looking for eggs, and stole a look up at the fo'c'sl deck. There was no one there, and there was no one aloft on the foremast. She went quickly up the ladder to the fo'c'sl deck, climbed quickly up on the railing, and then, very quickly, began to climb the portside foremast shrouds.

The shrouds on either side of each mast looked like part of a giant spider's web, a slice-of-pie-shaped section of webbing, their narrow ends at the mast-tops. The "threads" of the webbing were heavy, tarred line, rough against her hands. She was afraid that she would be seen and that Mr. Porter would put the megaphone to his lips and shout an order for her to come down.

The best she could hope for, Mary decided, was to make it to the foresail yard, the oak pole from which the foresail hung. If she could make it that far, she could pretend she didn't hear Mr. Porter's order to come down. He would send men aloft to bring her down, of course, but that would take a minute or two, and by then, she would have seen what she had gone aloft to see, been able to look down over the bowsprit to see *The Eleanor*'s prow cutting through the water, and been able to look aft and down and see what the sailors saw all the time.

She made it to the foresail yard without being seen and turned to look down and aft at the quarterdeck. Mr. Porter wasn't even looking in her direction. She took a breath and climbed some more, until the shroud ended at the foremast top. There was a small platform here where the foremast top was fastened to the foremast. She crawled onto it on her stomach, then gained her feet and wrapped her arms around the two masts where they joined.

She could feel *The Eleanor* sway side to side, and then from bow to stern, her movement magnified by the height of the foremast top from the deck. For a moment, Mary felt that shaming, uneasy sensation in her stomach.

But she forced down the urge to be sick and was pleased with herself that she had done it. She was aloft, and no matter what happened now, even another beating by Charley, or being put ashore in Boston, nothing could take that from her.

There was a safety line woven around the masts where the foretop mast was joined to the foremast, and she leaned against the foremast and tied it around her waist. Now, even if a sudden movement of the ship threw her off the top, she wouldn't fall to the deck, and if she stayed forward of the masts, hid behind them, there was no telling how long she could be up here before she was caught and ordered below.

Someone hissed her name, and for a moment she thought she had been discovered anyway. But then she realized that if her name had been hissed, instead of shouted, it was only Tony who had seen her from his perch in the crow's nest on the mainmast. Tony was in no position to order the captain's daughter around, or even to shout at her. She ignored him.

The fog, which had appeared a solid gray wall from the quarterdeck, from up here looked to be in patches. She could see, here and there, small areas where the fog had completely parted, exposing the black-looking swells of the English Channel.

There was the smell of salt water, and she heard, far off, the call of seagulls, and wondered if that was how Mr. Porter had known they would soon make landfall. A lot of seamanship was like that, she had learned. It was very simple once you knew the secret.

Within five minutes, she could see a hundred yards in all directions from *The Eleanor*, and ten minutes after that, there was hardly any fog at all, and the sun was all the way up, a great orange disc on the horizon off the starboard quarter.

"Ahoy, the quarterdeck! Land ho!" Tony called, as loudly as he could. "Land ho! Two points off the starboard bow!"

"Where away?" Mr. Porter shouted up at him through his megaphone.

"Two points off the starboard bow!" Tony shouted, He sounded, Mary thought, like a girl screaming. Tony was still a boy, Mary thought, a little bitterly. He was still a boy, and she was a woman, and yet Tony was routinely ordered aloft, and she was going to be in very bad trouble for having done so.

Captain Paul Selkirk, who had been sitting at the table in his cabin waiting for Mary to clean his breakfast away so that he could have a little talk with her about how she would be expected to behave when they went ashore, heard Mr. Porter calling to the lookout. He hadn't heard the lookout, but he knew where they were, and that the lookout had reported either another vessel or landfall; and in either case, he belonged on deck. He put his cup of cold coffee down, swore at his daughter for having failed to reappear with a second cup of coffee and for the talk he wanted to have, put on his tricorn, and climbed the ladder to the quarterdeck.

He was going to have to take her ashore, and he didn't want her to say something in innocent conversation, especially something about the three-hundred-stand rifles he had in the hold, that might call the attention of H.M. Customs, or for that matter, the Royal Navy, to him and *The Eleanor*.

The way to avoid the interest of H.M. government was to fade as far as possible into the merchant fleet by doing everything that merchantmen were expected to do, when and where they customarily did it, no more and no less.

He would discharge most of his cargo of ship's timbers at Plymouth, where it would be used by British shipmakers to construct small coasters, and by fishermen. He would take on provisions, of course, and some ship's ironwork, and whatever else he could buy at a reasonable price that would make his next ports of call, London and Amsterdam, seem perfectly natural places for a merchantman like *The Eleanor* to be.

It was no one's business that he would be out of Amsterdam for Tatta in Hyderabad, but even if it came to someone's notice, they would think he was carrying Dutch cheeses, not three-hundred-stand of Pennsylvania rifles and a hundred barrels of Pennsylvania ironwork that could not be told from English-made ironwork.

The crew could be trusted to say nothing about where they were bound, or what they carried, but Mary was liable to say something, unless he had a talk with her beforehand about not letting anyone know any of their business.

"What and where away, Mr. Porter?" Captain Selkirk asked, when Porter tipped his hat to him.

"Lookout reports landfall two points off the starboard bow, Captain," Mr. Porter replied, and handed Selkirk his foot-and-a-half-long brass telescope.

Captain Selkirk looked aloft and saw Tony gesturing with his arm in the direction where he had spotted land. He also saw someone on the foremast top.

"I'm glad the lad spotted it," Selkirk said to Mr. Porter, who had no idea what why a lookout doing what a lookout is supposed to do pleased the captain.

"Aye, sir," he said.

"Ahoy, the quarterdeck," Tony screamed in his boyish soprano. "Land ho, off the port quarter!"

Captain Selkirk put his glass to his eye, looked to port, and made out, faintly, land on the horizon.

Mr. Selkirk appeared on the quarterdeck as Captain Selkirk lowered his glass and asked, "What do you make it to be, Mr. Porter?"

"Probably Great Mew Stone, to starboard, Captain," Porter replied.

Mr. Selkirk put his glass to his eye, and announced, "Great Mew Stone it is, sir. And to port, Penlee Point."

"Thank you, Mr. Selkirk," his father said sarcastically, returning Mr. Porter's glass to him. "It is always rewarding to have one's judgments confirmed by a master mariner."

Mr. Selkirk took his glass from his eye and walked with what dignity he could muster to the binnacle to consult the compass.

"Once you have confirmed that we're headed through Plymouth Sound, Mr. Selkirk, would you see if you can find your sister? I think she would like to see us make landfall."

"Aye, aye, sir," Mr. Selkirk said. "Have you any idea where she is, sir?"

"Well, she's not in my cabin, and if she's not in yours, then I would suggest either the mess or the chicken house."

Mr. Selkirk put the leather megaphone to his lips.

"Go get her, Mr. Selkirk," the Captain said, stopping him. "The walk will do you good."

Angry, but doing his best to hide it, Mr. Selkirk went down the ladder to the deck, and checked both the mess and the chicken house for his sister. She was in neither place, and she hadn't been in his cabin, nor, his father said, in his. But she could have gone there as he was going up the ladder to the the quarterdeck. He checked first his cabin, then the captain's cabin, and finally, just to be sure, the wardroom. Mary was nowhere.

He returned to the bridge.

"Sir," he said, "I can't find her."

His father looked at him coldly.

"Now you may use your horn," he said.

Mr. Selkirk put the megaphone to his lips. "Mistress Selkirk to the quarterdeck," he said. "And lively now."

There was no response. He repeated the call.

Mr. Porter softly informed the captain that Miss Mary had been on the quarterdeck a half hour or so before, and that he'd seen her making her way toward the chicken house.

"Send for the bosun," Captain Selkirk said, as softly.

"Mr. Selkirk," Mr. Porter said, "The captain will have the bosun."

"Bosun to the quarterdeck!" Mr. Selkirk bellowed through his megaphone.

"Ahoy, the quarterdeck!" a feminine voice shouted. "I'm coming."

"Belay the call for the bosun," Captain Selkirk said. "Porter, where the hell is she?"

"Belay the call for the bosun, Mr. Selkirk," Mr. Porter ordered.

"Belay the call for the bosun," Mr. Selkirk bellowed.

Captain Selkirk snatched the megaphone from him.

"Where away, Mary?" he bellowed through it.

"At the foresail yard," Mary yelled back.

The three officers on the quarterdeck looked up at the foresail rigging. Captain Selkirk snatched Mr. Selkirk's glass from his hand and put it to his eye.

"By God, I'll kill her!" he said.

He bit back the temptation to tell her not to look down.

"Who had the watch?" he asked, icily.

"God, Captain," Chief Mate Porter said. "I never dreamed that she . . ."

"I'll go get her," Mr. Selkirk said.

"Stand!" Captain Selkirk said, sharply. "You'll distract her!"

"Drake's Island dead ahead!" Tony called out from the crow's nest, and then he screamed it again in his boyish soprano.

"Steady as she goes, Mr. Porter," Captain Selkirk said. "We'll hold what we have until she gets down."

"Steady as she goes it is, sir," Mr. Porter said.

The crew was on deck now, looking up at the foremast shrouds as Mary, very slowly, continued to climb down them.

"Nobody moves!" Captain Selkirk bellowed through the megaphone, to prevent any of the crew from climbing the shrouds to help her. That would likely distract her, cause her to lose her footing and fall nearly one hundred feet to the deck.

And then she was down. She turned from the shrouds, stood for a moment on the railing, and then jumped lightly to the fo'c's'l deck.

"I'll have all hands on deck, Mr. Porter," Captain Selkirk said, "and then all hands aloft."

The commands were given, and the crew scampered into the rigging.

"I'll have your sister on the quarterdeck," Captain Selkirk said to the third mate. But it was not necessary to issue the order through the megaphone. Mary was walking, not quickly, but not hanging back either, down the deck toward them.

She walked quickly up the ladder and to her father. As she approached him, she hung her head, but when she was standing directly in front of him she raised her face to his.

"So, mistress," her father said.

"I wanted to go aloft, and so I did," Mary said. "I waited until I was sure Mr. Porter wasn't looking."

"What was in your mind?" her father asked, incredulously. Then he looked around. The Hamoaze River was off their port quarter. The fog was now just about completely gone, and he could make out the houses of Capetown, beyond The Hoe.

"You have the helm, Mr. Porter," Captain Selkirk said. "Bring her around wide, if you have a mind to."

"I have the helm, sir," Mr. Porter said. "Steer north northeast."

"Nor' nor'east it is, sir," the quartermaster said, as the helmsmen hauled on the wheel.

Captain Selkirk looked down at his daughter.

"So you wanted to see what it was like aloft, even though you could have easily fallen to your death, is that it?"

"I didn't plan to fall," Mary said. "And I didn't."

"And you didn't think that I'd punish you, if you lived?"

"I knew that I'd be punished," Mary said.

"I'll think of something," Captain Selkirk said. "You can rest your mind about that. I'll think of something."

Then he grabbed the girl and held her against him, holding her head against his chest with his massive hand.

Over her shoulder, he saw Mr. Porter start to turn to Mr. Selkirk. He knew he was about to order a reduction in sails.

"Mr. Porter," he said, letting go of Mary. "I think it would be very nice if we sailed in there with everything flying. Let's show them what kind of sailors we have aboard."

"Aye, aye, sir," Mr. Porter said. "Steer southeast."

"So'east it is, sir," the quartermaster parroted.

"And then, Mr. Quartermaster," Mr. Porter said, "we're going to bring her around smartly to west nor'west, and then I want all the canvas reefed at once."

"Bosun," Mr. Selkirk called, making a megaphone of his hands, "make sure everybody on the yards is awake!"

There was laughter from the rigging.

All of her canvas flying, the merchantman *Eleanor*, with her namesake's daughter on the quarterdeck, approached the wharfs of Plymouth making a good seven or maybe even eight knots. When she was two hundred yards off shore, the word was given, her sails were reefed, and she began to slow.

She was directly off the wharfs when she lost way. Captain Selkirk nodded at Mr. Porter, who put the megaphone to his lips and bellowed, "Let go the for'd port anchor!"

A seaman who had been waiting with an axe poised swung it against the anchor rope, and the anchor chain rattled through its port. *The Eleanor*, thirty-two days out of Philadelphia, had made port.

119

Captain Selkirk, accompanied by his son Charles, made the calls that were expected of him by custom and required by law. He informed the harbormaster officially that he was out Philadelphia with a cargo of ship's timbers and pig iron and that he intended to pick up ironwork in Plymouth, then sail to London, where he hoped to be able to pick up a commission to buy Indian silk, raw and finished cloth.

He told the harbormaster that the absolutely reliable information he had been given about what the Indians would pay for good Pennsylvania oak, walnut, and pine had proved, when he actually got to Tatta on the Indus, absolutely unreliable. But he had found the Indians willing to part with their silk at a reasonable price, so the voyage had not been a total waste of time and effort.

It was a typical mariner's tale, and the Plymouth harbormaster accepted it as he heard it. He also accepted Captain Selkirk's invitation to dinner, and the three of them ate heartily at a tavern, called Pilgrim's Progress in reference to the early settlers of New England, the Pilgrims, having sailed from Plymouth.

Over dinner, the harbormaster learned that New England still reflected the Pilgrims' rather straitlaced views on life, especially insofar as consumption of intoxicating beverages was concerned. Pennsylvania, on the other hand, Selkirk told him, was populated by English and Germans primarily; and both the Church of England and the Lutheran church were too wise to put themselves between a good hardworking Englishman, or his German counterpart, and his pint of beer or ale.

Selkirk told the harbormaster that he was in no great rush to put out to sea, that he felt his men, for reasons of morale and health, should have the chance to spend several days ashore, and he would rather they do so in Plymouth than in London. There was a greater tendency for the men, he said, to get themselves in trouble along the Thames River in London than there was here in Plymouth.

And Selkirk asked the harbormaster if he could recommend an honest commission merchant to him to help him transact the business. He was not surprised to have the harbormaster tell him that his brother-in-law was in that line of business and that if Captain Selkirk happened to be free for supper, say at half past seven o'clock, he would be happy to make the introduction at his home. Captain Selkirk replied that he had promised to take his daughter Mary, whom he carried aboard, ashore for dinner, otherwise he would have been honored to accept the harbormaster's kind invitation.

Selkirk was not surprised when the harbormaster immediately included Mary in the invitation.

He was surprised, however, when the harbormaster's brother-in-law turned out to seem both competent and honest. He told Selkirk that he was sure he could get a price for the ship's timbers twenty percent higher than Selkirk had expected; and he said that if Selkirk could spend, say, seven days in port, he felt sure that he could have the ironwork Selkirk wanted to buy sent down from a goods warehouse in Bristol at a price substantially lower than the ironwork for immediate sale from the stores houses in Plymouth.

Selkirk, with a smile, told him he was always willing to exchange time for money.

The excuse he had wanted to spent a week in Plymouth had been handed to him.

As a courtesy, the harbormaster had provided Captain Selkirk and his children with a guard of the Plymouth Watch to escort them back to the wharf where *The Eleanor*'s longboat waited for him. When they got to the boat, its crew were not prepared to take the captain and his party back to *The Eleanor*. The members of the Plymouth Watch smiled at the tongue-lashing the Pennsylvania captain gave the bosun in the longboat for having permitted two of its crew to get off in a tavern.

Then the Pennsylvania captain climbed back up onto the wharf, and quite unnecessarily explained that two of his seamen were drunk in a tavern someplace and he was sending his bosun and some men to bring them back to the longboat, and there was no need for the watch to wait. He gave the sergeant of the watch three shillings and told him to buy the others a pint of ale with his thanks.

As soon as the watch started down the wharf, Captain Selkirk, surprising Mary, peeled off his powdered wig and put a knit cap on his head. He took off the jacket with its gold stripes and put on a seaman's simple black shirt. Bosun LaSalle handed him a pistol, which he put in his waistband and covered with the simple seaman's shirt. Then he and Theo LaSalle and two other seamen climbed up on the wharf.

The watch would know that seamen from *The Eleanor* would be searching the taverns for two drunken sailors. The heavy-set man in the knit cap looked nothing like *The Eleanor*'s captain, who was a fine gentleman, and even if he was seen entering the Golden Herring, one of the less reputable places on the Plymouth waterfront, it would be naturally assumed that he was a seaman in search of the two who had gone off to get drunk, or perhaps find a tart.

The Golden Herring, renamed when it was bought fifteen years earlier by a fisherman who had made one of those legendary catches at a time when the price of herring was way up, was now operated by that fisherman's widow.

She was a tall, stern-faced, thin woman who looked, Captain Selkirk thought, not unlike the woman he had married in Philadelphia. She was standing between the beer kegs in the rear of the smoke-filled, salty smelling public room when he entered. She moved her head just enough for Selkirk to be able to understand he was to go up the stairs to the second floor, where the Golden Herring provided tarts to those who had the money.

All the doors in the upstairs corridor were closed, so Captain Selkirk and Bosun LaSalle waited for her in the corridor. She came up a moment later, carrying three clay mugs in one hand and a clay pitcher of ale in the other. She nodded her head and gave Selkirk what could be a smile when she walked past them. She went to one door, found it locked, and then moved to the next one.

It opened.

"Out!" she ordered. In a moment, a tart, tucking her blouse into her skirt waist, and a drunken man, from his looks probably a seaman, came into the corridor, and went further down it.

The woman gestured with the hand holding the three clay mugs for Selkirk and LaSalle to go into the room. It held a bed, a table with a stubby candle, and two chairs. It smelled unpleasant.

She followed them in, held out mugs to them, and when they had taken them, poured the ale into them.

"I saw you in mid-stream this noon," she said.

"We came in this morning," Selkirk said.

"And from the harbormaster's house to the Golden Herring," she said. "Dressed like you are. And I don't think it's a trollop you're after."

"I'm after something I know will cost me a lot more than a trollop," Selkirk said.

"I always try to oblige, Captain," the woman said. "You know that. Especially if you're willing to admit right off that some things are very expensive."

"I want a steelworker," Selkirk said. "A crucible steelworker."

"You want to press a steelworker?" the woman, obviously confused, replied.

"No," Selkirk said. "I don't want him for the crew. I want him to come to Pennsylvania. I have work for him there at good wages."

"Captain," she said, "you've always been straight with me, and I'll be straight with you. I have no idea what you're talking about. I'm a fishwife and a saloonkeeper, and you're talking about things I know nothing about."

"I thought that it would be necessary to get somebody else involved," he said. "And I thought you'd be able to find the man I need."

"And if I got caught doing what you ask me to do, what kind of trouble would I be in?"

"You'd be facing seven years in gaol," Selkirk said.

"What in the name of Sweet Jesus is what you said, a ducible steelworker?"

"*Crucible* steelworker," Selkirk corrected her. "They're highly skilled craftsmen, and they're under a life's contract to their employers. They don't want their secret to leave England."

"But, so far's you're concerned, to hell with the contract, and for that matter, to hell with the law, right?"

"You have to pay for some things," Selkirk said. "I'm willing to pay for a craftsman."

She didn't reply for a moment, and then she said, "There's a man named Woodley."

"Philip Woodley?" Selkirk asked, and when she nodded, added, "I've dealt with him before. I don't like him and I don't trust him."

"As you like and trust me?"

"You know how I regard you, Mistress," Selkirk said.

"But you come to me with a proposition that would see me sent to prison for seven years?"

"I didn't come empty-handed," he said, and nodded to LaSalle, who took a small leather pouch he had worn hung

123

around his neck. LaSalle laid it on the table and stepped back.

"That much now. That much again when I have the man aboard *The Eleanor*," Selkirk said.

She picked up the pouch and opened it, and spilled the contents, gold coins, into her hand.

"They're Spanish," she said, biting one.

"Spanish and Russian," Selkirk said. "But you can get at a scale. A quarter ounce of gold is worth a pound sterling."

"That's one hell of a lot of money, Paul Selkirk," she said. "Are you telling me all there is to tell? Is there more than going to jail for seven years?"

"That's all the penalty I know," Selkirk said. "As God is my judge."

"But there is more?"

"I want a journeyman crucible steelworker. Someone who knows the trade, *and* the secret." She nodded. "I want an unmarried man," he went on. "The risk of trying to sneak a whole family out is too great, and so is the risk of having a married man willing to come alone and then changing his mind once I get him to Pennsylvania. And I don't want the king, or anyone else, to connect the disappearance of such a man up north with *The Eleanor* here."

"But seven years is the worst that can happen?"

"So I have been told," he said. "By somebody who knows."

He did not tell her that somebody was his new wife.

"I know no way to go except through Philip Woodley," she said finally.

"Then do what you can to keep my name out of it so long as you can."

"You want the man here? How would you get him on board?"

"Have him taken to London," Selkirk said. "And have Woodley contact me at the Cheshire Arms. There's enough money there to pay his expenses."

"And when do I get the rest of my money?"

"I'll get it to you, Mistress," he said.

She nodded. She picked up the pitcher and her mug.

"I'll go first," she said. "Unless you'll be wanting a girl?"

"No, thank you, Mistress," Selkirk said.

"Captain!" Theo LaSalle blurted.

"I will go," Selkirk said. "LaSalle will be staying."

124

"I'll go to the longboat with you, Captain," Theo LaSalle said. "And then come back."

"I'll make it to the longboat all right," Selkirk said. "Just you make sure that you're on the wharf at eight o'clock in the morning."

"I don't like the idea of you walking the streets alone," LaSalle said.

"And I don't like having to tell Mary what you're about when she asks, as she would, where you were going at near midnight," Selkirk said. He tugged at his seaman's shirt, freed it from his waist, and shifted the butt of the pistol so that it would be visible.

"Have a good time, Theo," Captain Selkirk said. "But be on the wharf when you're supposed to be." He turned to the woman. "Put that on my slate, Mistress," he said. "That way I'll be sure that no one's paying for something he didn't get."

The woman nodded at him, and walked out of the room.

Theo LaSalle took a pistol from his belt and held it out to Captain Selkirk.

"Theo," Selkirk said, patiently, "*if* there are footpads out there willing to take someone my size on, and *if* a pistol pointed at them doesn't discourage them, they'd not be discouraged by two pistols."

"Aye," LaSalle said.

"Goodnight, Theo," Captain Selkirk said, and walked out of the room. Three good-looking tarts came up the stairs as he went down.

They made him realize how long it had been since he had a woman.

"Damn!" he said, aloud, but he kept going down the stairs.

Chapter Seven

1

Plymouth, England
November 5, 1769

Captain Paul Selkirk considered a number of factors before making his decision about what to do next.

His plan for acquiring a crucible steelworker had been, he thought, simple, as most good plans are. He would pay more for a running-from-indenture craftsman than he was worth. That was both good sense and not really expensive. Money was relative. The gold coins Theo LaSalle had so casually thrown on the table before Mistress Hawley in the whore's crib in the Golden Herring had been worth 200 pounds sterling, give or take a couple of shillings. They had weighed out at three pounds two ounces. Given the relative inaccuracy of his scales, and the possibility that some of the coins weren't as pure as they were supposed to be, that was close enough. He was giving her two hundred pounds now, and he would give her gold worth another two hundred pounds when the craftsman was safely aboard *The Eleanor*. Plus what other expenses were necessary. The expenses, even considering the opportunity to cheat him he had offered Mistress Hawley and Woodley, shouldn't be more than 20 or 25 pounds sterling. A total of 425 pounds sterling.

He would have bought at the least possible risk a craftsman capable of doing what he wanted him to do. The reward for turning him in to the authorities for planning the running from indenture of a craftsman wouldn't be more than fifty pounds, if that. It was in Mistress Hawley's and Woodley's own best interests to see that the man was put safely aboard *The Eleanor*.

He was prepared to spend five hundred pounds. The other

money would be spent to provide the craftsman, when he was delivered aboard and they could make a port outside England, with a set of decent clothes, and passage for himself and Peter O'Keefe, *The Eleanor*'s quartermaster, on a ship to Philadelphia. O'Keefe was clever (Selkirk had in mind for him a promotion to third mate as soon as there was a spot for him), and he could get the steel maker aboard a ship and to Pennsylvania without trouble.

That plan, formed even before they had sailed from Philadelphia, had been modified: Mary would sail with O'Keefe and the crucible steelworker. That would get her home to Pennsylvania, and spare her the trip to Tatta.

The plan had to be reconsidered again and again. You shouldn't go around changing plans as you changed your shirt, Paul Selkirk believed, but neither could you afford to make a plan and follow it no matter what new development turned up. Unaware that he was being smug about it, Selkirk had concluded that his success was in some degree due to the fact that he knew when to change a plan and when not to.

One of the possibilities he had considered was actually getting caught with the three-hundred-stand of rifles aboard. Or with the running crucible-steel maker aboard. There was a chance (he had not, so far, come to the attention of the authorities) that he could explain away the rifles by saying that he thought the firearms prohibition applied only to military arms. It would be stretching credibility, but it was something to consider. If he were caught with the crucible-steel maker aboard, he could tell them he didn't know about the lifelong contract the man was under, and that he was carrying him simply as a passenger.

If, however, the English authorities searched his ship and found the rifles, and the crucible-steel maker, and one-hundred barrels of ironwork that had not come out of Birmingham or Leeds, he could plead neither innocence nor ignorance; they would catch him for what he was, someone in conscious defiance of a royal order.

He thought the latest change in plans was made for him when Mistress Hawley told him that she had been in touch with Woodley and that Woodley said it would be at least a month and probably more before he could safely come up with a crucible steelworker to Captain Selkirk's specifications.

There was no way he could stay in London for that long a

time without arousing the interest of even the dullest of George III's customs officers.

He wasn't canceling his plans, he told himself, just shifting them around, like pieces on a chessboard.

When *The Eleanor* moved through Plymouth Bay and into the English Channel, outbound for London with enough fresh provisions aboard only for a journey that long, Selkirk waited until they were out of sight of land. Then he motioned Mr. Porter over to the binnacle where Quartermaster O'Keefe stood.

"Bring her about," Captain Selkirk ordered. "Set a course that'll keep us out of the shipping channels, and out of sight of England, and make for the Atlantic coast of France. We'll reprovision at some small French port, and then we'll go to Tatta."

"Aye, aye, sir," Mr. Porter said, but he hesitated, waiting for an explanation.

"I've decided the safest thing for us to do is get rid of the rifles as soon as we can," he said.

"Miss Mary'll be pleased," Mr. Porter said. "She was not at all fond of being shipped home."

"Miss Mary'll do what she's damned well told to do," Captain Selkirk snapped.

The one thing he didn't like about the change of plans he had decided upon was that it meant Mary would have to stay aboard. He didn't like the idea of her being in Tatta, and he didn't like the idea of her coming back to England with them when he picked up the crucible-steel maker. It would have been much better to see her aboard a respectable Englishman bound for North America.

2

Tatta, Hyderabad
November 20, 1769

Colonel Sir Edgar Watchbury died of fever at Government House, Tatta, Hyderabad at two o'clock in the afternoon. At his bedside were his wife, Lady Caroline; Sir Charles Rewwe, vice governor of the Royal East India Company; and Surgeon Kenneth MacLain, of the Prince of Wales's Own Scottish Borderers.

128

Sir Edgar passed peacefully. He just sank, Surgeon Mac-Lain said, and there seemed to be nothing they could do to keep him afloat. Lady Caroline didn't at all like Surgeon MacLain's choice of words, but she had to admit privately that they aptly described what had happened.

She and her husband, and Sir Charles, a portly and dignified gentleman in his late fifties, had come to Tatta on horseback from Karachi four days before, after moving from Bombay to Karachi by ship.

At their first meeting, a dinner at Government House in Bombay, the governor of the Royal East India Company had told Sir Edgar that he believed he understood Edgar's mission to India. And that he had decided there was nothing like the truth, and no better way for Edgar to come by the truth than by seeing things with his own eyes.

"We have just regained control of our post in Tatta," he said. "It involved moving two companies of the Scottish Borderers and a battalion of native troops overland from Karachi, as opposed to sailing them upriver, I mean to say."

"Regained control from whom, Your Excellency?" Sir Edgar had asked.

"Tatta is nominally under the control of the maharaja of Hyderabad," the Governor had replied drily, "who periodically assures us of his fidelity to the crown. He is regrettably unable to keep certain nomadic tribesmen, who he believes are from Baluchistan . . . you know Baluchistan?"

"It is, I believe," Sir Edgar had replied, "to the northwest, in the direction of Afghanistan and Persia?"

"Yes," the governor agreed. "As I was saying, the maharaja professes to be unable to keep these natives from preying on his own people, and our posts, and so it was necessary for me to send the Scottish Borderers to pacify Tatta."

"Pacify?"

"There was a twelve-man post, twelve Englishmen, at Tatta. Protected by a company of native troops."

"Was?"

"Was."

"What happened to them?" Sir Edgar asked.

"No one knows. When the ship arrived on its scheduled call, they were gone. The English had simply vanished, and so had the 145 natives charged with their protection."

"Extraordinary," Sir Edgar said.

"We have reason to believe that the troops deserted with-

129

out firing a shot," the governor said. "And were paid off with proceeds from the silk and spices the company had gathered in anticipation of the arrival of our ship."

"The implication, then," Sir Edgar had replied, "is that native troops cannot be trusted."

"It is not, in my opinion, quite as simple as that," the governor had replied. "Properly officered, and under adaquate supervision, that is, serving with British troops, they are trustworthy, and they are splendid soldiers."

"Then why . . . ?" Sir Edgar asked, leaving the rest of the question unspoken.

"They are somewhat more pragmatic than devoted," the governor said drily. "When faced with the choice of simply vanishing into the countryside with some money in their pockets, or fighting to the death to protect a building housing only dead Englishmen, they are prone to do what they think of as the reasonable thing."

"You're saying the English were somehow killed, whereupon the native troops chose to desert without fighting?"

"I don't know that," the governor said. "But I believe that."

"I see. And had there been a larger detachment, or a detachment of any size, of British troops present, they would not have deserted?"

"Not, at least, until the last Englishman was dead."

"I see."

"As I said, we now have two companies of the Borderers in Tatta, and they will remain there as long as I can keep them there, until there is a more desperate need for them elsewhere. What I'm going to do, Sir Edgar, is send you to see for yourself. I have absolute confidence that an officer of your background and experience will be able to judge the situation for what it is. And make your report to His Majesty on the facts as you perceive them."

"I raise the question of the safety of Lady Caroline," Sir Edgar had said, and for a moment Caroline had thought she might be permitted to stay behind in Bombay.

"I am quite confident that Lady Caroline will be as safe, and certainly more comfortable, in Tatta than she would be here. Safe because with two companies of the Borderers present, one would be hard-pressed to find a more loyal ally of His Majesty than the maharaja, and comfortable, because it gives His Excellency great pleasure to have visiting dignitaries as his guests."

There had been a surprisingly good road from Karachi to Tatta, and a quite comfortable carriage had been made available to them for the trip. Edgar, of course, as a colonel of cavalry and personal representative of His Majesty, absolutely refused to ride in it, although he must, Lady Caroline thought, have been at least as aware of his illness as she was.

They were accompanied on the trip from Karachi to Tatta by a platoon of the Scottish Borderers, a twelve-man detachment of the Governor General's Troop of Light Horse, and a company of native troops.

And they had been attacked en route.

The truth of the matter was that Lady Caroline had had no idea of it until it was all over.

She had naturally been aware that some of the troops had not been up to the physical demands of the march, in particular the blinding heat. In just about equal numbers, Scottish Borderers and native infantrymen had either broken ranks to collapse at the side of the road or simply slumped to the road in their tracks.

Provisions had been made for this eventuality. There were three ox-drawn wagons at the tail of their column, and each had place to carry and care for troops who had fallen victim to the heat. The victims were either carried to the rear of the column while the column was halted or waited where they had fallen until the wagons came up to them and they could be placed on them.

She had been surprised but not startled when two soldiers, both of them Borderers, had dropped in their tracks almost together. She had not heard the shots the men had heard, nor understood why the detachment of the Governor General's Light Horse (Edgar, of course, right with them) had galloped off toward the hills that formed the valley in which the column stood.

She had learned later that natives were hiding behind rocks and shooting at the column of troops, then running away. She heard, but did not understand what it meant, that they had fired not native muskets, which were crude and generally ineffective, nor even the Brown Bess muskets they were presumed to have from the native troops who had deserted. It was a strange kind of a weapon, something apparently like those Edgar understood the colonists in North America were making, that threw a smaller ball at a higher velocity over a greater distance than even the standard Royal Army infantry weapon.

Edgar had been fascinated with that. He had talked about it to her even after he had been stricken by the fever. There was no question whatever in Lady Caroline's mind that Edgar had become sick (actually, that he had had a relapse) because of his galloping off with the detachment of Light Horse in their futile chase. She had at first been quite annoyed with him.

The annoyance had quickly turned to concern when it became almost immediately evident that Surgeon MacLain's ministrations were doing nothing for him. MacLain seemed not only as competent as the surgeon and the physician had been in Bombay, when Edgar had first been ill, but she was sure that he was personally concerned with Edgar. He had sat up with him through two nights, watching the leeches at work.

Edgar, who had been sleeping peacefully, just stopped breathing. That was all there was to it. One moment, she had been sitting there, waiting for him to wake up so that she could feed him some broth, and the next moment, he had stopped breathing and would never wake again.

She had never ever considered what would happen next in any specific detail until he was actually dead, and she had really been in a daze when Sir Charles had as tactfully as possible brought it up to her.

"Madam," he said to her in the sitting room (furnished, she was astonished to find, with fine English furniture) of the quarters assigned to her in the maharaja's palace, "first let me assure you that on the death of Sir Edgar, the Royal East India Company and myself personally have naturally assumed responsibility for your safety and well-being."

"Thank you very much, Sir Charles," she said, dabbing at her eyes with a handkerchief. "You are most gracious."

"You will naturally wish to return home as quickly as possible."

"Yes, of course."

"Which raises the question of Sir Edgar's remains."

"I beg your pardon?"

"While we could, of course, arrange for his interment in Bombay, in the cemetery of the cathedral there . . ."

"I hadn't thought of his interment," Lady Caroline confessed.

"Since," Sir Charles went on, with exquisite tact, "the preparation of the remains will in any event be necessary . . ."

She thought that through. Edgar was dead. Therefore, especially in this climate, Edgar would soon start to decompose. What could they possibly do about that?

"Perhaps you would be good enough to tell me something about that, Sir Charles," she said.

"Quite. The . . . uh . . . *normal*. That is to say, for someone of your late husband's rank and position, the normal procedure involves a lead sheathing within a wooden casket, and a sealed airtight tinned packing box for the casket."

"Lead sheathing?"

The necessity for getting into specific detail so embarrassed Sir Charles that Lady Caroline actually felt sorry for him.

"What it involves," he said hesitantly, "is covering the body, the *remains*, as it were, in lead. Sort of a leaden shroud, you see. And then that is placed in a standard casket. The casket itself is then sealed within a tinned shipping case. Do you quite understand?"

"Yes, I do," she said. "Thank you."

"What I'm driving at, rather badly, I fear, Lady Caroline," Sir Charles went on, "is that these preparations will be necessary in any case, except for immediate interment here . . ."

"I will not bury my husband here," she said, wondering why she felt so strongly about what she was saying.

"No, of course not," he said. "But whether Sir Edgar were to be interred in the British Cemetery in Bombay, is what I'm saying, or at home, the same *preparations*, don't you see, will be necessary."

"The preparations will permit me to take my husband's remains home for burial?" Lady Caroline asked.

"I have had occasion, Lady Caroline," Sir Charles said, "to review the King's Regulations concerning these matters." She had no idea what he meant.

"I beg your pardon?" she asked.

"The governor, or in the instant case, myself, is empowered to serve on the master of any vessel flying the English flag, that is to say, Royal Navy, Merchant Navy, or for that matter, a colonial merchantman, a warrant directing that he provide passage for you, in accommodations appropriate to your late husband's rank, either to England, or to such point

133

where you may transfer to another English-flag ship making for home waters by a more direct route. Do you follow me?"

"No," she confessed.

"The first ship that calls here will be required to take you either directly to England, you and Sir Edgar's remains, that is, or to transfer you to a ship that is proceeding directly to England."

"I see," she said. "Yes."

"I beg your pardon?"

"I would like to go home as soon as possible," Lady Caroline said, "taking my late husband's remains with me."

"I will execute the warrant this afternoon, and turn it over personally to Mr. Forbes myself."

"Mr. Forbes?"

"Mr. Edwin Forbes is the resident agent of the company here. I am going to turn you over, on my departure, to his capable hands."

"You are leaving me here alone?"

"Hardly alone, Lady Caroline," Sir Charles said, gently chiding her. "Under the protection of two companies of the Scottish Borderers, and personally in the hands of Mr. Forbes."

"And when, do you think," she asked, "might I expect a ship?"

"Perhaps within a matter of days," he said.

She sensed that he was lying to her. There didn't seem to be anything, however, that she could do about anything. Circumstances were quite out of her control.

3

Cape Town, South Africa
December 24, 1769

Once the sails of *The Eleanor* had been sighted, and the word passed, much of the population of Cape Town came out to see her anchor. They lined the shore and the wharfs, but none of the boats on the beach made for *The Eleanor*. Selkirk understood why; he knew (and admired) the Afrikaaners. He knew they not only did not want to appear overeager to deal with *The Eleanor*, or any other ship that called at Cape Town, they didn't have to. They had a sellers' market for their main exports, fresh water, goats, and cattle, for there was no other port within thousands of miles.

But once *The Eleanor*'s longboat had been put over the side and rowed ashore, Captain Selkirk, his son, and his daughter, were greeted warmly, if a little stiffly, and invited to the wide-porched home of Willem van Reibeeck, Cape Town's richest merchant, for "a little meal."

"My wife and I would be pleased, Captain Selkirk," he said, "if you and your daughter and son would spend the Christmas with us. Tonight a little meal, then church at midnight, and then tomorrow we make a little extra effort for Christmas dinner."

The "little meal" was a feast, roast pork and roast beef, veal, lamb, and fowl, washed down with limitless wine. Van Reibeeck's ancestors had come to South Africa more than a century before from the Netherlands, and the family was now firmly established among the colony's leaders. They thought of themselves as Afrikaaners, a separate nationality, rather than expatriate Dutch. They spoke a language, based on Dutch but flavored with some French words (pronounced as Dutch) from French Huguenot immigrants, called Afrikaans.

Except for the little trade there was with ships like *The Eleanor* the colony was just about self-contained. Members of the community raised livestock, grew corn, had vineyards, and distilled rum and brandy. Selkirk liked them but found them smug and more than a little hypocritical. They were devout and pious Calvinists, very concerned with morality and the penalties for earthly sin in the form of eternal punishment in the life hereafter. This did nothing to discourage them from drinking from first light of day, and of taking the more comely black Africans as mistresses.

As Captain Selkirk believed he would, van Reibeeck insisted that they spend the night ashore as his guests, and after the meal and midnight services in a church where the ritual of worship reminded Selkirk uncomfortably of his wedding in Saint Olaf's Lutheran Church in Philadelphia, they were taken to comfortable, well-equipped rooms in a wing of van Reibeeck's large and rambling home.

In the morning, Selkirk left Mary with van Reibeeck's wife and daughters and sent Charley with Theo LaSalle to see about water for *The Eleanor*. He took van Reibeeck himself on board *The Eleanor*, where he produced French brandy and they conducted their business. Christmas was Christmas, but business was also business, and if the women didn't know, what was the harm?

Both were pleased with their deal. Very little money changed hands. Van Reibeeck got plows, axes, wagon wheel rims, and other ironwork from *The Eleanor*'s holds. Selkirk gave him Pennsylvania-manufactured ironwork for two reasons, first that he personally thought it was better than the goods he had taken aboard at Plymouth, and second because it got the Pennsylvania goods off *The Eleanor*, leaving him with an ironwork cargo for which he had bills of lading signed by the Plymouth harbormaster.

Van Reibeeck knew Selkirk had given him the ironwork at a very good price, about half what he would have been willing to pay. That meant, he knew, that the ironwork had come from forges in North America, without having passed through anyone else's hands. If Selkirk was willing to take the risk of beating the English out of their tariff, more power to him. So far as Selkirk was concerned, of course, he had been paid more for it than he would have gotten selling it in Amsterdam, or elsewhere in Europe.

In exchange, Selkirk received, at what he considered were very good prices, barrels of wine and brandy. There was a surplus of wine and brandy in South Africa; it manufactured and distilled far more than could be consumed in the colony, and what it made was of good quality. When Selkirk sold the wine and brandy in Philadelphia, or for that matter, in Amsterdam or London, he would honestly report it for what it was, South African. It would be resold, he knew, as French. He, personally, couldn't tell the difference, and the deception therefore would be both easy and safe, and in any case none of his business.

With the business out of the way and a bottle of brandy before them, Selkirk's thoughts turned finally (and nearly too late, he realized with chagrin) to Christmas presents. There were certainly to be gifts from van Reibeeck, if not to him, then certainly to Mary, and he would be expected to reciprocate in kind.

He had no trouble with the women. Women could be pleased easily with one of two gifts, a bolt of silk or a gold trinket. If he hadn't given the chest of gold to Captain Ephraim Lewis in Philadelphia, Selkirk thought, he could have gotten everything he needed out of that. Well, there was some silk, but he would have to offer something of real value to van Reibeeck himself, since he couldn't offer it to his wife in the form of a gold trinket.

Looking at the Afrikaaner, sipping the brandy with genuine pleasure, he had an idea.

"Tell me, Willem," he said, "do you hunt?"

"Getting too fat," van Reibeeck said. "I go watch the boy and let him do the running after."

"Excuse me a moment," Selkirk said, and went and found Porter and told him to have two of the Pennsylvania rifles, and a supply of ball and powder and flints, taken from the hold, wrapped in a clean sheet of canvas, and put in the longboat, so that he could take them ashore when he and van Reibeeck went.

Selkirk was absolutely astonished at van Reibeeck's reaction to the rifles. The portly, dignified Afrikaaner bubbled over with enthusiasm at the very sight of the weapons, running his fingers lovingly over the smoothly oiled birdseye maple stocks and polished brass furniture. After they had gone outside, full of food and brandy, and Charley had demonstrated how accurate the weapons were, van Reibeeck had acted, Selkirk thought, smiling at the thought, like a small child at Christmas.

Well, I pleased him, Selkirk thought, at a very low price, indeed.

But it didn't end there.

Van Reibeeck got him in a corner of the wide veranda and told him that he wanted, for resale, a hundred, or better, *two* hundred of the rifles.

"They're very expensive, Willem," Selkirk said. "If you'll forgive me saying that."

"I can see that," van Reibeeck said. "Your gift overwhelmed me and my son. But I'm talking business now. We put our friendship aside. How much do they cost, wholesale?"

"Seven pounds six shillings," Selkirk said, solemnly. They had not cost him a quarter of that figure. "That's to me, Willem," he said. "Not to you. And without flint, or powder, or ball."

"Flint I got, powder and ball I can get anywhere. The rifles are something else. How many can you let me have?"

"I haven't even given you a price," Selkirk said.

"How many can you let me have at fifteen pounds?" van Reibeeck asked. "That's fair profit for you."

"What do you think you can sell them for?"

137

"That's my business, Paul," van Reibeeck said. "I am not a greedy man."

"I can let you have twenty-five," Selkirk said.

"I'd rather have a hundred," van Reibeeck said. "I'll pay in gold, if you like."

"I'll give you forty, Willem," Selkirk said. He had quickly decided several things. It was important that he try to give van Reibeeck at least part of what he wanted, but at the same time keep him from thinking that he was in the firearms trade. It was better to lie to his friend and tell him forty rifles was all he had.

Selkirk was pained to think that every rifle that he sold in Cape Town was a rifle he could not trade in Tatta for jewels, but there was nothing he could do about it.

The final thought he had was that if there was a market here for such rifles, there was going to be a market elsewhere. It was now absolutely necessary that he have a crucible-steel maker aboard when *The Eleanor* made Philadelphia.

On December 28, 1769, *The Eleanor* sailed out of Table Bay headed south, the three-hundred-stand of Pennsylvania rifles in her hold down to 260, to round the tip of Africa and enter the Indian Ocean, bound for Tatta, on the Indus River.

4

Marburg an der Lahn, Hesse-Kassel
January 16, 1770

His Royal Highness Wilhelm VIII, landgrave of Hesse-Kassel, son of Queen Ulrika Eleanora of Sweden and her consort King Frederick, was in a very good mood. For one thing, he had spent a very pleasant evening in the castle, physically and intellectually. Physically, because for once they had been able to build fires which made the castle warm without simultaneously filling it with smoke. Intellectually, because he had spent three hours in the middle of the clear, winter night, bundled comfortably in fur, peering at the wonders of the moon through an absolutely marvelous telescope designed and constructed by a member of the faculty of Philip's University.

Wilhelm took great pride in the university named for his ancestor, Landgrave Philip I, who, following the teachings of

Martin Luther, had taken the land and property of the Roman Catholic monasteries and turned them into a center of Protestant knowledge and study. He was always thrilled when someone on the faculty came up with some marvelous new scientific device. There had recently been some fascinating experiments with an air pump, and there had been some equally interesting experimentation with fluid electricity, based on the reports to the Royal Society of London of his experiments by an extraordinary American colonist named Benjamin Franklin, but the telescope was a Philip's University advance, if not actually an invention, rather than a duplication in Marburg of the scientific endeavors of others.

What it was, was the incorporation of clockwork in the base of the telescope itself. Professor Diehl had gone to Nürnburg, where the best clocks were made, and ordered manufactured a clockworks of sufficient strength to move the telescope mounting to compensate for the movement of the earth. Once the device was aimed at the moon (or for that matter, any celestial body) and focused, and the clockworks turned on, the telescope remained focused on the moon. It made the moon, or the celestial bodies, seem to stand still.

And Wilhelm had immediately seen a practical political use, in addition to the value the device would have scientifically.

"Professor, how long would it take to have other machines like this built?" he had asked, and had been delighted with the professor's response.

"Your Highness, I thought perhaps Your Highness might be thinking along those lines. I took the liberty of sending Muller und Thane instructions to begin the construction of three similar clockworks."

"And how far along are they?"

"Your Highness, they are virtually complete."

"We will send one to King George, who will probably give it to the Royal Society," Wilhelm said. "Make sure that it bears a plate with your name and that of the University. And we will send one to the tsar, who will probably use it to peer into the bedchambers of the ladies of his court."

He really should not have talked to a commoner so disrespectfully of the Tsar of all the Russias, but the behavior of the Russian court (and of the members of the Russian nobility who were students at the University) was well known to

139

Professor Diehl, and a brilliant astronomer and engineer was, moreover, something special, not bound by convention.

"Why three clockworks?" Wilhelm asked.

"Your Highness, I had the thought that the device might have a military as well as a scientific application," Professor Diehl had said.

"Yes, of course it will, and I feel like a fool for not having thought of that myself."

And when Wilhelm had come down from the tower of the castle where the telescope had been erected to his bedchamber, there had been proof of the normal, that is to say, scandalous behavior of the Russian nobility. Grand Duke Alexei, who was nineteen, had sent a small gift to Landgrave Wilhelm, who was fifty-one. She was in his bed, an exquisite Mongol, one of four the grand duke had brought with him to the University.

It was the grand duke's expression of gratitude for being invited to join the landgrave on a boar hunt today. Wilhelm would have preferred not to have the grand duke along. There were certain conventions to be observed, however. Furthermore, Wilhelm expected to receive a substantial contribution to the University from the grand duke's parents, presuming Alexei made it back to Russia without getting himself run through with the sword of someone whose wife or daughter the grand duke fancied in ways frowned upon in German noble circles.

Wilhelm was annoyed, however, when he walked into the courtyard of the castle and saw the entourage waiting for him. There were fifty horsemen and as many grooms and other servants milling around, including His Imperial Highness, the Grand Duke Alexei. The grand duke was engaged in conversation with Hauptmann Baron von Kolbe, commander of the Cavalry Squadron of the Hessian Regiment, who saluted the landgrave formally but at the same time raised his eyebrows.

What Wilhelm had asked von Kolbe to arrange was "a little hunting party," not this half troop of cavalry, complete with trumpeter and flag bearers. All these people were the idea of either the grand duke or his equerry, Colonel Prince Gdern. Von Kolbe knew better.

"Good morning, Your Highness," von Kolbe said to the landgrave. "I think we're going to have a pleasant day for our hunt."

"I thought perhaps you were planning to have me march against the king of Bavaria," Wilhelm said, drily. "Good morning, Alexei."

"I trust you slept well, Willi?" the grand duke replied, mischievously, nearly lasciviously. "And if not well, then warmly?"

"Something in my bed kept me awake, actually," Wilhelm said. Then he recognized the boy holding the reins of von Kolbe's horse.

"Ernst," Wilhelm said to von Kolbe. "Don't tell me that's your Willi?"

"That's Willi, Your Highness," von Kolbe said.

"Good morning, Your Highness," the boy said, taking one of his hands from the reins of his father's Arabian stallion to tug at his forelock.

"Ernst, he looks just like you," Wilhelm said, and then he looked around at the half-hundred horsemen.

"This is just not going to do," he said. "Alexei, do you want to hunt, or do you want to watch someone else hunt?"

"I want to hunt," Alexei replied. "Myself."

"Well, then, we'll dismiss this squadron of dragoons and hunt. You and I, Alexei, and Rittmeister von Kolbe. We'll take no more than three men with us to see to the game." Wilhelm saw the look of disappointment on von Kolbe's boy's face. His own son was about the same age. "Willi," he said, "you probably know where we can find the boar as well as your father. You pick a couple of grooms and as many pack horses as you think we'll need, and catch up with us." He raised his voice. "The rest of you may go home."

He put his foot in the stirrup of his horse, another high-spirited Arabian stallion, descendant of animals brought back from the Holy Lands by the Hessian regiment centuries before, and without assistance swung himself up and into the saddle. He put his hands to the horse-pistols mounted on either side of the saddle to make sure they were firmly inserted in their holsters, then spurred the stallion into motion. The Grand Duke Alexei followed him, and then von Kolbe.

Willi (Wilhelm Karl Philip von Kolbe), the sixteen-year-old fifth son and eighth child of Hauptmann Baron von Kolbe, was suddenly drunk with power. He had his orders from Landgrave Wilhelm himself, and everyone had heard them.

He quickly pointed out three of the cavalrymen to accom-

141

pany him as grooms, and as quickly identified three other cavalrymen's mounts he knew had been trained to carry the carcasses of boar, rehbock, and stag. He ordered their riders off, and their saddles replaced with a canvas blanket.

He would need a mount himself, of course, and that posed a problem. He looked around the courtyard and found himself looking into the stern, ruddy, broad-mustached face of Chief Sergeant Lahrner. Lahrner, it appeared, was glowering at him. Perhaps Lahrner expected him to come to him and ask him to pick grooms and pack horses. The Chief Sergeant of the Cavalry Squadron of the Hessian Regiment was a powerful and proud man.

But then Lahrner casually swung his leg across the saddle of his stallion, Prinz, and slid easily to the ground.

"Take Prinz, why don't you?" he called. "Save me the trouble of having to find someone to take his saddle off."

He led Prinz to Willi and handed him the reins.

"Be careful around the big shots, Willi," the old soldier said. "The same power they have to make you feel important can be used to make you feel like a fly on a pile of horse shit."

Then he gave Willi a hand-up onto Prinz, and walked away.

Willi and the two grooms and the three packhorses caught up with the landgrave, the grand duke, and his father in the marketplace. His father was riding beside the landgrave, and the grand duke's mount walked behind them. Prinz had been trained to walk beside whatever horse was in front of him, and Willi knew the only way he was going to be able to keep him from walking beside the mount of the grand duke was by constantly reining him in. That would be apparent to the grand duke.

The protocol of the situation confused him. He would have thought that the two noblemen would have ridden side by side, and probably the grand duke would have liked it that way. But Landgrave Wilhelm VIII of Hesse-Kassel, when he was in Hesse, did what he felt like doing. Willi remembered his father saying once that protocol was whatever Wilhelm felt like doing at the moment.

He certainly had paid little attention to protocol when he'd told the grand duke's entourage to go home, and he was treating the grand duke now like a young man allowed to be

142

with his elders, providing he kept his mouth shut, rather than as a member of the Russian Imperial family.

Willi decided to let Prinz have his head. Prinz edged up beside the grand duke, who looked at Willi curiously.

"Good morning, Your Imperial Highness," Willi said.

"That man is your father?" the Grand Duke asked, pointing ahead.

"Yes, Your Imperial Highness," Willi replied.

"Then what were you doing holding the reins of our mounts?" the grand duke asked, in honest curiosity.

Wilhelm turned around in his saddle.

"Ah, you made it, Willi," he said. "And where did you tell your father we could find boar?"

"Your Highness, there are some around the fields north, on the way to Kolbe," Willi said.

"Willi, I don't understand who this man is," the grand duke said.

"He is the son of my old friend and comrade-in-arms, Baron von Kolbe, here."

"But why was he holding the reins of our horses, like a serf?"

"Because his father, Your Imperial Highness," Wilhelm said drily, "thought that the mount of Your Imperial Highness was too important to be held by a serf."

"I see," the grand duke said, calmly accepting the explanation.

"And also because we have no serfs in Hesse," Wilhelm added.

"I suspect that you are mocking me!" the grand duke said, suddenly furious.

"No, Alexei, I am not," Wilhelm said, impatiently. "I'm simply trying to do for you what your father asked me to do."

"And what is that?" grand duke Alexei asked, mollified.

"Civilize you," the landgrave said, and laughed. Willi was sure that his father chuckled, but he couldn't be sure. He bit his lip to keep from smiling, much less chuckling. What Chief Sergeant Lahrner had said about the dangers of being close to the powerful had stuck with him.

Although Willi knew that his father and the landgrave were old friends, a baron was on the absolute bottom rung of the minor nobility. He was in no position to give a grand duke the idea that he was laughing at him.

143

They passed through the marketplace and entered on Stein-weg. It was not a market day, and the marketplace had been deserted. Steinweg was a street of stores, butchershops, bakeries, and craftsmen, and despite the very early hour, people, probably the merchants themselves on their way to open their shops, were on the narrow street. In places it was so narrow that the people had to flatten themselves against the walls to permit the two-abreast horses to pass.

The people recognized his father, first and far off. He was in uniform, the famous red tunic. He wore a glistening helmet, with a chain that caught under his chin. He had high black boots, and the saddle blanket under his saddle was red, embroidered in gold thread with the landgrave's coat of arms. The stocks of the horse-pistols in the saddle holsters were chased in silver. There was no mistaking an officer of His Highness's Squadron of Cavalry of the Regiment of Foot.

And then they recognized His Highness himself, despite the fairly ordinary clothing he wore. That sent the people against the wall, to get them to take off their hats, to bow their heads, and in the case of prominent burghers, to make a show of the bow, making the act of subservience itself an act of privilege. A peasant would not dare make a sweeping bow.

His Highness nodded from time to time at a familiar face, and gave a little smile to almost everyone else. His father saluted the more prominent of the burghers. And then Willi became aware that he was being greeted respectfully, and he didn't know quite what to do.

It was, he thought at first, because he was on Prinz, and Prinz wore the saddleblanket of a noncommissioned officer of the Squadron of Cavalry, but then he dismissed that notion. It was clear that he was not even a member of the Cavalry Squadron (for one thing, he had no mustache), much less a noncommissioned officer in it. He was being saluted because, if he was in the company of the landgrave, and the Russian grand duke, he must be someone important.

After a moment or two, he came to like being able to smile at people and grandly nod his head. Later (not too much later; he would enter the regiment at seventeen, and by the time he was twenty, a little over three years from now, he could hope to be offered the landgrave's commission as a junior officer), this sort of thing would happen to him all the time.

Willi thought that in all of Hesse there were very few boys

his age whom the landgrave himself called by their first name. Or asked to point out likely spots to encounter boar.

They rode down Steinweg, past the Posthotel, and then past Saint Elizabeth's Church. Elizabeth was a saint, and she had been a virgin. When the church was built in her honor, one of the two steeples had tilted crooked. The steeple was supposed to straighten itself the first time a virgin got married in the church.

The result of that (his father had told his mother that he wouldn't be at all surprised if the landgraves themselves had started the story) was that the church was very seldom used for weddings. If the steeple did not straighten itself, a girl would be disgraced.

Since few girls were willing to run the risk of not being miraculously able to straighten the steeple through their status of virtue, their weddings were held in their parish churches. Saint Elizabeth's was a symbol of the old times, when all Germany had been Roman. It was now a decent Christian, that is to say Protestant Lutheran church; but it had been Roman, and the landgraves were determined to undermine any symbol of past Roman glory.

The former Roman monastery—on top of the granite hill that gave Marburg its name, site of God alone knew what Romish revelry—was now doing God's work as the University. The former chapel was now the library.

They passed out of Marburg now, and came to the river. It wasn't a very wide river, even in the spring, when it was nurtured by falling snow. When Willi had been in Frankfurt am Main, he had been impressed with the Main River. His father had told him that the Rhine made the Main look like the Lahn, and that he had read of rivers in Africa and South and North America that made the Rhine look like a mountain stream.

When he was older, and an officer of the Squadron, Willi thought, he would see these places, for the Hessian Regiment of Foot was one of the most traveled regiments in the world. His father had twice been to Constantinople, as well as to places like Paris and Berlin and Vienna and Budapest and London.

Two miles out of town, Willi spurred Prinz and moved up next to his father, and pointed out a path leading into the pine forest.

"There's a field ten minutes in there where I saw a male with tusks as long as my forearm," he said.

"You're not to fire unless His Highness tells you to," his father said, behind his hand. "I think what His Highness wants is for the grand duke to have a shot at what we find. And then he'll have a go."

Willi nodded his understanding and dropped back beside the grand duke.

"What was that all about?" the grand duke asked.

"I was suggesting to my father where we should go," Willi said.

"I would like to have a large one," the grand duke said, "so that I could have the skull boiled and sent to my father."

"I'm sure that can be arranged, Your Imperial Highness," Willi said.

He remembered something else Chief Sergeant Lahrner had told him: "The nobility hunt for the sport; soldiers hunt for the practice; and other people hunt for the meat." By that definition, Willi thought, I am a commoner. I really want some roast boar.

Five minutes into the forest there were signs of boar: the marks of cloven hooves, scraped tree trunks, places where the light snow cover had been brushed aside. And as soon as they came out of the forest onto a field, there were boar in sight, a dozen or more of them. Willi offered a silent prayer of thanks. He would have hated to disappoint the landgrave.

Boar do one of three things when they spot humans, on foot or on horseback. They either ignore them completely, until they get so close that some action has to be taken. Or they attack. Or, most commonly, what they were hoping for now, they run. The sport had been, until fairly recently, facing driven boar with a spear. But then the horse-pistol had come into common use by cavalry officers, and their sport (now adopted by the nobility) was to run the boar down and shoot them with a horse-pistol. It was more sport, because boar are fleetfooted and can run swiftly where a horse cannot go, and they are very hard to hit with a pistol from horseback.

"There they are!" the landgrave called, and took one of his horse-pistols from its holster and cocked it; holding the pistol barrel up beside his head, he galloped toward the herd. A moment later, taking his horse-pistol from its holster and cocking it after he was moving, the grand duke galloped after him.

Willi waited with the grooms as his father followed the grand duke, holding his horse-pistol aloft as the landgrave had done. Willi knew that his father would fire only to "save the shot" for the grand duke, if, in other words, the grand duke fired and missed. His father would then kill the animal and insist that the grand duke had done it.

The landgrave would either make his kill or not. He did not expect, and would not, in fact, tolerate, having his shot "saved" by Rittmeister von Kolbe.

The field, in which corn was regularly sown (something else imported from America, via the landgrave's long-standing friendship with the King George III of England), was grown heavily with weeds. The stalks poked up through the snow, and it was difficult to follow the movement of the boar, although it was fairly safe to assume that they would head in the other direction, for the forest there, as fast as their surprisingly slender legs would carry them.

Willi saw the landgrave lower his pistol to his side and saw the puff of white smoke, a second before he heard the shot. Then he saw the grand duke, the reins of his horse in his teeth, a horse-pistol in each hand, fire twice, once almost at his horse's feet, and then a second time, with the pistol in his left hand held across the horse, behind his neck, at another boar.

And then the landgrave fired again. But this time, instead of galloping straight ahead, the landgrave turned sharply to the right. A moment later he was thrown, and the horse reared and then fell. There was a wild thrashing in the weeds, and the horse screamed.

One of the boar, or another boar, had chosen to attack. Willi saw his father spur his horse to the gallop toward where the landgrave, on his feet, seemed to be moving indecisively around in the weeds. His father fired, and wheeled, and then came galloping back to where Willi stood with the grooms.

Willi knew what he wanted, and took Chief Sergeant Lahrner's horse-pistols from their holsters and cocked them.

The grand duke, who had seen what had happened, galloped toward Willi too, jamming his horse-pistols in their holsters (one of them fell to the field) and clearly intending that Willi give him the pistols he had. Willi was reluctant to do that.

147

He spurred Prinz and Prinz broke into a canter and then a gallop as he entered the field. Willi's father saw that the grand duke was going to reach Willi first, and wheeled his horse again, back toward the landgrave, who was now obviously frighened, standing with his head cocked to better hear the sound of the boar he could not see advancing toward him.

The grand duke held his hand out for a pistol. Willi decided, in the flash of a moment, to try to hand him one of the pistols as they passed each other, but then realized that wouldn't work. He swerved to avoid the grand duke, who swore furiously at him, wheeled around, and galloped after him.

Willi could see the weeds moving as the boar stalked the landgrave. He reached up and caught the reins in his mouth and reined Prinz in, slowing him to a walk. Then he directed him with his knees toward the boar.

He couldn't see him until he was five feet from him, although he could tell where he was from the movement of the weeds. Then he aimed very slowly and deliberately and, as the boar pawed the ground preparatory to charging, shot him behind the front shoulder.

The boar thrashed a moment, thick arterial blood turning the snow to red, and then lay still. Willi rode over to the landgrave and slid off Prinz.

"Take Prinz, Your Highness," he said, handing him the reins. The landgrave looked at him a moment, and then swung himself into Prinz's saddle. He put his hand out for the second horse-pistol, and Willi handed it to him. The landgrave walked the now skittish animal toward where his screaming, gut-cut mount lay thrashing in the weeds, leaned out of the saddle, and shot him.

Then there was silence, except for the soft pounding of horse's hooves behind Willi. He turned and saw the grand duke cantering up to him. The grand duke reined his mount to an abrupt stop and then slid nimbly out of the saddle.

"It's all over," Willi said, with a smile.

The grand duke raised his left hand beside his face, made a fist, and then punched Willi as hard as he could. Willi's eyes filled with tears, and his ears rang, and then the grand duke hit him again. Willi lashed out first with his open left hand, and then with his right fist. He caught the grand duke square on the mouth. The grand duke's teeth opened the flesh

148

of his fingers. The grand duke let out a squeal of pain and outrage like an animal. The blow had knocked him down, but now he regained his feet and came at Willi, his hands open, obviously intending to choke rather than strike him.

And then the landgrave put Prinz between Willi and the grand duke, forcing the weeping, nearly hysterically furious grand duke to back and turn, back and turn.

Willi's father rode up, a stricken look on his face.

"Your boy has struck His Imperial Highness," the landgrave said icily. "Get him out of here while he's still alive."

Chapter Eight

1

Tatta, Hyderabad
January 17, 1770

Paul Selkirk found something new in Tatta when *The Eleanor* dropped her anchor midstream in the muddy Indus. There was a large British flag flying from the pole in front of Government House, and there was a rude guard shack on the wharf, a canvas and wood sunshade to shield the soldier standing under it. The Royal Army was obviously giving the Royal East India Company another stab at establishing its business monopoly in Hyderabad. His first reaction was that he was now going to have trouble with the rifles, but that quickly passed. Getting the rifles ashore would not be the first time he had broken the King's Regulations right under the nose of the King's Army.

It wasn't the Royal Army he had to worry about, but the Royal Navy. The army almost took pride in its ignorance about ships and what they carried. If they did come aboard *The Eleanor* (which was unlikely, since that would mean having to come out to her in a boat), it would not be hard to turn them from their official intention to look into his dirty, smelly, wet, rat-infested hold toward sharing some of the South African brandy.

He had no sooner come to this satisfying conclusion than a longboat, oared by Royal Navy sailors and with a large British flag flapping from a too short staff aft, put out from the shore. It was only after he had studied the longboat through his glass that he was able to relax again. There was only one Westerner in the longboat. The oarsmen were Indians wearing British Navy uniforms.

When the longboat came aside *The Eleanor*, Paul Selkirk

took one look at the officer who climbed up the ladder and saw him for a typical English colonial official, drunk with his own imagined power and authority.

"Who are you, sir?" the tall, thin, sharp-featured officer demanded formally. "And whence and where bound?"

"*The Eleanor*, sir, out of Philadelphia, via Cape Town, with ironwork for Tatta, and to take on raw silk for London," Captain Selkirk said, deciding he did not like this arrogant Englishman.

"Ironwork, you say?" asked the Englishman, who had not yet identified himself.

"My name is Selkirk," Selkirk said. "Whom do I have the honor of addressing?"

"My name is Forbes," the man said. "I am the resident officer of the Royal East India Company at Tatta."

"May I offer you a small libation, Mr. Forbes, and introduce my officers to you?" Forbes was the kind of man who enjoyed the social privileges of his position. If this type of government official were not paid the "respect" to which they devoutly believed they were entitled, they were quite capable of throwing one petty administrative rock after another in one's course.

"That would be very kind of you," Forbes said. He actually believes, Selkirk thought, that he is being gracious.

Forbes was surprised when Mary came into the captain's cabin and was introduced.

"May I suggest, Captain," he said, "that you keep your daughter aboard the ship while you're in port?"

"I have been here before, Mr. Forbes," Captain Selkirk said.

Is this man suggesting that I was about to turn my only daughter over to the Indians?

"Disease, you know," Forbes went on. "And I'm sure you know how a fair-skinned young woman affects the natives."

He says that right in front of the girl, the ass, and thinks nothing of it.

"Genuine French cognac," Captain Selkirk said, changing the subject by offering Forbes a glass of the South African brandy. "Near the end of it."

Forbes sipped, sloshed, and pursed his lips, and then, not surprising Captain Selkirk at all, announced that there was nothing like the real thing, that all other brandies were missing something, and that it all had something to do, probably, with the chalky soil of France.

"Or perhaps the French have a secret way of making it," Captain Selkirk offered, helpfully.

"You're carrying ironwork?" Forbes asked, getting down to business.

"Farm implements, heavy hinges, and some strap steel for wagon rims," Captain Selkirk said.

"British manufacture?"

"By loyal subjects of the crown, of course," Captain Selkirk said.

"I mean to say, all from the British Isles?"

"Pennsylvania is a British colony," Selkirk said, as if indignant.

"Yes," Forbes said. "Well, the East India Company follows the Navigation and Tariff Acts rather strictly, I'm afraid."

"There is nothing in the Acts which forbids the manufacture or transport of farm implements and tools," Selkirk said.

"*Within* the colonies, not *between* them," Forbes said, "is the way the Company interprets the Acts."

"You're not telling me that I can't off-load my ironwork?"

"Not without paying the import tariff," Forbes said, "I'm sorry to tell you."

"In that case, Mr. Forbes, perhaps what I should do is just keep them aboard and sell them for what we can get in Amsterdam. Where they'll really be in competion with the English forges."

"My dear Captain," Forbes said. "Certainly you understand that I don't make the laws; that I am just doing my duty in obeying them. And even paying the tariff fees, you'll get a better price here than in Holland."

I knew you would say something like that, you uniformed clerk.

"I understand the heavy responsibility you bear on your shoulders," Captain Selkirk said, getting his temper under control. He knew the way to deal with people like Forbes was to agree with their own opinion of themselves.

"And, of course, the tragic loss of Sir Edgar makes it worse," Forbes replied.

"I beg your pardon?"

"Doubtless you have heard about Sir Edgar," Forbes said.

Captain Selkirk had never heard about, or of, Sir Edgar.

"No."

152

"You know to whom I refer, of course?"

"You'll have to forgive me, Mr. Forbes. I confess I do not."

"Colonel Sir Edgar Watchbury," Forbes said. "More precisely, the *late* Sir Edgar."

"I have not heard what happened to the gentleman," Selkirk said.

"Gone," Forbes said dramatically, snapping his fingers. "Just like that. The fever, you know."

"I'm so sorry," Selkirk said.

"And with Sir Charles gone back to Bombay, of course, all the responsibility's fallen on my shoulders."

"I understand. A tremendous responsibility," Selkirk agreed. He had no idea whatever what the man was talking about.

"Yes," Forbes said, solemnly. "Yes, it is." Then he brightened. "You'll take dinner with me tonight, of course, Captain. At Government House. Seven-thirty?"

"That's very kind of you, Mr. Forbes," Selkirk said. There was no way he could refuse the invitation.

2

Forbes's boat, with its Indian oarsmen, pulled alongside *The Eleanor* at five minutes to seven. Selkirk wondered if that were simply courtesy or whether Forbes thought he might sneak an axehead or a wagon wheel tire past the East India Company's wharf if he went ashore in his own longboat.

Probably, he decided, Forbes had smugly decided he had killed two birds with one stone. Selkirk had decided against sending Theo, or going himself, to the maharaja's palace to inform him he was here, with the Pennsylvania rifles aboard. For one thing, the maharaja had certainly been told, if he had not seen for himself, that *The Eleanor* was at anchor in the Indus. It would follow that he had the rifles aboard. Selkirk did not want to appear too eager to contact the maharaja, either, and if there was going to be some problem about getting the rifles ashore, the maharaja would know about that too, and probably have the problem solved.

Government House inside was as Selkirk suspected it would be when he had seen it on his first trip: far less grand than the name implied, a two-story brick building serving as

153

both quarters and offices for the resident officer of the East India Company and his staff. There were two flagpoles in front, and two British soldiers, in sweat-darkened uniforms, on guard at the door. They carried Brown Bess muskets.

Forbes was wearing his dress uniform and obviously enjoying his role as the senior man on the scene. He advanced on them, wearing an insincere smile and a look of mild disapproval.

"I don't believe, Captain," he said, "that I have the privilege of this gentleman's acquaintance."

"May I then present my third mate, my son Charles?" Selkirk said.

"An honor, indeed, Mr. Selkirk," Forbes said.

He took them into a small, sparsely furnished drawing room and introduced them to two officers, Captain Edmond Peel and Lieutenant Francis Lange, of the Prince of Wales's Own Scottish Borderers.

Selkirk shook their hands. The last time he had seen officers of the Prince of Wales's Own Scottish Borderers was at the Battle of Culloden, nearly a quarter of a century ago. Amused by the notion, Selkirk thought that neither Captain Peel nor Lieutenant Lange was old enough to have been at Culloden, and even if they had been, it was unlikely that they would remember that an arrest order had then been issued for Paul Selkirk, outlaw.

An Indian servant offered sherry on a tray, and as Selkirk reached for it, another servant stepped to the door and made an announcement:

"His Highness, the prince of Hyderabad."

Selkirk turned quickly so that the prince would have a chance to recognize him, and make the decision whether or not to acknowledge they knew one another.

The prince bowed to Forbes, saying, "My dear Mr. Forbes, how gracious you are to include me," and then turned to Selkirk.

"And my dear Captain Selkirk, what a pleasure it is to see you and young Mr. Selkirk again."

Selkirk and Charley nodded their heads in something of a bow.

"Your Highness," Selkirk said.

"You met His Highness on your previous call here?" Forbes asked.

"Yes," Selkirk said.

154

"And when was that?"

"May of 1769," the prince answered for Selkirk. "I took it upon myself to suggest that because the Baluchistanis were infesting the area that it would be unsafe for him to try to conduct business ashore."

"And you immediately left?" Forbes asked Selkirk.

"No, actually, I took my chances, and swapped ironware for silk," Selkirk said.

"Oh, really?" Forbes replied, his tone implying he hadn't liked the answer. He could not ask for tariff fees after the fact.

"My father was happy to place Don Sidonio Arriaga at Captain Selkirk's disposal," the prince said. "I believe he was able to be of some small service."

"I'm sure he was," Forbes said, coldly. "And where is Don Sidonio?"

"He is escorting Lady Caroline," the prince said, and looked at the door, and as if it had been rehearsed, Don Sidonio Arriaga and Lady Caroline Watchbury came through it at that moment.

From her black mourning gown Selkirk deduced her to be the widow of Sir Edgar Whatsisname, and had the somewhat nasty thought that Forbes probably had trouble restraining a smile of satisfaction at the demise of the colonel. Forbes was a big fish in a little pond in this remote outpost of the British Empire, among whose prerogatives was the comforting of widows of Senior British officers. Comforting a widow as good looking as this one might very well be his most pleasant obligation.

"Lady Caroline," Forbes said, "may I present Captain Paul Selkirk, and Mr. Charles Selkirk, of *The Eleanor* of Philadelphia?"

Lady Caroline offered them, in turn, her gloved hand. The more chance Paul Selkirk had to examine her, the more Lady Caroline was a pleasant surprise. He would have supposed that the widow of a colonel would either be plump and comfortable or thin and dried out, and in any event at least his age, and probably older. Lady Caroline was neither plump nor dried out, and Selkirk thought she was no older than twenty-five, and possibly not even that.

Her hand was warm, even through the glove, when she gave it to him, and there was something in her eyes and behavior that told him that while Forbes might be doing everything in his power to comfort the widow, that comforting was not taking place in her bed.

This, he told himself, was the sort of widow I should have married, rather than the cold-blooded Swede who now carries my name.

"What an interesting coincidence to meet you, Captain," Lady Caroline said to him. "We are rather neighbors."

"How is that, Lady Caroline?" Selkirk asked.

"My late husband," she said, "came into a grant of land in the Pennsylvania colony as inheritance from his late father."

"Oh, I see," Selkirk said. He caught a glimpse of Charley. Charley was staring at the widow like a calf at his mother. Charley, his father thought, was at that age when time at sea really upset God's plans for the continued repopulation of the earth. He would have to keep an eye on him. There was no telling what foul disease he would likely contract if he got with a native woman here.

"And do you plan to take up residence in Pennsylvania, Lady Caroline?" Selkirk asked, straight-faced.

"I rather think not," she said. "But I thought perhaps you might be able to tell me something about my land."

In other words, Selkirk thought, tell you how much it's worth.

"I'm a simple seaman, ma'am," Selkirk said. "I know very little about land."

She was disappointed.

He could have told her, but did not, that if her late husband's land grant was like the others His Brittanic Majesty had passed out over the years to his unsuspecting subjects across the sea from it in England, it was wilderness, full of unfriendly Indians, and for all practical purposes worthless.

He reluctantly turned from Lady Caroline to greet Don Sidonio Arriaga and to tell him, very obliquely, that he had the rifles aboard. He could tell that Arriaga was pleased.

The dinner was disappointing, simple, tasteless, and not very much of it or the wine that came with it.

He and Charley were given a detailed report of the mission of Colonel Sir Edgar Watchbury to India, and of his demise. He wondered why, since the colonel was dead, the widow was still here, but he did not ask the question for fear it would trigger a too-lengthy response. Furthermore, he decided, it might later offer a subject for conversation in the unlikely case that he could corner the widow somewhere.

That made him decide that he was behaving toward her as Charley was, allowing him to draw the not unpleasant conclusion that there was apparently still some life left in his old carcass.

He was disappointed when Forbes did not ask them to spend the night at Government House. Selkirk thought that it was entirely likely that if he had, Lady Caroline just might have come to his room to discuss her land grant in greater detail. Forbes, he decided, sensed the same thing and had decided that if he wasn't going to get under the widow's skirts, neither was anyone else.

He felt something of a fool when the dinner was over and Lady Caroline begged to be excused to "go back to the palace." He should have been able to figure that out himself. She couldn't have stayed in Government House; that would have caused talk. Staying in the palace was something else again. It was simply presumed that no Englishwoman would share her bed with an Indian, even if he was a prince, and a good-looking man to boot.

Lady Caroline said something strange to him: "A pleasure to meet you, Captain. I look forward to our meeting again, as we obviously will." It could have been some sort of an invitation, but then again might have simply been what she said. She had treated Charley through dinner, and especially when they said goodnight, as if he were one of the servants. Probably, Selkirk decided, as young as the widow was, she had learned that young men weren't often any better than, and frequently not as good as, men in their middle years.

When they went back aboard *The Eleanor*, Paul Selkirk went directly to Mary and offered her a sincere apology for not taking her with them.

"I had no idea there was going to be an English lady there," he said. "Otherwise you'd have gone."

"What kind of an English lady?"

"A widow woman, actually," he said. "She was married to an English colonel who died a while back of the fever."

"You probably did me a favor," Mary replied. "I had dinner with Mr. Porter and Mr. Dillon. Then we played at cards."

"Playing cards with ship's officers is no life for a young girl," he said without thinking.

"I'll not tell your wife, if you don't," Mary said, mischievously.

"We still have adequate supplies of tarred line aboard, Mistress Mary," Selkirk told her, and then, surprising her, hugged her against him and kissed her forehead. Then he told her good night, and walked around the decks, checking the watches Porter had set, ending up at the fo'c'sl, where he checked to see that the crew, whom he had granted shore leave with orders to be back aboard no later than eight, were in fact back. When he was satisfied they were, he went to the quarterdeck, had a word with Mr. Dillon, who had the watch, and then climbed down the ladder to his cabin.

He had just finished making the entry in his personal log and was about to get into his bunk when a messenger from the quarterdeck told him there was an Indian boat alongside, asking for him by name. He pulled on a pair of trousers and a shirt and went on deck. When he looked down into the boat, he saw the Don Sidonio Arriaga and the prince of Hyderabad. He didn't recognize the prince at first because he was bareheaded and dressed in a simple white wrap-around (Selkirk thought of it as a sheet) rather than the jeweled turban, silk pantaloons, and gold-embroidered jacket he had worn at dinner.

He gestured for them to come aboard, and told the messenger to get Mr. Selkirk on deck.

There were several minutes of polite and meaningless conversation between Selkirk, the prince, and the Portuguese, something that Selkirk recognized as a necessary thing in the East, but which annoyed him nonetheless. He wondered why it was taking Charley so long to comply with a simple order to come on deck.

When Charley finally appeared, he understood why it had taken him so long. Charley had apparently been with Mary, giving her his report of the evening's doings, and the messenger hadn't been smart enough to understand the situation and to tell Mary to stay in her cabin. Selkirk could imagine what the messenger said, "Your father's talking with a couple of natives, Mr. Selkirk, and he wants you out there."

Mary, who considered everything not expressly forbidden to be permitted, had naturally tagged along with him.

"Your Highness will remember my son, of course," Selkirk said. "And this is my daughter, Mary. Mary, this is the prince of Hyderabad, and Don Sidonio Arriaga, who is in the service of the maharaja."

Mary curtseyed.

"She is quite lovely, isn't she, Don Sidonio?" the prince said.

Mary flushed. It was the first time that she had ever been paid what she thought of as a *woman's* compliment by a man.

"Let's go to my cabin," Selkirk said. "I could stand a brandy, and I would be pleased if you would join me. My son will show you the way, and I'll be with you in a moment."

He stood for a moment until they were almost at the passageway to his cabin, and then he quickly ascended the ladder to the quarterdeck.

"Very quietly, Mr. Dillon," he said, "wake Mr. Porter, rouse the crew, issue rifles, and put them aloft. Put some lanterns around her sides. Until I send word to the contrary, let no boat but the one now alongside come close."

"Aye, aye, sir," Mr. Dillon said. "Can I ask who those people are, Captain?"

"The white man's the Portugee I dealt with the last time, and the Indian with him is the son of the local king; they call them maharajas. I don't trust either of them so far's I can throw Theo LaSalle."

"The men'll be aloft in three minutes, Captain."

"Get them up there silently."

"Silently it is, sir," Dillon said.

Selkirk entered his cabin from the quarterdeck, and he saw that seeing him climb down from the overhead startled Arriaga and the prince.

Charley had poured brandy for Arriaga, and Mary was in the act of pouring coffee for the prince. She then watched with undisguised disbelief as the prince put five spoonsful of sugar into the mug.

"Coffee for me, too, please, Mistress Mary," Selkirk said. He saw both that Charley was surprised by that announcement and that he unsuccessfully tried to hide the brandy he had poured for himself.

The prince tasted his coffee, added a sixth spoonful of sugar, found it to his liking, took a tiny sip and set the mug on the table. Then he handed Selkirk a small, square, leather box.

"A small token of my father's regard," he said.

Selkirk opened the box. It contained two diamonds, one cut and polished, and another, larger, uncut stone. "Charley,"

159

he said. "Go to the weapons locker and fetch the fancy rifles."

"Aye, aye, sir," Charley said, but the prince put out his hand and stopped him.

"You have misunderstood me, Captain," he said. "These are simple gifts from my father. They are not, forgive me, offered in the expectation of something in return. Not, I mean to say, as part of the business arrangement we have previously discussed."

"You misunderstand me," Selkirk said, ordering Charley with a nod of his head to do what he had originally told him to do. "While I was about the business of collecting the rifles we discussed, I came across two rifles of, I believe, greater beauty than the ordinary, and put them aside to present to you and the maharaja as a token of my respect."

"That was quite unnecessary," the prince said, but Selkirk saw that he was pleased.

Nothing more was said between them until Charley returned with the rifles. They simply sipped their drinks and smiled at each other. The prince, Selkirk noticed, allowed his eyes to wander over Mary. It was, he told himself, simply curiosity that we strange foreigners permit our women to be around when men are talking. But he didn't like the way the prince looked at Mary.

Selkirk took one of the rifles from Charley and handed it to the prince. It was covered with a light coating of sperm oil, which seemed to bring out the extraordinary quality of the metal finishing, and the gloss of the light, yellowish birds-eye maple stock. The two weapons had come from a German gunsmith at Allen Town, twenty miles west of Easton, who had harnessed the flow of the Lehigh River to turn wheels that polished his metal work.

Selkirk was pleased at the skill with which the prince examined the rifle. The more the prince knew about firearms, the more he would appreciate the extraordinary quality of the two rifles from the Allen Town gunsmith.

The prince tested the lock by cocking it, but held the hammer with his thumb and let it down gently, rather than simply squeezing the trigger and permitting the hammer to fall against the anvil. There was no flint in the anvil, and damage could have resulted. Someone had been teaching the prince about fine firearms, Selkirk realized. Or, more likely, now that he thought about it, the prince had taught himself. He was intelligent. Highly intelligent.

When he had finished examining one rifle, he handed it to Arriaga, who was not very interested, despite the smile he put on his face, and then examined the second rifle as carefully as he had the first.

"They are works of art," he said. "Your generosity shames me."

"A deal is a deal, of course," Selkirk said. "But the price Your Highness has offered for the rifles I carry shamed me."

The prince was surprised, but smiled after a moment, confirming what Selkirk had suspected: if the prince did not know the precise value of rifles, even rifles smuggled in defiance of the British, he knew that he had agreed to pay far more for what Selkirk had aboard than they were worth.

"I confess," the prince said, "that I had in mind renegotiating our deal."

"I'm sure," Selkirk said smiling, but fastening the prince's eyes with his own, "that you mean renegotiating future deals."

The prince met his eyes and paused for what seemed like a long time before smiling even more broadly.

"Future deals, of course," he said.

"And now, how are we going to get this load ashore, without attracting Mr. Forbes's attention?" Selkirk asked.

"I have boats waiting," the prince said. "Would you take offense, Captain, if I had one of my men, who professes to know something about firearms, examine the weapons before they are taken ashore? I know, of course, that a gentleman such as yourself would never offer any but the highest quality merchandise. My father, unfortunately, has had bad experiences in the past, and he made it quite plain to me . . ."

"Your man can inspect the rifles while I examine the jewels," Selkirk said. "And he can bring one or two men aboard to help him."

The prince chuckled. "Of course," he said. "I had forgotten for the moment that you are, in addition to everything else, a skilled appraiser of jewels."

"Where are your men?" Selkirk said.

"In a boat waiting for my signal," the prince said. "In a place where they cannot be seen from Government House."

"Signal them," Selkirk said.

The prince gestured to Don Sidonio Arriaga.

"I'll need a lantern," Arriaga said.

"Go with him, Charley," Selkirk said. "Get him a lantern, and tell Theo to send four men into the hold, to bring the rifles up, two at a time, here."

"Aye, aye, sir," Charley said.

"And tell Mr. Dillon he may pass three men, no more, aboard."

"Aye, aye, sir," Charley said again.

"How many rifles do you have?" the prince asked.

"There is a stand of two hundred and sixty."

"That many!" the prince said. He was surprised. He obviously hadn't expected that many, and that pleased him. But on the other hand, Selkirk knew that he would have preferred to have fewer guns, with more to follow after the price was bargained down.

"That many," Selkirk said.

"Don Sidonio," the prince said, "will you arrange for more stones?"

Arriaga nodded.

"I will have to remember, in the future," the prince said, "how you do business, Captain Selkirk."

"I am," Selkirk said, "as I'm sure Your Highness is, a man of my word."

"We understand each other, Captain," the prince said. He looked at Mary. "Might I have some more coffee?"

I understand you, all right. And that look you're giving my daughter, as well.

The Indian who came into the cabin to examine the rifles was, Selkirk saw, something of an Indian Theo LaSalle. He wasn't a boatman, but rather a part of the prince's entourage, a landsman's bosun's mate. This snap judgment was confirmed when the man took the first rifle he was offered, examined it expertly, and then handed it to one of the other two Indians. He said something to him, and from the man's response, Selkirk could tell the rifle examiner was a competent man, used to giving orders and having them obeyed.

Once the first rifle had been examined and found satisfactory, Selkirk turned to the prince, wondering what he would do now. He had decided to let the prince continue to make the overtures.

The prince spilled the contents of the leather bag into his hand.

"I wasn't aware that you would be so obliging," he said. "These are all I brought with me."

"But you've sent for more," Selkirk said. "And I'm sure Don Sidonio will be back before we have run out of the ones you have."

The prince looked directly at him and smiled.

"I presume I have the same right," Selkirk said. "To reject your stones, as you have to reject my rifles?"

"Of course," the prince said, with a wide smile.

"Your Highness's way of doing business is very Western," Selkirk said, thinking to make it a compliment.

"I have studied Western customs," the prince said, and then added: "One should learn as much as one can about one's enemies."

"I hope that does not mean you consider me your enemy," Selkirk replied.

"You could be either," the prince replied. "Friend or enemy. Or what you are now, an Arab trader who happens to be white."

"I'm not fond of the English, either," Selkirk said. "But I am not their enemy. At least not any more."

"The English have not come to your country as they have come here," the prince said.

"No," Selkirk agreed. He considered telling the prince about the English and Scotland and decided not to. The conversation had gone as far as it should.

As the sailors brought rifles from the hold, the prince's man examined each of them carefully and then handed them over to be carried on deck and put over the side. Selkirk kept a mental count, making sure that no more rifles left his possession than there were jewels to pay for them.

Finally, it was all over. The 260-stand of rifles were all gone, replaced by a pile of jewels six inches wide.

Worth a small fortune, Selkirk thought, and then corrected himself: worth a *fortune!*

He was already worrying whether he would be able to dispose of them all at once in Antwerp. He was reasonably sure there were too many of them for his friend the Jewish diamond merchant to handle all at once, and he was reluctant to involve anyone else.

The prince caught him staring at the jewels.

"I mentioned renegotiating the price for further shipments," the prince said. Selkirk looked at him, and met his eyes. "I will pay you twenty-five pounds sterling for each of one thousand rifles like these," the prince went on. "Delivered into my hands here."

When Selkirk did not at first reply, the prince went on again, "Since I did not specify in our last agreement that the rifles were to come with flints and strikers, I will pay extra for those now. I presume you have them aboard. The twenty-five pound price, payable as you like in sterling or gold, a quarter ounce to the pound sterling, or in jewels, includes supplies of flint and strikers. I will also require bullet molds, and I will pay a fair price for them . . ."

Selkirk held up his hand, shutting him off.

"There are flints, molds, strikers, and spare ramrods to go with these weapons," he said. "My son has already had them loaded into your boats."

The prince pursed his lips. That had suprised him.

"And the twenty-five pound price?" he asked. "Do you think that's fair?"

"I would not presume to suggest that someone like Your Highness would offer an unfair price," Selkirk said.

"Selkirk, you are as devious as the Portugee," the prince said, smiling. Then, without a word, he got up and walked out of the cabin, onto the deck, and then climbed down the ladder into his boat.

Selkirk walked to the rail and watched until the boat was out of sight. Then he ordered the ladder brought aboard, and a double watch, armed with pistols and cutlasses, positioned all around the ship. It had occurred to him that a boarding party would have less trouble stealing a small bag of jewels than 260-stand of rifles. And he was still in no position to run to the British ashore for help. They would ask questions, and the prince, and more important, the prince's father, knew it.

But morning came and passed without sign of any Indians, except those in the employ of the East India Company, taking barrels of ironwork ashore in a steady stream of small rowboats. It wasn't until the next day, when Selkirk went ashore to inspect the raw silk that the East India Company proposed to sell him, that the prince was heard from again.

Don Sidonio Arriaga was waiting for Selkirk on the wharf when he got out of *The Eleanor*'s longboat. He handed Selkirk another square leather box, this one containing a very large uncut diamond, worth at least five times as much as any other stone offered so far.

"What's he want for this?" Selkirk asked. "I've no more rifles."

"It's symbolic," Arriaga replied.

"I don't follow you." Selkirk said.

"He wants the girl. A virgin jewel for a virgin."

"You tell that goddamned savage that girl is my daughter," Selkirk said, angrily.

"He knows that," Arriaga said. "They don't think as we do, Captain."

"Tell the bastard over my dead body!"

"It may come to that, Captain," Arriaga said.

"Tell him that if he, or anybody who works for him, comes within a hundred paces of my ship, I'll have them shot."

"You're making a mistake, Captain, you can't tell him things like that."

"That includes you, too, you son of a whore!" Selkirk said. "You tell him what I said." He pushed the Portugee out his way and headed toward the warehouse where the East India Company had raw silk waiting for his approval.

3

Captain Selkirk took possession of the raw silk on the East India Company wharf and had it transported out to *The Eleanor* in mid-stream in *The Eleanor*'s longboat, rather than in native boats owned or hired by the East India Company.

Cargo had an amazing way of disappearing in Eastern ports unless you kept your eye, and better still, your rearend, on it.

He would have been a good deal less happy with the draft Forbes had issued to his credit on the Bank of England for the difference between the worth of the cargo of ironwork he had off-loaded and the worth of the raw silk he was taking aboard if it had not been for the velvet sack of diamonds, emeralds, rubies, and pearls he now had hidden in a corner of *The Eleanor*'s strong box.

There was always a need for modern (that is to say, pure, and thus stronger than that made locally) ironwork in India, and especially the heavy hinges and straps and plowshares he had off-loaded. The East India Company was going to be able to get a good price for them, or barter them for a good deal of raw silk, or finished silk and cotton goods, and bulk material. It was going to make a profit for both seller and buyer, and even if that was the principle on which the company was founded, it didn't seem fair.

On his next trip, Selkirk told himself, he would have a long chat with the prince about getting legitimate goods, as well as contraband rifles, into India without having them pass over the East India Company's wharf, and getting silk out of India without paying the East India Company a tariff.

He had mingled feelings when he saw Lady Caroline Watchbury coming down the wharf on the arm of Resident Officer Edwin Forbes. Even in her widow's black, she was a good-looking female, and he was sorry that he hadn't had a chance to get to know her a good deal better than Forbes had permitted.

Forbes, now that he was close enough for Selkirk to take a good look at him, was obviously unhappy about something. Was it possible that he had somehow heard about the rifles? It was unlikely, but possible.

Captain Selkirk tipped his tricorn to Lady Caroline, who responded with a dazzling smile.

"Good afternoon, Captain," she said.

"Lady Caroline," he said. "Mr. Forbes."

"When do you sail?" Lady Caroline asked.

"With first light in the morning, ma'am," Selkirk replied.

"Oh, that won't give me much time," she said. "I don't suppose that you could delay sailing for a day, could you? I would be ever so grateful to you."

"I don't take your meaning, ma'am," Selkirk said.

"Lady Caroline will be sailing with you," Forbes said.

"I'm afraid," Selkirk said, "that that's quite impossible."

"Lady Caroline," Forbes said solemnly, and added, "and the remains of Sir Edgar."

"I beg your pardon?" Selkirk said, incredulously.

"Is there some problem, Captain?"

"I'm not equipped to take passengers, ma'am," Selkirk replied. "Especially a lady, such as yourself." He paused. "Nor the remains of your husband, either, ma'am, forgive me for being indelicate."

"Nonsense," she said, sharply. "Mr. Forbes tells me that you have your daughter aboard."

"I'm sorry," Captain Selkirk said.

"I am, too, that I'll be unwelcome aboard," Lady Caroline said, coldly angry. "But I'm going."

"I beg your pardon, ma'am, but you are not going."

"But she is, Captain," Forbes said.

Selkirk lost his temper.

"You can't order me, sir," he said. "Keep that in mind."

"I am about the king's business," Forbes announced, formally, solemnly, enjoying every syllable.

"And what might that mean?" Selkirk snapped.

"I serve you herewith, Captain," Forbes said, handing him a large, rolled-up sheet of paper. "This is a warrant, issued by Sir Charles Rewwe, vice governor of the Royal East India Company in the name of His Majesty the King. It states . . ."

Selkirk snatched it from his hand and unrolled it.

"I can read, thank you," he said.

Forbes, undaunted, went on, ". . . that you, as the master of a vessel sailing at His Majesty's pleasure, are commanded to transport Lady Caroline and the remains of Colonel Sir Edgar Watchbury to the British Isles in accommodations reflecting her late husband's rank."

Selkirk read the warrant. His Most Britannic Majesty King George III probably didn't know Lady Caroline Watchbury from a Cheapside tart, Selkirk thought. But some official of the goddamned East India Company had invoked the royal authority. The warrant he held in his hand was unquestionably genuine.

He was not going to be able to get away with claiming that he had sickness aboard, or questioning the seaworthiness of *The Eleanor*, either. Forbes was a fool, but not that much of a fool.

Lady Caroline, on the other hand, was just the kind of female who would take great delight in making an official report of the matter, if he just sailed off without her. Hell hath no fury like a woman scorned.

He handed the letter to her, not back to Forbes.

"We sail at first light, Lady Caroline," he said. "If you're aboard by that time, I will, of course, honor this warrant."

"But you won't give me a day to pack and settle my affairs here?"

"That warrant, ma'am, says nothing about my sailing at your convenience," Selkirk said. "I sail at first light, ma'am." He tipped his tricorn and walked away from them.

In the longboat, on the way to *The Eleanor*, he cursed himself for being a fool. What he should have done, once he knew he had to take her, was act as if he liked it. His temper

167

had cost him any chance of consoling the widow in his bed on the voyage to England.

On the other hand, it was at least forty days, often as many as sixty, from here to London, and a lot of things could happen on a ship between a man and a woman in sixty days. And nights.

Chapter Nine

1

Durham Furnace, Pennsylvania
January 19, 1770

The merchantman *Phoebe* of Philadelphia, Captain Zachariah Newton, had sailed from Plymouth for Boston and New York on November 4, 1769. Captain Newton had been pleased to carry with him a letter from Captain Paul Selkirk of *The Eleanor* of Philadelphia, which had made Plymouth the previous day, to his wife.

There was mail service, of course, to the American colonies, and a letter posted anywhere in England would more than likely eventually be delivered anywhere within the British Empire. Mail entrusted into the hand of one captain from another, however, to be posted (or indeed, sometimes delivered by messenger) when the ship made port literally cut months from the normal delivery time.

Captain Newton and *The Phoebe* had run into a little bad luck on the crossing. He had nearly been demasted off Cape Cod by an unusually early winter storm, and he'd put into Boston for repairs. He didn't want to run the risk of running into another storm without being sure of both the soundness of his masts and the condition of his rigging.

He had considered, in Boston, posting Captain Selkirk's letter to his wife there, but the initial shipyard survey of the damage to *The Phoebe* had indicated that no serious harm had been done to her and that he could expect to put to sea again in four or five days. Newton had aboard two men from upriver, and he thought the greater service to Captain Selkirk, an acquaintance he would like to have as a friend, would be to have one of his men personally deliver the letter on his way home once they made home port.

169

A closer examination of *The Phoebe*, however, revealed that her fore topmast had been cracked. There were two ways to go about handling that: making on-the-spot repairs, hoping they would hold long enough for her to make Philadelphia from Boston, or having the splintered mast replaced where she was.

Newton was a careful man, and his cargo was not perishable, so he ordered the Boston shipyard to set *The Phoebe* right. What they said would be a four-day job, five days at the most, turned out to be more like two weeks. It was December 27 before *The Phoebe* put to sea, and she made home port on January 5, 1770.

Kurt Suhlmann, *The Phoebe*'s carpenter, to whom Captain Newton entrusted Captain Selkirk's letter for delivery on his way home to Stroudsburg, above Easton, had to make his way home by road, for the Delaware River was frozen over. There wasn't much wagon traffic, either, along the Delaware. It was a bad winter, and the snow and ice kept all but the most determined draymen off the roads.

Suhlmann was lucky, however, for as he stood by the Post Road north of Philadelphia, he caught a ride in a covered wagon loaded with hams and bacon and lard, headed all the way to Stroudsburg. The wagon passed the Durham Furnace Road late in the afternoon, and Suhlmann knew that if he got off he would be stuck there, thirty, thirty-five miles shy of home at least overnight and maybe, if it snowed again, for several days. There was no guarantee that Mistress Selkirk would feel obliged to put him up just because he was delivering a letter; and after five and a half months at sea, Kurt Suhlmann was anxious to see his wife and family.

He stayed inside the warm wagon and told himself that just as soon as the weather broke, and in any event within the next week, he would send one of his sons by horse to deliver the letter. There was no way, he reasoned, that Captain Newton would learn, much less care, when it actually had been delivered. All Captain Newton would want to know, when Kurt went back to *The Phoebe*, was whether it had been delivered.

On January 19, 1770, Fritz and Eric Suhlmann, Kurt's fifteen- and seventeen-year-old sons, got stiffly off the back of a plow horse and knocked on the door of the fieldstone farmhouse Nils Johnson had left to his sons. It had stopped snowing, but it was bitter cold, and felt even colder when they

170

were out from under the bearskin robe and off the horse's warm back.

"Excuse me, mistress," Fritz Suhlmann said. "We have a letter for Mistress Selkirk."

Only then did Ingebord Johnson Selkirk open the door wide and motion for them to come in. She was a hard-working woman, left all alone with no one but two boys to help her run the farm and the forge, and she couldn't be expected to set a table for every hungry wanderer who saw the smoke rising from her chimney.

Nils and Luther, who were yet to learn the value of a penny, immediately started to set food before the two boys who had appeared at the door, and Ingebord opened the letter. It was sealed with an envelope, and the envelope with waxed paper, and the waxed paper within a square of oilskin.

At Sea, off Land's End
2d Nov. 1769

Dear Wife,

I hasten to inform you that Mary is with me and in good health. She stole aboard The Eleanor *at the wharf and was not discovered until we were well at sea. I will see about sending her home, for that is where she belongs, if I can arrange it.*

The passage was uneventful, and I pray the remainder will be likewise.

We make landfall at Plymouth tomorrow, and I hope to be able to send this letter on its way shortly from there.

I have been thinking over the business we talked about, and believe that what I seek in England can be obtained without too much difficulty. I therefore ask of you that you make all the necessary arrangements, in terms of land clearing, etcetera, so that work can commence as soon as possible once we have the means to do so.

In the meantime, I think it would do no harm to acquire another stock of the merchandise I carry aboard now, taking care to be discreet. If there is a question of money, see Captain MacMullen of The Mary *and tell him I said to provide you with whatever is necessary.*

171

*When there is something further to relate, I will
write again. I hope this finds you and your sons in
good health and spirits.*

Paul Selkirk

Ingebord Johnson Selkirk told her sons that the girl had
been with her father all along, and then she put the letter in
the Bible. She would show it to the Reverend Ingmar Sooth
when he came to visit. Pastor Sooth had written saying that
he was going to begin a circuit upriver, with an eye toward
establishing churches if that proved to be God's will.

She had written back that she would be pleased to have
him as a guest in her home when he was in the area. It
seemed to her to be her Christian duty. If Pastor Sooth was
willing to leave the comforts of Philadelphia to spread God's
word to the unchurched, the least she could was provide him
with decent food and a place to lay his head.

2

Tayffield, Nottinghamshire
January 19, 1770

The long lines of connecting houses were of dull red brick.
There were twenty-five houses in a row. There were two rows
of houses, back to back, separated by fifty feet, which area
was given over to outhouses and vegetable gardens, and here
and there a pigsty and a chicken house.

There were ten double rows of houses, making a total of
five hundred houses. The double rows began at the ironworks,
separated from the fence which surrounded it by only a narrow cobblestone street. They ran up the steep incline of the
valley until it narrowed and grew steep and building more
houses would have been impossible.

At the Works end of the rows, two houses in each double
row were given over to commercial enterprise. The first row
held a store. Doors had been opened in the walls between the
houses so that their first floors could be given over to the
store and their second floors to living accommodations for the
store manager and his family.

The first two houses in the next double row of houses had

been similarly modified by the opening of the walls between them. The first floors of these two houses had become a tavern, and their second floors, living quarters for the tavern manager and his family.

The pattern was repeated through the ten double rows, a store in one double row and a tavern in the next, five stores and five taverns in all.

The stores and the taverns, as well as the houses, were owned by the Works. There were no other stores or taverns available to the people who lived in Tayffield. There was a church, Saint Paul's, located at the north end of the fence which surrounded Tayffield Iron Works Company, Ltd., and beyond that was a smaller valley, in which had been ten small single houses, two slightly larger single houses, and one single house largest of all.

These houses, which were also owned by Tayffield Iron Works Company, Ltd., housed the general manager (in the largest house) and his staff, in houses reflecting their responsibility.

The south end of the Works opened on the Tayffield River, which flowed into the River Trent, ten miles to the south.

The West Housing Estate to the west of the Tayffield Iron Works very much duplicated the East Housing Estate, except that the somewhat flatter terrain on which it had been built had permitted the construction of thirty-five connected houses in a row, for a total of seven hundred houses, two hundred more than the East Housing Estate provided. The West Housing Estate also contained single men's accommodation, a three-story brick dormitory with mess.

Houses in both estates were assigned fairly, on strict seniority. When a worker in the single men's accommodation married (or when, rarely, an outside worker was brought int), he put his name on the waiting list. When a vacancy occurred, it was first made available for bidding, according to strict seniority, by those already occupying a house. (The desirable houses were those farthest from the noise of the mills and the taverns.) When the shifting around was done (sometimes one vacancy would result in fifteen or more moves), the man on top of the waiting list was given the vacancy.

Seniority itself was precisely defined. It was not simply a question of how long a worker had been employed by Tayffield Iron Works Company, Ltd.; it also considered his job in the works. There were six categories of workers, with master ironworkers constituting the senior and most prestigious category, and worker's helpers the lowest. Generally, it had evolved that the workers with the most time as employees also had the most responsible jobs, but there were exceptions.

George Sedge was such an exception. He was thirty-three years of age and had been an employee of Tayffield Iron Works for nineteen years. There were men in his class who had started at the Works with him who were still workers or firemen, and there were half a dozen who were still in the seven-year-long steel makers' apprenticeship. George had early on been recognized to be a bright, hard-working lad, and he had been the first of his class to enter steel makers' apprenticeship. He was now a journeyman, a year away from certification as a master ironworker. When he reached that status, he would be in the highest pay category and could look forward to annual increases in his pay, providing the works had made enough money during the previous year to justify such an increase.

Sedge had, as a condition to being permitted to enter the apprentice program, signed a contract that tied him to Tayffield Iron Works Company, Ltd., for his working life, unless released sooner. It was the satisfaction of the ambition he had had when he had come to the Works. A master ironworker could make enough money to put something away for his old age and not have to count on having his children look after him when he grew too old to work, or if he should be injured on the job.

An injured worker, obviously, could not work, and logically could not expect Tayffield Iron Works to continue to provide him with a house. Security came when your own children became old enough to go to work and thus qualify for a house in the housing estate on their own. The Company had a generous policy in its seniority scheme when a worker's household included a former employee who had either become too old to work or had been injured on the job and could no longer hold a job. A credit equal to ten years of service was added to the credits a worker was entitled to himself, if he had someone in his household who was no longer an employee of Tayffield Iron Works for either of those reasons.

George Sedge was a wiry little man, stronger than he looked, growing bald, and with bad teeth. He had taken a good deal of ribbing from his fellow workers over the years because of his family. "The little rabbit" had put a baby in the belly of his Janet every year but three of the thirteen years they had been married. Not only that, but eight of the babies had lived past their first birthday, which was really uncommon.

The size of their family kept George and Janet Sedge and their children just about as poor as the newest worker's helper living in single accommodations, for while it might be true that two could live as cheap as one, and three as cheap as two, and so on, when you had eight growing and hungry children, you had to watch your pennies. This meant not going to the tavern straight off when the shift ended, as most of the men did, and really trying to make a go of the vegetable garden, and feeding the pig, and selling all but a rare egg from the chicken house instead of eating the eggs.

Philip Woodley learned George Sedge's name from the manager of the tavern on Block III of the East Housing Estate. He had come to the tavern manager well recommended by a business associate of his who dealt with tavern keepers as a business. He took off the tavern keeper's hands those things workers had pledged for credit and had not redeemed as promised.

When a man was in the drink, as they tended to be when they got in their late twenties, or early thirties, and there wasn't enough money to both drink and support a family, they pledged things, things of value sometimes, brought to the mill and works villages from the farms they'd left. Generally, they did not know, nor did the tavern keepers who took the items, how much the things were worth. The tavern keeper gave the owner a fraction of what an item was worth to him, and Philip Woodley's friend, on a regular basis, took it off the tavern keepers at a fraction of what it would be worth in a city.

Philip Woodley was no fool, and in no mind to risk seven years in prison for encouraging an indentured craftsman to run from his contract; not even for his share of two hundred pounds, which was what Mistress Georgina Dale of the Golden Herring had told him a certain sea captain was willing to pay for a crucible-steel maker delivered aboard his ship.

He had not only paid the tavern keeper more for a collection of well-worn tableware, silver-plated trays, and a set of seven razors with gilt handles than they were worth, and bought him a lot of his own ale, but had been, he was sure, very discreet in making inquiries that just might turn up a crucible-steel journeyman who was single and who might be willing to run.

The tavern keeper liked to think of himself as a judge of human character, and Woodley had patiently sat through a nearly endless recitation of the quirks of the tavern's patrons before he had been able to separate the name of George Sedge from the others. Woodley liked to think of himself as a judge of human character, too, and from what the tavern keeper told him about Sedge, Sedge was the man he wanted, once it had become clear that there were no single men who were crucible steelworkers.

Sedge had a family that kept him poor, and since he was a journeyman already, years before he could ordinarily expect to be, he was more than likely bright enough to know that he wasn't going to make much more than he did now, if he spent the rest of his life in Tayffield Iron Works. What they actually paid their men, as little as that was, was supposed to be a secret. But unless Sedge was really stupid, he would know that if he had a lifelong contract with the company, and couldn't quit, the company was not going to be overanxious to pay him a lot of money.

The trouble was, and Woodley knew it, that many of these workers were stupid, as he saw it, with regard to the company, and got as angry if anyone tried to get them to run as the company would get. They had feelings of loyalty to the company and simply could not believe that the loyalty of the company to them was about as thin as the sheets of oiled paper the company gave them to replace broken windows in their houses.

Philip Woodley was disappointed to hear that George Sedge rarely came into the tavern after work, because he could not support both the tavern and his eight children. That meant he wouldn't be able to meet Sedge in the tavern and feel him out. On the other hand, it meant that Sedge was probably almost as smart as the tavern keeper made him out, and that, once Woodley figured out how to meet him, would likely make talking sense to him a good bit easier.

Woodley was smart enough to know that questions were going to be asked about him being in the village anyway, so the thing for him to do was get out of town for a couple of days. That would give him time to think, and while he was gone, the tavern keeper, who would be asked, could tell people that he was in the used goods business, just passing through, and would be coming again.

Then fortune smiled on Philip Woodley. He later thought of it as proof of what it said in the Bible about casting bread upon the waters; that if you did good to somebody, something good happened to you.

While it was true that he didn't see that the woman had a baby under her cloak when he stopped his two-wheeled cart to pick her up, the point, he told himself, was that he had done the gentlemanly thing, picked her and the sick kid up and took them out of the snow and slush even if he knew that with the kid she wouldn't be interested in what he had in mind, and anyway wasn't all that good looking.

And what do you know, but it was Mistress Sedge herself, taking a sick kid to Sheffield, where there was a charity hospital run by the Church where there were doctors who treated people for what they could afford, even if that meant nothing.

Woodley was the perfect gentleman with Mistress Sedge, telling her he was a traveling businessman and driving her in the cart right to the door of Charity Hospital, not even laying a hand on her.

He was tempted to wait until she came out to drive her back but decided that would be a little too obvious. He spent the night in Sheffield and drove back to Tayffield in time to get to the tavern and have the tavern keeper point out Sedge to him when the line of workmen went past the tavern at shift-changing time.

Woodley liked what he saw of Sedge when he walked by. Intelligent eyes, and also worried eyes.

He waited until the tavern keeper had gone back inside the tavern, and then he caught up with him.

"Mr. Sedge?"

"Do I know you?" Sedge asked, suspiciously.

"No, but I had the pleasure of driving Mistress Sedge to Sheffield yesterday, and when Charley said who you were, I thought I'd ask how that baby of yours came out at the hospital."

"Don't know," Sedge said. "Missus ain't come back."

"Oh," Philip Woodley said.

George Sedge nodded curtly at him, and walked away.

At first Woodley was disappointed and annoyed. He had

177

hoped, planned, on getting George Sedge into the tavern and filling him with alcohol, if that were possible. But after a moment, he realized that he now had an even greater opportunity to capture Sedge's confidence. The way to get to a man like Sedge, a devoted husband and father, was obviously through his wife and children.

Woodley went back to the tavern and told the manager that something had come up and he would have to have his cart right away. He had to go to Sheffield.

3

Susan Elizabeth Sedge, aged eleven months and three days, was laid to her eternal rest in the graveyard of Saint Paul's Church, Tayffield, at half past five in the afternoon of January 21, 1770.

Mr. Ernest Ward, assistant supervisor of the crucible steel hearth, gave her father the day off with pay and dismissed half the crew on which George Sedge worked at five, so that they could attend the services. He also arranged with the pay department to deduct from Sedge's pay, at the rate of one shilling every two weeks, the cost of the grave, and personally informed the Reverend Mr. Grable, Rector of Saint Paul's, that the Company would guarantee payment for the grave.

The carpenter shop of Tayffield Iron Works Company, Ltd., in keeping with long-standing custom, furnished both the casket, of neatly finished and varnished pine, and the grave marker, of oak, on which was carefully carved a cross, and cut out the legend, *SUSAN ELIZABETH Beloved Baby Daughter of George & Janet Sedge Feb. 24 1769–Jan. 20 1770 In The Arms of Jesus.*

Mr. Ward himself went after the ceremony to the tavern on the Sedge's block in the East Housing Estate and stood the cost of the drinks custom required be provided to the pallbearers. While he was there, he spoke with a very interesting traveling gentleman, a Mr. Woodley, who dealt in used items, and who, he was told by Sedge, had been really a Christian gentleman during the sad period, having carried Mistress Sedge and the dying child to Charity Hospital in Sheffield, and then carrying her and the body back to Tayffield when the child died.

Mr. Ward was grateful to Mr. Woodley when Woodley talked Sedge into leaving the tavern. Until Sedge left, Mr.

178

Ward felt obliged to stand the cost of the mourners' drinks, and too often that sort of thing got out of hand.

"I think," Mr. Woodley said to him, "that we'd better get George out of here."

"How're you going to do that?"

"Get him a bottle of whiskey and take it to his house."

Mr. Ward put a shilling in Mr. Woodley's hand.

"Let me help pay for it," he said.

"You're an understanding man, Mr. Ward," Mr. Woodley had said to him. "A real gentleman."

"One tries to help as one can when something like this happens," Mr. Ward had replied.

George Sedge drank most of the bottle of Scotch whiskey, sitting at the table in the kitchen of his house, with tears running down his cheeks, and from time to time laying his head on his arms and weeping, before he passed out. Two of his chums and Mr. Woodley carried him upstairs and put him to bed. Then the chums left, and Mr. Woodley started to leave with them, but Mistress Sedge asked him to stay behind a minute.

"Two of the others are sick of the same thing," Janet Sedge said to Mr. Woodley in her kitchen as she gave him a drink of the Scotch whiskey.

"Mistress," Woodley said, "I never did learn what ailed the child."

"Not enough coal to heat the house," Janet Sedge said. "And not enough clothes to keep her warm, and not enough food to give her strength."

"Mistress," Woodley said, "I hope you will let me help you, in your trouble."

He reached into his pocket, and letting her see all the crowns he had, gave her a dozen shilling coins.

She took them, wrapped them in a piece of cloth, and put them in a pocket of her black cotton dress. She did not say thank you.

"What is it you want, Mr. Woodley?" she asked.

"I don't think I understand you, mistress," Woodley said.

She shook her head impatiently, resignedly.

"What do you want of me," she asked. "Of us?"

Woodley took the chance.

"I want George to run," Woodley said.

"I thought as much," she said. She did not, in fact, Woodley saw, seem at all surprised.

"And if we run, where to?" she asked. "And what happens, when we're caught?"

"I do not plan that we get caught," Woodley yaid.

"I did not plan that Susan die," she said.

"Would George listen to me?" Woodley asked.

"No," Janet Sedge said, flatly. "He would not listen to you, no matter how many gold crowns you let him see you have in your pocket."

"Gold crowns buy coal and clothes and food," Woodley began to argue. Janet Sedge put up her hand and shut him off.

"George will listen to me," she said. "I'll tell you true, Mr. Woodley, I'll take a chance with my freedom, and George's, with us going to prison, I mean, if it means I will not lose another of my babies the way I lost Susan." She took a deep breath. "They'd have more to eat, and better clothes to wear, if they was in the asylum. I saw that in Sheffield."

"There's no reason that they should have to go to an asylum," Woodley said.

"You tell me what you have to offer, Mr. Woodley," she said.

4

Marburg an der Lahn
January 22, 1770

So far as the Grand Duke Alexei was concerned, there was no question of how to deal with the boy who had struck him. He had to be put to death, and the only question was how. In Russia, he would have been killed on the spot, and if he had run as this one had, they would have found him right away, or in any event, within a couple of days, and he would have been spread-eagled between posts where they ran him to ground, and beaten to death with a rod. Or, perhaps, if there was no snow or ice on the ground, he would be bound, and his body dragged behind the horse of one of the Cossacks who had caught up with him.

His body would then be left in a public place for the birds to pick over, a reminder to the people that assault on the body of a member of the Imperial family was about the same thing as an assault on the body of Christ, and had to be dealt with accordingly.

His Imperial Highness's equerry, Prince Nicholas of Gdern, Colonel of the Saint Petersburg Regiment of Cavalry, explained His Imperial Highness's position, and his feelings, to His Highness Wilhelm VIII, landgrave of Hesse-Kassel.

Prince Nicholas was himself a graduate of Philip's University and understood the difference in culture between the two societies. Under the circumstances, he said that he would try to reason with his Imperial Highness and get him to agree to a more humane death for the boy, hanging, or perhaps beheading.

"What we have here," Wilhelm said, "is either a sinful assault on the person of someone chosen by God, or a spat between two young men."

"Your Highness, a member of the Russian Imperial family has been assaulted by one of your subjects, while His Imperial Highness is under Your Highness's protection."

"The boy is not a serf, nor a peasant," Wilhelm replied.

"He is not of the nobility," Prince Nicholas insisted.

"His family has been in the military service of my family for three hundred years," Wilhelm replied. "I ennobled his father."

"As a baron," the prince said depreciatingly.

The prince received a look of disdain and anger from the landgrave.

"I repeat," Wilhelm said, "the boy is not a peasant."

"I had hoped that by the time this matter came to the attention of the tsar," Prince Nicholas said, "I would be able to assure him that it had been resolved in such a manner that there was no reflection on the honor of the House of Romanov."

"Where would honor be, Prince Nicholas," the landgrave asked, "if I ordered put to death the son of the commander of my calvalry, who rode at my side in Persia?"

"He assaulted His Imperial Highness," Prince Nicholas repeated, doggedly.

"Would you have me believe, Colonel, that when you were a young officer, you never raised your hand to a member of the nobility senior to yourself?"

"Not against a member of the Imperial family," Prince Nicholas replied.

"But if you had, would you have been executed?"

"The situation did not arise," Prince Nicholas said. "What is it that Your Highness suggests?"

"I would suggest that you talk with His Imperial Highness, and remind him that he has two options. He can either accept my assurances that I have dealt with the boy in such a way as to properly punish him for his inexcusable behavior, and accept my apologies for the insult to his honor. Or he can report to his father that he has been insulted and that I have refused to satisfy his honor. That would be tantamount to my having insulted His Imperial Majesty."

Prince Nicholas looked as if he was about to respond, but then changed his mind.

"The letter you brought me from His Imperial Majesty, Prince Nicholas, asked me to treat his son as he would treat one of mine," the landgrave said. "If His Imperial Majesty was forced to conclude that I had stood idly by while the honor of his house was soiled, there would be consequences far greater, I believe, than one young man striking another young man, with no lasting harm, justifies."

"I must repeat, again, that the honor of His Imperial Highness must be satisfied."

"By punishing the boy who struck him?"

"Precisely. As personally painful as that may be for the both of us."

"There have been von Kolbes in the military service of my family for three hundred years," Philip said again. "I cannot find it in my conscience to put one of them to death for this. I will punish him, in my own way."

"May I ask how?"

"You must take my word that the punishment will be in proportion to the offense," Wilhelm said. He locked eyes with Colonel Prince Gdern. "And that it satisfies honor in this case. Or you must let the tsar decide."

5

Baron von Kolbe had taken Willi to the cottage of a *forest-meister* twenty miles northwest of Marburg an der Lahn. There the boy had been whipped, with a riding crop, not hard enough to break the skin, but hard enough so that the welts would last for three weeks.

Willi understood the beating. Children were beaten, it was a way of life, and what he had done deserved, he knew, a worse beating than he received. He had not only brought whatever was to happen down on his neck, but had shamed and humiliated his father, his family, his heritage. His father, as his father's father before him, and his father's father's father before that, for generation after generation, had sworn fealty to the House of Brabant. They had literally pledged their lives to serve the landgraviate and whoever was the landgrave himself.

Striking the grand duke had been the same thing as striking the landgrave, or a member of the landgrave's family, a crime punishable (and, Willi thought, justifiably punishable) by death. He had thought about it and decided that the only reason he hadn't been shot on the spot was because none of their weapons was loaded; they had all been fired.

He didn't want to die, but what happened to him seemed less important than the trouble he was liable to cause his family. It was likely that his father would be dismissed from command of the Cavalry Squadron, if not dismissed from the Regiment itself.

It could even be worse. Over the centuries, the Kolbes had prospered under the Brabant landgraviate. The first Kolbe who had gone to war for the house of Brabant had probably been a sturdy peasant, clutching a spear or a lance in a rear rank. And then there had been underofficers and finally officers, and Willi's great-grandfather had been singled out as Friedrich, Riding Master of Kolbe. Friedrich, Rittmeister von Kolbe. Not nobility, but gentry.

It had taken three more generations for the von Kolbes to rise from the gentry to the minor nobility. Willi's father was the first Baron von Kolbe. And now he had brought shame upon the title in its first generation.

There had been rewards in property, too. His family, over the years, had been given small plots of land outright and bought others. They had been awarded the privilege of working plots of landgraviate land with peasant workers, on fair sharing terms, and they had been allowed the privilege of cutting landgraviate timber lands on shares. His father carried the title of master of the Marburg Hunt. All game on all lands of the landgraviate belonged to the landgrave. Being master of the hunt provided a tacit authority to the title holder to hunt what and when he wished, for he was answerable to no one but the landgrave himself.

All the privileges were at the pleasure of the landgrave, of course, and he had just earned the displeasure of Wilhelm VIII. He could only hope that the landgrave's displeasure would not include his father.

After the beating by his father, Willi von Kolbe was left in the cottage while his father went to face the landgrave's rage. The forest master and his wife were told to go someplace else for a few days, there being no point in their getting involved with the trouble the von Kolbes were in with the landgrave.

A half hour after his father left, one of the hunters appeared at the door and told him that he had come out of the forest and met his father, and that his father had ordered him to the forest master's cottage to stay with Willi. And then an hour after that, Baron von Kolbe had reappeared.

"If it comes down to it," his father said, "you'd be better running. If you see someone coming to fetch you, run. You understand?"

"Won't that get you in more trouble?"

"His Highness will not likely hold a father responsible for the running of a boy so wild that he would raise his hand to a nobleman," his father said. "You run, if they send for you. It is no sin to try to stay alive."

Early on the morning of the third day Willi was in the forest master's cottage, he heard the sound of horses' hooves on the stones of the creek bed below. He peered out a window and saw Chief Sergeant Lahrner and three troopers of the Cavalry Squadron. They were leading an extra horse.

Willi, without waking the hunter, grabbed the bag he had packed with sausage and bread and eggs, and raced out the back of the house and into the woods.

He ran far enough into the forest so that he thought he could not be seen, and then lay on his stomach in the snow-covered pine needles and watched as Chief Sergeant Lahrner rode up to the cottage, dismounted, and went inside. In a moment, he appeared at the back door, and looked out and cursed and called Willi's name.

"You can come out of the woods," he called loudly. "Your father sent me."

When there was no reply to this, he shouted it again, and then swore. And then he raised his voice to the troopers.

"Spread out and see if you can see his footsteps in the forest," he said. "Start at the back and circle around until you find them."

And then, as if he had magical vision, Chief Sergeant

Lahrner pointed his horse almost directly toward where Willi lay hidden. Willi lay motionless in terror, afraid that if he moved he would be surely seen, and afraid that if he didn't move elsewhere, Lahrner would ride right up on him.

Finally, he decided he had to take the chance of moving. He would try, he decided, to move silently out of Lahrner's way, and find some other place to hide.

But beneath the carpet of pine needles was a piece of ice, and when Willi stepped on it, it broke, making a sound like a horse-pistol shot. When he looked to see if Chief Sergeant Lahrner had heard the noise, if he could tell the direction of it, he saw Lahrner looking right at him.

"Stay right there, damn you, Willi!" Lahrner shouted.

Willi started to run. As his father had said, it was no sin to try to stay alive.

Chief Sergeant Lahrner swore when he saw the boy begin to run. He urged his stallion into motion, cantering into the woods, and swearing again as the branches of the trees whipped into his face. By the time he caught up with Willi, he was genuinely angry.

He took his right boot from its stirrup and raised his leg. When he caught up with Willi, he overran him, holding his foot so that it caught Willi between the shoulder blades. The boy went sprawling on his face, striking the mostly frozen pine needle carpet of the forest so hard that the breath was knocked out of him.

Lahrner brought his mount up short, wheeled, and trotted back to Willi, who had enough of his breath back to be able to try to crawl away.

"You want another boot?" Lahrner demanded.

Willi rolled over and looked up at Larhner.

"You're not to be hung," Lahrner said. "Though God knows you deserve to be."

"What then?"

"First, we're going to Nürnberg, and then we're going to England with a gift from the landgrave to King George. You're to be apprenticed to a gunmaker."

The three other troopers rode up. Willi now recognized them as the grooms he had picked to go on the hunt.

"None of you can come back until the landgrave says so," Chief Sergeant Lahrner said. "You should have listened to me, Willi, when I told you to be careful around the bigshots."

185

He motioned for the trooper leading the extra horse to bring it up.

"Get on," Chief Sergeant Lahrner said. "And don't give me any more trouble, Willi, than you already have."

Chapter Ten

1

Tatta, Hyderabad
January 20, 1770

As the early morning fog burned away, the red clay buildings of Tatta, the native houses and huts, and Government House and the East India Company wharf came into sight.

It was going to be a beautiful day, and Captain Paul Selkirk was anxious to take *The Eleanor* to sea. With the exception of its passenger, Lady Caroline Watchbury, the ship was loaded and ready to let the tide take her down the Indus River to the sea.

Captain Selkirk had just told himself that he had known, as sure as the sun comes up, that Lady Caroline would be late, when Charley walked up to him, tipped his hat, and announced that two boats had just put out from the East India Company's wharf.

Charley, he noticed, was all dressed up, complete to pigsticker and wig. That was obviously to impress Lady Caroline. Charley had not been at all unhappy to learn they were taking her with them. He told himself that that was perfectly natural. Charley had had virtually no chance to show himself off as a ship's officer. The crew might now be calling him Mr. Selkirk and taking his orders with a collective straight face, but in their minds he was still Charley the cabin boy and baker's helper. He was a young man and wanted to strut his new finery.

It occurred to Captain Selkirk that if Mary were with his wife in Durham Furnace, and Charley were still sleeping in the fo'c'sl and messing with the crew, he would have had a much better chance to have the widow in his bunk. With

187

them aboard, and messing in the wardroom, that was going to pose certain problems.

"Ask the bosun to see to her luggage, please, Mr. Selkirk," Paul Selkirk said, formally, the captain to the officer of the watch.

When he looked toward the East India Company's wharf and saw the boats, Forbes's "official" boat with its Indian oarsmen in British navy uniforms, carrying Lady Caroline and a native boat heavily loaded with her luggage, it occurred to him that he should have passed the word for the officers to wear their dress uniforms. If he had thought about that, he could have at least worn a wig and a decent hat and a pigsticker, if not gotten completely dressed up, instead of being dressed as he was, without his wig, in a simple, open-collared cotton shirt and trousers.

Forbes's "official" boat reached *The Eleanor* first. Theo had rigged a bosun's chair for Lady Caroline, for a lady could not be expected to climb a ladder, and she was hauled aboard.

"Good morning, Captain," Lady Caroline greeted him, with a warm and wholly insincere smile, when she had been freed of the lines holding her to the bosun's chair and had gained her feet.

Paul Selkirk responded with a far more elaborate bow that he ordinarily would have made. He thought that in the early morning light Lady Caroline looked even younger than she had ashore. Younger, he thought, but still too old for Charley. He wondered why that thought had suddenly popped into his mind.

Mr. Porter joined them.

"Lady Caroline," Selkirk said, "may I present my chief mate, Mr. Porter?" Lady Caroline gave Porter her hand. She had not offered it, Selkirk noticed, to him.

"Would you take Lady Caroline to the quarterdeck while we bring her things aboard?" Selkirk said.

"Aye, aye, sir," Porter said. "This way, please, ma'am, and watch the deck. It's just been stoned, and it's slippery."

Lady Caroline nodded her head at Selkirk, flashed him another insincere smile, and, extending her hand and arm to Porter, allowed him to lead her down the deck as if she were being presented at court.

Selkirk looked over the side. The boat that had brought her

188

out to *The Eleanor* was already heading for shore. Forbes had not come along to say goodbye.

Theo LaSalle appeared at his side.

"I could bear having that in my bunk, Captain," he said.

"Well, put that thought out of your mind," Selkirk said, firmly.

"Aye, aye, sir," Theo said, smiling broadly.

"All that stuff in the boat is hers, Theo," Selkirk said. "Get it aboard and then stack it somewhere on deck. We'll let her sort it out when we're underway."

"Aye, aye, sir," LaSalle replied. Selkirk was surprised that Theo hadn't said something about having a female aboard. Women were supposed to be bad luck. (Mary was different; she was the captain's daughter.) Theo was probably, Selkirk decided, taking perverse pleasure in his knowledge that Lady Caroline was aboard despite his wishes.

Captain Selkirk turned from the railing and bellowed, "Mr. Selkirk!"

Charley appeared at the quarterdeck railing.

"Yes, sir?"

"Make all preparations to get under way, Mr. Selkirk," Captain Selkirk ordered.

"Aye, aye, sir," Charley said.

Lady Caroline and Mr. Porter had reached the quarterdeck just as Captain Selkirk had called to Charley. Charley, a little confused about what was expected of him, tipped his tricorn to the chief mate.

"With your permission, sir, I'll order all hands on deck."

"You have the helm, Mr. Selkirk," Porter replied.

"I'll have all hands on deck," Charley said to Tony, and Tony shrieked the order through the megaphone. "Man the forward capstan."

"What are your intentions, Mr. Selkirk?" Mr. Porter asked.

"I'll bring the forward anchor aboard and let her swing with the current," Charley said, without much confidence.

Porter nodded. "Lady Caroline," he said. "I believe you know our third mate, Mr. Selkirk?"

"Yes, I do," Lady Caroline said. She extended her hand to Selkirk, who bowed awkwardly over it.

"A pleasure, ma'am," he said.

He's adorable, playing man, Lady Caroline thought. In just a few years, he will be practically irresistible to the ladies.

"And Mistress Selkirk," Porter said, introducing Mary.

The smile that had excited Captain Selkirk and made Mr. Selkirk flush had no effect on Mary Selkirk. She gave Lady Caroline a curtsy that was just as insincere as Lady Caroline's smile.

"Ma'am," she said.

"I'll leave you in Mistress Mary's care, Lady Caroline," Mr. Porter said. "I believe I'm needed on deck." He tipped his tricorn to Charley, the traditional sign of respect to whoever had the helm, and went down the ladder to the main deck.

Charley was astonished and a little unnerved by the realization, for there was no denying it now, that he was expected to turn *The Eleanor* in mid-stream and take her to sea. By himself.

He stepped to the quarterdeck rail and cupped his hands.

"Weigh the forward anchor," he called. "Let fly the foresail!"

Theo LaSalle saw to it that the capstan was manned.

"With a heart, lads," he said. "We don't want to make Mr. Selkirk look foolish in front of the lady. Heave, *ho!*"

The seamen heaved at the capstan. Very slowly, it began to move. The capstan gear dog slid into place with a clank.

"Heave, *ho!*" LaSalle called. The seamen heaved again, and the anchor chain rose eight inches. "Heave, *ho!*" LaSalle repeated, and the chain rose another eight inches. LaSalle repeated the litany every fifteen seconds until the anchor broke free of the suction of the mud, by which time the seamen at the capstan were covered with sweat and panting from the exertion. Once the anchor was free of the bottom, however, the mechanical advantage of the capstan made it possible to raise it out of the water and get it stowed aboard in a continuous shuffle around the capstan, rather than with the individual heaves to Theo's order.

The Eleanor's bow began to swing downstream with the current as soon as the anchor left the mud, and as soon as the forward anchor was aboard and tied down, the capstan crew trotted to the aft capstan and waited for Charley Selkirk's order to weigh the aft anchor.

How extraordinary, Lady Caroline thought, when she realized that Captain Selkirk's pretty young son was actually in charge. He's just a boy, but he seems to know exactly what he's doing.

It was the first time Charley had ever been permitted to

weigh *The Eleanor*'s anchor and get her underway. He had known that the responsibility was going to come eventually, but he had been quite sure that when it did, it would be under the eyes of his father and Mr. Porter, so they could quickly correct his errors.

But his father and Mr. Porter were studiously ignoring him. Charley understood what they were doing to him, throwing him in to let him sink or swim, as the most effective way to remind him of his responsibility. He didn't like it, but there was nothing he could do about it.

"Weigh the aft anchor," Charley ordered, when *The Eleanor*'s bow was pointed downstream.

"Weigh the aft anchor," Tony piped through the megaphone. The seamen began to heave against the stout oak arms of the capstan.

Charley waited until the anchor was aboard, and *The Eleanor* had started to move, and then he called for the bosun.

"Bosun to the quarterdeck," Tony shrieked, and then added, "look lively!"

When he saw Theo LaSalle bouncing up the ladder, his familiar scowl now directed at Tony, Charley felt a lot better. LaSalle would prevent him from getting into deep trouble.

LaSalle came and stood beside him.

"I'll have the main and mizzen masts manned," Charley ordered.

LaSalle snatched the megaphone from Tony.

"Hoist the colors," he bellowed through it.

Damn, Charley thought, I completely forgot about the damned colors.

"Prepare to let loose the mizzen and the fore!" Theo bellowed without waiting for Charley to give the order. He waited until the order had been complied with. Then he said, "Any time you're ready, Mr. Selkirk."

Charley didn't thank him. For one thing the officer of the deck did not thank the bosun. More importantly, the first time Charley had climbed the shrouds, Theo LaSalle had climbed behind him, in case he slipped or froze. Theo LaSalle knew him well enough to know when he was grateful. Profoundly grateful.

Charley ordered, "Let fly the mizzen and the main."

LaSalle handed the megaphone to Tony.

Tony shrieked, "Let fly the mizzen and the main."

191

The furled canvas sails dropped from the yards with a loud flutter.

"Rudder amidships," LaSalle said softly to the quartermaster.

Good Christ, I forgot that too! I forgot the goddamned rudder!

The Eleanor's sails filled with gentle popping sounds, and very slowly, she picked up speed and headed down the Indus River.

Third Mate Charles MacGregor Selkirk went and stood beside the binnacle.

"Keep her in midchannel," he said.

"Midchannel it is, aye, sir," Quartermaster O'Keefe replied.

2

"It would appear that Mr. Selkirk has turned us with the anchor in the channel," Captain Selkirk said to his chief mate.

"That would seem to be the thing to do with the current what it is, sir," Mr. Porter replied.

"I suppose," Captain Selkirk said. He and his chief mate exchanged subtle pleased looks.

"I notice that he summoned the bosun to the quarterdeck for his instructions," Mr. Porter said.

"Well," Captain Selkirk said. "Our Theo is a fairly bright man, and it's possible that he can learn something by watching the officer of the deck."

"Anything is possible, sir," Mr. Porter said.

Lady Caroline Watchbury had only sailed once before, on H.M.S. *Indomitable*, the forty-gun ship of the line on which she and her husband had come to India. She had not wanted to go to India. She had tried to convince her husband that since he would more than likely be returning in six months or less, it made little sense to close up their apartments in London, dismiss the servants, and shut everything down.

She had failed to convince him that it would make more sense for her to remain in London. He insisted that she accompany him. He told her that the voyage aboard H.M.S *Indomitable* would be quite pleasant, and that Bombay was actually quite civilized, and that she would enjoy her position there. What he really wanted, she knew, was to have her at his side, not because he was in love with her, or even especially fond of her, but because it flattered his masculine ego to have his attractive young wife standing at his side, and because he didn't want anyone wondering aloud who was accommodating her in his absence.

Lady Caroline had not broken her marriage vows since they had sailed from London. There had been no one aboard the ship in whom she had been in the slightest way interested. Nor had there been in India, either in Bombay, or especially, after they had come to Tatta. Even after Edgar had come down with the fever and died, there had been no advances toward her, not even from Forbes, which had rather frustrated her. She had been sure that Forbes was going to try to "console" her; and when he had not, it had for some reason annoyed her, although she had no intention of letting anything happen between herself and that pompous minor official.

The prince of Hyderabad, as forbidden as that thought was, was the only man she had met since she had left London that was in any way appealing to her. At least until she had met Captain Paul Selkirk. And his son.

That made three men who were interesting. And three men with whom she would not, could not, become involved. Getting involved with an Indian, prince or no prince, was something that a respectable Englishwoman simply did not do. And it would be the height of folly to get involved with Selkirk, *père*, or, more absurdly, *fils*, when her future seemed quite clear.

Captain Sir Richard Trentwood had professed, before she left England, to be in love with her. It was perfectly reasonable to presume, now that she had been widowed, that he would propose marriage. She didn't love Trentwood. She had concluded that the one love of her entire life would be Grand Duke Alexei; it *had* to be love, to produce the reactions in her that their relationship had. Now that that had ended, as it had to end, being practical about the matter, she understood that she was going to have to settle for another marriage of practicality.

If Richard Trentwood loved her (and why would he say he did, if he didn't—not to mention that the proclamation had come *after*), that would allow her to begin her second marriage with a good deal more than there had been in the first. It would be a practical marriage, of course, but a practical marriage of the best possible kind.

For one thing, she would not enter it empty-handed. She was the lawful heir of poor Edgar; she had gone to her first marriage with a very small dowry. Edgar had not loved her. Certainly not in the way she understood bridegrooms, at least as they were supposed to love their brides at first. Richard not only professed to love her but had demonstrated an ability to affect her in that delicious way. Not as much as Alexei had, of course. There would never be another man like Alexei. But affecting her the way Richard had done was far better than not being affected at all, even if it wasn't the divine, perhaps even satanic, madness she had known with Alexei.

It would be the height of folly even to consider dallying with either of the Selkirks aboard a ship carrying her, more than likely, to the man with whom she would spend the rest of her life. There was no denying, however, that when she had met Captain Selkirk, the thought of dallying with him had almost immediately passed through her mind. There was a certain roughness, a certain *vitality*, about him that she found appealing.

Now that she was thinking clearly, the forbidden notions seemed quite absurd. For one thing, they were on a ship. Where could they do it in anything remotely resembling privacy?

There was more shouting from the quarterdeck now, from a dark-skinned boy screaming through a leather megaphone, repeating whatever orders young Mr. Selkirk issued. Seamen scurried through the rigging, and more canvas fluttered down from the yards of the masts, and filled with a popping sound.

Lady Caroline stole a look at young Mister Selkirk. He was standing with his hands on his hips, his head bent far back as he looked up into the rigging. His white trousers, the way he was standing, were drawn tight against his middle. Lady Caroline had heard that, like money, a man's size had little to do with happiness, but it was nicer to have than not to have.

Captain Paul Selkirk was considerably less appealing, however, now that he could be compared with his son. Boy or not, young Mr. Selkirk was tall, and well put-together, altogether physically attractive, a peculiar combination of man and boy. He looked so handsome, rather like a young stallion, on the quarterdeck of *The Eleanor*, his hand on the handle of his sword, issuing orders. She remembered how, at

194

dinner at the resident officer's table, young Selkirk had colored so quickly when she had looked into his eyes. When she thought about that now, she wondered if it was possible that he could be a virgin. She decided that it was entirely possible, and she found *that* possibility shamefully exciting. She couldn't imagine what had come over her, except, of course, that the Devil himself was working on her again.

That's what it had to be. There was no other explanation. Only the Devil himself, working on her when she was weak and vulnerable, would put thoughts like that in her mind.

She felt the girl's eyes on her, and smiled at her. The girl did not smile back. Had the girl seen where she was looking? Could she tell what she was thinking?

An officer she had not yet met appeared at her elbow.

"Lady Caroline," he said. "I'm Peter Dillon, the second mate. If you're ready, ma'am, you can show me which of your bags you'll require in your cabin."

She smiled at him, and then at the girl, and finally at Charley Selkirk, getting him flustered again, and then followed Mr. Dillon off the quarterdeck.

With my luck, Lady Caroline thought, I will be forced to share a cabin with the girl. But it didn't turn out that way. She was given a cabin to herself, and when she asked Mr. Dillon where Mistress Mary's cabin was, he told her that the girl had taken over her brother's cabin in officer's territory.

"You don't mean that I have turned Mr. Selkirk out of his cabin?"

"Mistress Mary done that, ma'am," the seaman told her. "Mr. Selkirk's right beside you, in with the small arms."

"Thank you for your kindness, sir," Lady Caroline said, and got rid of him. She closed the door after him and unpacked her trunks. She laid three dresses on the bunk and spent some time looking at them before she picked the one she would wear that night at dinner.

3

They were fifteen miles downstream from Tatta when Mr. Dillon relieved Charley, still a good seventy-five miles from the point where the main mouth of the Indus River opened onto the Arabian Sea.

Charley had hoped that Lady Caroline, who was, he thought, the most beautiful woman he had ever seen, as well

195

as the finest lady he had ever been close to, would return to the quarterdeck, but she did not.

Perhaps, he thought, he would see her now, and if not now, then certainly at dinner. He sought out the ship's carpenter, and took him with him to the passenger cabins. He had a cabin, but no place to sleep.

The design of *The Eleanor* was such that there was space for two large cabins on the deck below the one where the master's and officers' cabins were located. Since his father had not intended to carry passengers, he had had the cabins built nearly twice as large as the cabins on the deck above, so they could serve as storage rooms for cargo that he did not wish to put in the holds. One of them had been fitted out as the storeroom for the "ready stores." The ship's carpenter had built racks on which were stored two dozen balls for the aft cannon, and their powder charges. He had built other racks for the small arms, the cutlasses, swords, pistols, Pennsylvania rifles, axes, and grappling hooks Captain Selkirk wanted immediately available in case they were needed.

The Eleanor mounted twenty-four guns, but her master relied far more on her speed and his notion of defense at sea than on firepower. Captain Selkirk had told Charley that *The Eleanor* was a merchantman, and the purpose of a merchantman was to carry cargo. Every pound of cannon and shot that she carried reduced her cargo-carrying capacity by precisely that much. Furthermore, Captain Selkirk had pronounced, a cannon without a highly skilled crew was just so much useless iron.

Captain Selkirk never spoke about it, but Charley was no fool, and he was convinced that when his father talked about defending a ship at sea, or really the science of *attacking* a ship at sea, he was speaking from experience.

Charley had heard the rumors of how his father had come into the money to buy *The Mary*, and he knew that his father hadn't made enough money with *The Mary* to build *The Eleanor*. There was no question in Charley's mind that his father had been a privateer on at least one voyage. Charley suspected that the strong box in his father's cabin, built into the frame of the ship itself, iron-wrapped and secured with four sturdy locks, contained more than the ship's papers and what gold and other currency were necessary to pay the ship's routine expenses.

There was more: Captain Richard McMullen, now master

196

of *The Mary*, and Chief Mate Porter and Bosun Theo LaSalle of *The Eleanor*, had all been shipmates of Chief Mate Selkirk on that untalked-about voyage from which Selkirk had returned with at least enough money to buy *The Mary*. And ashore, they lived much better, and, strangely, far more quietly, than other seafaring men.

McMullen owned a dairy farm outside Chester. Porter had an interest (how large Charley didn't know, but it was substantial) in the ship chandler's firm from which supplies for *The Mary* and *The Eleanor* were purchased. Theo LaSalle acted as if he owned the seaman's tavern and hotel on First Street, and Charley had concluded that he probably did. He might not be married to the red-haired Irish woman who ostensibly operated the place, but he slept with her, and not with the trollops who frequented the place.

And almost all of the more than four dozen seamen aboard *The Eleanor* remained aboard voyage after voyage. That was highly unusual. Ordinary seamen almost always left a ship after a voyage, staying ashore until their money ran out and only then looking for another berth. If two voyages were aboard the same ship, that was simply coincidence. But ordinary seamen shipped again and again aboard *The Mary* and *The Eleanor*. Their pay was a secret between the master and the chief mate and themselves, but it was evident that they were being paid more than the going wages.

Over the years, since he'd first gone aboard *The Eleanor*, Charley had figured out that his father often carried cargo that didn't appear on the manifest. That was not at all uncommon. American seamen deeply resented the Maritime Navigation Acts passed by the English Parliament, and violated them whenever they thought they could get away with it. It wasn't a question of morality, it was a question of getting caught by H.M. Revenue Service.

But it wasn't until this voyage, his first as an officer, that Charley had been told even a little about what *The Eleanor* carried in violation of H.M. Law:

"A Durham boat will appear at our stern tonight, Mr. Selkirk," his father said, the night before they sailed from Philadelphia. "She'll have three hundred Pennsylvania rifles for us. I want them aboard and in the powder magazine, and I don't want anyone on shore to know we loaded them."

They had been on the way to Tatta from Cape Town before his father had told him what he hoped would happen with the rifles in Tatta, and that explanation had been very simple: he intended to exchange one rifle for one jewel, dealing with an Indian prince and a renegade Portugee who would probably love to slit their throats.

"You're going to have to tell the men to keep quiet about it," Charley said, trying to show that he understood what an officer must consider.

"The crew doesn't have to be told that," his father had replied, humiliating him. "I called you in here to make sure *you* kept your mouth shut."

Four of *The Eleanor*'s twenty-four guns were mounted aft, directly under the poop lantern. The "ready stock" of powder and shot stored in the unused passenger cabins was for those cannon. Captain Selkirk's tactic for an engagement at sea was to simultaneously order all canvas aloft and the aft cannon run and primed, and then to run with the wind.

On the half dozen times Charley had been aboard, as cabin boy, as baker's helper, as apprentice seaman, and a ship had appeared which raised his father's suspicions, they had run with the wind, and that had been the end of it.

Later, when the sea was empty from horizon to horizon, the cannon had been fired, one at a time, to clear them. Each time, the boom of the firing, the tremor that ran through *The Eleanor*'s hull, and the cloud of acrid smoke that rose from the open ports and spread through the superstructure had been at once thrilling to Charley and a little frightening.

Charley had heard again and again from his father that "the only sure way to win a fight at sea is to run from it, and thank the Good Lord, *The Eleanor* so far always had been able to do that," or paraphrases of that.

"And what if the other ship is faster?"

"Then we'll try to take down some of her canvas with the aft guns," his father had told him. "You'll notice they're elevated for distance."

"And if we can't?"

"Then we see if these Pennsylvania squirrel hunters are as good as they say they are." It was said that with a rifle, a good shot could knock a squirrel from a tree at a hundred yards. The "squirrel hunters" aboard *The Eleanor*, armed with Pennsylvania rifles, would try to knock the officers and helmsmen from the quarterdeck of a pursuing ship if it came within two hundred yards.

It was this accuracy, Charley reasoned, so far superior to

that of the Brown Bess muskets common to the British Empire, that made the maharaja of Hyderabad willing to pay such an enormous price for them.

"And if that fails?" Charley had pursued. "And they come alongside?"

"By then we'll have the other cannon loaded," his father said. "And we'll fire right into whatever's alongside. They'll not have my ship and theirs too."

The first discussion of the defense of *The Eleanor* with his father was the first time he had sat at his father's table by right. They had been lying off the mouth of the Delaware, waiting for the tide, and Theo LaSalle had him at work whipping a hawser, and he had been so intent on doing it if not perfectly then at least well enough to escape some of Theo LaSalle's contempt, that he hadn't seen Theo walk up to him.

Charley had finally noticed him and scrambled to his feet, nodded his head in a bow, and waited for the bosun's wrathful contempt. His father demanded the outward signs of respect from his crew toward their superiors, and since his son was a member of the crew, from his son to his son's superiors even more than from any other young seaman.

Theo LaSalle had glowered at him for a long moment before speaking.

"Get yourself cleaned up and onto the quarterdeck," he said. "You're supposed to think you're to help, but don't faint if your Dad tells you to sit down."

Then Theo had walked away, and it was a good three minutes before Charley dared to believe what he had heard. He had expected to spend another year at least, probably two, in the fo'c'sl, probably on the next voyage as helmsman (a promotion from his present status as able seaman) and then after that several voyages as helmsman and maybe as quartermaster before being promoted mate.

But it was true. After dinner that night, he did not return to his hammock in the fo'c'sl. He'd slept that night on the deck of the ready stores cabin, for there was neither bedding nor hammock in there, but an officer, once he crossed the line, could never again sleep with the crew in the fo'c'sl.

He would be sleeping in the ready stores cabin from now on, too, he thought wryly, with Mary installed in his cabin and Lady Caroline occupying the other "passenger cabin."

"You'll notice, Mr. Selkirk," said the ship's carpenter, who

199

was as old as his father, and yet another old sailor who had been with his father before his father had bought *The Mary*, "that there's place for a bunk where that rack of rifles is."

"So I see," Charley said.

"And it won't be any trouble at all to make you a table and some chairs. But that doesn't answer what we'll do with the ready stores."

"It's a question of priorities," Charley said, realizing that his father had not given specific instructions for what he wanted done, because he wanted Charley to make the decisions. If he made the wrong decision, which was likely, the correction by his father would be part of his continuing education.

"Aye," the ship's carpenter said, and waited for Charley to make up his mind.

"Most important is the ready stores and the rifles," Charley said.

"Aye," the ship's carpenter repeated.

"What it looks like we're going to have to do," Charley said, "is make provision to move the rifles from where they are, so I'll have a bed, against the other bulkhead."

"I can do that," he said. "But there won't be any place for a chair, much less a table."

"I know," Charley said.

"Where am I to put the powder?"

"Under the bunk," Charley said.

"I don't think the captain will like somebody living in here with the powder kegs."

"And if the captain were doing this, where do you think he'd put the powder?" Charley asked.

The ship's carpenter thought that over for a long moment.

"I expect he'd store it where you say," he said.

"Then that's what we'll do," Charley said.

"Aye, aye, sir," the ship's carpenter said.

Charley then went out of the cabin and down the companionway. The door to Lady Caroline's cabin was closed. He walked past it, then turned around and knocked at it.

She opened it.

"Yes?" she asked.

"I just wanted to say, ma'am," Charley said, "that I'm right next door, and if there's anything you need, I'd be happy to be of service."

"That's very kind of you," Lady Caroline said.

He could think of nothing else to say.

"Is there something else, Mr. Selkirk?" Lady Caroline asked.

"No, ma'am," Charley said, and made an awkward bow and fled. He could hear her chuckling behind him. He was furious with himself for making an ass of himself. He should have known that a lady like that would have no interest in him.

He was too embarrassed to face her at lunch, and fed himself standing up in the galley. When he went in to dinner, he found himself sitting directly across from her at the wardroom table. He avoided meeting her eyes, stayed out of the conversation, and was horribly embarrassed when his knee accidentally brushed against hers under the table. She was likely to think he had done that on purpose.

Chapter Eleven

1

The Free City of Nürnberg
February 2, 1770

They dismounted on the bank of the Pegnitz and waited for the ferry to return from the opposite shore to carry them across to the city, the walls of which rose from almost the opposite bank.

Willi von Kolbe was not even very tired, much less saddle-sore, although he had been sure when Chief Sergeant Karl Lahrner had announced they would make Nürnberg in eight days, no more than nine, that the pace would kill them.

It hadn't been an easy ride, but it hadn't been killing, either. They had started out early every morning after breakfast, and they had ridden, at a walk, for two hours, then dismounted and walked their horses for half an hour, then ridden two more hours. Then they had stopped for lunch, most often in a roadside *Gasthaus*, but sometimes just along the road, for cold sausage and bread and beer out of their saddlebags. In the afternoon, they repeated the routine: two hours riding, a half hour walking, then two more hours in the saddle. Then they had stopped for the night, most often just about the time the sun started to sink, but sometimes having to ride until it was near dark until they found a *Gasthaus*.

"Just because a cavalryman, worth the title, can make himself, and his mount, comfortable wherever he finds himself," Karl Lahrner had announced that first night, when they were reining up outside a *Gasthaus* near Bad Nauheim, "does not mean that he should lay on the ground if a bed can be found. Especially, when he's spending the landgrave's money."

Larhrner had always rented two rooms. He occupied one and Willi and the three troopers from the Cavalry Squadron slept in the other. But that was the only time Willi was left alone with the cavalry troopers, or spent much time out of the saddle with them. He took his meals with Chief Sergeant Lahrner as soon as they stopped for the night, and first thing in the mornings. While they were eating the troopers took care of the horses, and ate and drank later by themselves.

Willi was not sure if the special treatment he was getting was because of his father's long friendship with Lahrner or because, although he was in disgrace, he was still his father's son, the son of the Commander of the Squadron of Cavalry, and basking in reflected privilege; or whether, as Lahrner sometimes hinted, the landgrave himself had ordered Lahrner to keep an eye on him.

In any event, he did not question what was happening. It was the first trip of any distance he had ever made in his life, and it wasn't all that hard to imagine he was participating in a military movement. Their saddle blankets bore the embroidered coat of arms of the landgrave, and the troopers all carried lances, one of them flying a little triangular pennant, signifying they were about the landgrave of Hesse-Kassel's business.

When they rode through villages, the hooves of their mounts striking sparks from the cobblestones, the villagers pulled their forelocks to them as they passed, and the burghermeisters and constables came out of their houses and saluted Chief Sergeant Lahrner, and then, often, not sure who the young man in regular clothes, riding a horse with a landgraviate saddle blanket was, but not willing to risk that he might be someone important, saluted Willi as well.

Willi dared to begin to hope that he might, if not soon, then eventually be pardoned. That the landgrave had not only not had him executed, or even beaten, for having assaulted the Grand Duke Alexei, seemed to be a good sign. If he was pardoned, then he could join the Cavalry Squadron and ultimately he would be entitled to a salute from the peasants and minor officials in his own right.

The ferry came slowly back across the Pegnitz River, powered by the flow of the river. The Pegnitz was wider than the Lahn, which flowed through Marburg, but it wasn't really much of a river compared to the Main, which they had crossed at Frankfurt am Main. The icy water was, however, too deep to ford, and the ferry was necessary.

When the ferry finally inched up to the bank and the ferryman had tied it against the flow of the stream, Lahrner led his horse through the crowd of peasants and one or two businessmen and merchants in line ahead of them. They gave way to the cavalrymen without argument, or even rancor, but the ferryman was not equally impressed with their importance. He went to Lahrner and quoted his fee to carry them across the river.

"I am on official business for the landgrave of Hesse-Kassel," Lahrner told him, an amused smile on his face.

"And I am on duty for myself, and that's what I charge," the ferryman said. "Pay me or swim."

Lahrner looked over his shoulder.

"Wohler," he said, to one of troopers. "If this illegitimate son of a river rat says one more word to me, put your lance through his belly."

Willi knew that there was nothing behind the threat, and that Lahrner had previously paid whatever ferry and toll bridge fees had been demanded of him, making note of what they were in the notebook where he listed what had been spent for overnight accommodations and other expenses. But the ferryman had no way of knowing that, and Lahrner was an impressive-looking man, and not only because of his uniform. He was tall, heavy and broad-shouldered, and his flowing waxed mustache would have been the pride of any cavalryman.

Muttering, but not at all loudly, the ferryman stepped out of the way, and they led their mounts aboard the ferry.

"You give little men authority, Willi," Lahrner said to him, "and it goes right to their heads. It's necessary to put them in their place from time to time."

Willi nodded his agreement and wondered if that was a veiled reference to himself and Grand Duke Alexei, implying that his being permitted to go along on the hunt, and being addressed by his first name by the landgrave himself, had gone right to his head.

On the far side of the Pegnitz, they led their animals off the ferry, and then mounted. They rode through a portal in the wall surrounding the city, where the guard, an old man with a rust-stained sword scabbard at his waist, eyed them suspiciously but said nothing.

They rode single file into the marketplace, where Lahrner turned in his saddle to call their attention to an enormous, ornate clock, with life-sized statues as part of it, mounted on a large brick building.

"Believe it or not," he said, "that thing, the *Mannlien-laufen*, has been up there, keeping time, for near three hundred years."

There was nothing anywhere like it in Marburg, and Willi was genuinely impressed. They turned at the Market Hall onto Koenigstrasse, and a hundred yards down the street, Lahrner raised his hand for his small detachment to halt. He swung easily out of his saddle.

They were in front of a not very appealing *Gasthaus*. Lahrner disappeared inside and came out a few minutes later with the announcement that this was where the troopers would be staying.

"Willi and I will be up the street in the Golden Ram," he said. "One of you go with him, and when he takes the saddlebags off, bring the animals back here. We'll be here overnight, anyway, and I'll get word to you when I'll need you."

Two of the troopers dismounted and collected all the lances and their saddlebags. The third would follow Willi up the street.

"I'll be over there, Willi," Lahrner said, pointing at a sign carved with a clockworks and the words, "Muller und Thane Uhrmachermeisters" hanging over the street fifty feet away. "When you get us settled in our rooms, meet me there."

"Yes, sir," Willi said.

"At the Golden Ram, ask for Trude, give her my name, and tell her I'll be along after a while."

Willi found the Golden Ram without any trouble and, putting the saddlebags from his mount and from Lahrner's Prinz over his shoulders, crossed the narrow sidewalk and pushed open the door. Inside was a large room, filled with mostly unoccupied large plank tables and benches. A few tables with chairs by them were against one wall, and another wall was lined with kegs of beer and wine. The rear wall was mostly taken up by an enormous fireplace. A boy of about ten, dirty and weary, was patiently turning a spit, on which was hung the loins, hams, and ribs of a large hog. Willi's mouth watered at the smell of the roasting meat.

A plump, attractive woman of about thirty, her blonde hair in braids, came up to him.

"I'm Wilhelm von Kolbe," he said, "I'm travelling with

Chief Sergeant Lahrner, of the Hessian Regiment. He sent me to arrange for rooms with a woman named Trude."

"I'm Trude," she said. "And that's what I do, rent rooms. Where's Karl?"

"Up the street," Willi said. "He'll be along after a while."

She nodded, and motioned for him to come with her. Inside a door there was a key cabinet on the wall. She unlocked it, then looked at him curiously and a little uneasily.

"You're pretty close to Karl Lahrner, are you?" she asked.

"No, ma'am," Willi said. "I couldn't say that."

"He's not 'a very close friend' of yours?" she asked.

"He's a good friend of my father's," Willi said.

"Aha," the woman said. "And who is your father?"

"He's Hauptmann Baron von Kolbe, and he commands the Cavalry Squadron of the Hessian Regiment of Light Foot," Willi said.

"God forgive me for what I was thinking," the woman said, and then she patted Willi on the cheek. "But you're pretty enough for that, blondie."

Willi finally understood what she had been thinking, and he was humiliated and angry. How many other people in the *Gasthauses* on the way down here had thought the same thing? Probably many of them, which explained why he had been put in with the troopers at night.

But why hadn't he been put in with them here?

The woman took two large keys from the cabinet, locked the cabinet, and led him up a narrow flight of stairs to the third floor of the building.

"You didn't understand what I meant before, did you?" she asked him, as she unlocked a door.

Willi met her eyes.

"Yes, I did," he said.

"Well, I'm sorry," she said. "You don't have to say anything to Karl Lahrner, do you?"

"It's all right," he said. "When I first saw you, I didn't think you were the innkeeper's daugher, either."

She glowered at him, then smiled.

"You've got quite a mouth on you, don't you?"

"A pretty mouth, you mean?" he replied, still angry.

"That, too, but that's not what I meant," she said. "This is for you. I'll put Karl next door."

"They look all right," Willi said, condescendingly.

"Look, I was wrong, and I said I'm sorry," she said. "What else do you want me to do?"

"Nothing, forget it," Willi said.

"Get rid of the bags, and I'll get you a glass of wine," she said. "You *are* old enough to drink wine?"

"I'm old enough to do practically anything," Willi said.

"If I were to take you up on that, blondie," she said, "you'd turn and run."

"Try me," Willi said.

"Humph," the woman snorted, and handed him both keys. Then she went back down the corridor to the stairs.

He put Chief Sergeant Lahrner's saddlebags on the bed in the second room, carefully locked the doors, and went downstairs. The woman was standing behind a counter, her arms folded on her chest, watching him. He walked over to her.

"Something?" she asked.

"Where's the wine?" Willi demanded.

"I don't think you're old enough," she said.

"I'm old enough," Willie said.

She looked at him and raised her eyebrows.

"Maybe you are," she said. She poured a glass of wine for him from a keg mounted on the wall and watched him as he drank it down.

"Thank you very much," he said.

"You're welcome," she said. Then, "Don't say anything to Karl, all right?"

"About what?" Willi asked. She raised her eyebrows again and smiled.

"You going to be here long?" she asked.

"Not long," Willi said. "We're on our way to London."

"London, England?" she asked, and when he nodded, she seemed to be very impressed. "Then maybe you aren't a boy after all," she said. Willi was now very uncomfortable. He had been able to be fresh to her, but she had been right. When she seemed to be treating him as a man, it made him want to run. Even the way she was looking at him made him uncomfortable. He set the wine glass down on the counter.

"I've got to go," he said.

"That's a shame," she said. She gave him a broad, inviting smile. Willi fled out onto the street and walked quickly down the narrow sidewalk to Muller and Thane's place of business.

A clerk there expected him and led Willi to the second

floor, where he found Chief Sergeant Lahrner with the proprietors.

"You get us someplace to stay?" Lahrner asked him, and when Willi nodded, Lahrner introduced him to the clockmakers as "the son of my officer, Hauptmann Baron von Kolbe." The clockmakers shook his hand as if he were an adult, and one of them led him to a telescope set up to focus out a window.

It was the first telescope Willi had ever been permitted to touch, and he was fascinated with what he could see when he looked through the eyepiece, out the window, across the Pegnitz to fields beyond. It really did bring everything close.

The landgrave had equipped Lahrner with a draft on gold in the hands of the Rothschild Bank in Frankfurt am Main. Neither Muller nor Thane seemed comfortable with the piece of paper Lahrner had handed Muller, who had then passed it to Thane.

"Forgive me," said Thane, the older of the two, a tall and bony-faced man. "But we normally conduct our business in cash."

"You aren't suggesting that the landgrave would issue a worthless piece of paper, are you?" Lahrner demanded.

"It will be all right, I'm sure," Muller replied, signaling with a motion of his head for his partner to say nothing more. "It will take us a week, ten days, maybe a little more, to check the instruments out and to have shipping crates built," he went on. "And to have the plate engraved to the landgrave's order for the one he is sending to Russia."

"What you're really saying is that you doubt the landgrave's word," Lahrner accused.

"What I'm saying, Sergeant, is that I treat your landgrave as I treat the king of Bavaria. I'm honored with his business, and I deliver my goods on payment. I am going to send one of my sons with this draft to Rothschild's Bank in Frankfurt am Main. By the time he returns with word that the landgrave's draft has been credited to our account, the instruments will be ready for you to take them."

"That still amounts to doubting the word of the landgrave," Lahrner said.

"Not at all, my dear Sergeant. That is merely good business."

Lahrner laughed, giving in, and handed over the draft.

"I wish your son a pleasant journey," he said. "I'll expect

the devices to be finished and packed for shipment two weeks from today."

Muller showed them out of his shop, and Lahrner led them up the street to the Golden Ram.

When Trude saw Lahrner, she ran to him and threw her arms around him, and acted as if they were friends, maybe more than friends, of long standing. Willi saw, though, that when Lahrner dropped his hand to her behind, she freed herself from his embrace.

"What can I get you, Karl?"

"What does any cavalryman want when he's just off a long ride?" Lahrner said.

"A glass of wine and something to eat," she said.

"That, too," Lahrner leered.

"All you'll get from me is wine and food," she said. That, Willi thought, was for my benefit.

She opened the tap and filled two glasses, and, after a moment, half-filled a third glass for herself.

"I need some information, Trude," Lahrner said. "Where can I get this lad some decent clothes? He left home in a hurry, you see."

"What did he do, get some girl in trouble?"

"Nothing like that," Lahrner said, and Willi was astonished to see that Lahrner was embarrassed. Trude was now looking directly at Willi. "But we're bound for London and the hauptmann, his father, the commanding officer of the Squadron, gave me some money to get him some decent clothes, first chance we got. And this is it."

"There's some fancy stores on St. Sebaldstrasse," Trude said.

"Well, give us another glass of wine, then, and we'll go over there and get that out of the way, and then we'll think about getting ourselves some dinner."

"I think he could use something to eat right now," she said. "A growing boy needs his food, you know."

"Can you wait?" Lahrner asked Willi.

"Could I have a piece of meat and some bread?" Willi asked.

"Give it to him, and while you're at it, give me something too," Lahrner said.

Trude served them roast pork and potatoes and kept Lahrner's glass full of wine while they ate. She drank sparingly, and was purposefully, Willi saw, giving him as little wine as she could. Like his mother did, Willi thought.

They finally left the Golden Ram and found a clothing store near Saint Sebald's Church. As they passed the church, a file of choirboys under the control of a pair of nuns came out of the side of the building and crossed the street. Willi thought that they didn't look all that different, despite their professed Popishness, from the choirboys under the nuns at Saint Elizabeth's in Marburg an der Lahn.

Willi noticed a change in Karl Lahrner in the store. He behaved as if he knew he were in the presence of his betters. There were some aristocrats in the store when they went in, and another came in while they were waiting to be served. Karl Lahrner waited until the latecomer had been served before he spoke to the man who ran the place, then he identified himself only by title, as the chief sergeant of the Landgrave's Squadron of Cavalry, rather than by name, and then identified Willi as the son of Baron von Kolbe. He explained that Willi was bound for London, "for some months," and that he had been instructed by his father to get him sufficient clothing until other arrangements could be made there.

Willi came out of the shop thirty minutes later with a broad-brimmed hat from the band of which curled a long feather, dyed purple. He had everything else in a box. Three linen shirts, the nicest he had ever owned, two pairs of good woolen trousers, and four pairs of knee-length stockings to go with them. There was a cape, warranted resistant against all but the heaviest of rains, a pair of high, black leather boots, and a pair of shoes with silver buckles.

It was more clothing than he had ever owned at one time in his life. But it didn't make him as happy as he thought it should. He interpreted it as a sign that he would be in London for a long time.

What he would do, he decided as they made their way back to Koenigstrasse and the Golden Ram, was get Karl Lahrner a little drunk and see what he could find out from him. Aside from the remark Lahrner had made in the forest, when he'd run him to ground, about his being apprenticed to a master gunmaker in London, there had been no other discussion about what was going to happen to him.

2

The tavern room of the Golden Ram, which had been nearly deserted when Willi first went in the *Gasthaus*, was half full of people when he returned with Chief Sergeant Karl Lahrner, and within an hour of their return, it was jammed.

They were given a small table against the wall, not far from the counter where the wine and beer were dispensed. Trude joined them and left them only to greet what Willi sensed were her best customers. Lahrner paid his respects to some sergeants of the Nürnberg Regiment of Horse, explaining to Willi that while the regiment wasn't much, the sergeants were pretty good fellows.

Then a sergeant of the King of Bavaria's Household Cavalry came to the table to pay his respects to Lahrner, and it was while Lahrner was boasting about the Hessian Regiment that Willi learned what was planned for him.

"My Hauptmann has convinced the landgrave that the days of lances and sabers are about over," Lahrner said. "And the proof of that is this lad. He's the Hauptmann's son, and I'm taking him to England for training as the squadron's artificer."

"The squadron's *what?*" the Bavarian sergeant asked.

"Artificer," Lahrner explained. "When he comes back, when his training is finished, he'll be commissioned as our firearms officer. In charge of the pistols and muskets and cannon."

"In the *cavalry?*" the Bavarian sergeant asked. "Muskets and cannon in the cavalry?"

"You'll come at me one day, Heinie, at the gallop," Lahrner said, "swinging your saber. And when you're twenty steps away, I'll put a ball through your breastplate and you'll be dead before you fall off the horse."

"What will happen is that you will point your pistol at me, and pull the trigger, and it won't go off, and then you'll take your other pistol and shoot it and miss me. Then I'll chop your arms off," the Bavarian said. "You don't have to reload a saber."

"If I shoot my pistol, and it doesn't go off," Lahrner said, and nudged Willi, "then I'll chop Willi's arms off."

They laughed.

"Seriously, Heinie," Karl Lahrner said, "King George III of England sent the landgrave a rifle. You know what a rifle is?"

"Certainly."

"This one was made in Pennsylvania, in the American colonies. It shoots a ball about half the size of musket ball, but you can hit a man at two hundred-fifty paces with it."

"Horseshit!" the Bavarian said.

"God's truth," Lahrner said. The Bavarian looked at him in surprise, and Lahrner went on, "so help me. I've seen him shoot it."

"You believe that, lad?" the Bavarian asked.

"Yes, sir," Willi replied.

"You learn how to handle a saber, lad, and pay no attention to Lahrner."

The conversation was interrupted by the appearance of a gypsy band. First they passed the hat, and then they played wild music on violins and tambourines, and then their women danced briefly, to shouts of approval, and then they passed the hat again, and the women danced some more.

Willi was excited by the dancing, by the way the gypsy women threw their bodies around, exposing lots of leg and letting their breasts flop around.

And then the women came to the tables (ignoring the benches, because the money was at the tables) and offered to tell the future with either tea leaves or playing cards.

"Give her money, Karl," Trude said to Lahrner. "I know what your future is, and I don't want to hear about mine, but let Willi find out what's going to happen to him."

The gypsy woman smelled like a horse when she was close, and there was black grime under her fingernails when she took Willi's hand. She traced one of the creases on the palm and told him he was going to have a long life, with many changes of direction. That seemed likely, Willi thought, considering that three weeks ago, he wouldn't have dreamed of being here in Nürnberg, much less going to London, England.

Then she took playing cards in her hands and laid them out in a ritual. First, she picked out every third card and laid it face down on the table until she had run through the pack. Then she turned the cards over one at a time to study them.

212

She frowned, smiled, grunted, looked horrified and pleased, and finally finished.

"You are on a journey," she announced dramatically. "It will turn out to be a very long journey, and you will not return home for a very long time."

Willi was awed. There was no way the gypsy woman could have known that about him.

"I see water," the gypsy woman said. "Lots of water."

That was the North Sea, Willi understood, and the English Channel.

"And I see trouble and death. Someone very close to you will die."

Willi saw that Lahrner was looking at her with distaste.

"And I see love," the gypsy woman said. "You will soon have your first woman, your first real woman."

Trude laughed.

Willi was now absolutely convinced that the gypsy woman had magical powers. How else could she have known that he had never been with a woman?

The gypsy woman took his hand again, looked once more at his palm, and then nodded her head. "You are just beginning your journey through life," she said. "It will be long, and take many paths."

Despite what she had said about not wanting to know what her future was, Trude put her hand out for the gypsy woman to consult. Willi didn't pay any attention at all to what the gypsy woman said to Trude. He was considering his own future, as laid out by the woman, both what she had said about the long journey and what she had said about his soon having his first woman.

Lahrner refused to have his fortune told, and judging by the loudness with which he made his refusal known, Willi saw that all the wine he had been drinking was finally having its effect. Trude seemed a little noisy herself. It was time for him to go to bed, and he did.

He was wakened by noise in the corridor outside his room. He recognized Lahrner's voice, jovially incoherent, and there were the sounds of other male voices, and Trude's voice, a little thick. It wasn't hard to put together from those clues what was happening. Trude, with some help from some men (now that he thought about it, one of the men's voices belonged to Heinie Kramer, the Bavarian sergeant), was putting, or dragging, Lahrner to bed.

He smiled, and turned on his side and put his hand under his cheek, and listened to the faint sounds from the room next to his. And then he went to sleep.

3

When Willi woke hungry the next day, sure that Sergeant Lahrner was not going to get out of bed before noon, if then, he went down to the tavern. Trude fed him a very good breakfast and caught him looking down her dress.

"Like what you see, do you?" she mocked.

Faced with the choice of fleeing back to his room, or onto the street, Willi chose the latter.

He wandered almost aimlessly around the town and eventually, circling back, found himself back at Muller und Thane. The front of the establishment was covered with panes of glass, behind which they exhibited their wares. There was a fascinating display of telescopes of all sizes and shapes, magnifying glasses, and other optical devices, as well as clocks of all descriptions.

He was startled when someone barked, "Good morning, Herr von Kolbe," in his ear. He snapped his head around and found himself looking at Herr Thane.

"Good morning," Thane said. "You don't have to stand on the street, looking through the glass. Come in, if you like."

Thane proved to be as flattered by Willi's awe as Willi was awed by the clockmaker's fascinating trade. Thirty minutes after he had entered the store, Thane had him in a basement workroom where the mirrors for the telescopes, and the lenses, were being ground and polished by apprentices and journeymen.

Chief Sergeant Lahrner found him there at two in the afternoon. Lahrner wasn't nearly as annoyed as Willi thought he would be when he remembered he had left no word where he would be.

"I thought you might be here," Lahrner said. "When he gets in the way, Herr Thane, send him back to the *Gasthaus.*"

"He's not in the way at all," Thane said. "As a matter of fact, since he is so interested, I was thinking of suggesting to you that he spend a couple of days, as long as he wants, with me in the shop. I'm going to check the instruments, which

214

means take them apart and put them back together, and I thought it might be something he should see."

"I was going to take him with me to Munich for a week or ten days," Lahrner said. "But as you say, learning how the telescope goes together would be a good thing for him to know."

"I think so," Thane said.

"But could I rely on you to stay out of trouble, Willi?" Lahrner asked.

"Yes, of course," Willi said, making the instant decision between going to Munich (he had never been to Munich) or staying here and being taught something about telescopes.

"I'll watch out for the lad," Thane said. "See that he's fed and so on."

Lahrner grabbed Willi's hair and held his face close to his own.

"You know you're in trouble as it is," he said.

Furiously embarrassed, Willi nodded his head.

"If you can't be trusted alone in Nürnberg, you certainly couldn't be trusted alone in London," Lahrner said. "You heed Herr Thane while I'm gone," he added, and let loose of Willi's hair. "If you need me, Herr Thane, I will be at the barracks of the Royal Bavarian Cavalry Regiment."

"I'm sure," Thane said, "that there is no cause for concern. I'll watch out after him as if he were one of my own."

"It's settled then," Lahrner said. He reached into his pocket and gave Willi some money. "Don't spend it all on hard spirits and wild women," he said. "Try to remember that you have to eat on this until I return."

So far as Herr Thane was concerned, looking after Willi as if he were one of his own meant taking him to dinner at a *Gasthaus* right across from his place of business, and then depositing him in front of the Golden Ram at half past eight that night.

The place was jammed, and Willi was surprised that Trude had seen him as he walked to the stairs to his room. But she had, for she came running after him.

"And where do you think you're going?" she asked.

"To my room," he said, surprised at the question.

"You're supposed to be halfway to Munich by now, with Karl Lahrner and Heine Kramer," she said.

"I didn't go with them," Willi replied.

"You were supposed to," she said.

"No, I wasn't," he said. "I'm staying here and learning about optical instruments."

"Staying here and sleeping on the street," she said. "I let your rooms to somebody else."

"You had no right to do that!" Willi said.

"Right or not, I did it," she said.

"What am I supposed to do?" he asked. He realized that he didn't know where Herr Thane lived, even if he wanted to appear at his door, looking like a fool and announcing he had no place to sleep. Then he thought of his clothing. "Where's my clothing?"

"I wondered why he left that," Trude said. She took his arm. "Come with me," she said, and led him up the stairs, past the second floor where his room had been, to the third floor, to her apartment.

"Your things are in the wardrobe," she said, pointing to it.

"Thank you," Willi said.

"You'll have to make do, until a room comes free, with a featherbed on the floor," she said. "But it's better than the street."

She pinched his cheek.

"You look like a little boy when you pout that way," she said, and laughed, and left him alone.

He made himself comfortable on the floor with blankets and the featherbed, arranged a candle by his head, and tried to read a book Herr Thane had lent him, explaining the principles of bent light and how those physical properties could be used to make things appear larger. He didn't understand any of it and gave up, and blew the candle out and went to sleep.

He was awakened by the sound of footsteps coming up the stairs. Then came the rattling as someone worked the latch at the door, and then Trude was in the room. He rolled over and saw her standing there with a bottle of wine and two glasses.

"You awake?" she asked.

"Now I am," he said.

"I brought you a glass of wine," she said.

"What time is it?"

"After midnight. The place is closed," she said. "If you're sleepy, you don't have to drink it."

"I'm not sleepy," he lied.

She poured wine into the glasses and handed one to him.

216

"I hope you realize how lucky you are," she said.

"About not having to sleep on the street, you mean?"

"About sleeping where you are," she said. "There's not many men who can say they've been in here. And no boys."

He flushed. She smiled at him and stepped over him and went to a chest of drawers. She used the candle to light a second candle, and then she unfastened her braids, unwound them, and picked up a brush and began to brush her hair.

When she was finished, an act Willi found strangely erotic, although he had often seen his mother and sisters brush their hair and thought nothing of it, she picked up one of the candles and went into the next room. He wondered if she had left the second candle burning on purpose, or whether she had simply forgotten it. He was just about to get out from under the feather bed and blow it out when she reappeared, now wearing a nightdress.

She picked up the wine bottle, and the glass, walked to him and sat on the floor beside him. He could see her breasts moving under the nightdress.

"Not so cocky, now, are you?" she asked.

"I don't know what you mean," he said.

"Oh, yes, you do," she said. "You heard what the gypsy woman told you."

"About what?" Willi replied, unable to believe that she was making reference to what had immediately come into his mind, that he soon was to have his first real woman.

"About the long trip you're going to take," Trude said, making fun of him. She reached down and put her hand on his face. "Didn't you hear what she said about you taking a long trip?"

"Yes, I heard her," he said.

"And did you believe her?" Trude asked, and without giving him time to answer, put her hand on the back of his neck, and pulled his face up to hers, as she lowered her own.

Her mouth was warm, and tasted of peppermint. Then, astonishingly, her tongue forced its way into his mouth.

"I wanted to do that the first time I saw you," she said, when she finally let him go. "And I've been thinking about it all night."

Willi looked at her, aware that he was frightened.

Trude caught his hand and moved it through the opening of her nightdress to her breast.

"Are you a man?" she asked. "Or aren't you?"

217

Willi wondered if this was another of the dreams he had been having lately, where he woke up all sticky. But when Trude slid her hand up under his nightshirt, and grabbed him, and said, with obvious pleasure, "Oh, you're a man all right, aren't you?" he realized that the gypsy woman had been right in that prophecy, too. He was about to have his first real woman.

4

Durham Furnace, Pennsylvania
February 4, 1770

What Ingebord Johnson Selkirk had had in mind when she wrote to the Reverend Ingmar Sooth offering him the hospitality of the farm, was that he would spend a night or two with her and the boys, either on the beginning of his circuit or at the end of it.

The Reverend Mr. Sooth had written back that he would be proud to accept her kind offer of a place to stay while he was bringing God's word to the villages and farms upriver. The tone of his letter had made Ingebord suspect that he was accepting more hospitality than it had been her intention to offer. Her suspicions were immediately confirmed. Instead of staying at the farmhouse for a day or two, he had immediately begun to use the farmhouse as his base. He returned to Durham Furnace every Sunday after services he held somewhere in the area, and stayed there, resting up by sleeping late and eating everything she put in front of him through Sunday and Monday, and sometimes late into Tuesday as well, if the weather was bad, before getting on his horse and starting off again.

It was, she told herself, her Christian duty to provide him whatever accommodation he required, especially since she could afford to do so. And especially since she could see how spent and tired he was when he rode up to her door.

The truth seemed to be that Ingebord enjoyed feeding him and took pleasure in the knowledge that it was a Christian thing to do. It was pleasant to have a man around the house, even if the Reverend Ingmar Sooth could not be expected to do what other men would have done, carry firewood, or help

218

feed the animals. He was, after all, a man of God, and he knew that she had two healthy sons.

The problem there, Ingebord saw, was that neither Nils nor Luther Johnson liked the Reverend Ingmar Sooth. As soon as he rode up, the boys found some excuse to leave. Whenever they thought they could get away with it, they stayed away from the farmhouse as long as he was there, even if that meant they missed a number of meals.

That had given Mistress Selkirk and the Reverend Mr. Sooth the opportunity to be alone a good deal, and with the boys gone, the Reverend Mr. Sooth had been able to talk more frankly about the sin he had seen, and was dealing with, than he would have been able to if they had been sitting at the table, or in front of the fire after dinner.

The more she came to know the Reverend Ingmar Sooth, the more Ingebord understood what a true Christian man of God he was. A *compassionate* man of God. The difference, she thought, was that the Reverend Mr. Sooth felt genuine pity for the sinners he was trying to bring to Jesus Christ's forgiveness. He felt no anger toward the thieves, and the usurers, and the blasphemers and the drunkards and the gluttons and the adulterers. Anger, he told her, was reserved for God, and God was more merciful and understanding, in the final analysis, than angry, even if some sinners seemed to have missed breaking only the Commandment about making graven images.

The Reverend Ingmar Sooth was also a believer in the theory that everyone had a cross to bear. His cross, he confessed to her one evening when they had been sharing a squirrel-and-hare pie alone, was that although he yearned for the comforts of a good Christian home, a Christian woman to share his life, he could not, considering he was devoting his life to spreading the Gospel, ask a woman to put up with both the near poverty a clergyman's life demanded and share him with his calling, which of course meant that he could not be home as much as a husband should be home.

He told her that she must know, with a seafaring man for a husband, how difficult it was for women to be separated from their mates for long periods of time. He could not find it in himself, he told her, to ask a woman to be as brave and self-sacrificing as she had proved herself to be.

She confided in him that her marriage was one of convenience, that she and Captain Selkirk had joined in marriage for business reasons and so that she could provide a good Christian home for the girl, Mary. She confided further that not only had it proved impossible to provide a home for the girl, who had run off to sea with her father, but that she had come to believe that she had exaggerated the value of marrying for business purposes. She had found, she told him, that rather than being a convenience to her, being married was something of a burden.

The Reverend Mr. Sooth had not pressed her for details, and she had offered none, for the discussion had taken a turn that made her uncomfortable.

"But he will come home again to your bed, Mistress Ingebord," the Reverend Mr. Sooth had said. *"You* have that to look forward to. We must be grateful for the compensations God does provide."

Alone in the house now (Nils and Luther, aware that it was Sunday, and that the Reverend Mr. Sooth and his lengthy prayers were due to be at the farmhouse, were spending the night at the furnace, to "keep the heat up"), Ingebord thought of that conversation, and how she would have liked to tell the Reverend Ingmar Sooth he was wrong. That there had been no physical relations between her and Captain Selkirk. There was, of course, no way that she could say something like that. Even to a man of God.

The boys had butchered a hog the day before, and she had kept one of the loins (sending Luther with the other to the next farm, who would repay in kind the next time they butchered) to roast. Confident that the Reverend Mr. Sooth would appear in time for supper, as he habitually did, Ingebord had roasted the loin while she prepared the bacon and hams for the smokehouse and chopped meat for sausage.

She was more than a little annoyed when the Reverend Mr. Sooth did not appear by dark, when the loin and the potatoes were done. She ate a solitary meal, and her annoyance turned to concern. It was a bitter cold night, after a sunny day, and the roads would be icy. She had mental pictures of the Reverend Mr. Sooth falling from his horse and lying injured and perhaps freezing to death along the road.

It was after nine when she heard the heavy thump of his fist at the door. When she opened it, her relief that he was all right was immediately replaced with concern for his chill. Even though he was wrapped against the cold in a bearskin rug, worn over his greatcoat, and even though he had wrapped a woolen scarf over his head, he looked nearly frozen.

"You should have stayed where you were," she chided him. "Stand by the fire, and I'll get you hot milk."

He unbuttoned his greatcoat, but did not take it off. He held it open to catch the heat from the fire, as she warmed milk and put two tablespoons of honey in it.

"Thank you, mistress," he said, taking the mug from her and holding it in both hands.

He turned and stood facing the fire until he'd finished the milk, and then he took off the greatcoat and sat on the rug and pulled off his boots.

"Have you any spirits?" he asked her.

"I should have thought to offer you some," she said. "There's plenty here. I don't use them, of course, and I forgot about them."

She went into the cupboard and took from it one of the six gallon-bottles of New Jersey applejack that Captain Paul Selkirk had bought from a traveling merchant.

"How will you have it?" she asked.

"With hot water and sugar," he said. "If you have some. A toddy."

She splashed a good two inches of applejack into a mug, added two large lumps of maple sugar and as much hot water as spirits, stirred it until the sugar dissolved, and then handed it to him.

He sipped at it gratefully.

"You're not having some?" he asked.

"I think of myself as a Christian woman, Reverend," she said.

" 'Take a little wine for thy stomach's sake, and thine other infirmities,' " he quoted. "Corinthians."

"I'm certain there's no harm in taking spirits for medicinal purposes," she said.

"There's no harm in taking them, in moderation, for pleasure," the Reverend Mr. Sooth said. "Or for charity."

"Charity?"

"You make me feel a sinner, Sister Ingebord," the Reverend Mr. Sooth said.

"I don't mean to," she said.

"Christ made wine, you will recall, at the wedding," he said. "The sin is drunkenness, not drinking, as gluttony is the sin, not eating."

221

He offered her the mug.

"I'll make my own," she said. "You drink yours, you need it, as chilled as you are."

Ingebord had had spirits before. Medicinally. When she had her teeth pulled, the barber had given her a full glass of rye spirits for the pain; and when she'd delivered Luther and Nils, Widow Thorpe, the midwife, had given her applejack. And she took it sometimes when she had the curse, for the cramps, a couple of burning swallows straight from the neck of the jug, but never before had she had it for pleasure.

She made a drink exactly as she had made it for the Reverend Mr. Sooth, applejack and maple sugar and hot water, and when she sipped at it, she was really and pleasantly surprised at how good it tasted.

She sat with the Reverend Mr. Sooth for a few minutes, listening with horror to the story he told her of a burial service he had conducted in Tatamy.

"Burial to me means in the ground," he said. "And I confess to you, Sister Ingebord, that when they told me they couldn't open a grave, I thought they didn't want to go out in the wind and snow and do the work. Pride, you know, goeth before a fall. So I took a pick and a shovel, and said that I would show them how it was to be done. So I swung the pick with a mighty effort. And bent the point and broke the handle, all at once."

"So what did you do?"

"I left the casket where they had it," he said, and laughed. "By the end of the barn. He'll be put to his rest at the first thaw."

She was a little ashamed of herself for being irreverent, but it was a funny story.

She asked him if he would like another sugared applejack toddy while she warmed the sauce for the roast pork and potatoes, and he said he did, and while she was making his, she decided she would have another one herself.

He ate his supper as if he were starved, and she told herself again that he really was a good man of God, subjecting himself to all he did to spread the Gospel, and act as shepherd to a flock of people who otherwise would not have the comfort of religion.

And looking down into her fourth applejack toddy, she told him that he had been wrong, the last time they had had

222

a conversation, when he told her that she could at least look forward to having a husband in her bed.

"God's truth," she said, "is that I have no more of the physical comforts of marriage than you do. Captain Selkirk has never touched me. That way, I mean."

"That's a sin!" he responded.

"It is?"

"Absolutely," he said. "As it is a sin for a wife to deny her husband, it is a sin for a husband to turn his back on his wife."

"I didn't know that," she admitted.

"He's never . . . ?"

"Never," she said softly.

"Then it's no marriage," the Reverend Ingmar Sooth said.

"You mean, legally?"

"Legally, maybe," he said. "But in the sight of God, it is not!"

"Oh, my!" she said.

"It would appear, Sister Ingebord," the Reverend Mr. Sooth said, reaching out and taking her hand, "that we both bear the same cross."

She nodded her head. She did not withdraw her hand.

"Do you know the theological difference," the Reverend Mr. Sooth asked, "between the sin of fornication, and the mortal sin of adultery?"

"No," she said.

"Adultery," the Reverend Mr. Sooth explained, "is sexual congress between two people bound by holy matrimony. For the obvious reasons, it is a far more serious sin than fornication, which occurs when two people, not bound by holy matrimony, give in to the natural temptations of the flesh. When they are lonely, for example."

"Natural temptations?" she asked.

"Natural," he said. "Much of the evil of the Church of Rome is because their clergy deny, or try to, God's natural urges to be with the opposite gender. Martin Luther himself saw that. He saw that abstinence is unhealthy, and by extension, a sin."

"He did?" Ingebord had never heard matters like this discussed before. But Ingmar's reasoning was right. She could sense that.

"Do you think that God thinks Martin Luther to be a sinner?"

223

"Of course not!"

"Even though he took into his bed a woman?"

"I didn't know that. I thought he was married."

"Marriage came later," the Reverend Mr. Sooth said. "When they first gave in to their natural hungers, were drawn to each other by loneliness and need, he was a Popish priest sworn to celibacy, and she a Popish nun, sworn to chastity."

"I don't know what to think."

"Do you think God would have permitted Martin Luther to lead so many Christians from the hypocrisy of Rome to the faith that I now preach if He were angry with him?"

"Of course not," Ingebord said firmly. "It's just that I never thought of these matters before."

"I understand," he said, and squeezed her hand.

"You say, that in the eyes of God, I am not really married?"

"Not if what you tell me about the relations between your husband and yourself are true," the Reverend Mr. Sooth said.

"They're true!" Ingebord said firmly. She seemed to be having trouble forming her words. She wondered why that should be.

"Where are the boys, Ingebord?" the Reverend Mr. Sooth asked.

Ingebord felt her face color. There was no mistaking his meaning. She looked at her mug of applejack toddy. It was nearly empty. She drank the rest of it. She raised her eyes to Ingmar.

"They'll not be back this night," she said.

Chapter Twelve

1

Aboard The Eleanor
West longitude 15°25', north latitude 2°15'
February 15, 1770

Lady Caroline Watchbury found life aboard *The Eleanor* very different from the shipboard conditions she had experienced on H.M.S. *Indomitable* on the way to India. Many of the differences, she thought, were because *The Eleanor* was a merchantman, carrying her owner aboard, and the *Indomitable* a Royal Navy man-of-war. Others were because *The Eleanor* was American and the *Indomitable* British. She had almost immediately begun to understand that Americans were not simply English who lived in a colony, but almost a different nationality.

The food aboard *The Eleanor* was much better than it had been on the *Indomitable*. Breakfast in the wardroom, for example, consisted of fresh eggs, bacon and ham, fresh baked bread and rolls, tea and coffee. On the *Indomitable*, it had been bacon and ham and hard crackers and tea.

There were of course fewer officers eating in *The Eleanor*'s wardroom, never more than three at table, and she and Mary Selkirk were the only two passengers. It was considerably less formal, too. The only special etiquette of the sea that was observed around the table was that no one sat down until Captain Selkirk either appeared or sent word that he would not be eating. And except for the first night, when the captain's son, Charley, obviously for her benefit, had shown up in a uniform, none of the officers wore uniforms. Or for that matter carried either swords or pistols on deck.

On the *Indomitable*, the quarterdeck had been available to Sir Edgar and Lady Caroline because of their rank. Aboard

The Eleanor, she had been told to stay on the quarterdeck as much as possible because she would be in the way on the main deck.

Her cabin on *The Eleanor* was four times the size of the cabin she had shared with Edgar on the *Indomitable*, but, incredibly, she was expected to clean it, and make the bed, and clean the slops bucket herself. She had learned that, to her astonishment, the first morning at sea. Since she was a lady, and it was a rather delicate subject, she had sought out Mistress Mary and raised the question with her.

"What you do with it, Lady Caroline," the girl had told her with a smile of amused tolerance, "is take it to one of the slop chutes and throw it over the side."

"Myself?"

"None of the men'll do it for you," Mary said, smiling even more broadly. "So it's either that, or leave it where it is. Watch the wind. Throw it to leeward."

"I don't know, I'm sure," Lady Caroline had said, "what that means."

"It means if you try to throw it over the side into the wind, you'll get it splattered all over you," Mary had told her.

"And what of bathing? I mean to say, when do I get water?"

"Any time you want it," Mary had told her, pointing to one of several barrels marked "Sweet Water" lashed in place along the deck. "We're on the honor system," Mary explained, obviously enjoying her discomfiture. "The ration is a bucket a day for drinking and washing. Bosun LaSalle told me that since I'm a lady, and expected to smell sweeter than the men, I could take an extra bucket, from time to time, provided I didn't make a pig of myself, and I suppose the same applies to you. You could ask him."

"I'm expected to carry buckets of water to my cabin, is that what you're telling me? And to empty my own . . . ?"

"That's right. When you think the sheets on your bunk need washing, I'll show you how to do that."

"There are no servants?"

"Two," Mary said.

"Oh?" Lady Caroline had asked, falling into the girl's trap.

"Tony, who's learning to be an apprentice seaman," Mary explained, "takes care of my father and serves at table. And me. Mostly I help Tony and care for the chickens."

"You care for the chickens?"

"It's either that or chance that the egg'll break. Or disappear," Mary said.

The girl was quite as impossible, and, in her way, as amusing as her brother. Oblivious to her position (she was, after all, the captain's daughter) as well as to the fact that she was a female supposed to be a lady, Mary spent more time with the men than she spent with her social peers. At night, she sat spraddle-legged on the deck and played the violin when the men danced to amuse themselves. She was often barefoot, and seldom without a lethal-looking dagger in a leather scabbard suspended on a cord around her neck. A particularly ferocious sailor, obviously with the captain her father's approval, was teaching her how to carve with the knife. Her current project was a poor imitation of *The Eleanor*'s figurehead.

The brother, Charley, Mr. Selkirk, the third mate, was similarly amusing and impossible. He was actually infatuated with Lady Caroline, and had been, Lady Caroline realized when she thought about it, since they had first met at the dinner at Government House in Tatta.

Oblivious to the snickers not only of his father and sister and the other officers but the crew as well (Lady Caroline could not imagine a British sailor having the temerity to even suggest that he was laughing at one of his officers), he had started following her around whenever he was off duty, staring at her out of calf's eyes.

Whenever she glanced up from her plate in the wardroom, there he was, looking at her with childlike adoration. Whenever she went to the rail and looked over the side, she could count on having him standing, a discreet three feet away from her, his hands folded against his back in conscious or unconscious mimicry of his father, waiting for an opportunity to speak to her.

A week or ten days out of Tatta, when he had become quite a nuisance, she had called him on his behavior. It was late at night, and she had come on deck to empty her slops, something to which she had not yet become accustomed, and something she would have preferred to do in absolute privacy. It was before she had come to fully understand when the officers were on duty, and when they were relieved. In her ignorance, she had carried the bucket onto the main deck just as Mr. Selkirk was being relieved of his watch.

And he had, of course, come down the ladder from the

227

quarterdeck and practically trotted over to where she stood flushing the bucket with waste water from the galley.

"Good evening, Lady Caroline," he'd said. "Beautiful evening, is it not?"

"Mr. Selkirk," she said, turning to glower at him, "do you think it is seemly for you to pursue me whenever you see me?"

He had been struck dumb by her remark. His face had flushed, and his whole body had stiffened, and he had pretended to be fascinated with the horizon. She had pressed the advantage.

"I fear, Mr. Selkirk," she had gone on, "that you might be giving others the impression that you are courting me."

Still no response.

"Certainly," she had said, actually feeling a little sorry for him, "you can see the absurdity of the situation."

"Why is it absurd?" he had croaked.

"I would remind you of two things," she said. "The disparity of our ages and positions, and that I am embarked on this vessel with the sad duty of taking the remains of my late husband home. I am, of course, still in mourning."

That, she had thought, while it might be cruel, would serve to run him off.

"You're not that much older than me," he had replied, his voice on the edge of cracking. "And, as you point out, he's dead."

"You won't actually," she had said, annoyed, "dare to presume to press your attentions on me, now that I have made it perfectly clear I am offended by them?"

"I'm sorry they offend you, but there doesn't seem to be much I can do about it. The way I feel about you, I mean."

"I'm sure," she had replied, "that I have no idea what you mean, sir."

"I mean that I can't eat, I can't think of anything but you, and from what I've heard about it, that means I'm in love with you."

"You are insane, sir," she said, although she was touched. "Insane and insulting."

"I'm sorry you're insulted," he said. "But I can't help being crazy."

She had snorted and marched away, and then had to march back to where he stood, with as much dignity as she could muster, to pick up her slop pail.

It was a pity, she thought later, for there was something undeniably attractive about the boy, that he was but a boy, and that he was what he was, an American colonial seaman rather than someone of decent English birth.

He reminded her in many ways of Viscount Malvern; and, she admitted to herself, if Third Mate Selkirk of *The Eleanor* had been Viscount Selkirk, and they had been in England, then she might have *considered*, just *considered*, dallying with him.

But here, of course, that sort of thing was quite impossible. She would be branded a whore if anyone ever *suspected* that there was anything more between her and the lovesick young man than the to-be-expected relationship of a respectable upper-class English widow escorting the remains of her late husband home, and an officer of the ship on which they were traveling. If they stopped laughing at Charley, they would start laughing at her, and the laughter in the latter case would be neither innocent or pleasant.

After her encounter with Charley, when he told her he loved her and she had told him he was both insane and insulting, he never spoke to her alone again. She continued to catch him looking at her in the wardroom, on deck, whenever she was in his sight, but he no longer tried to catch her alone, and when he spoke with her, he was absurdly formal and distant.

While she was pleased that she had turned him away from his embarrassing pursuit, she was, in fact, a little disappointed that he had given it up so easily, and sorry that she had so hurt his feelings.

2

Early in the morning, a rain squall appeared on the horizon, nearly dead ahead, a dark gray, sharply outlined column connecting the clouds with the waters of the equatorial Atlantic.

"What in the world is that, Mr. Selkirk?" Lady Caroline Watchbury asked, laying her hand on his arm to make sure she had his attention. When he was sulking, he often pretended that he didn't notice her at all. He had, she knew, made a point of not noticing her when she had come onto the quarterdeck after breakfast.

"I would venture the opinion, my lady," Charley Selkirk

229

said very formally, "that it is entirely likely that we're to experience a moderate storm."

Lady Caroline pressed her lips to keep from smiling at his solemn pomposity.

Charley Selkirk was, in fact, furious with her. He had come to the conclusion that not only had she laughed at his profession of love but that she was going out of her way to make a fool of him. She always seemed to be brushing against him, looking deeply into his eyes, and touching him with her hands, at the same time playing the role of respectable older widow woman. He was convinced that that's what she was about now: she wanted to tease him when he had the helm, with the quartermaster and the helmsmen standing ten feet from them.

"Not a bad storm, I hope?" she asked, standing so close to him that he could smell the cloves on her breath.

"No, Lady Caroline," Third Mate Selkirk said. "It will be, in my opinion, a moderate storm of short duration." He looked down at the hand on his arm and stepped away from her. "Might I be so bold as to suggest, Lady Caroline, that it might be best if you went below?"

Lady Caroline, suppressing another smile at his language, saw that he was really angry, and wondered why. It had not been her intention at all to tease him, but obviously he felt that she had.

"Where do rain clouds come from?" she asked, deciding to ignore his pointed suggestion to go below. She didn't want him to be angry with her, but when she thought about this, she could think of no reason why that should be important.

He looked at her, and for a moment, she was afraid that he was not going to respond. His blue eyes could sometimes be quite icy.

"I believe, Lady Caroline," he said, archly formal, "that the physicists' theory holds that when the sun heats the water, or the land, this causes the air to rise. The theory further states that there is generally some water, in the form of an invisible vapor, in the air. As the air rises, the air thins, until a point where it will no longer support the invisible vapor. The vapor becomes visible."

"How do you mean, 'visible'?" Lady Caroline asked, hoping that she sounded far more sincerely interested than she was.

"Clouds, you might say, Lady Caroline," Charley went on, "are visible vapor."

"Oh, yes," she said. "How fascinating!"

"At a certain point further, the visible vapor, which no longer can be supported by the air, if you follow me, becomes raindrops and they fall to earth."

Despite her almost total lack of interest in where rain clouds came from before she had opened the conversation, she now really found this fascinating. She was surprised again at the depth of his knowledge. Since he didn't really seem old enough to be a ship's officer, the temptation for her had been to treat him as if he were just playing at it. The fact was, she reminded herself, that he *was* the third mate, and that he was possessed of the skills and knowledge that responsibility required. In that, he was not a boy. Perhaps not the grizzled old salt that his father and Mr. Porter were, but a good deal more than a boy in uniform.

He looked at her, without being embarrassed, to see if she had understood his little lecture, and then he walked away from her. She walked after him and looked at the horizon again. The storm clouds, seemingly immobile, seemed much closer than they had been a moment before.

He looked down at her, and there was still a flicker of annoyance in his eyes. He had as much ordered her below, and she had disobeyed. The man in him, Lady Caroline said, is angry with me. The boy in him is afraid to say anything.

Selkirk turned his head. "I'll have the watch on deck," he called to Tony the apprentice seaman, who relayed the order by shrieking through a leather megaphone.

"May I?" Lady Caroline asked, pointing to Charley's telescope. When he handed it to her, she carefully avoided touching his hand or looking into his eyes.

"Thank you, Mr. Selkirk," she said politely, and drew the tube open and looked at the dark clouds. She could see nothing with the telescope that she had not seen with her naked eyes, except, perhaps, she thought, it appears a bit darker.

Bosun LaSalle came up the ladder from the deck, paused at the top step until Mr. Selkirk nodded permission for him to come on the quarterdeck, and then went and stood beside Charley. He managed an approving look at Lady Caroline.

"Little broad to run around, do you think?" Theo LaSalle said.

"I think we'll do better to run through it," Charley Selkirk said.

Theo LaSalle nodded his agreement.

Lady Caroline wondered if LaSalle were seeking an opinion or tactfully offering one.

"Is it going to be rough, Mr. Selkirk?" she asked. For some reason, her question had startled him. He turned quickly to her, accidentally but firmly brushing her bosom with his arm. He withdrew it as if the contact had burned him. He stole a quick look at her, his face flushed, and he looked away. Like a frightened fawn, she thought.

"There will be, I fear, a quickening of the winds, and an increase in the seas," he said pompously. "It was for that reason, Lady Caroline, that I suggested, and suggest now, that you will be more comfortable below decks."

He nodded at her, a gesture of dismissal, and turned to the bosun.

"I think we had better start taking in canvas, everything, I think, above the main yards," he said.

"Aye, aye, sir," Theo LaSalle said. "And the sprit?"

"Take everything down from the sprit," Mr. Selkirk ordered.

"Watch aloft the bowsprit," Theo LaSalle called out, making a megaphone of his hands. "Take in the bowsprit topgallant, and the sprit topgallant!"

Seamen began to make their way forward and onto the footlines below *The Eleanor*'s bowsprit. Then they climbed out over *The Eleanor*'s figurehead, a twice-lifesized carving of a lady with her arms folded modestly over her naked bosom, so that there was nothing beneath their feet but the ocean, and then even further out, and further up, to the bowsprit yard. They reefed the sail there up against its yard by hand, because there was no way to apply the power of the capstan to the bowsprit rigging.

Lady Caroline watched with interest, impressed again with what she thought of as the organized confusion involved with operating the ship. It reminded her, in many ways, of ants scurrying back and forth around an ant heap.

And then there was a cry, an excited cry that she couldn't quite make out. She saw Charley Selkirk, a look of horror on his face, step quickly to the rail.

Then another cry, an excited shout: "Man overboard on the port side!"

"Careless son of a whore!" Theo LaSalle exploded, forgetting Lady Caroline's presence.

"Ahoy on deck, throw a barrel over the side!" Mr. Selkirk shouted.

Bosun LaSalle rushed to the port rail of the quarterdeck and looked down into the water.

"He's swimming, Mr. Selkirk," he reported.

"Bring her around, Mr. O'Keefe, hard to starboard," Mr. Selkirk said.

"Hard to starboard it is, sir," the quartermaster replied, and the helmsmen literally jumped on the wheel, using their weight to turn it.

"I'll have all hands on deck," Mr. Selkirk said. "Prepare to launch the longboat."

"All hands on deck and aloft," the bosun shouted. "Longboatmen to the longboat!"

"Take in everything as soon as we're about," Mr. Selkirk said, and walked to the skylight hatch over the master's cabin. He pulled it open and called, "Man overboard, Father!"

He forgot himself then, Lady Caroline saw. It was the first time she had ever heard him refer to his father as anything but "Captain."

He then ran to the fantail rail and looked over the side.

"Where away?" he called, as he frantically examined the water for the missing seaman.

"He should be directly aft," Theo LaSalle called, as he moved quickly to join Charley at the rail.

The Eleanor was heeling sharply as she turned. Lady Caroline had to steady herself against the rail to keep her footing.

Mr. Porter, the chief mate, bounded up the ladder to the quarterdeck, with Mr. Dillon, the second mate, on his heels. Both were hatless and showed signs of having just jumped up from their beds. A moment later, Captain Selkirk came up the ladder from his cabin, stepped on deck, stopped and tucked his shirt in his trousers, and looked first up at the rigging, then at the storm approaching from what was now starboard. Then he joined his son and the Bosun at the stern rail.

"I've ordered a barrel over the side, and the longboat readied, sir," Mr. Selkirk said to his father. Lady Caroline saw his enormous relief that his father had shown up to take charge. But no sooner had she thought this then she saw that

233

Captain Selkirk had no intention of taking responsibility from his son's shoulders.

"You have the helm, Mr. Selkirk," Captain Selkirk said coldly. "Do whatever you think is necessary."

With maddening slowness, *The Eleanor* made her turn, reversing direction.

"There's the barrel!" Theo LaSalle called. Lady Caroline walked to the side of the quarterdeck and looked out over the ocean. She saw the barrel, and saw for the first time that ropes were fastened to it, making loops, and for the first time she understood its purpose. It would keep the man who had fallen into the sea afloat. *If* he could swim to it.

But she saw nothing else on the gently rolling swells of the sea. The man who had gone overboard was nowhere in sight.

The turn was completed.

"Reef all sails!" Mr. Selkirk ordered, and the bosun shouted the order to the men in the rigging. Immediately, the mizzen, main and foresails began to be pulled up to their yards. The other sails were let loose, to flap in the wind. *The Eleanor* immediately began to lose way.

"Look alive up there, for God's sake!" Mr. Selkirk called up to the men in the rigging. His voice was tinged with anguish and impatience. Lady Caroline understood that he was urging them to find the seaman who had gone overboard, rather than to greater effort with the sails.

"Can't see a thing, Mr. Selkirk," a voice called down.

"You take the longboat, Theo," Mr. Selkirk said. "Launch it when you're ready."

"Aye, aye, sir," the bosun said, and ran down the ladder to the main deck, and to where the longboat, normally stowed upside down over the main hatch, was already dangling from block and tackle over the starboard rail. The sailors who would man it were already in it.

Selkirk watched as Theo LaSalle clambered aboard, and the boat dropped out of sight. Then he turned to look at his father.

"Can you think of anything else to do, Mr. Selkirk?" his father asked, coldly. From the tone of Captain Selkirk's voice, and the stricken look on Charley's face, Lady Caroline decided the question was a criticism of Charley's performance, and she felt terribly sorry for him and angry with his father for not helping him when he needed help.

Charley shook his head no.

"No, Captain," he said, when he found his voice. "I cannot."

"Longboat's in the water and under way!" someone shouted from the deck. In a moment, Lady Caroline saw it bobbing on the surface of the sea, with the bosun on his knees at the tiller and the six sets of oars dipping regularly into the water as it crossed the water to the lifesaving barrel.

There was no sight of the seaman.

"If you were to take the helm, sir," Mr. Selkirk said to his father, "I could go aloft and look for myself."

"You are the officer of the deck, sir," his father said, icily. "Your place is on the quarterdeck."

Charley, Lady Caroline saw, tried hard not to show it, but she could tell that what his father had said was like a slap on the face.

The Eleanor was now dead in the water. Lady Caroline could hear the sea slapping at the flat expanse of the rudder.

Selkirk looked at his father, who met his glance but said nothing. Lady Caroline knew that the son was wordlessly asking his father for assistance, for guidance, and that Captain Selkirk was refusing to give either.

Charles Selkirk looked away, and then at the approaching storm, which now filled a quarter of the horizon, and then at the longboat, and then up at the rigging, and finally back at the storm. Caroline could now see bolts of lightning.

She looked at Charley. His face was white and strained. She sensed that he had to make some kind of decision, but she had no idea what.

Charley took a breath, let it out, and then issued the order: "Let fly the main and the mizzen. Mr. O'Keefe, when we have way, turn her into the wind."

"Into the wind, aye, sir," the quartermaster replied.

The main and mizzen mast sails fluttered down and filled with dull popping sounds.

Lady Caroline wondered why they were going to start moving again, if they hadn't found the seaman who had gone overboard. And then she understood: the ship had to be moving, so it could be controlled, by the time the storm reached them. Even, she understood, if that meant abandoning the search for the man in the water.

"Aloft!" Mr. Selkirk shouted, impatiently, desperately. "What see you?"

There was no reply.

235

Mr. Selkirk took the leather megaphone from Tony and walked to the rail.

"Bosun!" he bellowed. "Leave the barrel, and bring the longboat alongside."

Lady Caroline was surprised, at the sound of his voice. She wondered why, and then understood. To judge from the predicament he was in, and his pained face, she had expected that he would sound like the boy he was. But the command, she understood, had been issued by a man, and had sounded like it.

The Eleanor now began to crawl through the water, as the full sails began to move her. As soon as there was steerage, the quartermaster began to turn her so that she would be heading into the approaching storm.

She looked at Charley, and found him looking at her.

"Lady Caroline," he said furiously, "if you don't go below now, I will have you carried below."

When she stared at him in disbelief that he would talk to her in that tone of voice, he made a gesture foreward. She looked where he gestured. The black clouds, laced with lightning, were now a wall reaching up to heaven, no more than a hundred yards or so away. She went quickly down the ladder to the main deck. She heard the first drops of rain strike the canvas with a little popping sound as she reached the deck, and by the time she reached the passageway to the cabin, it was raining hard.

3

The storm struck suddenly. By the time she reached the wardroom, intending to have a cup of tea, it was apparent that drinking tea was out of the question for the time being. *The Eleanor* began to shudder as her bow encountered wind-driven waves, and then she began to dip her bow in the troughs between them. Then, for reasons Caroline did not understand, the ship began to rock from side to side.

She made her way with difficulty to the wardroom table, sat down, and then had to hold onto the table, which was fixed to the deck, to keep her chair from sliding, with her in it, with the movement of the ship. She could hear the pounding of the rain on the ship, and the creaking of the rigging, and there came a series of blasts of thunder that sounded as if lightning were striking just outside the wardroom door.

None of this, Lady Caroline noticed with annoyance, seemed to bother Mistress Mary Selkirk, who moved around the room as if the pitching deck were neither moving or slippery. Mary actually opened the port and looked out of it as if it were a window in a country cottage somewhere, not a hole in a ship with towering foam-crested waves inches away.

No more than thirty minutes after it had struck, the storm ended as suddenly as it had begun. The thunder stopped, and then the pitching and heaving of *The Eleanor*, and then Lady Caroline became aware that the steady drumming of the rain could no longer be heard.

Final proof that they were through the storm came when *The Eleanor* heeled steeply again, obviously turning around again. Lady Caroline got to her feet and went to the passageway.

"It will be slippery on deck, I fear, Lady Caroline," Mary Selkirk warned.

"I'll manage, thank you," she said. She wondered why it was so important that she rush on deck again. She was, she then understood, concerned with Charley Selkirk. With his father so coldheartedly refusing to help him, letting him sink or swim, it was natural, she told herself, for her to be concerned. With Charley, and, of course, the seaman.

The deck was slippery wet, and she nearly lost her footing on the ladder to the quarterdeck. The instant she reached that, she was suddenly drenched with water that had gathered in the folds of the reefed mizzen sail and was spilled out as the mizzen sail was let fly.

Charley was the only officer on the quarterdeck, and she saw that he had been soaked by the rain but was otherwise apparently all right. She was relieved and concerned at once. His hair was plastered to his head, and his shirt and trousers to his body. If he didn't get out of his wet clothing, he was liable to catch a chill.

She wondered where the other officers were, and why they weren't on the quarterdeck, helping Charley. When she looked around, she saw that Mr. Porter was on the main deck, looking over the rail on one side, and Mr. Dillon on the other. It took her a moment to locate Captain Selkirk, who had climbed the rigging of the foremast. She saw that they were now in pursuit of the wall of rain of the storm, going back where they had been.

No one paid a bit of attention to her, or to Mary Selkirk when she appeared on the quarterdeck a moment later.

"Ahoy the quarterdeck!" a voice from aloft shouted. "The barrel bears dead ahead."

"Steady as she goes," Mr. Selkirk said to the quartermaster, and then shouted to the men in the rigging to keep a sharp eye.

They sailed for ten minutes. The sea was now almost glassy smooth, and almost without swell. Lady Caroline saw the lifesaving barrel float past them. They sailed ten minutes beyond the barrel. Mr. Selkirk looked into the rigging where his father was hanging from the shrouds.

Why doesn't he help him? Lady Caroline thought angrily.

They sailed another five minutes. If we haven't found that man by now, Lady Caroline thought, we're not going to find him. And then she realized that was precisely the thought Charley must have in his mind. The difference was that he was going to have to make that opinion into a decision.

Damn his father! she thought. Why is he doing that to him? Why doesn't he say, "You've done all that can be done"?

There were tears in Charley's eyes when he finally, a minute later, made the decision himself.

"Bring her around, Mr. O'Keefe," Charles Selkirk ordered. "Steer north nor'west."

"North nor'west, aye, sir," the quartermaster said.

Lady Caroline thought that Mr. Selkirk appeared to be on the edge of losing control of himself. She saw that his hands, balled into white-knuckled fists, were shaking. She watched as he forced them open, until the fingers were spread. She saw him swallow hard, and then walk to the railing overlooking the deck.

"Bosun," he ordered matter-of-factly in his under-control man's voice, "as we pass the barrel, see if you can get a hook on it. And when we've passed it, stow the longboat."

Lady Caroline became aware that she was being chilled as the wind blew against her water-soaked dress. She could feel water running down her chest and down her legs. She would just have to put up with that, she decided. She was determined to stay on the quarterdeck and see this through. She watched as Bosun LaSalle stationed three men with grappling hooks fastened to coils of rope along the port railing. They straddled the railing, one leg hanging over the side, and then, as *The Eleanor* came up to the lifesaving barrel in the water, they began to swing the grappling hooks in vertical circles. Then, one at a time, they let loose the ropes, dropping the hooks into the sea, trying to catch the lines of the barrel.

The first two hooks missed the life-saving barrel's life-lines, but the third hook caught one of them. The barrel began to move with the ship, bouncing against the force of the water.

"Get two hooks on it before you try to bring it aboard," Mr. Selkirk called out.

That was a simple matter, and soon the barrel was being pulled over the side. As if that were some kind of cue, the quartermaster stepped to the binnacle and stepped on a little lever. The ship's bell rang, clang-clang, and then a double clang three more times.

"Eight bells it is, sir," the quartermaster called out.

"I relieve you, sir," Mr. Porter said to Mr. Selkirk, tipping his tricorn to him.

Selkirk looked at him, and then turned to examine the compass.

"The ship is underway and on a north nor'westerly course, sir," Selkirk said to the chief mate. "I report the loss of Seaman Dooley."

"You'll enter it in the log, sir?"

"Aye, aye, sir," Mr. Selkirk said. "I stand relieved, sir." He tipped his tricorn to Mr. Porter, and looking at no one, walked down the ladder to the deck.

"Mr. Porter," Captain Selkirk said. "Please muster the crew at the next change of watch. We'll say a service for Dooley."

"Aye, aye, sir," Mr. Porter said.

Lady Caroline had not seen him come down from the rigging and onto the quarterdeck. He had waited until Charley had gone through the whole silly routine. She looked at him with disdain in her eyes. He smiled at her.

"Lady Caroline," Captain Selkirk said, "you're soaking wet."

"I had noticed, Captain," Lady Caroline said icily. "But thank you for your concern." Then she went down the ladder, onto the main deck.

4

Lady Caroline had hoped she would meet Charley Selkirk in the passageway on her way to her cabin. She felt terribly sorry for him and wanted to say something to him that might comfort him. Perhaps something nasty about his father's callous treatment of him, so that he would know he was not just feeling sorry for himself.

But he was not in the companionway, and she went to her cabin and started to take off her wet dress. Then she stopped, and went back out of her cabin and made her way to the arms locker cabin where he lived. She had her hand raised to knock when she considered what she was doing and stopped. She leaned her head against the door, trying to make the right decision.

And then she heard him crying.

He wasn't sniffling, he was sobbing, crying like a woman. Her first urge was to go inside and comfort him like a mother. Then she realized that would be exactly the wrong thing to do. He did not need to be reminded of his youth and vulnerability.

She turned from the door and ran back down the companionways to her cabin, and rummaged through her cases until she found Edgar's silver cognac flask. She took two glasses from the chest of drawers and went back to Charley's cabin door. She raised her hand to knock, then lowered it, and worked the latch instead.

He was standing against the bulkhead, still dressed, leaning on both hands and looking out the porthole. He turned around when he heard her. His eyes were cold on her, but they also gave evidence that he had been crying.

"I thought," she said, surprised at the timidity of her voice, "that you might like to have a drink of brandy."

"I am in no mood for you right now," he said flatly.

"All right," she said, and started to leave.

"Leave the cognac," he said. "Maybe that's what I need."

She walked to him, handed him a glass, and then poured cognac into it.

He drank it down.

"Dooley was a friend of mine," he said. "The man we lost overboard."

"Was that his name?"

"Yes," he said bitterly. "That was his name. And God forgive me, if it wasn't for me, he'd still be alive."

"Don't be a fool," she said. "It wasn't your fault."

"But it was," he said. "I ordered him out there. And then I couldn't handle the ship well enough to find him and pick him up."

"You're being a fool again," she said. "Your father may be a cold-blooded bastard, but he would have stopped his training of you short of losing a seaman to make his point."

"You don't understand the sea," he said. Then he smiled. " 'Cold-blooded bastard'? Is that what you think of him?"

"I did before," she said, and smiled back at him. "But I just realized that he was right. He let you make your own decisions. The proof that you made the right ones is that he didn't countermand any order you gave."

He looked at her out of his light blue eyes as he considered that, and then he nodded. She could see the salty track a tear had left on his cheek, and it was all she could do to stop herself from taking a handkerchief and wiping it away.

" 'Cold-blooded bastard,' " he quoted again, and smiled again.

"You're embarrassing me," she said.

"Don't mean to," he said. "I'd never do that."

"It's all right," she said.

"Will Dooley was a year older than me," he began to explain. "From a farm upriver. I mean, upriver from Philadelphia. His family's farmers . . ."

And then the sobbing burst out of him again, surprising her. He turned from her in embarrassment, and leaned against the bulkhead. She put her arms around him, as well as she could, not quite succeeding because of his bulk.

He got control of himself in a moment and found his voice.

"I dreamed of you holding me," he said, trying to make a joke. "But it wasn't quite like this, what I was thinking."

"Turn around," she said.

He didn't move for a moment, and she felt his back swell against her breasts as he took a deep breath. Then he turned around.

He put his arms around her, very gently, as if he was afraid he would hurt her.

"You must think me a fool," he said.

"I thought you were magnificent this morning," she said.

241

"Goddamn you, don't make fun of me!" he said.

She had become aware that he was erect.

"Charley," she said.

He looked down at her.

She raised her face to be kissed. As if it had a mind of its own, her right hand dropped off his arm, and moved between them.

5

Lady Caroline Watchbury had just stepped out of her dress when there was a knock at her cabin door.

"Who is it?" she snapped.

"Captain Selkirk."

"One moment, please, Captain," she said, and looked for her robe. When she put it on, she noticed that her nipples were erect and sensitive. Probably from the chill of her wet dress, she decided. Then she thought, wet dress, hell, Charley Selkirk was responsible. She tied the robe and went to the door.

"I saw how soaked you were on deck," Captain Selkirk said. "How'd that happen?"

"Water, rain, spilled from one of the sails," she said.

He gave her a smile. She knew that kind of male smile. It meant that a man wanted something. She did not return it.

He held up a narrow-necked, flat-bottomed flask. "This is French cognac," he said. "The real thing. Not the South African stuff I usually pass off as French."

"That's very kind of you, Captain," she said, stiffly. She would normally have refused it, she thought, but taking it seemed to be the easiest way out of the situation. She reached for the bottle. Instead of giving it to her, he stepped into her cabin and closed the door behind him.

Lady Caroline immediately concluded, furiously, that he was going to make some kind of an advance to her, and assumed what she hoped would be a sufficiently aloof manner to discourage him.

"Forgive me, Captain," she said, haughtily. "But is it seemly for you to be in here with the door closed?"

He turned and looked at her, then turned and took a glass from a rack and poured cognac into it, and handed it to her. Then he tilted the bottle up and drank from the neck.

"If you have not noticed, Captain, I am not dressed."

"Seemly on my ship is whatever I do, Lady Caroline," he said.

She flushed, and wondered if he had been drinking. Was he going to rape her? Why now, of all times, without overtures of any kind?

She remembered that Alexei had taken her the first time by force. That had been very exciting. This would be obscene. Captain or not, she decided that Captain Selkirk was going to have to fight her. Perhaps, if she screamed loud enough, someone would come. But that someone might be Charley. She had half expected it to be Charley when she'd heard the knock. She couldn't have Charley and his father fighting over her.

Was this the way God was punishing her for what she had done?

"I have watched what you have been doing to my son," Captain Selkirk said.

What did he say?

"I beg your pardon?"

"I'm an observant man, Lady Caroline," Captain Paul Selkirk said. "But I didn't have to be to see you always rubbing up against him, and breathing on his ear, and the like."

"How dare you speak to me that way?" she demanded, now genuinely angry. She had done nothing of the kind. Not until forty-five minutes ago, anyway, when the Devil had taken her hand and guided it to Charley's swollen hard organ.

"You didn't hear me," he said. "This is my ship, and I do what I will, and say what I will, without permission from anyone."

"I'll thank you to leave my cabin," she said, and stopped herself just in time from threatening to call someone if he didn't.

"When I'm through saying what I came to say," he said calmly.

"Which is?"

"You're through teasing him," Captain Selkirk said. "You'll either give him what you've been promising, or you'll not go near him again."

"How dare you?" she hissed.

"He has just now crossed a bridge that few men cross," he

243

said. "A man has died at his orders. A man who was a friend of his."

"I know," she said, "about him and Dooley being friends."

"Do you now?" he said. She had the feeling he wasn't listening to her. "And he has enough weighing on him right now," Captain Selkirk went on, "without the torment of wondering whether an older woman is playing with him. Do I make my point?"

"You have the . . . the *audacity,* the *audacity* to come in here and make a suggestion that I . . ." she was having a hard time choosing her words, but she plunged on, "that I have been *enticing* your son?"

"Aye, I am," he said. "What I'll saying to you, and you'd best heed me well, is that you make up your mind between going into him now, taking this with you." He set the flat-bottomed bottle of cognac on her chest of drawers. "And making good on your promise, or staying away from him."

She glowered at him, unable to think of anything to say to him.

"So far as I know, he's never been with a woman," he said. "So this is a good time for him."

And then she began to laugh.

"What's funny?" he snarled. "There has to be a first time for every man."

"You're a little late, Captain," she said.

"I don't take your meaning," he said.

"I just came from Charley's cabin," she said.

He looked at her a long moment, without expression.

"Then perhaps you're not quite the selfish bitch I thought you were," he said. Then he nodded his head at her and walked out of her cabin.

She couldn't understand her behavior. She could never remember having been so insulted, so humiliated, in her life, as she had been just now by Captain Paul Selkirk. Nor could she really believe that she had said to him what she had. Nor that she wasn't crushed with shame now that she had.

But she wasn't.

She became aware of the untouched cognac in the glass in her hand. She tossed it down, and felt the warmth spread through her stomach.

"*Goddamn* you, Paul Selkirk," she said aloud. She poured cognac in her glass again and drank it down.

The really incredible thing, she thought, was that it had

244

been better with Charley Selkirk than it had ever been before. Even better than with Alexei. She couldn't understand that, or explain it, but that's the way it was.

6

Durham Furnace, Pennsylvania
February 16, 1770

So far as Captain Richard MacMullen, master of *The Mary* was concerned, it was one hell of a lot of wasted effort he was about, carrying three dozen Pennsylvania rifles (actually, they were Connecticut rifles, for that's where he'd found them, at Mystic, in a ship chandlers) all the way upriver from Philadelphia to Durham Furnace, when they would just have to be hauled back downriver again when Captain Selkirk wanted them.

He hadn't asked Selkirk what he was doing with the rifles. If Paul Selkirk had wanted him to know, he would have told him. He'd found a market for them somewhere, at a good price, and that was all that counted. All Richard MacMullen knew was that he was supposed to buy as many of the rifles, best quality, as he could, someplace where no questions about them would be asked. That was all he had to know, and all he wanted to know.

He had the rifles packed six to a roll of canvas. The rifles were generously coated with sperm oil, then wrapped in cotton cloth, then tied together, then wrapped in oilcloth, and finally in sturdy canvas. There were six rolls of six rifles each, and he was pleased with the packing. It would protect the rifles no matter where Paul Selkirk hauled them, after they had been hauled back and forth upriver to the woman whom Selkirk, for reasons MacMullen could not fathom, had married.

The Delaware wasn't frozen over at the moment, but it was likely to be anytime, so he'd been unable to go upriver by boat. He'd had to rent a dray wagon, two horses, and even a driver to haul the rifles, and he had to bring with him two men from *The Mary* who made it plain without saying out loud that they would have much preferred to spend all of the two weeks *The Mary* would be in home port with their families, instead of wasting four days, maybe five, taking some rifles to the woman Captain Selkirk had married.

MacMullen had liked the forge operator, Nils Johnson, the few times he had met him before he died, and he had disliked, every time he'd met her, the woman he was married to. But now that she was married to Paul Selkirk, he had to stay on the right side of her and keep his opinions of the cold-blooded Swede bitch to himself.

As the dray wagon rode the last several hundred yards from the road they'd turned onto from the Bethlehem Pike, he had the first pleasant thought he'd had since leaving Philadelphia. The present Mistress Selkirk, unlike the first, was more than likely not going to insist they stay for dinner. If that was the case, just as soon as they got rid of the rifles it seemed worth the chance to go the other five miles to the Delaware, to see if it was not frozen, and maybe catch a riverboat back to Philadelphia. It would be quicker than returning with the dray wagon, even if he had had to pay for a round trip, and if he could get them on a boat, they could have something to drink to make the journey pass more quickly. He did not enjoy drinking in a wagon.

And he had not been able to take a drink on the way up, for the new Mistress Selkirk had, even before she'd married Paul Selkirk, let him know what she thought of masters who drank with their men.

If luck was really with him, he thought, Mistress Selkirk would not be at the house at all. He could then just turn the rifles over to one of her sons and be on his way. He could get his money back for them later.

Mistress Selkirk didn't seem to be at home, but neither did her sons. Captain MacMullen thought that was strange, for farms were seldom left entirely deserted. It was too easy to steal things from a deserted farmhouse.

He checked first in the barn, and there was nothing in there but the animals, including Paul Selkirk's mare, Lucy. As he walked back toward the dray wagon, which he had ordered stopped by the barn, closer to the road than the house, he saw what looked to him like the flicker of a candle, or an open fire in a hearth, in the back room of the farmhouse.

Maybe she was in her bed, he thought. Sick. And hadn't heard his knock at the door.

There was a crack in the shutter over the window, and he glanced through it as he made his way to the back door.

He was right about the open fire, and he was right about her being in bed. But Mistress Selkirk wasn't sick, and the skinny, naked, red-headed son-of-a-bitch shoving it to her wasn't Captain Paul Selkirk.

MacMullen ran quickly back to the dray wagon and told the driver that something had come up, they would be going back to Philadelphia right away.

"What's up, Captain?" one of his men asked.

"If I wanted you to know, I'd tell you," MacMullen said.

"Oh," the sailor said, suspecting what MacMullen had seen through the window. "Wasn't expecting callers, huh?"

"You say one more word, I'll feed you your balls," MacMullen said.

Chapter Thirteen

1

Nürnberg
February 17, 1770

Chief Sergeant Karl Lahrner of the Cavalry Squadron of the Hessian Regiment spent nine days with Sergeant Heine Kramer of the Bavarian Household Cavalry in Munich before starting back to Nürnburg. Near two weeks, he had decided, was long enough a time for Willi to be with Trude of the Golden Ram.

Lahrner was very fond of both Willi and Willi's father. So far as he was concerned the only real mistake Hauptmann Baron von Kolbe had made in all the years Lahrner had known him, and that was a *long* time, one shy of a dozen campaigns, was that he had let his wife lead him a little too deeply into the arms of Martin Luther.

Lahrner himself was a good Protestant, who once a month marched into Saint Elizabeth's with the troopers of the Squadron of Cavalry in full dress uniform behind him. And he would quite literally have laid down his life for Baroness von Kolbe, if it came to that. But the woman paid a little too much attention to what Luther had to say about earthly pleasures.

As devoutly as he believed that having been baptized in Jesus Christ would see him, when his time came, passing before Saint Peter at the gates and being admitted to heaven, he believed that cavalrymen were entitled to a sound horse, a Solingen saber (maybe now, a saber *and* a pair of English horse-pistols), a mug of beer, a flask of wine, and a woman's body, with or without marriage.

He found nothing wrong with a man being faithful to his wife. *He* didn't have one, but he could see the logic in that sort of arrangement, providing you were in garrison. But on a campaign, a cavalry trooper was as much entitled to relax with a woman under his blankets as he was to the blankets themselves.

Frau Baron von Kolbe believed that being with any woman you didn't happen to be married to was a sin, and she used her unfortunately strong influence on the Hauptmann von Kolbe to keep his married troopers as faithful to their wives at home as he was, and to keep the young troopers "unsullied" until they were married. So far as Lahrner was concerned, a virginal cavalry trooper was as unnatural as a three-headed horse.

So far as Wilhelm von Kolbe was concerned, Chief Sergeant Karl Lahrner thought him a good lad, as bright as they came, and brave, and when he was a man, he would be as good a man as father. But as sure as the sun rose, he was going to get himself involved with women when he was left all alone in England. He was a good-looking, sturdy young man, attractive to women, and one of them, unless Willi knew what the whole arrangement was about, was sure to get her claws in him.

What Willi had to learn, Lahrner had decided on the ride down from Marburgan an der Lahn, was first what it was like to be with a woman, and second, that as much fun as it might be, that getting a woman in your bed was not really important enough to get yourself in trouble over.

He had explained the situation to Trude before he left for Munich. He had to pay her, of course, and that was money well spent, but he knew Trude well enough to be able to tell that her interest in Willi was not entirely professional. Mixed business and pleasure, so to speak.

Lahrner rather smugly decided from the look on Willi's face when he walked into the Golden Ram that things had gone as he intended them to go. Willi was disappointed to see him. Well, that was another lesson he had to learn: sooner or later, every woman you got in your bed you had to get out.

"Why aren't you at Muller und Thane?" Lahrner demanded.

"The son's back from Frankfurt am Main," Willi reported. "And the instruments are ready to go."

"Let's have a look," Lahrner said.

As they crossed the street to Muller und Thane's establishment, Lahrner asked Willi if he had been behaving himself.

249

Willi blushed. Karl Lahrner did not press it.

Willi led him to a rear room in the building and showed him the crates. There were three telescopes, each of them packed the same way in sturdy wooden crates, their parts cushioned with straw and cloth padding. The telescopes themselves went into long crates; the three-legged mounts into longer, thinner crates; and the clockwork mechanisms which somehow made the moon and the stars stand still all night went into rather elaborate, well-finished chests. Willi explained, very seriously, that he had learned from Herr Thane that the clockworks were the most delicate of all the parts and had to be handled accordingly.

They went next to the riverfront, where Lahrner arranged for the charter of a riverboat, a flat-bottomed affair more a barge than a boat, large enough to carry all of them, and their horses, and fodder for the horses. It came with a crew of two skilled riverboatmen. The troopers would be pressed into service as sailors.

Lahrner then took Willi aside and told him he was obliged to spend that night with the three troopers, both to make sure they were prepared to begin the journey in the morning and to buy them a good meal, to make them feel good. Willi would have to fend for himself that night, Lahrner said, and he should not wait up for him to return, because he would be out late.

Willi, Lahrner saw, had more than a little trouble concealing his surprise and pleasure that he would have one more night with Trude.

The next morning, after a hearty breakfast at the Golden Ram, they left Nürnberg. There was a mast and a sail on the boat, but they were not of much use until they reached the Main River at Bamberg. From Nürnberg to Bamberg, the boat was propelled by their horses, harnesses attached to a stanchion on the boat, walking along the bank.

From Nürnberg to Furth, where the Pegnitz River flowed into the Regnitz, was only a few miles, and they reached it within hours of leaving Nürnberg. From Furth to Bamberg was a two-day trip, following the curves of the river at the slow pace of the walking horses.

It took a week from Bamberg to Frankfurt, half the distance being dragged by the horses and the second half with the horses aboard the boat, the sail moving the boat only slightly faster than the current itself.

Some nights, they stopped at riverside *Gasthauses* for a hot meal, but they always slept aboard the boat. Lahrner considered himself back on duty now and wasn't drinking at all. The telescopes were worth a good deal of money, and he explained to Willi that when things were stolen along the river, they were seldom recovered, for it would take an army to search all of the boats along the major rivers.

Almost as soon as they reached Frankfurt am Main a detachment of the Cavalry Squadron trotted up, led by Willi's father. The Cavalry Squadron commander would not normally accompany a detail sent to pick up three crates for the landgrave, and Willi knew his father had come to say goodbye.

They had an hour together, surprisingly awkward. His father said that he was going to accompany Grand Duke Alexei to Petergrad in the spring, more to accompany the telescope than the grand duke, and for that reason Willi had better prepare to spend the next summer in England.

"Actually," his father said, "the longer you stay away, the better. I suspect that His Imperial Highness is going to try very hard to think of a good reason he should not return to the University. You can't come home of course, while he's still there."

Baron von Kolbe gave Willi a purse of gold from the landgrave, to pay his expenses, and then a smaller purse of gold from himself, and finally a package from Willi's mother. "There's a Bible in there, and some other things."

As soon as the crates with the telescope intended for the tsar had been unloaded from the boat and strapped (with considerable difficulty) onto pack horses, his father and the cavalry detachment headed for Marburg. Willi was able to keep back his tears when he said goodbye to his father, and to manfully shake his hand, but he felt terrible. This was really goodbye. There was no telling when—or if—he would see his father, or his mother, or his family again.

Before the cavalrymen were out of sight, Lahrner ordered their journey resumed, and by nightfall, they were tied up east of Mainz, where the Main flows into the Rhine. Lahrner produced a bottle of wine as Willi sat disconsolate on the bow of the riverboat, watching the black water of the river swirl past.

Lahrner's kindness made things worse, and Willi, a little

drunk, blurted out the confession that he had been in bed with Trude.

"You little bastard, you!" Lahrner said. "The minute you get a chance you pull up the skirts of your friend's doxies, do you?" Then he laughed. "I know that you've been taught all your life, Willi, by good Christian believers in the teachings of Martin Luther, that if you put your thing in any woman without some pastor giving you his and God's permission, that it's somehow worse than stealing, or murder. But don't you believe it."

"You're not mad?"

"With Trude in heat, and you feeling your oats, God himself couldn't have stopped it from happening."

He punched Willi in the arm. It was a painful blow, but it was at the same time a rare gesture of affection. Willi felt his eyes began to tear again.

It took them almost two weeks to get from Mainz to Nijmegen, on the Dutch border, including a three-day layover in Cologne to care for a sick horse, and another three days from Nijmegen to Rotterdam.

They had trouble in Rotterdam. The master of the ship on which Lahrner first booked passage had flatly refused to accept one of the landgrave's drafts on the Rothschild Bank in Frankfurt, and sailed without them. So did the next two masters Lahrner tried to deal with.

Lahrner then spent two days seeking audience with the prince of the port, who normally did not deal with noncommissioned officers. But when he finally agreed to see Lahrner, and Lahrner explained his problem, the prince arranged for a Rotterdam banker to promise to make good the landgrave's draft, and they finally got a ship.

It wasn't what Lahrner wanted. He was furious to learn that most shipmasters regarded horses as filthy beasts and refused to carry them aboard at any price. They finally settled for a fishing boat, whose master rigged a sling to lower the animals into a hold reeking of dead fish.

On the twentieth day of March, 1770, the *Queen of Peace* raised her sails and made her way out of Rotterdam harbor and into the North Sea, bound for London.

They sailed close by the Hook of Holland, and then turned west. When the *Queen of Peace* began to dip her bow into the waves, her master saw the look of concern on Chief Sergeant Karl Lahrner's face, and told him that they were about to have a little weather, but there was nothing to worry about.

<h1 style="text-align:center">2</h1>

London
March 5, 1770

Two letters from Durham Furnace, one six weeks old and one not quite four weeks, the latter fresh that day from Pennsylvania, awaited Captain Paul Selkirk at the East India Company's docks in London. They were delivered to him aboard *The Eleanor* by the senior of H.M. customs officials who came to inspect the vessel.

Having aboard the widow of Colonel Sir Edgar Watchbury, and the body itself—having sailed, in other words, under a Royal Warrant—changed very little so far as H.M. Customs was concerned. Beneath a veneer of courtesy, a pretense that as a Pennsylvanian, Captain Selkirk was just as much a loyal Englishman as any H.M. customs officer himself, and as eager to comply fully with both health regulations and the Tariff and Navigation Acts, *The Eleanor*'s log was carefully examined to see if she had indeed come to London from Tatta via Cape town, when she said she had. Her holds were carefully searched to confirm that her cargo was indeed Indian raw silk and piece goods, and not finished goods manufactured against the law (and more important, to the detriment of industry in the home islands).

Selkirk had played the game with H.M. customs officials in London before. He knew full well that among the "workmen" going down into his holds was at least one officer who would identify himself to members of *The Eleanor*'s crew and remind them that H.M. government was prepared to pay a bounty of at least ten percent, and sometimes more, of the value of a confiscated cargo, or vessel, to whoever reported violations of the law to H.M. Customs.

He wasn't worried about his cargo, for there was nothing illegal aboard, and he wasn't worried about his crew, for their mouths were sealed, both out of loyalty to him personally and for fear their crewmates would slit the throat of an informer. Selkirk suspected that H.M. customs officer, who was

253

no fool, knew that he wasn't going to find a violation aboard *The Eleanor*, but they had to play out the game.

He had the officer to his cabin and offered him the South African "French" brandy while the inspection was being carried out. The customs officer sent one of his men as a messenger to the Household Cavalry Barracks to inform them that Colonel Sir Edgar Watchbury's body was aboard.

Selkirk, very formally, begged the custom officer's leave to read his mail.

"By all means, Captain."

In her first, older, letter Ingebord Johnson Selkirk wrote that she had been relieved to learn that Mary was with him. He had expected something like that, references to God's mercy, and to ungrateful children being like a serpent's tooth, and skimmed over the rest of it.

The second letter was strange and disturbing. Ingebord wrote that she was "very disappointed" that he had "taken advantage" of her "ignorance of certain matters" and that it had only recently "been made known to her" by a "certain unquestionable source" that the penalties for violation of H.M. Tariff and Navigation Acts were far more severe than he had led her to believe. "Conscious disobedience of lawfully constituted authority was as much a sin as conscious disobedience to the laws of God," she wrote, and urged him to reconsider, both for the sake of his children, for whom he professed such love, and for "the sake of his own immortal soul," his role in the certain matters that he would understand she meant. For her own part, she was "grateful to God" that her own involvement in certain matters had been "so innocent" that "her own conscience was clear." He would understand, she knew, that now that she "understood the consequences of certain matters," she would "no longer participate in anything like that."

Although he instantly regretted it, he crumbled the letters up and threw them out his porthole. Goddamned fool had been talking to some Bible-beating preacher, that was clear. Of all the mistakes he had made in his life, and God knew how many there had been, marrying that woman had been the worst.

There was a real danger, he understood, of her running off at the mouth to this "unquestionable source" of hers before he got to Pennsylvania and shut her up. But the rifles were gone, and so was the Pennsylvania-made ironwork, so there was no immediate danger.

The problem was that the "unquestionable source" might alert the authorities, and the authorities might pay more attention to him than they should. That could pose serious problems about getting the crucible-steel maker out of England. But that had gone too far to call off now. He would just have to take special pains to make sure that the steel maker wasn't on board when *The Eleanor* made Philadelphia.

By the time he'd thought all this through, he really regretted having thrown the letters out the port. He would have liked to be able to study them, to see just how much she lost her senses.

The inspection of *The Eleanor* took nearly two hours, but finally one of the "workmen," obviously an officer, came to Selkirk's cabin and told H.M. customs officer that all was in order.

"Will you have a glass of brandy with us?" Selkirk said, unable to resist the temptation to let H.M. customs officer know that he hadn't been fooled for a minute by the disguise.

The "workman" hesitated, then smiled.

"You are very kind, Captain," he said, discarding the pretense and taking a glass of the brandy.

"I presume that I may now begin to off-load my cargo and permit my crew to go ashore?"

"Certainly."

"Tony," Captain Selkirk said, "please inform Mr. Porter that he may begin to discharge our cargo."

He entertained H.M. customs officers with another glass of brandy, gave each of them a case of it, which they expected, and then started to see them ashore. As he reached the gangplank, two British cavalry officers rode onto the wharf and dismounted. There was no question who they were, officers to see about the casket he carried in the forward hold. He said goodbye to the customs officers and greeted the cavalry officers, then personally led them to Lady Caroline's cabin.

None of their business with her was any of his concern, so he went to the quarterdeck.

Mary was sitting on a three-legged stool, her back against the wheel, watching Charley supervise the unloading of the bales of raw silk. There were two ways to do it, one using a sort of human chain, with each forty-pound bale passed hand to hand from the hold to the deck and then down planks to the wharf. This method would have required an army of stevedores, and London's stevedores were known around the world for being able to steal anything that was not nailed down.

Selkirk had devised a system involving the use of the main sail yard and the capstan, which picked up half a wagonload of raw silk bales (or any similar cargo), a thousand pounds at once. It took six men on the windlass to raise the cargo from the hold; two men to swing it over the side and position it over the wagon on the wharf; one man on the wagon to loose the line when the material was in the wagon; and one officer, to issue the necessary orders.

Selkirk was pleased with his system, not just for here in London, but for other ports, especially African and West Indian, where if they suspected you were in a hurry to get unloaded, they would charge an arm and a leg. *The Eleanor* was self-sufficient. Her crew could load her and unload her, and that cut out theft of either cargo or ship's fittings just about completely. It also served to keep strangers from nosing around in *The Eleanor*'s holds, where they might see something Selkirk didn't want anybody to see.

He always paid into the trip fund what he would have had to pay for stevedore services, instead of putting it in his pocket. That kept the crew happy, for the trip fund money was divided on shares among the officers and men when they made home port.

"Mary, why are you wearing that dress?" Selkirk asked. The dress was much too small for her.

"It's one of the only two I have that come close to fitting me," Mary replied.

"Well, get your bag, or whatever else you need to go ashore, and come with me."

"Right now?" she asked.

"Aye," he said. "As soon as I can change my clothes. I've had two carriages waiting for an hour."

"Two?"

"One so your brother can see Lady Caroline safely to her home," he said.

Mary snorted.

"Don't mock things you don't understand, mistress," he said.

"I understand perfectly," she said.

256

"You just think you do," he said. "In any event, in thirty minutes you'll have seen the last of her."

"I'll go brush my hair," she said, and got up from the three-legged stool. He noticed that every time he looked at her, she seemed to be taller. And from the curves of her bosom and chest, it was evident that she was no longer a child, even if she sometimes acted like one.

"I'll have you in a bonnet," he said.

"I don't have a bonnet," she replied.

"Then we'll have to get you one," he said. He walked to where Charley stood at the quarterdeck railing directing the unloading; he waited until Charley sensed his presence and turned and tipped his hat.

"They've cleared us," Selkirk said. "I'll be taking Mary ashore with me. I've got to go to the bank, and on the way, I'm going to drop her at a seamstress where your mother bought her clothing. Mary's outgrown everything she brought aboard."

"She's no longer a little girl, is she?" Charley replied.

"No," Selkirk said.

"Who were those English officers?" Charley asked.

"Come to see Lady Caroline about the body," Selkirk replied. "Find out what's going on. If necessary, you see Lady Caroline to where she's going. There's a carriage waiting on the wharf. But be back here by four-thirty. We have some business to attend to."

"Yes, sir."

"Who will you have relieve you here?" Captain Selkirk asked.

"Mr. O'Keefe," Charley said.

Selkirk nodded his approval and walked off the quarterdeck.

When Paul Selkirk emerged on deck ten minutes later, he was wearing his pig-sticker and his wig and his silver-buckled shoes, and otherwise dressed to conform with what London expected of a shipmaster. He saw that Charley had found Mr. O'Keefe, the quartermaster, and put him to supervising the unloading of the silk. And when he looked down to the main deck, he saw Mary sitting on the railing by the gangplank, swinging her legs.

He went down to the deck, and when he was close enough to her that no one else could hear him speaking softly, he snapped, "You're a lady. Or supposed to be. Stand up."

257

She immediately slid off the railing. There was a shrug of her shoulders that was painful to him. Her mother had shrugged her shoulders in precisely the same way when she was giving in to him when he was being foolish.

3

Lady Caroline Watchbury recognized the knock of Charles Selkirk's knuckles at her cabin door and had a mental image of the way he was holding his hand, rapping the door with the back of his knuckles.

She went to the door and opened it, and looked up into his face, and then backed away from the door to admit him.

"I came to see about getting you safely ashore," he said. "My father sent me."

He looked, she thought, quite handsome in his gold-buttoned blue jacket and white shirt, with his powdered wig accenting his tanned face. His muscular legs filled out his silk stockings, and the material of his trousers was drawn tight against the bulge at his crotch. She felt somehow wicked that she had noticed that, although five hours before, as they entered the Thames estuary, she had lain naked and satiated in his arms, cupping his manhood gently in her fingers, even giving it a name, and cooing to it that Poor Little Rooster was all worn out.

She had been telling herself, since he'd risen from her bed when the ship's bell had called him to his watch, that that had been the end of it, that they were just hours from London, that the interlude, however charming, was now over.

Charles Selkirk was nineteen, nothing more than a boy, with no money except that which he had at the pleasure of his father. He had no position, and the brightest future he could expect, years from now, would be as master of one of his father's ships. She had reminded herself that she was nearly twenty-three, a widow of rank and position, and that it was simply absurd even to consider that their relationship could go further than it had aboard *The Eleanor.* . . .

But oh, God, she thought, when she saw him here, ready to put her ashore, how she was going to miss him!

"Where are the English officers?"

"They've gone," she said. "They're going to send men for the casket and then call on me tonight at my apartments to tell me of the arrangements."

"I must have missed them leaving while I was changing," he said.

She stepped behind him and latched the door, and ran to him, putting her arms around him, her face on his chest, feeling the biceps of his arm on her torso as he put his arms around her.

"Touch me, Charles," she whispered. He chuckled and ran his fingers down her hair and over her face. That wasn't what she had been asking, but she couldn't correct him. She suspected that he thought she was loose and lewd, and she didn't want him to think that of her now, as they were saying good-bye.

"Are you going to miss me?" she asked, the words coming to her lips seeming of their own volition, and making her furious with herself.

"Sure," he said. "But we've talked that subject to death. We know how things have to be."

She pushed herself away from him, got control of herself.

"You'll be coming to London again," she said.

"Probably," he said.

He doesn't care, she thought. A week from now, he won't even be able to recall my face clearly. There will be other women, I'm certainly not the only woman who will take note of his good looks, and his eyes, and his body, and his quiet strength. In a year, I will be that woman, what was her name? The one we carried from Tatta in Hyderabad to London, the one who had me in her bed, the one who had this extraordinary habit of talking to my Poor Little Rooster.

"Perhaps," she said, "you'll be able to find time to come see me before you sail. They're going to have a memorial service in Guard's Chapel for my husband. Perhaps you could be my escort for that."

"I wouldn't want to do that," he said matter-of-factly. "Even if there was time, and there won't be."

"No time?"

"The agent came aboard with H.M. Customs. Our cargo'll be discharged here, and then we'll go downstream to load our Philadelphia cargo from Patterson's Docks."

"What are you going to take to the Pennsylvania colony?" she asked. She didn't care. She just didn't want the conversation to end.

"Fabric," he said. "But we're not headed straight home. First, Amsterdam, and then Naples and the West Indies."

"Amsterdam?"

"We're going to load some spices and lace in Amsterdam for Philadelphia," he said. That wasn't the whole truth. They would pick up some lace, and some spices, and whatever else was needed to allay suspicions about their call there. But the real reason they were going to Amsterdam was to sell some jewels his father had acquired in Tatta. They were going to Naples to pick up some metal-working equipment, necessary to the making of rifles. It was forbidden under the Tarriff and Navigation Acts to export from England machinery of that complexity, or to import such equipment, no matter where made, into the North American colonies.

Captain Paul Selkirk had need of the equipment and planned to smuggle it into Pennsylvania. But there was no reason to tell Lady Caroline about that. As his father pointed out, she was a woman, and women had big mouths and empty heads, and the only secret they could be trusted to keep was one they didn't know.

"I guess it's time to go," Lady Caroline said.

Charles Selkirk turned and unfastened the door, opened it, then made a little bow, a gesture for her to go ahead of him.

"You will, won't you, dear friend, write from time to time?" Lady Caroline asked brightly.

"Yes, of course," Charley replied.

It's not that he doesn't believe what he's saying, Lady Caroline thought, but he'll never be able to find the time. And then when he eventually finds the time, he will be embarrassed about not having written earlier, and he will put off writing then, until he can think of an excuse, and eventually, he won't even be able to think of an excuse for not writing.

But what, she asked herself, would be the point in his writing anyway?

For his part, Charley Selkirk felt quite mature about the decision they had reached. As she had pointed out, it was absurd even to consider a marriage between them. She was a widow of position and rank, and he was a colonial sailor.

God had sent him, she had told him, to comfort her in her hour of grief and loneliness. They should be happy for what they had, and not be greedy. She had told him that it was perfectly understandable, especially considering that she was his first woman, that he should fancy himself in love with her. But that's all it was, a fancy. They would remember each

260

other always with fond memories, and be grateful to the other for having the wisdom to know what could not be.

It was a true tragedy, Charley thought, like *Romeo and Juliet,* a romance that was not meant to be. He would love her forever, he told himself, no matter what else happened in his life, and she would, from time to time, think of him. He had had a very clear picture of the future. He would be in London, Captain Charles Selkirk, old, of course, forty years old, anyway. And he would see her, in her carriage, with her husband, a viscount, or a duke, or maybe even a prince. She would recognize him, and he would bow. And they would both recall the month they had spent in her bed a long time ago.

Lady Caroline went ahead of him onto the deck of *The Eleanor.* She glanced over her shoulder to the quarterdeck, expecting to see Captain Selkirk, but Quartermaster O'Keefe was the only officer in sight.

But as they reached the gangplank, she saw him. He was on the wharf, standing beside a carriage, one of two in line. Mary Selkirk was in the first carriage, looking at her but not smiling. Charley helped her onto the gangplank, and Captain Selkirk walked quickly to the lower end and offered his hand.

"This is farewell, I suppose, Lady Caroline," he said.

"Captain," she said, "permit me to wish you Godspeed."

"Your luggage is in the carriage," he said. "Charles will see you safely to your apartments."

"That's very kind of you," she said. "But unnecessary."

Why did I have to say that?

"I can do no less, my lady," he said. "Unless you object?"

"Thank you, Captain Selkirk," Lady Caroline said, "for all of your courtesies to me."

"Having you aboard, madam," he said, bowing, "gave pleasure to all of us. May I wish you good luck for the future?"

"You're very kind, Captain," she said, and smiled at him. She walked to the first carriage. "Goodbye, Mary," she said.

"Goodbye, Lady Caroline," Mary replied. Obviously, Caroline thought, the girl is pleased to be rid of me.

Captain Selkirk helped her into the second carriage. Charley was already in it, sitting straight and looking a little uncomfortable, with his hands resting on the hilt of his sword, the sword between his knees. When she was sitting beside him, and Captain Selkirk closed the door, he took one hand off the hilt and reached up and tapped the coachman on the back. The carriage began to move away. Lady Caroline looked up at *The Eleanor*, and then again at Mary Selkirk. Their eyes locked, but Mary neither smiled or waved.

It's all right Mary, Lady Caroline thought. You'll soon have him all to herself.

"Do you know London well, Charles?" Lady Caroline asked, as they rode past St. Paul's Church.

"I have been here twice before," he said. "But never before with a lady, and never this far from the Thames."

"This is the first time we have ever really been alone," she said. "Have you thought about that?"

He looked at her with confusion in his eyes.

"We don't, for the first time, have to listen for footsteps in the passageway, or a knock at the door," she said. He blushed. She wanted to curl up against him, to nuzzle his neck.

The carriage carried them up Ludgate Hill, past the Royal Courts of Justice, and she tried to convince herself how happy she was to be back in civilization, and what a fool she was, the way she was acting about Charles, who was nothing more, really, than a provincial boy in excellent physical condition. She told herself that while he was dressed as a gentleman, an officer, he was not a gentleman. He was the son of a Scottish peasant who had been lucky enough in the colonies to come into possession of a ship.

Nothing more.

As soon as she got back into the swing of things, she would forget him as he would forget her. He would simply become in her memory that sweet boy she had taken into her bed to pass the time when returning from Tatta, in Hyderabad.

When Sir Edgar and Lady Caroline had gone to India, they had left the Irish maid, Bridget, to serve as caretaker of the apartment in their house on King's Way until they returned.

The maid was apparently on duty, for as the carriage made a turn on King's Way to pull up before the building, Lady Caroline looked up and saw curtains blowing out open windows.

When she came into her inheritance from Edgar, she decided, one of the first things she would do would be to sell the leasehold in this building and buy a suitable house. (She had a tangential thought: the first thing she would sell was

Edgar's land in Pennsylvania. Keeping it would be a painful reminder of Charles Selkirk.) If one were to move in the circles in which she intended to move, in which she intended to find a husband (if not Sir Richard Trentwood, then someone at least as well-to-do and prominent), she would have to have a larger, more prestigious, London residence than the top third of a house on King's Way.

She wanted to be thought of as the daughter of the marquess of Kelden, thus Lady Caroline Watchbury in her own right, rather than as the widow of a soldier who had earned a knighthood. There was a distinct difference, socially. Widows who were daughters of marquesses were able to remarry well. Widows of soldiers were just widows of soldiers. They had little money and no prospects of a good marriage.

"I have no idea how I'll get the luggage inside," she said. "There is only a housekeeper here."

"I'll see to it," Charles said. "You go inside, and I'll see to it."

When the maid, Bridget, opened the door, her hair was mussed, and from the look in her eyes and her slurred speech, Margaret saw that she was drunk.

"Make up my bed," Margaret snapped. "And then get food for my dinner. And when you return, you'd better be sober."

She followed the maid into the bedroom and watched her make the bed.

She would take Charles Selkirk into this bed now, she decided, for one last time with him. A London memory, she thought, as opposed to the memories she would have of her cabin on *The Eleanor*. She was entitled, she thought, to one London memory. What they had had had been wonderful, even if she had known from the start that it could have no lasting meaning.

She went into the kitchen of the apartment and helped herself to the remains of the bottle of wine the maid had been drinking. And then she heard the knock at the door.

It was two boys, carrying her trunk between them. She showed them where she wanted it, in the bedroom, and when they went downstairs to get the rest of her luggage, she opened the trunk and took from it a nightdress, and unfolded it, smelling the salt of the sea on it. The boys delivered her other cases and went back down for what was left.

She closed the bedroom door, and stripped off her clothes and put on the nightdress.

She heard the boys return, and one of them called, "That's the lot of it, m'lady."

"Just put it by the door," she called. She waited until she heard their feet going down the stairs, and then she waited for the sound of Charles's footsteps coming up. When she didn't hear them, she opened the door to the corridor and listened, and when she heard nothing, when there was no reply when she called his name, she went back into the apartment and to the window and looked down at the street to see what was holding him up.

The carriage was gone, and Charles Selkirk, she realized, with it.

First, she was angry, and threw the wine glass in her hand to the floor, and the bottle after it. And then, as she felt the tears well up in her eyes, she ran into the bedroom, slammed the door behind her, and threw herself on the bed and wept.

4

Captain Paul Selkirk, his head sweating and itching under his wig, was pleased and a little surprised to find Charley waiting for him on the quarterdeck of *The Eleanor* when he and Mary returned from their shopping. He had fully expected that even if Charley didn't keep him waiting, he would show up as the last minute of the two hours he had been given to take Lady Caroline to her apartment expired.

"There's Charley," Mary said. "Where are you two going?"

"To the Cheshire Arms," he replied.

"May I come with you?"

"Ladies do not go to the Cheshire Arms," he said. "We'll have time ashore, you and I, I promise, before we sail."

"Gentlemen should not go where ladies do not," Mary said.

"Go aboard, mistress, and tell your brother I'm waiting for him," he said. "And you're not to leave the ship. Understand?"

She didn't reply. That was something else she had inherited from her mother, a habit of replying with silence to an order in a way that made her displeasure clear, and was intended to make the order-giver feel guilty. You're not your mother, mistress, he thought, I don't give a damn if you like it or not.

Charley had seen the carriage drive up and was across the

gangplank before Mary reached it. He walked to the carriage, and his father motioned for him to get in.

"Take us to the Cheshire Arms on Portpool Street," Captain Selkirk said to the coachman.

After a good deal of thought, Paul Selkirk had decided that Charley's relationship with Lady Caroline Watchbury had been the right thing to happen to him at the right time. The boy was not only a man, but his father's son. The juices of life flowed in Charley at nineteen as they had flowed in him when he had been nineteen. He had been able to keep a taut line on Charley so far, but it had been apparent that Charley was going to have to be cast adrift even before Lady Caroline had shown up in his life in Hyderabad.

It had been for some time Captain Selkirk's intention to deal with the problem of Charley's inexperience with women when they got to London. The Cheshire Arms Inn on Portpool Lane did a good deal of business with ship's officers because they had clean rooms, set a fine table, and provided a better class of tart than could be found elsewhere. It was all accomplished in the best of taste. You weren't expected to dicker price with the tart, which was a hell of a thing for a man and an officer to have to do. The innkeeper, a jovial Irishwoman, made all the arrangements. The subject of money never came up with the tart. She was just there, for you alone, as long as you were in London and as long as you wanted her.

You were billed for all services rendered when you left. It wasn't cheap, unless you thought it through, and considered the alternatives, going to a house, exposing yourself to God alone knows what, maybe getting into your cups and throwing money around. And worse. In the Cheshire Arms, you were with your own kind. Only officers and gentlemen were admitted, and the games were honest, and you didn't wake up stripped of everything you owned if you had a little too much to drink.

The Cheshire Arms was something else, too, beneath the semirespectable officers' brothel facade. It was the contraband runners' equivalent of Lloyd's Coffeehouse, although it took the same pains to conceal its business that Lloyd's did to advertise its insurance underwriters.

His business at the Cheshire Arms, in other words, was of greater importance than guiding his son's love life. But there was no reason he couldn't try to kill more than one bird with a stone.

Mistress Grogarty would understand the problem and tactfully arrange for a nice, clean young tart for Charley, to dull the immediate pain he was sure the boy was feeling over leaving Lady Caroline. He would find some excuse to spend tonight aboard *The Eleanor* and to leave Charley at the Cheshire Arms. Then, tomorrow morning, when he went to the Cheshire Arms, he would have a father-to-son talk with Charley about physical hungers and the way wise men went about dealing with them.

Selkirk was sure that if Eleanor were still with them, she would have brought up the subject of Charley's manhood herself. She too would reason that a good whore was far better than a bad one, or some loathesome disease or an impetuous marriage. The boy was going to have a woman, and there was no denying that (although the present Mrs. Selkirk would probably have advocated a cold bath and prayer), and she would have seen that his clear parental duty was to help him over that hurdle as best he could.

But when the Widow Watchbury had come aboard that had changed things. She had found Charley interesting from the moment she'd laid eyes on him, and Charley would never in his life have greater need of a woman than he had had the day that damned fool Dooley had lost his footing and gone over the side. There was no doubt, afterward, of course, that poor Charley fancied himself in love with the woman. The poor calf looked at her as if she gave milk, and she, of course, had done nothing to discourage him, taking pleasure in the young man's infatuation, even if she knew, as well as Captain Selkirk did, that nothing could come of it.

Captain Selkirk didn't believe for a moment that Lady Caroline Watchbury needed the protection of his son to cross London. She was the kind of woman who could cross the African jungle by herself. He had sent Charley with her to let them be alone, to let Charley see for himself that what had happened was now over. Charles Selkirk might be the cock of the walk, in his own mind, on the quarterdeck of *The Eleanor*, but he was a bright lad, and he would quickly come to realize what a bumpkin he was in London.

One of two things would happen when he took her to her house. There would be an emotional parting, with him professing love undying, and the woman letting him make a fool of himself that way. Or, and it was possible, for he was his father's son, Charley would find out right then that the way to end something that had to end anyway was quickly, as one lanced a large boil with a large needle, to get the pain and bleeding over and done with once and for all. Either way, Charley would end up with a lesson learned.

But looking at him in the carriage, with his hands on the hilt of his pig-sticker, and his chin somewhere down around his knees, Captain Selkirk could tell only that his son was unhappy, but not why. Just as soon as their business was over, he decided, he would have a word with Mistress Grogarty. Charley might not be a virgin anymore, but he was the next thing to it, and the best way to straighten him out now was to get him another woman.

Charley finally noticed the brace of pistols his father was wearing.

"What are you doing with those?" Charley asked.

Captain Selkirk patted his vest. If you looked closely, as Charley did, you could see the outline of a purse under his vest. Captain Selkirk, looking at the coachman, put his index finger over his lips.

"You get Lady Caroline safely to her house?" he asked.

"Yes, sir," Charley said.

"And you think you'll live, do you?" Captain Selkirk asked, not unkindly.

"Sir?"

"Deprived of your place in the lady's bed?" Captain Selkirk said.

Charley blushed, and then grew angry. "I'll thank you, sir, to watch how you speak of Lady Caroline."

"You'll not tell me, Charles, what I will say."

With a great effort, of which his father was aware, Charley bit off his intended reply to that.

"Sir," he said, "couldn't I be of assistance to Mr. Porter?"

"If I thought so, I would have left you aboard," Captain Selkirk said.

"May I ask where we're going?" Charley asked.

"To the Cheshire Inn," Captain Selkirk said. "Didn't you hear me direct the coachman?"

Charley's face was now quite red.

"And may I ask why?"

"If I wanted you to know," his father said. "I would have told you."

Captain Selkirk worried for a moment that he had gone too far, that Charley was about to erupt. But he didn't. He gripped the hilt of his pig-sticker so hard that his knuckles turned white, but he didn't open his mouth. Captain Selkirk was pleased. Charley's temper was as bad as his own, and he had been a good deal older than nineteen before he had learned to control it. He'd gone into marriage with a temper, and only much later had managed to get it under control.

They went back up Ludgate Hill, then turned up Saint Bride Street to Shoe Lane, and then over to Gray's Lane, and up that to Portpool Lane, and the Cheshire Inn. Mistress Grogarty greeted Captain Selkirk like a long lost lover, more than a little embarrassing him, and then took a long, approving look at Charley.

"Paul," she said, "you said you'd bring me a present, but I didn't dream it would be anything like this." She patted Charley on the cheek, and he blushed like a girl.

"I've warned my son that you're an evil woman, Mistress Grogarty," Captain Selkirk said.

"And I've never denied it," she said. "Has your father told you that he's always after me to give up my inn and come to the colonies?" she asked. Charley, somewhat embarrassed, shook his head no. "When did you land, Paul?" Mistress Grogarty asked.

"Early this morning," Captain Selkirk said.

"And ye came directly here? I'm flattered."

"I was hoping that Mr. Woodley would be about," he said.

"Ah, then, 'tis business and not me you're after?"

"Everything in its proper time," he said, smiling back at her.

"I believe I could send someone to fetch Mr. Woodley," she said. "He has been asking for you in the last couple of weeks."

"I would be grateful."

"Will ye be spending the night?" she asked.

"Aye. And I'll need someplace where we can talk in private."

"Come on upstairs," she said. "And I'll show you what rooms I have open. And then I'll get you something to drink."

When she had left them alone in a room overlooking the street, Paul Selkirk turned to his son.

"You're not going to ask me what we're doing here?"

"In your good time, I'm sure, you'll tell me," Charley replied.

"Aye, I will," his father said, smiling at him. "But I thought you might be a little curious."

"I can wait," Charley said, but he smiled back at his father.

Mistress Grogarty returned with an attractive scullery maid, as obviously Irish as she was, carrying a tray with bread, sausage, glasses, and two bottles on it.

"I know what you want," she said. "That awful, raw Scotch whiskey. But your son looks like a gentleman, and I thought he might like wine."

"How thoughtful of you, mistress," Captain Selkirk said, drily.

"I'll see you later?" she asked.

"That you will," Selkirk said. She left. Selkirk noticed that Charley had looked down the maid's dress-front when she had been bent over the table. Perhaps he wasn't as lovesick as he looked, he thought. He picked up the wine bottle and offered it to Charley, who shook his head.

"Scotch whiskey, then?" Captain Selkirk asked.

"If that's what that is," Charley said.

"You know what happens to a lovesick pup if he drinks Scotch whiskey?" Captain Selkirk asked, as he poured whiskey into a glass and then sniffed it appreciatively.

"I have no doubt you'll tell me," Charley said.

"He becomes a *drunk* lovesick pup," Captain Selkirk said, smugly and handed the glass to him. "Who'll cry into his cup."

"I'm sorry to disappoint you, sir," Charley said. "But it never entered my mind that I was in love with the lady."

"I'm glad to hear that," Captain Selkirk said. He added mentally: even if I don't believe a word of it.

"Your health, sir," Charley said, and took a large swallow of the whiskey.

"If I didn't know better, I'd swear you do that all the time," his father said.

"What I would like to know is why you're trying to provoke me," Charley said. "Have I done something wrong?"

Captain Selkirk turned from pouring whiskey into his glass and looked at his son.

"You're perceptive," he said. "I guess that's what I have been doing. Trying to find cause to send you back to the ship as a boy."

269

"Instead of permitting me to stay with you in this brothel?" Charley replied.

Now it was Paul Selkirk's turn to control his temper.

"Ye've not been reading your Bible," he said, finally, drily sarcastic. "The part where Jesus said, 'Let him who is without sin cast the first stone.'"

"They seem to know you pretty well in here."

"I'll let that pass," he said angrily. "What I do and where I go is none of your business."

"You've brought me here to help me get over Lady Caroline?" Charley asked. "Is that your thinking?"

"No," his father said. "At least, that isn't the main reason."

When he saw the look on his son's face, Selkirk was pleased that he hadn't professed innocence.

"Why, then?" Charley asked, smiling.

"This is a good place to meet someone and not call attention to it."

"That Mr. Woodley you sent for?"

Selkirk nodded. "Mr. Woodley is a sort of purchasing agent for me," he said.

"And that's why you're carrying a purse of money?"

Captain Selkirk nodded. "Mr. Woodley's goods are often very dear," he said, but stopped there. He offered no further explanation, and Charley Selkirk asked for none.

Twenty minutes later, Mistress Grogarty ushered a man into the private dining room.

"My son Charles, Mr. Woodley," Captain Selkirk said. "My third mate."

"A fine-looking lad, Captain Selkirk," Mr. Woodley said. Charley took an instant dislike to him. He was oily, Charley decided, devious. He wondered what kind of business his father had with a man like this.

"I understand H.M. Customs gave you a pretty good working over," Woodley said.

"How do you know that?"

"Word gets around."

"I presume things are arranged?" Selkirk asked.

"Got just the merchandise you asked for."

"Where is it?"

"Not far from here."

"How long will it take to get him here?"

"When do you want him?"

"I will talk to him now," Selkirk said.

270

"If you've got the gold, you can have him here in fifteen minutes." Woodley said.

"I've got the gold," Selkirk said.

"And I've got just the man you want," Woodley said.

"Why does that make me uneasy, Woodley?" Selkirk said, "Why am I afraid that's a goddamned lie?"

Woodley looked uncomfortable. "I'm telling you the God's truth, Captain," he said.

"You wouldn't recognize God's truth if it were branded on your forehead," Captain Selkirk replied.

"You've no cause to talk to me that way, Captain."

"Have your man here in an hour, Woodley," Captain Selkirk said. "If he's what I ordered, I'll give you your money. If he's not here in an hour, or he's not what I said I wanted, I'll tell our mutual friend that she owes me a refund on the advance I gave her."

"I'll have him here in an hour," Woodley said. "And you have my word he's what you're after."

"Fetch him, Woodley," Selkirk said coldly, impatiently.

Chapter Fourteen

1

"What do you think of Mr. Woodley, Charley?" Captain Selkirk asked when Woodley had gone.

"I'm surprised you trust him."

"I don't trust him."

"Why do you deal with him?"

"Because he can arrange things I can't arrange for myself," Captain Selkirk said.

"I don't understand what you're doing now," Charley confessed.

"I intend to take a crucible-steel maker back to Pennsylvania," Paul Selkirk said.

"Is that some sort of problem?" Charley asked.

"The next time I make Tatta," Captain Selkirk said, "I intend to have a thousand-stand of rifles aboard."

"You'll draw attention, buying that many rifles," Charley said.

"Not the way I'm going to go about it," Captain Selkirk replied. "I'm not going into the open market. What I'm going to have to do is go all over the Lehigh and Wyoming valleys, to all the gunsmiths, and have them make rifles out of my steel."

"I still don't understand."

"Gun barrels are made of high-quality steel strips," Captain Selkirk said. "They're formed by beating them around a mandrel."

"I know," Charley said. "I've watched gunsmiths at work."

"The authorities keep track of how many guns are being

made by who is buying a lot of steel. If a gunsmith buys a lot of steel strips, he'll be asked where the guns are."

"Well?"

"If a man were to have his own source of steel strips," Selkirk said. "And were to offer it to the gunsmiths at a good price, in addition to the good price he paid them for finished pieces . . ."

"And no questions asked?"

"Right."

"You're going to have this man make steel strips?"

"He knows a secret process, something called crucible-steel making, that makes high-quality steel in large quantities."

"You're going to have him do this at Durham Furnace?"

"No. That's the last place."

"I don't understand," Charley said, confused.

"Mistress Selkirk has . . . The truth of the matter is, Charley, I had a letter from her, as much as telling me that not only am I going to burn in hell for my sinful ways, but that she'll have nothing to do anymore with helping me with the gun trade."

"So what are you going to do?" Charley asked. Captain Selkirk noticed that Charley had not seemed at all surprised to hear about his stepmother.

"I have an interest," Paul Selkirk said, "in a ship's iron-work forge outside Chester. I'll probably set up there."

"I didn't know you had 'an interest' in a forge in Chester," Charley said.

"My wife knows nothing of it. And I don't ever want her to."

"Why are you telling me now?" Charley asked.

"I'm beginning to think I should have kept ragging you until you lost your temper and I would have had reason to send you back to the ship."

"You almost did," Charley said.

"The reason I'm telling you, son," Selkirk said, "is that you're now a man. And a man has the right to know what his father is up to, if what his father is up to is against the law and can land them both in prison."

"Is it worth the risk?"

"That's for you to decide," Selkirk said. "The prince says he'll pay twenty-five pounds a rifle. I think I can have them made for about three pounds."

"But to buy a thousand-stand would be three thousand

273

pounds," Charley said. "Where are you going to get that kind of money?"

"I've got it," Paul Selkirk said. "Or I will have when I sell the jewels in Amsterdam."

"You're talking about a profit of twenty-two thousand pounds," Charley said.

"I'm also talking about seven years in one of His Majesty's prisons," Paul Selkirk said. "They generally put seamen in ex-Royal Navy man-of-war hulks outside Liverpool. After you've had six months or so of being chained and of fighting rats and other prisoners for rotten food—what they feed prisoners is condemned Royal Navy rations—they offer you a pardon. If you enlist for twelve years in the Royal Navy. And just so you don't forget you've been pardoned, so you don't think about running away, they brand a six-inch *P* on your arm."

"You're trying to frighten me, is that it?"

"I'm trying to tell you how things are," his father said.

"And if I didn't want to get involved?"

"Then I would arrange your passage, yours and your sister's, to Philadelphia."

"I'd like to ask you a question," Charley said.

"Ask. I may not answer it, but ask."

"Why do you do it? Take chances, since you don't have to?"

"I gave it a good deal of thought, on the way to Tatta," Paul Selkirk said. "And I came to an unpleasant conclusion about myself."

"What?"

"I do it for the money, Charley. For what the money can buy. I'm a greedy man."

"But you have money," Charley said. "You said you have three thousand pounds. And you own *The Eleanor* free and clear. And part of *The Mary*. And you said you have an interest in a forge . . ."

"I own the forge," Selkirk said. "And a lot more. There's no reason I would ever have to go to sea again. Nor you, with what you'll get from me. Nor would your sister's husband ever have to do a lick of work, with the dowry I'll give her."

"*Just* for the greed of it, is that what you're saying? And not because you like to twist the English lion's tail?"

274

"There's some of that in it," Paul Selkirk admitted. "But what it really is is that I like the money."

"It's disgraceful," Charley said. "That's what it is. You really should be ashamed of yourself."

Paul Selkirk looked at his son in absolute surprise. That was the one response he had not expected.

"You can leave me now," he said. "Take the carriage back to the ship, and wait word from me there."

"The only way, sir," Charley said, "that I'll go back to the ship is if you carry me there. You're not the only one who likes money."

"Heed me well, Charley," Paul Selkirk said. "I was not exaggerating when I told you of the risks we face. There's a very good chance that my greed, and yours, will see us both chained to the ribs of a prison hulk."

"And then again, there's a very good chance that it won't," Charley said.

He met his father's eyes.

"I'll be damned," Paul Selkirk said.

"Yes, sir," Charley said. "Probably."

Captain Paul Selkirk's eyes filled, and he turned away from his son so that the boy would not see.

"Could you handle another glass of these spirits without falling down?" he asked, when he could again trust himself to speak.

"I think so, sir," Charley said.

Woodley returned in less than an hour with an uneasy man in simple clothes in tow.

"This is Captain Selkirk and his son," Woodley said. "This man's name is Sedge."

Sedge tugged at his forelock, first at Captain Selkirk, and then, after a moment's hesitation, at Charley as well.

Selkirk gave him his hand.

"What's your Christian name, Sedge?" Captain Selkirk asked.

"George, sir," Sedge replied.

"Mr. Woodley tells me that you're a journeyman steel maker, George, is that so?"

"Yes, sir."

"How long have you been at it?"

"Since I was a lad, sir. I was apprenticed in '58."

"And how long have you been a journeyman?"

"Since '65, sir."

"Can you make crucible steel, George?"

"Aye, sir."

"And you could run a crew of men?"

"Aye, sir. I had a fourteen-man crew at the works."

"You know that leaving England is against the law?"

"Yes, sir, I know."

"How much does your father, or your mother, or your brothers and sisters know about your running?" Selkirk asked.

"My Dad and Mum is dead, sir. And I don't see nothing of my brothers and sisters. The missus's told them I just took off, sir. Left *her,* is what I mean. She's a good woman, sir. No need to worry about her."

"The missus? You're married?" Selkirk asked, disbelievingly.

"Yes, sir."

"You sonofabitch, Woodley!" Captain Selkirk said, furiously. "I told you no married men!"

"I couldn't find a single man," Woodley said. "It wasn't for lack of trying."

George Sedge, obviously frightened by Captain Selkirk's outburst, looked back and forth between him and Woodley.

"Goddamn you," Selkirk said to Woodley. "I knew you couldn't be trusted!"

"Sedge plans to send for his family later," Woodley said. "At his own expense, I explained to him. He's prepared to go with you now, is what I'm saying, Captain."

"No," Selkirk said. "That won't do. There's too much of a risk that they could locate him that way."

Sedge now looked very frightened.

"I can't go back now, sir," George Sedge said to Captain Selkirk. "They already know I'm gone. I've been run near a month."

"Can you read and write?" Selkirk asked.

"Some, sir."

"And your wife?"

"No, sir."

"Damn!" Selkirk said.

"My oldest lad can, sir. Read and write, I mean. I taught him myself."

"How old is he?"

"Twelve, sir."

"How many children do you have?" Selkirk said.

"Eight, sir," Sedge said.

"Good God, Woodley!" Selkirk said, angrily.

"Excuse me, sir," Sedge said, gathering his courage. "If I didn't have them, I wouldn't be running."

"What do you mean by that?"

"I can't care for them proper on my wages, sir," Sedge said.

"You've talked this all over with your wife, have you?" Selkirk asked.

"Yes, sir."

"And she was willing to stay behind?"

"Until I would work out getting her to follow me, yes, sir."

"Would she be willing to just pick up and leave, do you think?"

"I don't know what you mean, sir."

"Just what I said. If you sent for her, sent a note to your son, the one who can read, that said for her to just walk out of the house with the children and the clothes on their backs and nothing more, would she do that? Without saying anything to anyone?"

Sedge thought that over for a long moment before replying. "There's no turning back," he said. "She knows that. Yes, sir."

"By now, they're watching her, I'm sure," Woodley said, worriedly.

"Of course they are," Selkirk said, impatiently. "And if he sent for them later, they'd be watching her then, too, and if he sent her money, they'd find out where it came from, too."

Then he turned to Sedge. "I'm going to take a chance on you," he said. "I'm going to give you money. It will be enough money for you to fetch your family and carry them to Amsterdam. If you make it to Amsterdam, our agreement will hold."

"I'd hoped to go aboard your ship here, Captain."

"Don't you think His Majesty's customs is going to be watching to see who goes aboard my ship here? They'd just love to catch me trying to smuggle a journeyman steel worker who knows the crucible steel out of the country."

Sedge looked uncomfortable to the point of pain, but said nothing.

"There's no way they would miss a woman and eight children, and I'll not risk losing my ship," Captain Selkirk said, firmly.

"I can't go with you, then," Sedge said. "They'll be looking for me at the ports. It's seven years in prison for me, as a convicted runner. And if my family didn't go to prison, they'd starve while I was there. I'll not risk it."

Captain Selkirk glowered at him. And then he said, "You wouldn't be much of a man if you felt otherwise, Sedge. We'll have to come up with a way to get you all aboard *The Eleanor* after she's sailed from England."

He looked at Charley, and saw the concern on his face. "It can be done," he said. "It won't be the first time I've had to take on H.M. Customs. It'll be the first time I've had to smuggle a woman with eight children out of the country, and I'll have to give exactly how some thought."

"Could I have my money, Captain Selkirk?" Woodley asked.

"You didn't deliver the goods I asked for," Selkirk said.

Woodley's face screwed up as he framed a reply.

Selkirk took his purse from under his waist coat. He counted out gold coins into his hand but did not offer them to Woodley.

"Are you a Christian man, Woodley?" he asked, in a surprisingly gentle voice.

"I like to think of myself as one, yes, sir," Woodley replied.

"You pray, do you?"

"Yes, sir," Woodley said, now confused by the direction the conversation was taking. "From time to time."

"You'd better pray hard tonight," Captain Selkirk said. "That I'm able to get this man, and his family, out of England safely. Because if I don't, I'm going to believe that you turned me in for the reward. If I'm caught, in other words, keep looking over your shoulder, Woodley, for however long it is before one of my friends cuts your heart out."

He put the coins in a neat little stack on the table, then pushed them to Woodley with the back of the fingers on his left hand.

"There's your money," he said. "Take it."

Woodley snatched the money up and scurried from the room.

"Charley," Captain Selkirk said. "You go back to the ship, and send Theo LaSalle to meet me here. Tell him to bring his best clothes, for here, and some working clothes, as well. And a brace of pistols."

"What are you going to do?"

"I'm going to do my damnedest to get this man's wife and children out of wherever the hell they are and onto *The Eleanor,* and at the same time keep Theo and myself out of those prison hulks I was talking about."

"Let me go with you," Charley said.

"No. We've got Mary with us. With both of us in chains, I don't like to think what might happen to her. No matter what happens, you don't know anything about any of this."

Charley nodded his head in agreement.

"You got that, George Sedge?" Paul Selkirk asked. "You never saw my son before."

"Yes, sir."

"And you don't tell Mary anything, either," Selkirk said. "Just entertain her while I'm gone. Take her to dinner. Maybe even to a play."

"Yes, sir," Charley said.

"Don't look so sad, Charley," Paul Selkirk added. "You'll have plenty of time to see Lady Caroline, if you've a mind to."

2

London
March 16, 1770

Captain Paul Selkirk and Bosun Theo LaSalle had been gone for ten days before Charles Selkirk went to see Lady Caroline Watchbury.

He had gone ashore several times, to eat, to buy shirts, to look at but not buy pistols at James Jeffrey & Sons, Ltd., on New Bond Street; but he had not returned to the Cheshire Arms at all, and he had slept aboard *The Eleanor.* . .

He didn't need a whore, he told himself, and he certainly didn't want one. No whore could give him what Caroline had given him. And he told himself at first that he would not go see Caroline, that there were a number of reasons why he should not.

The first, he was honest enough to admit, was purely selfish. For one thing, the way he had left her when he had delivered her to her apartments had been childish and immature and he was now embarrassed. For another, there was no reason to reopen a wound. It had been bad enough, running away the way he had. It would be worse to see her, perhaps even have an intimate session with her, and then go away again.

But it was the prospect of another session with her that finally saw him asking Mr. Porter for permission to leave the ship.

"You're all dressed up, doubtless," Mr. Porter said, "so as to be suitably attired while visiting London's cultural and educational attractions."

Charley could think of no withering response, so he stood there and took it.

"Bound for the Cheshire Arms, are you?" Mr. Porter pursued. "Now that Lady Caroline, back among her own kind, has no more time for you?"

"No, sir, I am not," Charley replied, keeping his temper with a conscious effort. "I'm going ashore for supper and a little shopping."

"Yes, of course you are," Mr. Porter said. "How could I even think otherwise? Permission granted. Four hours."

"Thank you, sir," Charley said, and tipped his hat.

He caught the tip of his pig-sticker scabbard in a loop of line as he stepped up on the gangplank, and behind him heard laughter, and then applause. He spun around angrily, but no one seemed to be looking at him. They all seemed to be in earnest conversation with each other, or simply fascinated with the rigging.

He walked down the wharf until he came on a cab sitting in front of one of the waterfront restaurants. No sooner had he given Lady Caroline's address than the cab driver began a sales pitch for an inn that catered to young gentlemen, where the prices were right, where they would treat the young gentleman right, and where were located the finest doxies in London town.

"Just take me to Number 101 King's Way, if you please," Charley snapped.

"Forgive me, Your Lordship," the cab driver mocked him. "You didn't look at first as if Your Lordship could afford an address like King's Way."

"Just drive the cab!" Charley snapped. "I'm not interested at all in your opinion of what I can afford."

That was the end of the cab driver's sarcasm. Charley's annoyance vanished and was replaced with self-satisfaction. In his anger, he had behaved like an officer, someone used to giving orders, and someone who would not tolerate impudence.

He was similarly satisfied with himself at Lady Caroline's apartments when he stared down the doorman who had been on the edge of asking him what he wanted. Charley looked at him as he would have looked at a dockhand. The doorman just humbly held the door open for him and bowed his head as Charley passed through it.

There was the sound of a pianoforte or a harpsichord (Charley wasn't sure which was which) when the door to Lady Caroline's apartment was opened to his ring by a maid.

"Mister Charles Selkirk to see Lady Watchbury," he announced.

"Does her ladyship expect you, Sir?"

"Please be good enough to tell her ladyship that I am here," Charley said.

"I'll see if her ladyship is at home, sir," the maid said, and closed the door in his face. Of course she was home, Charley thought. Who else would be playing the harpsichord, if that's what it was? The cook?

He just had time to consider that Lady Caroline might refuse to see him when the maid opened the door again.

"Please to come in, sir," she said. "Lady Caroline will receive you."

Charles Selkirk was the last man Lady Caroline Watchbury had expected to see, now or ever again. She had waited for him to return the day he had brought her from *The Eleanor,* and the day after that. And the days after that. She had this very noon considered going to *The Eleanor* to "look for a missing brooch" and only the appearance of Captain Sir Richard Trentwod at her door had spared her from making a fool of herself.

With Richard in her drawing room, she realized that the affair with Charley Selkirk was really all over. By now, she realized, *The Eleanor* had certainly taken on its cargo for the Pennsylvania colony and sailed. He was *gone.* The affair was *over.* She would have to get on with her own life. In time, she would believe what she was telling herself now, that she should be grateful she hadn't made more a fool of herself than she had.

Charley Selkirk's surprise, almost his shock, at seeing her was visible on his face. She realized that he had never seen her properly made up before. She had spent most of the morning having her hair arranged. It was now piled high on her head, exposing her neck and the triple loop of pearls that circled it and then disappeared between her breasts.

When she saw him, her first reaction was anger: he had no right to come back now!

"Well, Mr. Selkirk," she said coldly, when he walked into the drawing room. "What may I do for you?"

"I came to collect your passage money," he said, pleased with his wit. The crown would pay a fair price for the transport of Colonel Sir Edgar Watchbury's remains, and his widow, from Tatta, and they both knew it. He was completely oblivious to her cold reception, she thought. Now that he had nothing better to do, and had come calling, he expected a warm reception.

He obviously expected her to smile warmly and then rush into his arms, and when she showed no sign of being ready to do either, he walked toward her.

"Mr. Selkirk," she announced to Sir Richard, "is an officer of *The Eleanor,* on which I came home from India."

Selkirk snapped his head around to see whom she was talking to.

"Mr. Selkirk," Lady Caroline said formally, "may I present Captain Sir Richard Trentwood? Richard, this is Charles Selkirk."

Charley Selkirk found Sir Richard to be a pleasant-faced man in his late twenties. He saw that while the spectacular cavalryman's mustache was full, his hair was already thinning. Lady Caroline had separately noticed the same thing. Richard's hair, she had thought, was nowhere as attractive as Charley's had been.

She thought of this again now, and wished that Richard hadn't taken off his uniform cap. He looked much better with the cap, a little round affair with a chin strap, on than he did without it. Seeing the two of them standing together, she was also aware that Richard had the beginning of a paunch pressing against the tight material of his uniform trousers.

But despite his faults, Lady Caroline reminded herself, Sir Richard Trentwood had many desirable characteristics, high among them the very good chance that he would inherit an earldom. He was the second son, and his elder brother was sick. She told herself again that there was nothing that young

282

Selkirk could bring to a marriage but his interest, whatever that was, in his father's ship.

"How do you do, Captain?" Selkirk said.

"How do you do, Mr. Selkirk?" Sir Richard said, and there was a smile on his face.

"I apparently have said something wrong," Charley said, picking up on it.

"No harm done," Sir Richard said.

"The correct form of address, Charles," Lady Caroline said, "would be for you to call Sir Richard 'Sir Richard.' "

"I'm sure Sir Richard," Selkirk said, "will forgive the poor drawing-room manners of a rough sailorman from the colonies."

"My dear fellow," Sir Richard said, pleasantly, "it's not worth mentioning."

Lady Caroline felt her temper rising. Telling herself that her anger was without reason and that it was foolish to lose her temper didn't do any good. She wanted Charley humiliated as he had humiliated her.

"While I fetch my passage money," she asked bitchily, pleased with herself, "may I offer you a glass of sherry?"

He looked at her and smiled, which made her even more angry.

"That would be very nice," he said.

She realized that Charley wasn't at all jealous of Richard, and suddenly she realized why: he thought Richard was an old man. The arrogance of him!

She flashed Charley her most dazzling smile. She bent over facing him to pour the sherry, to let him look hungrily at her bosom beneath the low collar of her dress. When she stole a look at him, he wasn't even looking at her.

"My ignorance is so overwhelming, Sir Richard," Charles Selkirk said, "that I don't recognize your uniform."

"The Life Guards of Horse, actually," Sir Richard said.

"And you're stationed here in London?" Charley asked, politely.

"Yes," Sir Richard said, with a smile at Charley's naiveté. "Actually, the life we guard is that of the king."

He did not take offense, Caroline saw, somewhat disappointed. Charley had disarmed him with the admission that he was a sailor from the colonies.

"The uniform is really quite something," Charley said to him.

283

"Oh, I'm sure your dress uniform is 'quite something' too," Sir Richard said.

"I'm wearing my dress uniform," Charley said. "Wig, pig-sticker, and clean stockings."

Sir Richard laughed. Damn him, too! Lady Caroline thought.

"One could assume that work dress is soiled stockings?" Sir Richard asked.

"No stockings at all, sir," Charley said.

"I envy you, sir," Sir Richard said, chuckling. He obviously found this young sailor from the colonies refreshing. "But how can the other ranks recognize you?"

"In my case, sir, they knew me when I was in the fo'c'sl. This is my first voyage as an officer."

Caroline had to make sure that Sir Richard did not get the impression that she had let into her drawing room a member of the lower classes.

"Charles's father is *The Eleanor*'s owner and master," she explained.

"And he had you serve with the men to learn the profession?" Sir Richard asked.

"Yes, sir," Charley said. "My father says that a man should never order another man to do something he can't do himself."

"He's absolutely right," Sir Richard said. "Absolutely right."

Lady Caroline handed Charley a glass of sherry.

"Thank you," he said. He glanced down into her décolletage now. "You really look beautiful today," he said.

"Thank you," she purred. She hated him. He wasn't talking about the totality of her appearance, but specifically of her breasts, and worse, he was sure that she knew what he meant.

"I'll get your money," she said. The obvious thing was to get rid of him now, right away. Otherwise, Sir Richard was liable to sense that they had been more than passenger and ship's officer on a voyage. "How much was it?"

"Five guineas even," he said with a smile. "Including cartage from the ship here."

Goddamn him, she thought, he just made that up.

As she went out of the room to her bedroom, she heard Sir Richard ask him where they were bound.

"Amsterdam first," Charley replied. "Then Naples, with a

cargo of woolen cloth, and then the West Indies, and then home."

"The trouble with the Household Cavalry," Sir Richard said, "is just that. Household. The king seldom leaves London, and even more rarely England. I envy your travels."

"I envy you," she heard Charles reply. "I would like to spend some time here in London."

I'll bet you would, Lady Caroline thought angrily. And then she went into her bedroom.

The bed was turned down. She remembered having it made the day she had come home, so she could take Charley into it. And then he had simply vanished, without so much as a single word of farewell.

She rang for the maid and told her to ask Mr. Selkirk to join her.

He appeared a moment later. She held out her hand, clutching the five gold coins. When he reached for them, she intended to drop them, to make him get down on his hands and knees to pick them up.

"Here," she said.

"I don't want your damned money," he said.

"Then what is it you want?"

He smiled at her.

"Damn you!" she said. "How dare you?"

His smile grew even wider.

She raised her arm back over her shoulders and threw the five gold coins at him. He ducked them and laughed at her. She turned and picked up a bottle of scent and threw that at him. It hit him in the arm, and he winced.

"God*damn* you!" she hissed. "Get out of my home!"

He bowed to her and walked out of the room. Furious, she ran after him. She stopped herself at the last moment from throwing herself on his back and scratching his eyes out. Instead, she leaned against the corridor wall, for some reason out of breath. She listened as he spoke with Sir Richard.

"I've got to get back to my ship, Sir Richard," he said. "I apologize again for my ignorance."

"Don't be absurd," Sir Richard replied. "It's been an honor to meet you, Mr. Selkirk. I shall be offended only in the event that the next time you're in London you don't look me up."

And then he was gone. She heard the door close after him,

and then his footsteps on the stairs. She tiptoed back to her bedroom, splashed her face with cold water, dried it, then powdered it. She put scent behind her ears and between her breasts, checked to see that her hair was still in place, and then went back to the drawing room.

Sir Richard commented that Charles Selkirk was a fine young lad, and that it had been his experience that there was generally something quite refreshing about North American colonists.

She played the pianoforte for him again, and grew tired of that, and then she sat beside him on the couch, drawing him out about what had happened to people in their circle of acquaintance while she had been gone. They finished what was left in the decanter of sherry, and Lady Caroline called for the maid to bring more.

"None for me, thank you, Caroline," Sir Richard said, getting up. "I have to be going."

She made pro forma objections, but when he had left, she realized that she was glad he was gone. She didn't want him, or any man, in her bed today. And then she realized he had made absolutely no reference whatever to what had passed between them before she had gone to India, or to what might happen now that she was free, after an appropriate period of mourning, to marry.

Five minutes after Sir Richard had left, there came another knock at the door. A moment later, the maid appeared to announce, "It's the young gentleman again."

Her heart beating, she was still trying to make up her mind what to do about that when he appeared behind the maid.

"I waited across the street, in that park or whatever . . ."

"Lincoln's Inn Fields," she supplied.

"Until he left," he finished.

"Thank you, Bridget," Lady Caroline said. "That will be all."

The maid left them alone.

Lady Caroline met Charles's eyes for a moment, then turned and walked down the corridor to her bedroom. He followed her inside, and closed the door and leaned on it.

"I don't know what I would have done if you hadn't come back," she confessed. He tossed his tricorn onto her chaise longue, then ducked out of the leather strap that crossed his chest and held his sword. He threw his jacket onto the chaise, and then his shirt. She waited until he sat down to take off his stockings, and then she put her finger to the buttons of her dress.

3

The maid knocked at the bedroom door.

"There's a man here for the young gentleman," she called.

"What the hell!" Charles said, and got out of bed naked and walked to the chaise and pulled on his trousers. Wearing those, he walked out of the room.

Lady Caroline got out of bed and ran naked to listen behind the open door.

"Mr. Porter sent me for you, sir. He said if I couldn't find you at the Cheshire Arms, I should look for you here. We've had word from the captain. We have to make the evening tide."

"I'll get dressed," Charles Selkirk said.

He came back into the bedroom, saw the empty bed, and looked around for her.

"I've got to go," he said. She nodded.

She leaned against the wall, watching him dress. It took him no time at all, for he didn't bother with his stockings, or his sword strap, or his tricorn. Holding them in his hand, he looked at her.

She went into his arms, pressing her body against his. His hand dropped and cupped her buttocks possessively.

"I love you, Charles," she said.

"That's going to cause some problems, isn't it?" he said, after a moment. Then he let her go.

"Write to me from Amsterdam," she said. It was a plea.

"All right," he said.

And then he nodded at her and was gone.

She waited until she heard the door close after him, and then she got back in bed, and lay on it face down. There was a suggestion of warmth still on the sheet, and the smell of him.

Chapter Fifteen

1

Aboard The Eleanor
East longitude 1°32', north latitude 51°45'
(The North Sea, off Clacton-on-Sea)
March 20, 1770

Tony the cabin boy was sulking on the quarterdeck. Mr. Selkirk, who had the helm, had just ordered him down from the crow's nest and replaced him with an able-bodied seaman. No explanation had been given, but Tony knew what it was. There was a little weather and *The Eleanor* was dipping her bows into an oncoming sea. Mr. Selkirk had been afraid that Tony would lose his footing aloft.

Tony was absolutely convinced that he was at least as sure-footed aloft as anyone aboard *The Eleanor,* and a good deal more nimble-footed than most. He had convinced himself that once a boy learned to control the feeling of dizziness that came to everybody aloft, a boy was safer and more efficient up there than a man, because he didn't have so much weight to move around.

He had proposed this theory to Mr. Selkirk on their way from Tatta, when he and Mr. Selkirk had shared a watch in the middle of the night. Mr. Selkirk had agreed with him then, even told him he had felt the same thing himself when he'd been in the fo'c'sl. And now he had ordered him down.

"Tony, ask Cookie for a mug of tea for me, will you?" Mr. Selkirk said.

At that moment, Mr. Porter came onto the quarterdeck. He tipped his hat to the officer of deck, although, as acting master, he didn't have to pay this courtesy, and Mr. Selkirk tipped his hat back to him.

"Will you have a cup of tea, Mr. Porter?" Selkirk asked. "I'm just sending Tony."

"Ask Cookie to put some soup in a mug, will you, Tony?" Mr. Porter said.

Tony said "Aye, aye, sir," and went down the ladder to the main deck. All of a sudden, *The Eleanor,* for some reason, didn't recover from dipping her bow as Tony anticipated she would, and he lost his footing and went sprawling on his face on the deck.

He slammed painfully into a cannon carriage, and as quickly as he could regained his feet. Not soon enough: when he glanced back at the quarterdeck, both Mr. Selkirk and Mr. Porter were solemnly tipping their tricorns to him.

"Don't you mind them, lad," Cookie said. "Charley Selkirk went sliding on his ass a couple of years ago, just the way you did, and we had to cut the splinter out with a razor." He held up his hands to show the length of the splinter.

"I don't know what sent me off my feet," Tony asked.

"The North Sea did that," Cookie said. "She's a bitch, Tony. She waits until you're not paying attention, and then she sends you flying. Look at this," he said, gesturing at the sky forward. "An hour ago, it was all smooth and blue, and now look at it."

"We're going to have weather," Tony said professionally, having recovered some of his dignity.

"Aye, that we are," Cookie said. "And I don't suppose you heard where are we supposed to meet the captain?"

"They didn't say," Tony said. They hadn't said, but he wouldn't have told Cookie anyway. What was said on the quarterdeck stayed on the quarterdeck, unless one of the officers elected to tell the men. Tony had been taught that as his first lesson when they began to let him learn seaman's duties.

Tony was halfway back down the deck to the quarterdeck, a mug of tea in one hand, a mug of beef-and-vegetable soup in the other, when the lookout sang out.

"Ahoy, the quarterdeck! Sail ho! Three points off to port!"

Tony, to make up for his shaming tumble, had very carefully planned the nimble run he made up the ladder to the quarterdeck. He made it, he was sure, with more grace and speed than anyone else aboard could have made it, but no one saw him. Mr. Selkirk and Mr. Porter had their glasses to their eyes, and the eyes of the quartermaster and the helmsmen were scanning the horizon.

"What do you make of it, Mr. Selkirk?" Mr. Porter asked.

"I don't know. It would help if we knew what we were looking for." He turned his head over his shoulder. "Steady as she goes," he said.

"Steady as she goes, aye, sir," the quartermaster replied.

Miss Mary came onto the quarterdeck. She came, Tony noticed, up the captain's private ladder from his cabin through the skylight. When the captain was aboard, she came up the ladder from the deck, like everybody else.

"Did I hear the lookout call?" she asked. Charley handed her his glass.

"It's a sail," he said. "We don't know what it is."

She looked through the telescope, handed it back to her brother, and then spotted Mr. Porter's mug of soup.

"That smells good," she said, and smiled at Tony.

"I'll get you a cup, Miss Mary," Tony said.

"She'll get her own," Mr. Selkirk said. "I'll have you here, Tony."

Tony nodded, embarrassed. Mary gave her brother a dirty look and went down the ladder to the maindeck.

"Tony, when you get an order, you don't nod your head," Mr. Porter said, not unkindly. "You say, 'Aye, aye, sir.' It means you understand the order."

"Yes, sir," Tony said. "I didn't know that was an order."

"Anything the officer of the deck says is an order," Mr. Porter said.

"Aye, aye, sir," Tony said. Mr. Porter handed him his glass, and Tony, after a moment, found the sail on the horizon.

"A one-master," he said. "A fisherman."

"Aye, but is it the fisherman we're looking for?" Mr. Porter said.

"And are we going to get to it before that?" Mr. Selkirk said, gesturing toward the darkening clouds ahead.

"Ahoy, the quarterdeck!" the lookout in the crow's nest called out. "She's coming about."

The officers put their glasses back to their eyes.

"It could be she's spotted us," Mr. Porter said, glancing up at the mainmast, where, at Captain Selkirk's order, a long white pennant flew from the mainmast top gallant.

"And it could be she's running from the squall," Mr.

Selkirk said. "I'd hate to be caught out here in a small ship like that."

"Ah, but you've been spoiled, Mr. Selkirk," Mr. Porter said. "There's real sailormen aboard vessels that size."

Charley Selkirk turned to the quartermaster.

"Make for her, Mr. O'Keefe," he ordered.

"Aye, aye, sir," Mr. O'Keefe replied, and made a gesture with his hands to show the helmsmen how far he wanted the wheel moved.

"Ahoy, the quarterdeck!" the lookout called down. "She's hoisted a white pennant."

"That's them, then," Mr. Porter said, pleased.

"I'll have the watch on deck," Mr. Selkirk said. "And the longboat crew."

Tony shrieked the orders through the leather megaphone.

"Ahoy, the quarterdeck!" the lookout called. "She's hoisted more sail. She's a cutter of some sort, could be a fisherman."

Mr. Selkirk and Mr. Porter looked through their glasses again. *The Eleanor* and the other ship were approaching each other at their combined speeds, and they could see more of the smaller ship now. When they had first seen her, she had had only one sail aloft. Now she was also flying a jib and a staysail.

"She was probably just making headway, waiting for us," Mr. Porter said, "with only her mainsail."

"She's not going to make it," Mr. Selkirk said. "Look at the seas. I'm not going to order the longboat over the side in these seas."

Mr. Porter looked at Mr. Selkirk for a moment before he replied, long enough to make Charley Selkirk wonder if his decision was about to be overridden.

"The one nice thing about a North Sea squall is that they're over about as quick as they sneak up on you," Mr. Porter said, finally. But then he added, "Sometimes, they are."

Mary came back on the quarterdeck with two mugs of soup, one of which she handed to Tony.

"Is that Father?" she asked.

"Yes, but he's going to be out there a while longer," Charley said. "I'll have the watch aloft. I'll have everything in but the main and the mizzen mains."

Tony shrieked the orders through the megaphone.

"What are your plans, Mr. Selkirk?" Mr. Porter asked.

"I'm going to maintain way," Charley said. "What I think he'll do is bring her about into our lee. Maybe, when he does that, we could put a line on her and bring her alongside. If we can't, we'll just have to wait until the seas go down."

"Aye," Mr. Porter said.

Charley guessed right about his father's intentions. As the two ships approached, the smaller came around again, to head in the same direction. When *The Eleanor* came abreast the sails of the smaller ship, except her mainsail, fluttered loose.

"I don't think he's got a crew aboard," Mr. Porter said. "The captain's at the wheel."

Charley put his glass to his eyes. Getting the images of the people on the deck of the smaller ship was difficult, because of the way *The Eleanor* was rolling, but he picked out his father, and then, on deck, Theo LaSalle. There was no one else in sight.

"I wonder what happened to the ironworker and his family," he said. Then he asked the obvious question, "I wonder what he plans to do with that ship?"

Mr. Porter shrugged his shoulders. Then he glanced up, a reflex action, as the first drops of the rain squall hit him.

The squall lasted forty-five minutes, and it was another twenty-five before Charley, torn between the safety of his men and the risk that another ship would appear on the horizon and see what they were doing, felt safe in ordering the longboat over the side.

He watched the longboat as her crew rowed her across the swells. He could not see them take on the passengers of the smaller vessel because the longboat had gone to her lee side for smoother water. And then the longboat reappeared. Charley saw his father making his way aft, and taking over the tiller from Mr. Dillon.

"May I make a suggestion, Mr. Selkirk?" Mr. Porter said to him.

"Yes, of course, sir."

"You might muster all hands, so that you could have one watch aloft and have the others rigging a bosun's chair to bring them people aboard. Little kids like that can't climb a ladder, and the yard blocks won't take the longboat, loaded the way it is."

"Thank you, sir," Charley said, furious with himself for his demonstrated ignorance. "I'll have all hands on deck."

"All hands on deck!" Tony shrieked through the megaphone.

Charley walked to the quarterdeck railing and told one of the able-bodied seaman to rig a bosun's chair.

When the longboat came alongside, the deck blocked Charley's view of it, and he was surprised when the first person to be hauled over the side in the bosun's chair was his father. His father was soaking wet, and for a moment Charley thought that he had been injured. But when he untied himself, he walked quickly down the deck and disappeared into the passageway beneath the quarterdeck, intending, Charley thought, to get out of his wet clothes.

The next passenger in the bosun's chair was Theo LaSalle, who had his arms wrapped around a small, whimpering child in his lap.

"My God," Mary said. "That poor child!" She ran down to the deck, and took the crying child from LaSalle before he could get out of the bosun's chair.

Three more seamen, each holding a child in his lap, came back aboard next. And then two larger children, together, and then a woman, sick and frightened, then a boy of twelve or so, and finally Sedgé himself.

Then the bosun's chair was put to one side, and the seaman on deck turned to the windlass to hoist the longboat itself, with Mr. Dillon and the remaining seamen in it, aboard.

"Belay bringing the boat aboard," Captain Selkirk said, into Charley's ear. Charley hadn't seen him come onto the quarterdeck. He saw that his father had not changed out of his wet clothes.

"Belay bringing the boat aboard," Charley called out.

"I relieve you, sir," Captain Selkirk said. "I've got something else for you to do."

"Yes, sir."

Captain Selkirk handed him a small, oilskin wrapped package.

"Matches and fuse," he said. "About five minutes' worth. Put it somewhere where it won't get wet or lost."

"Aye, aye, sir," Charley said.

"First, you go aboard her," Captain Selkirk ordered. "And pry her name plate off the stern. Throw it into the sea. Then you go into her bilge, and put powder on her keel. Then fuse it, and light it, and get the hell off."

293

"We're going to sink her?" Charley asked.

"That squall we just came through sent her down," Captain Selkirk said. "That's what they'll think when her name plate and the loose deck gear float ashore. We're lucky; the current'll do that."

"That's a valuable ship!" Charley protested.

"I know what it cost, Mr. Selkirk," his father said drily, "I bought and paid for it."

"Would you like me to go with him, Captain?" Mr. Nelson asked.

"No," Captain Selkirk said, firmly. "Thank you." He handed Charley a small wooden keg, ten inches tall and six inches in diameter. Branded into its sides was the legend, *"Poudre pour fusiliers Levoisie et Cie. Nantes."* It had come from the ready stores for the aft-facing cannon.

Charley tucked the keg under his arm and went down to the deck.

"Theo," he said to LaSalle. "I'll have a crew for the longboat."

"I'll go with you, Mister Selkirk," Theo replied, as he pointed his finger at seamen, ordering them to the rail to get into the longboat.

"No, thank you, Theo," Charley said.

"Where are you going?" Mary asked. He turned to look at her and saw that she was holding one of the children in her arms. The child was thin, dead-fish white, with bulging eyes.

"I'll be back shortly," Charley said. "You better get that kid below."

"Don't tell me about children," Mary snapped. "What did you think I was doing?"

Charley walked to the rail and looked down into the longboat. Two seamen were already in it. Charley pursed his lips and whistled, and they looked up at him. He mimed dropping the powder keg to them, and when he was sure they understood his meaning, dropped it. Then he climbed down the rope ladder into the longboat. He started aft on his hands and knees in the wildly pitching boat and then realized there was no point in his taking the tiller. He would board the ship, and someone would have to be on the tiller when he did that, while he was aboard, and when he was ready to come back into the longboat. He jerked his finger at the seaman nearest the tiller, ordering him to take it, and then squatted down just in front of him.

Other seamen came down the rope ladder and took their positions at the oars. They worked without orders, first finding a place, then unshipping the oars, then hoisting them out of the water, and then waiting for the order to put them in.

"Cast off," Charley called, when he saw they were all in place.

A seaman forward stood up and shoved the longboat away from *The Eleanor*'s hull with his oar.

"Ready!" Charley called. Then, "Stroke!"

The oars dipped into the water. Charley made cups of his hands, and then clapped them together to set the rhythm.

And then, startling him, Theo LaSalle tumbled into the longboat beside Charley. The rope down which he had slid scraped across Charley's face and shoulders.

"Don't you take orders, LaSalle?" Charley said, furiously. He had told LaSalle he could not come.

"Yes, sir," Theo said. "And the next time, Mr. Selkirk, you order me into the longboat, I'd deeply appreciate a little more notice. I damned near went in the water."

Theo LaSalle, his face a study in innocence, took up the clapping hands rhythm for the oarsmen.

Charley looked across the swells at the fishing boat. All but her mainsail had been taken down, and that fluttered loosely in the wind. She was drifting sideways. There was a rope ladder over her side. Charley wondered how his father and Theo had gotten the woman and the children safely over the side and down that into the longboat.

He thought about that again when they were alongside, and he was, with great effort, making his way aboard. They were lucky they hadn't put the children into the water.

When he gained the deck, he turned and saw Theo climbing the ladder. There was a great bulge in Theo's shirt, so that he had to dangle precariously sidewards, with his shoulder, instead of his belly, against the hull when the waves rolled her. The bulge was obviously the keg of powder, solving the problem of how to get that up from the pitching, rolling longboat.

Theo made it to the deck, pulled his shirt from his trousers, and handed Charley the powder keg.

"If you'll see to opening this, Mr. Selkirk, I'll see about tearing loose the name plate."

"Did my father order you along, Theo?" Charley asked, as he took the keg.

"Not exactly, but I don't think he'll mind, Charley," Theo said. "Careful with that, now."

Theo reached into his pocket and came out with a length of iron, sharpened on one end, and then walked purposefully aft.

Charley examined the powder keg in his hands. He knew what it was, and what it was for, but he realized he had no idea how to get it open. He'd seen the cannon loaded and fired three dozen times from the silk bags the keg contained. He had himself been taught to slit open the bag after it had been inserted in the muzzle, before ramming it down the barrel. But he had no idea how to open the keg he held in his hands.

Smashing it open was liable to see it blow up in his hands, for powder was notoriously temperamental. And then he saw, on the wooden lid, a double indentation, dividing the lid into thirds. He put the point of his knife to the indentation. It penetrated easily, and when he shoved just a little harder, the lid split down the indentation. When he'd split it along the second indentation, it was easy to get the point under the center piece and split that upward. He saw the black silk powder bags underneath.

Then he opened the main hatch cover, heaved it to one side, found the ladder, and went down into the hold. There were six inches of water sloshing around in the bilge, but the top of the keel, while wet, was out of the water. Slipping against the slimy hull, he made his way admidships, and then began to stack the powder bags on the keel. There were ten powder bags in the keg, and he laid four of them on the keel, and then laid two layers of three on top of those.

Water sloshed up against the silk. The silk was tightly woven, and wouldn't pass much water quickly. But it would pass some. He took one of the bags off the top layer and put a hole in its top and bottom with his knife point. Then he threaded the fuse, a length of quarter-inch, pitch- and powder-impregnated cotton line through the holes. Then he buried the fused bag in the center of the stack and carefully laid the fuse along the keel back toward the ladder.

He had expected all along that Theo would come down into the hold once he had managed to rip loose the name plate, but he didn't. Charley climbed the ladder to look for him. He found him on deck, hoisting sails.

"What the hell are you doing?"

"She was an honest ship, and she'll go down with her sails flying," Theo replied. "You finished already?"

"It's not lit, if that's what you're asking."

"Give me until you count to a hundred, then," Theo said, and turned his powerful back again to hoisting, alone, the sail. Charley realized that Theo was doing, without very much effort, what would have had two or three normal men straining all their muscles.

He went down the ladder again, counted to one hundred, and then, after some difficulty, managed to get a match lit. He touched it to the fuse and watched it burn until it was clear that it would not go out. There was something nearly hypnotic about the spluttering fuse, and it was almost with reluctance that he turned and started to climb the ladder out of the hold.

Theo was waiting for him at the rail.

"Get over the side, Theo," Charley ordered. Theo didn't like that, but it was an order, and he climbed over the rail. Charley followed him down the rope ladder as quickly as he could. The moment his foot touched the boat, he sensed the boat being pushed away from the hull of the fisherman, and immediately there came the clap of Theo's cupped hands, setting the fast rowing beat.

Charley turned and watched the fisherman as the longboat rowed back to *The Eleanor*. Her mainmast filled, and then the jib and mainsail. She began, very slowly, to turn with the wind, and then to move.

Just when Charley had grown convinced that something had gone wrong, that she had wallowed deeply and bilge water had sloshed up and doused the fuse, there was a puff of flame on her deck, followed a moment later by the sound of the explosion, a dull, surprisingly small boom, and then, several seconds later, they could feel the shock of the explosion strike the hull of the longboat.

For a long moment, that was all that happened. She kept turning with the wind. Then she seemed to slow down. She began to heel to port, and it was now evident that she had lost headway. And then, suddenly, her bow came out of the water, and she began to slip into the sea, stern first.

"Pity, that," Theo said, softly. "But it had to be done."

"Why didn't we put a crew on her and sail her to Amsterdam, and sell her there?" Charley asked.

"Because your father bought and paid for her, and she was legal, you mean?" Theo replied.

"Yes."

"Because the man we bought her from waited until we were out of sight of land, and maybe an hour more, and then went and told the harbormaster that she'd been stolen," Theo said. "That way he gets your father's money, and then he gets it again from the underwriters at Lloyd's Coffee House."

"Didn't my father get her papers when he bought her?"

"If she'd come with papers, she'd have brought four times her worth, not just twice it," Theo said. And then he started rhythmically clapping his hands. "Heave at them, lads," he said. "It's in your interest, too, to get away from here as fast as we can."

2

Janet Sedge had been seasick from the moment the fishing boat had encountered the swells of the Thames estuary outside Gillingham, and she had been convinced that she was going to die, that she and the children and George were all going to be drowned at sea during the squall.

She understood that she and George were being punished by God, her for having talked George into running and George for having listened to her and then having willfully broken his solemn oath of secrecy and service, sworn on the Bible. She understood that, and she had understood why George had decided to do it. George was a good man, and it ate his heart to see his family hungry and cold. And when the baby died, he had really been shamed and upset and willing to listen to her.

But he had broken the oath he had taken before God, and that was an offense against His Majesty's law, punishable in this life, if they were caught, by seven years in prison and punished in the hereafter as a sin. She was willing to take her punishment, now and in the hereafter, for she had talked George into it, but she had wept with the unfairness of the children having to die with them.

When the squall passed, and they were still alive, and *The Eleanor*, huge in comparison to the little boat there were on, was lying five hundred yards across the sea from them as the longboat made its way across the swells to them, the seasickness seemed to pass. Her mind had then been full of new fears, of crossing the ocean, which was full of sea monsters, and from which more than a few ships had disappeared without a clue; of wondering how many of her children, none of them really strong and healthy, would die en route to the Pennsylvania colony.

She had been sure that at least two of them were going to fall into the ocean and drown as they went over the side into the longboat, and once she was in the longboat, she got seasick again, and retched again and again, although the time had long since passed when there was anything in her stomach to come up.

She had wanted to scream when they were alongside *The Eleanor*, the very size of which terrified her, and again when they lowered the little seat over the side and began to haul her babies high in the air over her.

And she didn't at all like the men she saw when she herself was swung, stiff with fear, over the side of the ship and onto the deck. She had heard all the stories about seaman and pirates, and if these men were willing to defy the law of God and King George III, didn't that make them outlaws and pirates?

There was no question that they were outlaws. Not only because they had aided George in running, which was crime enough. In the wagon on the way from Sheffield, they had been stopped by a constable's patrol, two men on horses who had wanted to look in the wagon. And she had been terrified when Captain Selkirk had told them to look all they wanted, terrified that she and the children would be discovered. And then there had been terrible sounds, grunting and gurgling sounds, and no one had pulled aside the canvas wagon cover.

Captain Selkirk and the man with him had killed those two men, there was no question about that, cut their throats with knives, or run them through with swords, one or the other. That was murder.

Wasn't it possible that men who would kill constables would rape her and slit the children's throats and throw them all over the side? They would keep George, because they needed his trade skills, but if they cut their throats and threw them over the side, they could be sure that no one would tell the authorities where George was, and who had arranged for him to run.

And then Janet Sedge saw the girl. She was surprised to see another female of any kind, and here was a pleasant-faced girl, fifteen, sixteen years old, in a clean dress, her hair brushed, and with Jasper in her arms.

"Bring the children to Lady Caroline's cabin," the girl said to the four pirates holding the terrified Sedge children. "And have Cookie bring some tea and some meat broth." Janet could tell the girl was somebody important, for she had issued orders, not asked. Then the girl had turned to her.

"You'll be a lot more comfortable on board *The Eleanor*," she said with a sweet smile. "Once we get the children and you out of your wet clothing, and you have something to eat, you'll feel much better."

When they had gone aboard the fishing boat, they had been hurried into the hold, down a ladder into a dark, foul-smelling hole with rats scurrying away from the light of their lantern. Janet Sedge had expected more of the same here. But when she followed the girl carrying Jasper in her arms, she found herself in a sort of room, with a bed built into the walls, and even a window opening out onto the sea.

George came into the room on the heels of a fat man who carried a pot of broth and a ladle and bowls and loaves of bread, and even real butter.

He took Jasper from the girl and started to spoon broth into him.

There was a boom, an explosion of some kind, and then a few moments later, the whole ship trembled.

The girl saw the look on Janet's face.

"My brother just blew a hole in the bottom of the fishing boat," she said, matter-of-factly. "To sink her. Nothing to worry about."

George got up and looked out the window, and then motioned to Janet to join him.

She looked out the window. At first it looked as if the boat they had come on was sailing away. But then she saw that it wasn't moving. And then the front end of it came out of the water, and it slipped backward into the sea and then disappeared. Janet could see pieces of the ship floating on the surface of the sea.

She could hear shouting on the deck above her, and then she felt the ship began to turn.

"Everything will be all right," the girl said to her.

"Thank you, mistress," Janet Sedge said.

"You embarrass me, missus, when you call me that," the girl said. "My name is Mary Selkirk. Please call me Mary."

"Yes, mistress," Janet Sedge said.

"When we get the babies fed," Mary said, "I'll show you where the galley is, and you can get something to eat for Mr. Sedge and yourself."

"Yes, mistress," Janet Sedge said. "Thank you, mistress."

"For God's sake, Janet," George said. "Did you hear her? She asked you to call her by her name."

She looked at him.

"Janet," he said. "We've left the works, and England, and that life, once and for all. Get that through your head."

Captain Selkirk came into the cabin. He had changed out of his wet clothes. But what he was wearing now wasn't what Janet expected. She had expected that the captain of a huge ship like this one, someone with enough money and power to do what he was doing with George, would be dressed at least as fancy as the manager of the mill had dressed, and probably a lot fancier. But Captain Selkirk was dressed simply in a shirt and trousers and rough boots. He held a battered and dirty tricorn in his hand.

"You'll be a little crowded in here, Sedge," he said. "But it's the best we have to offer. If you need anything, you just tell Mary."

"Yes, sir," George said. "Thank you very much, Captain."

"Mistress Sedge," the captain said, "I didn't want to risk suspicion by bringing a cow aboard in London, but we'll make Amsterdam in three days or four, no more than five, more than likely, and we'll put a couple of animals aboard there."

"Animals, sir?" Janet Sedge asked, confused.

"Cows," Captain Selkirk said, as if surprised at the question. "Milch cows. For milk. For your babies."

"Oh, they won't be needing anything like that, Captain," George said, holding up the mug of beef broth. "This'll do just fine for them, sir."

"What the hell's the matter with you?" Captain Selkirk said. "They're babies. They need milk. They'll have milk."

He turned and walked out of the cabin, motioning for his daughter to come with him.

"Everything's going to be all right, Janet," George said, when he saw the worried look on her face. He put his arm around her.

She sniffled into his chest for a moment, and then she realized how terrible she must look. Just as soon as they got the babies settled down, and she got something for George to eat, she would see about washing, and brushing her hair.

And then she decided that George would just have to wait for something to eat until after she'd washed her face and brushed her hair and made herself as presentable as she could.

3

Amsterdam
March 26, 1770

It had been cold overnight, and the smoke from the stoves used to warm the cabins was unbearable. *The Eleanor* was docked nose in, with a ship on either side of her, and even if the ports had been open and there had been a breeze, the ships would have blocked it, and it would not have done much to clear the smoke from the cabins. Still, Janet Sedge would have stayed in her cabin, for *The Eleanor* herself, and the prospect of one of the children getting hurt on deck or falling over the side frightened her. But there was so much smoke that her eyes watered, and she really couldn't work her needle.

When Mistress Mary had walked down the hallway (they called it a "companionway" on the ship, but Janet was having trouble remembering the terms they used on a ship, "deck" for floor; "bulkhead" for wall; "port" for left; she forgot what for right; and so on), she'd caught her attention.

"Why don't you go on deck?" Mary had asked. "The sun's out, and it's warmer on deck than it is below."

"I fear for the children," Janet said, stopping herself just in time from adding, "mistress."

"They'll get sick from the smoke down here," Mary said.

"And if they fall over the side?" Janet replied.

"You gather them up and bring them topside, and I'll take care of that," Mary said.

When Janet went on deck, two of the pirates were waiting for her and the children. She no longer really thought of them as pirates; calling them that in her mind was making fun of herself. They were good men, and gentle, and she felt a little foolish about what she had first thought of them.

They were family men, the majority of them, and obvi-

302

ously hungry for children and children's laughter, and the older Sedge children were already being spoiled by them. Joseph had even shown up with a knife as sharp as a razor sticking out of his stocking, aping the sailor who had given it to him.

The problem of keeping the toddler-sized Sedges from falling overboard or from the fo'c'sl deck was simply solved. One by one, they were set on the lap of one seaman, while another, working quickly and surely, tied thin rope into a harness. There was no way even the most diligent toddler could get out of the harness, for the only knot was high up, between the shoulders, in the back. The harness was tied to the foremast shroud, far above where the children could reach. In just a few minutes, they had either grown used to the harnesses and were ignoring them, or, as in the case of Sarah and Anthony, had joyfully discovered that a sharp tug on the harness line brought the wearer abruptly back on his or her rear end.

There was enough sun on the fo'c'sl deck to make Janet warm, and one of the pirates brought her a stool, and she turned to her sewing. She was surprised when Mary came and offered to help her, and even more surprised that Mary was skilled with a needle. Not as skilled as herself, of course, but far more skilled than she would ever have believed the only daughter of a fine gentleman like Captain Selkirk would be. Janet had, from the time she was younger than Mary, earned the odd penny sewing for the families of the owners and the managers of the mill, and she had simply assumed that people like that, who could hire the work of others, did not bother to see that their daughters learned how to sew, or for that matter, to cook or wash clothes.

The Selkirks continued to surprise Janet and even George. No sooner had they docked in Amsterdam than Captain Selkirk had called for George. He had given him a bag of money and not even asked for a signed receipt, and told him to go ashore and get what he needed in the way of clothing for the journey and material and household goods, pots and pans and the like, to take with them to Philadelphia.

"Take the missus with you, Sedge," he said. "Don't buy any furniture, for that's cheaper in Philadelphia than here. But get what you need to set up housekeeping."

He had even sent one of the pirates ashore with them, a hulking blond-headed man who spoke enough Dutch for them to deal with the merchants. Janet was surprised first when he bought dishes and two large copper kettles for himself, and then even more surprised when he told them he always tried to bring his missus, who worked their farm, something she either couldn't get in Pennsylvania or which, like the copper kettles, cost much more there.

Janet had two brothers in the British Merchant Navy, and she knew they never had near enough money to buy expensive kettles, much less a farm for their families.

Two hours after she had gone onto the fo'c'sl deck with the children, she saw a milch cow, eyes wide in fright and mooing in terror, legs askew in a sling, being hoisted from the dock, swung over the fo'c'sl, and then lowered onto the deck. The children were fascinated with the operation, but less pleased when a second cow, while flying over the fo'c'sl, elected that moment to empty its bowel.

The cows were followed by a half-dozen goats and then by a half-dozen, enormous crates of cackling, wing-flapping, excited chickens. Janet freely admitted that she knew next to nothing about going to sea, but it was obvious, even to her, that they were about to go to sea.

The Eleanor moved away from the dock early the next morning and started back out into the Inland Sea. But then, practically in the middle of it, the sails were reefed and she dropped anchor. *The Eleanor* sat there all afternoon in an icy wind that made things so cold that when Janet touched the knob of the door from the maindeck to the cabin companionway, her skin stuck to it. When darkness fell, *The Eleanor*'s poop lantern was lit, and in its light Janet could see tiny snowflakes.

At about midnight, Janet was awakened by the sound of male voices outside the window of her cabin, and with a vison of pirates in her mind, jabbed her elbow into George's ribs.

"They'll be sending for me," he replied mysteriously, and sure enough, no sooner had he pulled his trousers on than there was a seaman knocking at the door.

"Mr. Sedge, if you please, sir, on deck," he called.

Janet could never remember ever before hearing anyone call her husband mister or sir.

He was gone an hour, and when he returned to the cabin, he was chilled and blowing on his fingers to warm them. Janet took a blanket from the bed and draped it over his shoulders. She knew better than to ask questions. If he wanted her to know, he would tell her.

He turned out the light and got in bed beside her, and put an icy hand on her bosom. She fought down the urge to push it away.

"We're on our way," he said. "Captain Selkirk found pouring pots and blowers here. We just brought them aboard. I checked them out. Fine equipment, all of it. The captain buys the best."

"Oh?" she asked to draw him out.

"Me, too, I guess," he said, pleased with himself. "He let it slip how much he paid that bastard Woodley to find me. I had no idea I was worth that kind of money." He paused and then told her, "Four hundred pounds, is what he paid for me."

"You're a good man, George," she said.

"Plus what he spent to buy that wagon and horses, and that ship he used just to get us out of England."

"You're a good man, George," Janet Sedge repeated.

"I feel pretty much like a good man right now, Janet," he said, mischievously. He let his hand slide under her nightdress and cupped her buttocks. "And, if you don't mind me saying so, you feel pretty much like a good woman."

"What happens now?" she asked.

"In the morning, we sail into the North Sea. Then through the English Channel, around France and into the Mediterranean Sea. The Captain told me we're going to stop at Naples just long enough to discharge cargo and pick up some machinery, and then we're off to Pennsylvania."

She had other questions, but he was not in a mood to hear them. He was really feeling like a man. More than once, when he had been feeling like a man the way he was now, there had been a child. If there was to be a child now, she decided, and it was a girl child, she would call it Eleanor. And if it was a boy, she would call it Paul Selkirk.

When she woke in the morning, she found that she was huddled close to her husband for warmth. The window (she corrected herself: the *port*) was closed tight, but there was enough icy air leaking around to chill the cabin. She got out of bed and went to the port and looked out. It was nasty-looking out there, with a black and overcast sky, and the seas were deep, with white froth being blown off their crests.

305

But she wasn't sick to her stomach, she realized with surprise, and then, with even greater surprise, she realized that she was no longer frightened, either with being at sea, or for the future.

Chapter Sixteen

1

London
March 25, 1770

The morning after Colonel Sir Edgar Watchbury was finally, and with appropriate pomp, laid to his eternal rest in the cemetery of Saint Martin's in the Fields Church, Lady Caroline Watchbury woke feeling vaguely nauseated. When she pushed herself up to a half-sitting position in the bed, the nausea struck, violently and so quickly that she barely had time to get out of bed, drop to her knees, pull the chamber pot from beneath the bed, and bend over it.

She hadn't dared to hope that Edgar would be interred in Westminster Abbey, for he really hadn't been that much of a soldier, much less a hero, even if he had been equerry to the king. But she had hoped that, because of his long service with the Life Guards of Horse, *and* because he had died while on a mission for the king, that he would have been granted grave space in the cemetery behind the Guards' Chapel.

The official decision by the Army Council to bury him in Saint Martin's in the Fields had been a genuine disappointment. The services themselves, however, left little to be desired. There was a memorial service first, at Westminster Abbey, with the Archbishop of Canterbury himself conducting the service. That was certainly because the king had announced his intention to come to Westminster, rather than a tribute to Edgar. But that didn't matter, the point being that the king and the archbishop had participated in Edgar's final rites.

Neither the king nor the archbishop, to be sure, had gone from Westminster Abbey to the graveyard (the graveside prayers had been offered by the rector of Saint Martin's in the Fields), but it would be remembered that they had been at the Abbey.

She had entertained the mourners afterward with a cold supper at her apartment. All the officers of the Life Guard of Horse had felt obliged to attend, which meant that Captain Sir Richard Trentwood had come. So had her father, who had immediately evidenced an interest in her financial affairs, with the clear implication that he intended to "manage things" for her.

She had suddenly perceived that his idea of management probably meant the diversion of Edgar's assets to his own purposes. She had made two instant decisions when that had come up. First, that she wouldn't tell him a thing about what she had come into from Edgar, much less let him "manage" anything; and second, that quarreling with him about it on the day of the funeral would not have been a good idea.

Captain Sir Richard Trentwood had gotten a little drunk on the champagne, and patted her fondly and possessively on the bottom, and she, a little tipsy herself, had entertained the notion that perhaps he could stay after the others left.

But that hadn't happened. Her family outstayed all the officers, and Sir Richard would have been conspicuous indeed had he remained behind.

Even as she threw up, she realized that she was glad that it had turned out the way it had. For one thing, she didn't want to appear too eager, either to have him in her bed or to marry him, and it *was* the evening, although he had been dead for so long, of Edgar's funeral. It might have been all right when they were both full of champagne, but it would not have been all right in the morning. Or if someone had sensed what was going on and started gossiping about it.

Finally, if Richard had spent the night, he would have been there when she became ill. She was aware that a retching woman is not the most attractive sight in the world.

She naturally wondered why she had become ill. She was rarely ill at all, and almost never sick to her stomach. She had not, she recalled, been sick once all the way from Tatta even in the nastiest weather. She first thought that there must have been a bad oyster among those she served when they came to the apartment from Saint Martin's. Or, if it had not been a bad oyster, then it had been the combination of good oysters and a great deal of champagne, because there certainly had been enough of that.

As quickly as the nausea had struck her, it passed, and she put it from her mind as being caused by a combination of nerves, oysters, champagne, the funeral itself, and her relatives, especially her greedy father.

But when she was sick the next morning, too, she suspected even as she knelt over the chamber pot that what was wrong with her was not nerves, nor something she had drunk or eaten. It was just too possible, indeed likely, that she was with child, and she was with child by a nineteen-year-old boy whom she would probably never see again.

She worried about it all day and all night, and the following morning she was not sick. She permitted herself to think that the nausea meant nothing. And neither, more than likely, did the fact that she had missed a monthly inconvenience. She had been irregular since leaving England. The first inconvenience she had experienced for three months had come the day after she boarded *The Eleanor*. Missing another one, she tried to tell herself, meant nothing.

The next morning, she was sick again.

Her self-diagnosis was confirmed by a doctor two days later. He told her that there was absolutely nothing to worry about, that morning sickness was to be expected, and that he actually believed it to be a good sign, indicating that her pregnancy would more than likely be without problems.

She almost laughed in his face. She couldn't imagine a worse thing happening to her, and cursed Charles Selkirk, his father, and herself, in particular, for being such a fool.

She asked the first doctor, and three others, to help her get rid of the unwanted child, and they flately refused, two because of religious beliefs and two because they considered that it would pose threats to her health they were not willing to risk.

Oh, God*damn* you, Charley!

Captain Sir Richard Trentwood was a fool, a sweet fool, and for a couple of days she considered letting him into her bed right away, so that she could later make him believe that he had done it to her. She came to realize that while she could probably initially convince him of that, because he *was* a sweet fool, and enamored of her, he would know the truth eventually. Sweet trusting fool or not, Captain Sir Richard Trentwood could count to nine.

She would have to do something else, and her thoughts kept returning to Charley Selkirk and the Selkirk family. He

309

was, after all, responsible, and he should assume his share of the responsibility. She was annoyed when she found herself, when thinking of Charley practically, thinking of him romantically as well. She wanted to rest her face against the muscles of his chest, to run her hand over the smooth, tight muscles of his legs, so different from the hairy sticks which supported Captain Sir Richard Trentwood.

While her only practical course of action did not come to her immediately, when it did come to her, she wondered why it had taken her so long to think it up.

She had to get out of England before her pregnancy became evident. That was absolutely essential, if she ever intended to make a decent marriage. Her position on the fringe of the Court and of London society was by no means secure. A duchess could get away with carrying a child out of wedlock, but not the second daughter of a marquess and the widow of a soldier. If her pregnancy became common knowledge, she would be, if not banished from the Court, simply not placed on the invitations lists.

She also had to consider what to do with the child after it was born. She wished that she had the coldness of character simply to get rid of it, but she knew she could not just dump it on the steps of an asylum for bastard babies. She would have to make arrangements for it, pay for its support and education. And she knew that even if she could somehow manage to have the child secretly in England, it would be impossible, over the years, to conceal it.

Marriage to Captain Sir Richard Trentwood would be absolutely out of the question if he learned she had carried an illegitimate child.

Going to America seemed a splendid, as well as the only, solution to her dilemma. To begin with, she had the perfect excuse to go. What better way to spend her period of deep mourning (during which she would not be invited out anyway) than traveling to Pennsylvania to examine her late husband's lands?

It would be expected that she would sell the land in America. That gave her the perfect excuse to go to Pennsylvania. Going there to examine the land, and to arrange for its sale, would simply take a little longer than she had planned it would. And then she could return either in a position to marry Sir Richard (without the problem of an illegitimate child) if he could be kept on the hook, and she believed he could, or with the proceeds from the sale of the land to make her a more desirable catch if he could not.

The child, of course, would be turned over to its father, or, more practically, to the Selkirk family. She knew that she would have no trouble with either Charley, who was a boy, or with his father. His father had sent her to Charley's bed, and it wouldn't be hard to convince him that he had a moral obligation to care for the child. Especially if the alternative was having Charley marry her. She was sure that Captain Paul Selkirk would not want his son to marry her.

And the child, of course, most important of all, would be well cared for. The Selkirks were kind and decent working people. If it was a boy, he could learn the mariner's trade, as his father had before him. The child would be far better off as a Selkirk, with that kind of honest, working-class future, than it would be in a home here in England. The Selkirks could easily not only invent some story of its origin, an adopted orphan or something, as an excuse to take it into the family, but they would really raise it as one of their own. For, obviously, it would be.

Far better the adopted child of a simple seagoing family, than the secret bastard of the wife of Captain Sir Richard Trentwood. It was as simple as that.

Lady Caroline Watchbury immediately made inquiries concerning suitable accommodations on ships bound for Philadelphia and took it as a good omen to learn that the Hanoverian merchantman *Prinz Wilhelm*, a fine, large ship in which it was common knowledge the king himself had a personal investment, would sail for Philadelphia in three days. That was just about enough time to tell Sir Richard what she was going to do and make all the other necessary arrangements.

2

East longitude 1°42', north latitude 51°20'
(The North Sea, off Cap Gris Nez)
April 2, 1770

The English Channel was choppy, with six- to eight-foot seas. *The Eleanor* dipped her bow frequently, sending a cascade of white water over the fo'c'sl to run down onto the milch cows and the goats tethered in an open cabin built against the fo'c'sl bulkhead. Because of the weather, the chickens had been taken into the fo'c'sl itself. The men had decided that if the price of an occasional egg now, and fresh chicken later, was the smell of the fowl, it was a cheap one to be paid. The cows would be all right, for they were used to the cold and rainy weather of Holland, but Charley had his doubts how long the goats could endure constant soaking with cold sea water.

Once they were around the curve of France, into the Atlantic, it was likely that the seas would not only run smoother but that the warmer air of the southerly latitudes would overcome the cold air coming down from the Poles. And bring with it fog, of course, he thought.

He was cold and miserable, and when he had taken the helm, he had felt sorry for the three lookouts he had had to order aloft. It would be even colder and more miserable above the yards than it was on the exposed quarterdeck. There was haze and fog, and ordering lookouts aloft was necessary, even if it was unlikely that they would be able to see much of anything.

In his time in the fo'c'sl Charley had stood his turns as lookout aloft, and he knew what it was like to spend two hours in weather like this, tied to the mast-junction, soaked to the skin, chilled to the bone, peering out into an impenetrable grayness while the ship did her damnedest to make you lose your footing and send you crashing to the deck to cripple or kill you.

But they had to be there. There was no alternative. Three men at a time being chilled and miserable was far better than having a shipful of people drowned when the ship ran aground, or sank when rammed by another ship.

"Would you like a mug of soup, Mr. Selkirk?" Tony asked him.

Charley had no appetite at all, and was on the edge of saying no, thank you when he realized that Tony was asking because he wanted something warm for himself, but didn't want to ask for it for fear that Selkirk would think he was unmanly.

He had done the same thing to Mr. McMullen on *The Mary*, on his first voyage as a cabin boy. He had attached himself to McMullen as Tony had lately attached himself to him.

"Will you have some soup?" Charley asked the quartermaster's mate and the helmsmen.

"Aye, that'd be fine, sir," one of the helmsmen immediately responded.

"Fetch a bucket and some mugs, Tony," Selkirk said. "And if there's someone in the kitchen, ask them to make sure it's hot. I don't want you fooling with the fire, understand?"

"Aye, aye, sir," Tony said, and ran down the ladder to the maindeck.

Selkirk walked to the port railing and looked out at the fog. It was a little after sunrise, and the sun had begun to burn the fog off, so that instead of a solid wall, it was in patches.

The sun was reported to be some sort of huge, permanent ball of fire, like the earth itself burning up. Charley had heard that from his father, so he believed it. He wondered how they knew. They also were supposed to know that it was several million leagues, or some other impossible-to-comprehend distance away. He wondered how they knew that, too. How were they sure it wasn't just, say, a hundred leagues up here in the sky?

"Ahoy, the quarterdeck!" a lookout called out. "Something in the water, off the starboard quarter."

Charley walked quickly across the quarterdeck to the opposite side and looked out over the rolling seas. It was a section of mast, with some canvas still attached. For a moment, until he considered how impossible that would be, he wondered if it was part of the fishing boat he had sent to the bottom off the English coast. That hadn't been far from their present position, but by now, certainly, what wreckage hadn't gone to the bottom had long since washed ashore.

"Piece of mast," Charley called up at the rigging. "Something went down around here. Keep a sharp eye."

The last thing he needed was to ram a half-submerged hulk, or for that matter, to run over what they had just passed, and have it foul the rudder. This would be a hell of a place to hove to and send men over the side to cut line free from the rudder.

He had a quick mental image of Dooley, who had lost his footing and gone over the side.

"Ahoy, the quarterdeck! Debris in the water, dead ahead!"

"Hard to port," Charley said.

313

"Hard to port it is, sir," the quartermaster's mate called, as the helmsmen strained to turn the wheel.

"Ahoy, the quarterdeck! Debris off the port quarter!"

"Rudder amidships," Charley ordered. Damn! He stepped to the railing, cupped his hands, and called, "Watch on deck!"

Theo LaSalle bounded on deck and then up on the quarterdeck, pausing at the head of the ladder to wait for Charley's nod of permission. Then he came and stood beside him.

"What do we have, Mr. Selkirk?" he asked.

"Debris in the water," Charley said. "We damned near ran over part of a mast."

"Goddamned channel's a garbage dump," LaSalle said, and then looked around for Tony, and, not finding him, picked up the leather megaphone.

"I want two men, port and starboard, on the foremast shrouds," he bellowed, "and two men onto the bowsprit topgallant yard!"

Charley, remembering Dooley falling to his death again, was tempted to countermand the order. But LaSalle, of course, was right. If you wanted to know what was lying dead ahead, you put lookouts on the bowsprit, as far forward as you could get them.

Tony came onto the quarterdeck with a bucket of soup and a handful of handled mugs.

"If that's soup, you're forgiven for not being where you're supposed to be when you're needed," LaSalle said to him.

"Mr. Selkirk ordered up the broth, Mr. LaSalle," Tony protested.

"When you answer me back the next time, I'll take a tarred line to your ass," LaSalle said, meanwhile winking at Charley.

Tony handed Mr. Selkirk a cup of soup. Mr. Selkirk, turning his head so that the bosun couldn't see, winked at Tony, who replied with a grateful smile.

To Charley's surprise, no further reports of objects in the water were called, either from the lookouts or from the seaman now hanging from the foremast shrouds and the bowsprit rigging. He turned and looked at LaSalle.

"If I see something float by you people missed," LaSalle bellowed, "I'll have you all stoning decks for a week!"

The exhortation produced nothing. As the fog continued to

314

break up, *The Eleanor* smashed through the waves, apparently alone on the sea.

"I think you can bring the men down, Theo," Charley said. "We're apparently through whatever it was."

"Another five minutes won't hurt them," LaSalle said. "What it probably was was a Frenchie or English fisherman. They lose them all the time out here in weather like this. That's what your father is counting on them thinking when they find the nameplate of that ship we sent down."

"Why do they do it, Theo?" Charley asked. "Knowing what the channel is like?"

"To eat, lad," LaSalle said. "You were raised in America. You don't know what it's like to be really hungry."

"The Sedge children," Charley said. "They looked really hungry."

"And they damned well were," LaSalle said. "You can count on it. I expect that getting his young enough to eat is why Sedge took the risk he did running the way he did."

LaSalle walked to the port railing and looked over the side, and then crossed the quarterdeck to look off the other side. Then he walked to where Charley stood and put the megaphone to his lips, obviously about to order the watch to come down from the shrouds and the bowsprit.

"Ahoy, the quarterdeck!" a lookout at that moment called. "Debris in the water, dead ahead!"

"We'll pass it to port," Charley shouted back. "Keep me advised."

He looked at LaSalle. LaSalle again had been right, had kept him from making another potentially serious mistake.

"Debris directly dead ahead, sir!" the word was passed back from the lookout on the bow sprit.

"Nudge her to starboard," Charley said to the quartermaster's mate.

Charley went to the port rail of the quarterdeck and looked forward. There was a break in the patchy fog on the water's surface, and he saw what looked like a crate in the water, and what looked like a body on the crate before he heard the call from the bowsprit lookout.

"The debris . . . Christ, there's a body on it! Body on the debris! Body on the debris!"

"Where away?" Theo LaSalle called.

"It'll pass to port, sir," the lookout replied.

LaSalle joined Charley at the port railing, and peered

ahead. Charley could see it clearly now. It was a wooden crate, a foot and a half thick, maybe five feet square, making a sort of raft. He could now see the body on it more clearly too. It was lying face down on the crate, tied to it, its legs hanging over the side and into the sea, making that side of the crate sink almost beneath the surface.

"Tony," Charley called, "I'll have all hands on deck."

Theo LaSalle put his hand on Charley's arm. "Charley," he said, "he's dead. You'll just be wasting time and effort."

Charley felt his temper flame.

"I'll have all hands on deck, Theo," he said, icily. "And make all preparations to bring her about and hove to. Ready the longboat crew."

There was scorn in LaSalle's eyes, and Charley thought he saw the seeds of defiance for a moment before the bosun finally said, "Aye, aye, sir."

"If that man is dead, Theo," Charley said to him, "then we'll give him a Christian burial. I'll not leave him floating around like that for the gulls to work over."

"Aye, aye, sir," LaSalle repeated, his tone a razor's edge from insolent. Charley was aware that his explanation had been wasted on LaSalle. LaSalle thought he was being foolish, sentimental, wasting time and effort, acting like a boy, rather than as an officer. He made no effort to conceal his feelings.

But this time, Theo, Charley decided angrily, *you're wrong!*

They lost sight of the floating crate and the body as *The Eleanor* moved in a wide circle to reverse course, but the lookout on the foremast spotted it again as Captain Selkirk, wakened by the movement of *The Eleanor* as she turned, came onto the quarterdeck from his cabin.

"There's a body in the water, sir," Charley said to him.

"Mr. Selkirk wants to give it a nice Christian burial, sir," LaSalle said sarcastically.

"I don't recall speaking to you, LaSalle," Captain Selkirk said icily. "Nor was I aware your position is on the quarterdeck when we're about to launch the longboat."

LaSalle looked as if Captain Selkirk had slapped him in the face. Captain Selkirk continued to glower at him. LaSalle tugged at his forelock and then ran down the ladder from the quarterdeck.

Paul Selkirk waited until LaSalle was out of hearing, and

then he spoke to Charley. "The main reason Theo's still in the fo'c'sl, Charley," he said, "and the reason he never should be allowed out of it, is because he's an animal. A great, hulking, loyal, stupid beast, who thinks with his stomach."

Charley looked at his father in surprise.

"Men like Theo, Charley," Captain Selkirk went on, "have to be led. They can never lead, and they should never be allowed to."

Charley nodded, still surprised at what his father had said.

"What did you do to him when he went in the longboat with you to blow up the fisherman, after you told him to stay aboard?" his father asked.

Charley flushed. He had done nothing to him.

"That led to this, Charley, can't you see?" his father said, not unkindly. "You let him get away with that, and that made him think he had not only the right to make fun of you, which is bad enough, but to ignore, even disobey you."

"Theo still thinks of me as the boy he taught in the fo'c'sl," Charley said.

"You're not a boy any more," his father said. "You were the officer of the deck when he made sport of you. You can't have that."

"Yes, sir," Charley said. He stepped to the railing. "Bosun! I'll have everything in but the foremast main!"

"Aye, aye, sir," LaSalle boomed in reply, and issued the necessary orders.

When *The Eleanor*, with only enough sail aloft to give her steerage, had slowed nearly to a stop, Charley ordered the longboat over the side.

The way the ship was lying, he couldn't see the recovery operation until the longboat was nearly back alongside the ship.

"It's a lad, sir, and he's alive," LaSalle called up from the longboat.

Mr. Porter, also wakened by the unusual movements of the ship, had come onto the quarterdeck.

"Take the helm and see what else you can find, please, Mr. Porter," Captain Selkirk said. "You come with me, Mr. Selkirk, and we'll have a look at your Lazarus."

They reached the deck as the unconscious body of a large, obviously young, man was hauled aboard. He looked near death, Charley thought. He quite clearly would not have lasted much longer in the water. The tip of his nose and his ears were white with frostbite, and the skin on his face and on his neck was puckered and raw.

Theo LaSalle, when the body was taken from the sling, picked it up in his arms.

Charley walked alongside him as LaSalle carried the body down the deck. He felt fury sweep through him.

"You were right, LaSalle," Charley said, angrily sarcastic. "A funeral will probably be unnecessary." Then his temper took over. "God*damn* you! Don't you *ever* question an order of mine again!"

LaSalle looked as unhappy as he had when Captain Selkirk had run him off the bridge.

"What do I do with him, sir?"

"Put him in my cabin," Charley ordered.

Captain Selkirk caught up with them, looked at the limp body, and then turned to look around for Tony. Tony trotted up to them.

"Go to my cabin," Captain Selkirk ordered. "Get a bottle of brandy, and in the lower right drawer of my port chest is a jar of whale suet. Meet me in Mr. Selkirk's cabin with it. And then have Cookie bring us some hot beef broth and some warm milk with rum in it."

Charley walked to the rail to see what was delaying bringing the longboat back aboard. He heard Mr. Porter shouting to the lookouts from the quarterdeck that they should keep a sharp eye. If they had found one man, there were likely to be others.

When Charley looked over the side, he saw the seamen fixing a cradle to bring aboard the crate on which the man had been half-lying.

"Do we need that?" he called down.

If there were more men in the water, the men should be looking for them, not devoting their attention to salvaging a water-logged crate.

"It's a fine crate, sir," one of the seamen called back. "You never can tell what might be in it."

"Well, hurry it up," Charley said, and turned and went into the companionway to his cabin.

The rescued man was on his bunk. Theo LaSalle was pulling his clothing off.

"You'd not needed here, Mr. Selkirk," his father said curtly, dismissing him. Charley went back to the quarterdeck.

"I can relieve you, sir, if you wish," he said to Mr. Porter.

"I stand relieved, sir," Mr. Porter said. "We're underway, under just enough sail to give us steerage, and on course."

Charley looked at the compass. When he looked up, Mr. Porter was looking at him.

"Can you take a little advice, Charley?" he asked.

"Yes, sir. Of course."

"The next time you want to curse out Theo, take him somewhere out of hearing of the men."

"Yes, sir," Charley said. "That was stupid of me."

Mr. Porter met his eyes a minute, then tipped his tricorn and went off the quarterdeck.

Goddamn it, I can't do anything right, Charley thought.

For some inexplicable reason, a mental image of Caroline, naked in her bed in the apartment on King's Way popped into his mind. God, how he would like to be with her there, rather than here. He forced Caroline from his mind and walked to the railing and looked up at the lookouts. He could see them clearly now.

"Ahoy, aloft!" he called. "Anything?"

One by one they reported there was nothing in sight.

Charley walked to the forward rail of the quarterdeck to see if the longboat was ready to be brought aboard. It had been hoisted out of the water and was hanging from its davits, over the side.

Half a dozen men were watching a seaman about to rip open the crate they'd taken from the sea.

"Belay that!" Charley called. "Bring it up here."

It was liable to contain wine or spirits, forbidden to the men under way. If it did, and no officer was present, the contents of the crate would vanish within seconds.

The crate was carried to the quarterdeck.

"Open it up," he said, "and carefully."

Inside a rough outer crate, there were two smaller crates. Charley saw that something was painted on them: Muller und Thane. Uhrmachermeisters. Nürnberg.

Inside the inner crates, packed in cotton wool, protected by oiled silk, was a telescope, the largest Charley had ever seen, and a three-legged stand for it.

"Put that in the captain's cabin," Charley said. "On his bunk. And stow those smaller crates somewhere handy. We'll probably need them again."

319

2

London
April 7, 1770

Karl-Friedrich Christian von und zu Wetterich-Dryden
held his handkerchief to his nostrils as he made his way
through the wards of Saint Anne's Hospital for Seafarers.
Wetterich-Dryden, a tall and bony man of thirty-six, was personal representative of Gerlach Adolph von Munchhausen,
Privy Councillor of Hanover, to the Court of Saint James.

The smell in the wards of Saint Anne's was almost over-
powering, and Wetterich-Dryden was about as concerned that
he would vomit all over his silk trousers as he was about the
danger of contagion. If anyone else had been available at the
Residence, Wetterich-Dryden would not himself be making
his way to meet a man plucked out of the English Channel
by a fishing boat and who was incredibly protesting that he
was about the business of the landgrave of Hesse-Kassel. But
there was no one else in town, and here he was.

The sister led him to a bed halfway down one of the long,
high-ceilinged wards, and pointed to a large man asleep in
one of the beds, his head lolling to one side. The man showed
terrible signs of long exposure to the water. And he showed
no signs whatever of being aware that someone was standing
by his bed.

Finally, almost timidly, Wetterich-Dryden reached down
and pushed the man's shoulder with a gloved hand. And
when there was no response, he pushed again, and harder.

The lolling head suddenly snapped erect, and the eyes
opened. The eyes were terribly bloodshot.

"Who're you?" the man demanded.

"The question, my good fellow," Wetterich-Dryden said,
"seems to be, who are you?"

"Chief Sergeant Karl Lahrner, Cavalry Squadron, the
Landgrave of Hesse-Kassel's Regiment of Light Foot,"
Lahrner said.

"You're a long way from Kassel, Sergeant," Wetterich-
Dryden said drily.

"I am about the landgrave's business," Lahrner said.

"Are you, now?"

320

"I said I am."

"Say 'sir' when addressing your betters," Wetterich-Dryden said.

"I do when I know who they are," Lahrner said.

"I am the Baron von Wetterich-Dryden," he said. "Personal representative of the Hanoverian Privy Councillor."

"Then, in that case, Herr Baron, please excuse my manners."

"Tell me how you happen to be here, and what it is you want of me," Wetterich-Dryden said.

He had come as duty required, but prepared to be bored and annoyed with a story of mishap among the lower classes. But his ears immediately began to perk up when Lahrner told him that he had been assigned to bring a gift, a telescope, from the landgrave to King George III. A present from one royal to another was important.

He grew fascinated when Lahrner told him that he had been accompanied by the son of the Baron von Kolbe. Wetterich-Dryden had heard that story not four days before.

"The boy who struck the Grand Duke Alexei?" he asked.

"Yes, sir."

"And you say he was lost at sea?"

"No, sir. He was picked up at sea, him and the telescope, by a ship."

"You're sure?"

"I saw it."

"And was the boy alive?"

"I don't know," Lahrner said. "We were out there a long time after that goddamned boat sank under us."

"But how do you know about the gift from the landgrave to His Majesty being picked up?"

"Herr Baron, I tied the boy to that crate myself."

"How commendable, Sergeant," Wetterich-Dryden said.

"The landgrave himself told me to keep an eye on that boy, Herr Baron," Lahrner said.

Wetterich-Dryden looked at him with still more interest. He's quite telling the truth, he thought. Philip was entirely capable of taking a personal interest like that. He had spared the boy's life, and written to George III that he was sending, together with the telescope, a young man to whose father he owed a great deal, and who had earned the displeasure, which was an interesting way of putting it, of Grand Duke

321

Alexei, and whom, he was sure, George III would protect while he was in England.

"Why weren't you picked up, Sergeant," Wetterich-Dryden asked, "when the boy and the telescope were?"

"It was not, Herr Baron, because I did not wish to be," Lahrner said sarcastically. Wetterich-Dryden was offended by the man's insolence, but more important, he was impressed with it. He would not have dared such insolence were he not telling the truth, or if he were not used to dealing with his betters on a personal basis.

"What is it you wish of me?" Wetterich-Dryden asked.

"I saw the name of the ship that picked up the boy," Lahrner said. "I want to know where I can find out where it went, so that I can go there. And I will need the means to follow it."

"Money, you mean?"

"Yes, Herr Baron, money. I am empowered to draw on the landgrave's funds at the Rothschild's bank in Frankfurt am Main."

"I will discuss the matter with my superiors," Wetterich-Dryden said, to give himself time to think, for he had no superior at the moment in London. "And tell you of their decision. In the meantime, is there anything I can do for you?"

"I would be deeply grateful if the Herr Baron would get me out of this charnel house. I am tired, not sick. Brandy is what I need, not warm gruel."

"I will bring that request to my superiors' attention as well," Wetterich-Dryden said. "I should have word for you in a day or two."

Lahrner nodded at him.

"You would guess, would you," Wetterich-Dryden said, "that despite its being in the water for some time, if you could get your hands on the telescope, it would be all right?"

"I would think so, Herr Baron. Some parts of it are lost, but the main parts, the glass and the stand for it, will be all right."

"How can you be so sure?"

"After they packed it, the Uhrmachermeisters, I mean, I had it packed inside still another crate, before we sailed from Holland."

"I will get back to you just as soon as my superiors make their decision," Wetterich-Dryden said.

He made his decision almost as soon as he was back in the fresh air. It was quite an opportunity for him, when you looked at it carefully. He would give the man some money and send him on what was sure to be a fruitless pursuit of the telescope and the boy. He would both earn the landgrave's gratitude, and get his money back, too, for the landgrave would consider it a debt of honor. And at the same time, he could made interesting conversation at court. The boy who had struck the Grand Duke Alexei, and whom the landgrave of Hesse-Kassel had incredibly protected, had been shipwrecked at sea. And picked up. And he, Karl-Friedrich Christian von und zu Wetterich-Dryden, had given the sergeant who accompanied him money to chase after him. He could probably make wagers about whether the boy, or the telescope, or both, would ever be found.

He went the same afternoon to the shipping company, where he sent the man in charge to deal with the Admiralty, to learn what he could about the ship *Eleanor* of Philadelphia. Where she was bound, and who her owners were.

He learned that the ship had left London bound for Amsterdam, Naples, and then Philadelphia. More than likely, they had picked up the telescope outbound from Amsterdam. If he could find a ship directly bound for Pennsylvania, on which he could dispatch the sergeant, the sergeant could be waiting on the wharf in Philadelphia when *The Eleanor* docked. In that case, he could lay claim to the telescope . . . or could he?

Wetterich-Dryden sent the man back to the Admiralty to ask that question. Did the laws of salvage apply to royal property? He was more than a little annoyed to learn that they did. But on reflection, that, too seemed to be a blessing hidden beneath some minor inconvenience. He would simply give the sergeant more money, enough to buy the telescope back from the Americans, who probably wouldn't know what it was and would be glad to get rid of it. He would get all his money back from the landgrave, no matter how much it was.

He asked the man at the shipping office about ships sailing for Pennsylvania. The answer seemed to be one more proof that what had begun as an unpleasant duty had turned into a stroke of good luck. The *Prinz Wilhelm*, a Hanoverian in which he himself had a one-eighth interest, was sailing in plenty of time to be in Philadelphia before *The Eleanor*.

He had another thought: if Chief Sergeant Lahrner were

323

important enough to be personally entrusted with a dual re
sponsibility by the landgrave of Hesse-Kassel, he should b
provided with accommodations according to his responsibil
ity, not his rank. He ordered that the *Prinz Wilhelm* reserv
the best available cabin for Lahrner. The landgrave woul
certainly regard that cost, too, as a debt of honor, and ther
would be the profit from the passage, his one-eighth share o
it, as well.

He was tempted to return to Saint Anne's Hospital th
next morning, but after thinking that over, decided it woul
be better if Lahrner stayed there another day or two, regain
ing his strength. He would then be even more grateful whe
he showed up and told him what he was going to do for him.

If necessary, he could arrange to have Chief Sergean
Lahrner carried aboard the *Prinz Wilhelm* on a stretcher. H
could recuperate at sea.

Chapter Seventeen

1

Philadelphia, Pennsylvania
April 2, 1770

Ingebord Johnson Selkirk, who had come down the Delaware by boat two days before, was waiting at the house at the corner of Arch and Third streets when the wagon, pulled by oxen and driven by her son Nils, lumbered slowly up Arch Street and stopped before the white picket fence.

Nils climbed down from the wagon seat, opened the gate in the picket fence, walked up the walkway to the door, which Ingebord opened as he reached it.

He did not look into her face.

"I can't unload this by myself," he said, offering no other word of greeting.

"Reverend Sooth has arranged for men to be here to help after lunch," she said. He nodded.

"I bought bread and sausage," Ingebord said to her oldest son, "if you're hungry."

"I'm going down to the waterfront and look at the ships," he said. "I'll get something to eat there."

"I don't want you going into a tavern," she said.

Nils didn't even reply. He walked back to the wagon, took wooden buckets from it, carried them to the well in back of the house, filled them, and set them before the oxen, who drank noisily from them. He filled the buckets twice before the oxen had their fill. Then he spilled what little water was left onto the cobblestones and filled the buckets with corn from a bag in the wagon. When the oxen had been fed, he walked down Arch Street toward the river without once looking at the house, or his mother, who stood in the doorway.

It was foolish, Ingebord decided, watching him walk away,

to deny to herself that Nils knew what was going on between her and Ingmar. Or to hope that Luther didn't know, either. If Luther hadn't known, Nils would have told him. Both of her sons knew, disapproved, and were shamed, because they didn't understand. They were hardly more than boys, and there was just no way they could understand.

She was still astonished to realize that she had gone all those years and borne two sons, not knowing what she had been missing, what incredible pleasure there could be in being with a man, what a wondrous feeling afterward. Ingmar had opened a whole new world to her, a world that once she knew she could not turn away from.

For all those long years, until Ingmar, she had known almost nothing of carnal pleasure. Until the first time with Ingmar, she had been a good, modest, faithful Christian woman. She had gone to her wedding bed a virgin, prepared for it by her mother only with references to the Biblical admonition that man and woman were meant to be of one flesh, and that it was a sin for a woman to deny her husband.

Sometimes she felt shamed at what she had done and was doing. She couldn't believe that what she and Ingmar were doing was quite as sin-free as he suggested, although he offered arguments that were convincing: if God was joy and love, how could it be a sin to give joy to someone you loved? If Captain Paul Selkirk had turned his back on her and gone to sleep, rather than mated with her, on the night of their marriage, how could they possibly, in the sight of God, be married? And if she was not married, how could what was going on with her and Ingmar be a terrible sin?

They had, Ingmar had explained to her, pledged themselves to one another from now on. That was in a very real way a marriage vow. The vows that she had exchanged with Paul Selkirk had been a sin, because they meant nothing. Paul Selkirk hadn't wanted her as a wife, and she hadn't wanted Paul Selkirk as a husband. She had wanted a husband in name only to protect her now that she was a widow, and he had wanted a wife in name only to take care of his daughter. That had been pure selfishness on his part, as Ingmar had pointed out. Selkirk had been shirking his responsibility to care for the girl now that the girl was motherless. It had been sinful for him to take advantage of Ingebord's good-willed ignorance and talk her into accepting a responsibility that was his and his alone.

326

Shouldering it himself would have meant a sacrifice on his part. He would have had to give up the life he lived and stayed home. And, as Ingmar pointed out, unless Paul Selkirk was some kind of saintly exception, which he doubted, to the rest of the mariners he had come to know, the life he would have had to give up was a life of sin and wantonness, carrying on with women at each port.

There was no question in Ingebord's mind that Paul Selkirk, used to wild and degenerate women in the waterfront taverns, had looked at her and found her wanting, and that was the reason he had turned his back on her. It was interesting to consider (although thinking about it made her somewhat uncomfortable) what would have happened had Paul Selkirk taken her as he took the loose and wanton women he met in his travels.

Would she have responded to him as she had responded to Ingmar?

She thought not. The only man she had known before was her husband, and Nils, she now understood, had been the exception among men, a man not interested in what happened in bed between men and women because he wasn't thrilled by it. Nils had been something like a partial gelding. He had taught her none of these *new* things, in all the years of their marriage. If Paul Selkirk had wanted those things from her, he certainly would have been disgusted and repelled. But, she told herself, as a Christian woman, she would not have denied her husband, and if he had come to her with love, she would have eventually responded to him. In that sense, it was Paul Selkirk's fault that she had taken Ingmar into her bed and would eventually marry him.

Ingmar was a special kind of man, with the unusual ability to bring something to a woman that could not be fully described by words like pleasure and joy, who had been able to recognize the passion in her and bring it out. But if Paul Selkirk had done what a husband was supposed to do, she would never have permitted what had happened between her and Ingmar to happen.

The difference was that Ingmar had come to her bed with love. The *new* things had come later. But now that what had happened had happened, there was no turning back. She was sorry that the boys knew, and sorry that they didn't understand, but that simply couldn't be helped.

Ingebord Johnson Selkirk and the Reverend Ingmar Sooth

had had long talks about what to do about their situation. An annulment of the marriage between herself and Captain Paul Selkirk was the obvious solution. Ingmar had spoken with a solicitor (not giving him any hint, of course, that the parishoner of whom he spoke was Ingebord Johnson Selkirk), who had confirmed what he had told Ingebord. An unconsummated marriage was not valid. When Paul Selkirk returned from this voyage, all that would have to be done to end their marriage and free her to marry Ingmar would be for her and Paul Selkirk to appear before a judge and swear to the truth: that they had not known one another.

If Paul Selkirk was reluctant to appear in court, as was likely, Ingmar was then prepared to reason with him. Reasoning with him would mean letting him know that his taking advantage of a good woman was at an end. He would either appear in court, to do the decent thing; or the authorities would be made aware that he wasn't quite the upstanding, law-abiding merchantman captain he represented himself to be.

Ingebord saw no problems about that. She knew enough about his illegal dealings to have him sent to prison and to see the courts confiscate his precious *Eleanor*. Paul Selkirk was no fool. He would see where the path of reason led.

But all that had to wait until he returned to Philadelphia, and God alone knew when that would be.

Now that she had found Ingmar, she could not live without him. She was fully aware that that would paint her as both weak and wanton in some people's eyes, but she didn't care. She was, as Ingmar pointed out, a woman who could make her own decisions about right and wrong.

And she had made her decisions, and Ingmar had agreed with them.

In discharging her moral and legal obligations to her late husband and the sons she had borne him, she would see that their sons came into the farm, share and share alike. The farm, free and clear of all loans and other indebtedness, was more than large enough to provide both of them (and their families, if and when they married) with a fine livelihood. If the boys couldn't get along together, that was their problem, not hers.

She had no obligation, moral or otherwise, to turn the forge and the mines and the furnace over to them. She and her late husband had built that business, and it was hers alone now by right.

Once her marriage to Paul Selkirk was annulled, she would put the forge and the mines and the furnace on the market, and bring the money to Ingmar as her dowry. She would use part of the money to buy the house at the corner of Third and Arch streets from Paul Selkirk. She would be able to buy it, Ingmar suggested, at a very good price, as sort of compensation to her for the humiliation Paul Selkirk had subjected her to. It was for that reason that Ingmar suggested that she occupy the house now, before he returned. She was entitled to live in her husband's house, and possession was nine-tenths of the law.

That her moving to the house in Philadelphia would also permit them to be together far more often than was possible when he was riding the upriver circuit was understood but not put into words between them.

Ingmar intended to have a long, personal conversation with Paul Selkirk immediately *The Eleanor* tied up. He was sure he could settle all these points at one time.

She wished, on one hand, that the boys were older, so that they might be able, as men, to understand her needs as a woman. But on the other hand, if they were men, they might presume they had a right to the furnace and the forge and the mines, which she wanted to take to Ingmar as a dowry.

She was grateful that she had Ingmar to advise her.

She was not surprised when Nils did not return from the riverfront until long after what had been Eleanor Selkirk's furniture had been unloaded from the wagon and put back into what had been Eleanor Selkirk's home.

Neither was she surprised, or disappointed, when Nils did not come into the house when he finally came back. She watched as he untied the team of oxen from the iron gatepost, then climbed onto the wagon, flicked the whip, and started back on the long road to Durham Furnace.

He just couldn't understand, and therefore could not approve of, what she was doing. And if he had come in, it might have been awkward. Ingmar had said he would be coming to supper, and Ingmar knew that Nils did not like him.

2

Aboard The Eleanor
West longitude 1°45', north latitude 49°50'
Off Cape de la Hague, the English Channel

April, 5, 1770

Wilhelm Karl Philip von Kolbe opened his eyes and found a pretty red-headed young woman looking down at him. He tried to lick his lips. He didn't seem to be able to get his swollen tongue through his lips.

He wondered if he was dreaming again. He had dreamed a lot lately, dreamed that he was in his bed at home in Marburg; dreamed that he was in Trude's bed in the Golden Ram in Nürnberg; dreamed that he was aboard the flat-bottomed boat on which they had gone from Nürnberg to Holland. Sometimes the dreams had been very real.

But he'd always woken up. There had always been a fire in the dreams, no matter where he had dreamed he was. And he had been burned in the fire, and woken up to find himself floating on the surface of the water. He had wondered how it could be that he could feel as if he was burning and feel so cold at the same time.

He decided that he was just about to wake up again. That he was dreaming there was a really pretty young woman looking down at him, and soon there would be a fire and he would wake up again floating around on the water. God knows, he could feel the burning already. His shoulders and arms felt as if they were on fire. His throat was so dry it hurt, and when he moved his eyes, that hurt, too. He closed his eyes. It did no good to keep them forced open.

He heard a woman's voice.

"He's awake, Mr. Selkirk," Janet Sedge said. "Or he was a moment ago. His eyes were open."

Willi, who spoke no English, had no idea what the woman's voice was saying. He forced his eyes open.

There were now two faces looking down at him. A woman's face, not the girl's face he had seen before, and a young man's. He wondered what had happened to the pretty girl.

"Hello, there," the young man said. That sounded like "Hallo."

"Where am I?" Willi croaked, in German.

"What did he say?" Janet Sedge asked, and leaned closer to him.

"I don't know. Sounds like Dutch. Maybe German."

"Hello," the woman said, and smiled at him.

"Wasser," Willi croaked.

"That's Dutch," Charley Selkirk said, positively. "He wants water."

The woman put a glass to his lips, and water went into his mouth, and trickled down his throat. He tried to find the strength to move his hand to hold the glass and failed.

When the water reached his stomach, he threw up. It was very painful.

"I'll tell my father he's awake," Charley said. "And get Stern. He speaks Dutch."

Willi moved his head and forced his eyes to focus. The pretty girl sat down on the edge of the bed. She dipped her fingers into a jar and then, very gently, rubbed some kind of salve on his face. Her fingertips were soft and cool. He looked at her face, met her eyes. He just had time to see that her eyes were green when she quickly, modestly, averted them.

Two other men and the young man he had seen before came into view, looking down at him in the bed.

"Are you Dutch or German?" one of the newcomers asked, in German.

"German," Willi said. Then he asked the obvious question. "Where am I?"

"He's German, Captain," Stern translated. "He wants to know where he is."

"Tell him," Captain Selkirk ordered. "Tell him who I am."

"This is Captain Selkirk, master of the merchantman *Eleanor*, of Philadelphia, out of Amsterdam for Naples," Stern said to him. "We picked you out of the sea."

"Did you pick up anybody else?" Willi asked.

"You were the only one we found," Stern said.

"What did he say?" Captain Selkirk asked.

"He wants to know if there were any other survivors."

"Ask him what ship, and where bound," Captain Selkirk said.

It took Willi a moment to recall the name of the *Queen of*

Peace. He gave it, and then he said, "Please tell the captain I'm in the service of the landgrave of Hesse-Kassel, en route to the Court of King George III with a gift."

Stern made the translation, and Captain Selkirk nodded his head to show his understanding.

"Tell the captain, please," Willi went on, "that the gift for the king of England was in the crate to which I was tied."

"Tell him," Captain Selkirk said, when that had been translated, "that the telescope is now in the service of Captain Paul Selkirk, Esquire, of Philadelphia."

Mary, surprised at the coldness of the answer, looked at her father in surprise.

"The one thing we don't need, mistress," Captain Selkirk said, "is someone aboard who's headed for Buckingham Palace, where he can tell the king's people, or maybe the king himself, that *The Eleanor* is carrying a running journeyman ironworker to Pennsylvania."

"God, I didn't think about that," Charley said. "I was trying to think of the nearest port where we could put him ashore."

"He's not going to be put ashore just yet," Captain Selkirk said. "We can't risk it."

"But his family," Mary protested. "They'll think he drowned at sea!"

"They already think that, mistress," Captain Selkirk said.

"It's not right!" Mary said, angrily, "for you not to put him ashore."

"Not putting him ashore for a while is a whole lot better than putting him back in the sea," Captain Selkirk replied drily. He looked at her and smiled. "Don't look so distressed, mistress. See to him, and when he's better, we'll figure out what's to be done with him."

Mary turned to Willi and resumed rubbing the whale grease into his raw skin. She felt his eyes on her, and then she felt her face flush. She wondered what made her do that. She forced herself to meet his eyes. He had very nice eyes, she thought. Terribly bloodshot from being in the salt water, but very nice eyes. Pretty, and *nice.*

3

Willi's strength returned quickly. He slept, on and off, for three days, waking when either the woman or the girl had something for him to eat, or when they wanted to rub the greasy salve on his raw, ulcerated skin.

From time to time, the man, Stern, who spoke German, and the young man whom Willi came to understand was the officer in whose room he was, came to help him onto the chamber pot, and to ask, but not answer, questions. Willi learned nothing from either of them beyond what he had learned when the captain has come to see him.

Willi had time to think, to reconstruct in his mind what had happened their third night at sea. There had been a terrible storm, tossing the fishing boat around like a cork. The boat had lost its masts, and then there had been water coming into it, more water than the pumps could get out of the hold.

He remembered Karl Lahrner manhandling the crates with the telescope parts out of the hold and into a small boat. Lahrner had sensed long before it happened that the fishing boat was going to sink. They had gotten the boat into the water, Willi remembered that, and when Lahrner had told him to jump into it, he had done so without question. Two of the troopers had jumped in too, but the third had been afraid, terrified, and refused to leave the larger fishing boat for the small rowboat. The last time Willi had seen him, he was standing on the deck of the fishing boat, in the process of tying himself to the mast.

In the rowboat, Lahrner had roped them to the telescope crates. They would float, he said, if the rowboat sank. He had roped Willi to the larger crate, the one holding the telescope and its stand, and he had roped himself to the smaller chest containing the clock works.

They had been in the rowboat perhaps half an hour (it seemed like a long time, but there was no way to tell) when it capsized. One moment, Willi had been cowering in the bottom of the boat, and the next moment, he had been underwater. When he gained the surface, he was floating beside the telescope crate, and he'd hauled himself up onto it with the rope.

He could see nothing, neither Lahrner nor the two troopers

who'd gotten into the rowboat with them nor the rowboat itself. The waves were enormous, steep and black. The rain was falling in sheets, and the wind was blowing icy salt spray from the tops of the waves into his eyes.

After several hours, he had decided that he was going to die out there, either freeze or drown, and that his body would end up at the bottom of the sea. He hadn't been as terrified with the realization as he would have thought he would be. If that was the way it was going to be, so be it. He would see if it was really true that he would meet Saint Peter at the gates of Heaven and that he would there be asked to explain all his earthly sins.

Aside from talking back to his parents, and some petty thievery from the stalls in the marketplace in Marburg, there had been only two major sins of the type that would likely see him sent to Hell. He had struck the Grand Duke Alexei, and he had done *that* with Trude every night (and some afternoons) for more than a week in the Gasthaus of the Golden Ram in Nürnberg. Not only had he done it, but in his heart, he wasn't even sorry about it. If God really knew all the secrets in men's hearts, then God knew he really didn't heartily repent his sin. He would have to take his punishment, whatever that was. He had avoided earthly punishment for having struck the Grand Duke Alexei, but now he would be punished in death for that and for being in bed with Trude.

And that was all he remembered, except that as he had grown drowsy, the pain in his neck and shoulders and the cramps in his middle had stopped, and when he had realized that, he had welcomed the drowsiness, even if it was the prelude to the sleep of death.

On the day he had been aboard *The Eleanor* a week, he waited until he was alone and then got out of bed. He was dizzy for a moment, and he was very weak, but he was all right otherwise. He made his way to a window and looked out. There was nothing out there but endless rolling seas. He could hear men's voices above him, and he could smell roasting meat of some kind. And, incredibly, he could smell cow manure. That, obviously was impossible. What would a cow be doing here in the middle of the ocean?

When the girl, whose name Willi now understood to be Mary, and who was the captain's daughter, and sister to the young officer they called Charley, came to the cabin and

334

found him out of bed, she somewhat arrogantly ordered him back into bed. When he smiled and shook his head, she had walked quickly out of the cabin.

She had apparently immediately gone to tell the captain, for he came into the cabin, with Mary and Charley behind him, just as Willi sat down at the table to eat the bowl of stew Stern had brought to him.

Willi stood up as a mark of respect.

"Tell him to sit down," Captain Selkirk said, and Stern translated the command.

"Tell him to get back in bed!" Mary said.

"I give the orders here, mistress," Paul Selkirk said. "If he feels well enough to get out of bed, let him."

Then the captain, through Stern, asked him how he felt.

"Much better, thank you, Captain," Willi said.

Then he drew out of Willi, once again, for what was, Willi thought, the fifth or sixth time, the whole story of the telescope, and what Willi had been doing with it. Willi finally understood that for some reason, the captain suspected he was not telling the truth and was making him repeat the story again and again to catch him in a discrepancy. Willi didn't like that at all but realized there was nothing he could do about it.

Finally, Stern said, "The captain asks me to tell you that he will see that you are returned to your people, as soon as it can be arranged. In the meantime, you have the freedom of the ship. It will not be necessary for you to work. The captain says that he believes impressment is a sin."

"How do you say thank you in English?" Willi asked. Stern told him.

"Thank you, thank you," Willi said, and made a little bow. Captain Selkirk bowed back and walked out of the cabin. Then he turned and said something else.

"The captain says you will continue to share this cabin with Mr. Selkirk, and that you will take your meals, when you feel up to it, with the officers in the wardroom. He says that Mr. Selkirk will give you some clothing."

"Thank you, thank you," Willi said, again.

Captain Selkirk smiled at him as if he had said something funny and walked out of the cabin.

"Eat your stew," Mary Selkirk said, gesturing with an imaginary spoon.

"My sister thinks you're a child," Charley said.

335

Willi looked at him without understanding. Charley pointed at Mary and then at Willi and mimed a mother spoon feeding an infant. Willi smiled his understanding. Mary glowered at both of them and stormed angrily out of the cabin.

"I have sisters," Willi said.

Charley could make the translation from the German "Schwester" to English.

They exchanged a smile of understanding, the commiseration of young men with sisters.

"Well, since my father is giving away my clothes," Charley said, "I suppose I might as well get it over with." He opened the chest beneath the bunk and took out trousers, a shirt, a belt, and a pair of shoes.

He put them on the table and waited for Willi to finish his stew.

"Clothes," Charley said. "For you."

"Thank you, thank you," Willi said.

"Ah, then you do speak English, do you?" Charley said.

"Thank you, thank you," Willi repeated.

"Two words of it," Charley said, and laughed. Willi looked at him curiously, wondering if he was being mocked. But there was nothing cruel in the other young man's eyes.

Charley held the shirt against Willi.

"Well, the shirt'll fit, anyway," he said.

"Thank you, thank you," Willi said.

Charley laughed. "I wonder how you say you're welcome in German?" he wondered aloud.

He made signs to Willi that he should put the clothes on, and that they would then leave the cabin. Willy hurriedly pulled the nightshirt he had been wearing over his head, modestly turning his back, and then pulled on the clothes Charley had given him. They were a little large on him, but they would do.

Charley made a sign for Willi to follow him, and they left the cabin, going down the passageway to the maindeck.

Willi was impressed with the size of *The Eleanor*. It was many times the size of the *Queen of Peace*, which was the only other ocean-going vessel he had ever been on. He looked up in awe at all the sails, enormous sheets of canvas drawn taut by the wind. He looked at her cannon and saw that the ropes that held them in place were as thick around as his arms.

336

And he was pleased when he saw the cows and goats. They were the last thing he expected to find on a ship, despite the unmistakable odor of manure he had smelled in the cabin.

But despite everything, when he first went onto the deck he was a little uneasy. There was nothing in sight from horizon to horizon but water. He knew how unpleasant water could be.

But then the uneasiness passed. There was no reason he should be afraid of being where he was when everybody else he could see showed no signs of fear at all. Quite the contrary, they seemed happy, and many of them smiled at him, apparently aware of who he was, and pleased to see him on his feet. Within a couple of minutes, he went from uneasiness to embarrassment for having felt uneasy to experiencing a strange feeling of pleasure. He couldn't understand it, but he liked being where he was.

Then he saw Mary, sitting on a stool, milking one of the cows. Willi had milked many a cow in Marburg, and he saw that she wasn't very good at it. He thought it over a moment, and decided that it had been impolite of him to join her brother in mocking her in the cabin. She really had worked very hard to make him feel better when he had first been brought aboard.

He walked up to where she was milking the cow, tapped her on the shoulder, and gestured for her to get up. He had always hated being forced to milk cows, but now it seemed to be a good skill to have. He sat down on the stool and went to work.

"Thank you," the girl said, and smiled at him.

"Thank you," Willi said to her, and smiled. He milked the cow until she was dry, and then got up. Mary took the bucket and walked away.

Charley Selkirk, obviously unhappy about something, touched Willi's arm to get his attention, and then made a motion for him to follow him to the back of the ship, where there was a deck a level higher than the one they were on.

He followed Charley Selkirk down the deck and up a flight of stairs. There were half a dozen men on the deck, one of whom was obviously an officer. Willi saw Charley tip his hat to him, obviously some kind of salute. And he saw that the two men standing at either side of the huge steering wheel pulled at their forelocks in a gesture of respect to Charley Selkirk.

337

The older officer smiled at Willi and put out his hand.

Willi stood to attention, bobbed his head, and said, "von Kolbe."

The officer persisted in offering his hand. Willi finally took it.

"Porter," the man said. "How do you do?"

"Von Kolbe," Willi repeated, to make sure that the man had really given him his name.

"Porter," the officer repeated, and smiled. They understood each other.

Willi turned to Charley Selkirk, smiled, and put out his hand.

"Von Kolbe," he said.

"Selkirk," Charley replied with an understanding smile, and shook Willi's hand.

Willi fingered his shirt, and then nodded his head in approval.

"Thank you," he said.

"You're welcome," the young man said.

"Thank you," Willi said, again.

"You're welcome," Selkirk said again.

Ach, so! Willi thought. *Bitte schön.*

Charley Selkirk took Willi von Kolbe's arm and led him in front of a huge wheel. There was a compass there.

"Understand?" Selkirk asked, pointing down at the compass. Willi studied the instrument. He knew what a compass was, and there had been some large and elaborate compasses in Muller and Thane's establishment, but nothing as large or substantial looking as this.

And nothing really like it, either, he saw when he looked closer. The compasses at Muller und Thane, and the compasses with which his father and the other officers and some of the senior sergeants of the Hessian Regiment were equipped had a needle in the center that always pointed north. To tell the direction in which you were headed, you turned the compass case so that the "north" mark on the case was lined up with the point of the needle. This ship's compass was different. Instead of a needle, it had a flat moving plate inside, on which the points of the compass were printed. The compass case, which was fixed to the deck and obviously couldn't be moved, had only an indicator point. It didn't take Willi long to figure out how that worked. Where the indicator pointed to

338

he markings on the plate was the direction in which they
vere headed.

"Ja," Willi said, "Ich verstehe. Sud."

"South," Selkirk said.

"South," Willi repeated. He pointed at north. "Nord," he
aid.

"North," Selkirk said.

"North," Willi repeated.

Charley turned to locate Tony the cabin boy.

"Tony," he said. "Go to the chart room and get me an English Channel/North Sea chart."

"Aye, aye, sir," Tony said, and ran to fetch it.

Selkirk looked onto the deck. Mistress Sedge was sitting in
he lee of the fo'c'sl, sewing. He pointed at her. Willi looked
to see where he was pointing, then nodded.

"Woman," Charley Selkirk said. Willi looked at him curiously, having no idea at all what he meant. Charley pointed
at himself, at Willi, at the quartermaster's mate, at the helmsmen, each time saying, "Man."

"Thank you," Willi said, understanding. "Man."

"Woman," Charley said, pointing at Mistress Sedge.

"Woman," Willi repeated, wondering what this was all
about.

"Man," Charley Selkirk said, pointing to himself and Willi.
Then he went to the wheel and mimed turning it. He smiled.
Then he mimed the milking of a cow. "Woman," he said,
smiling and nodding his head. "Yes." Then he pointed to
Willi again. "Man," he said, frowning and making signs of
distaste as he mimicked the milking motions. "Man, no."

Willi understood him. Milking cows was not man's work.

"Thank you," Willi said. "Man, no," he shook his head.
"Woman, yes." He made milking motions.

"By God," Charley Selkirk said, smiling broadly. "I'll have
you speaking English before you know it."

"Thank you," Willi said.

Tony returned to the quarterdeck with the chart he had
been sent for. He handed it to Charley, who spread it out on
the table in front of the binnacle. He laid his finger on the
"north" symbol and asked the question by raising his eyebrows.

"North," Willi said.

"Right," Charley said. Then he pointed to the English
Channel, off Cap Gris Nez. Willi looked at him with interest,

but without understanding. Charley put his hands on Willi'
shoulders and made a gesture of picking him up.

"Ach, so!" Willi said. He bent over the map and foun
Rotterdam. He put his finger on it, waited until Charley
nodded, and then moved it to London. Charley nodded. Ther
he put his finger on London, drew a course to Amsterdam
then back out through the North Sea, through the English
Channel, around the coast of France, and through the Med
iterranean to Naples.

Willi nodded, then asked, by turning his palms up and
shrugging his shoulders, where they were. Charley pointed t
their present position, and Willi nodded.

"Thank you," he said.

Charley smiled and then pointed to the chart and turned
his palms upward and shrugged his shoulders and then
pointed at Willi. After a moment, Willi understood. He ben
over the chart, then frowned. It was a mariner's chart. Areas
where there was no navigable water or ports had been lef
blank.

But he found the Rhine, and Cologne, and then the Lahn
He could make a good guess where Marburg was.

"Marburg," he said. "Marburg an der Lahn." Then he
moved his finger just barely and said, "Kolbe."

Charley nodded his understanding. But he actually misun
derstood. He thought Willi wanted to say "me." There fol
lowed several minutes of confusion, while Charley tried to
teach Willi the word. He of course got nowhere, but compre
hension finally dawned on Willi.

He pointed at himself, and said, "Me, *von* Kolbe. Me, *von*
Kolbe." Then he pointed at the map, "Cologne," he said
"Marburg." And, finally, "Kolbe."

"Do you have any idea what he's trying to say?" Charley
asked Mr. Porter.

Porter shook his head.

"Mr. Selkirk," Quartermaster O'Keefe, who had beer
watching the exchange with a broad smile, said, "I think
know what it may be."

"Well, speak up, I'm getting nowhere," Charley said.

"I think he may be some kind of aristocrat," O'Keefe said.

Charley snorted.

"Stern told me he said he was on official business for som
bigshot," O'Keefe said.

"So what?"

"What I'm saying is that he could have the same name as the place he lives," O'Keefe said.

That seemed pretty farfetched, but it was an intriguing idea.

"Tony," Charley Selkirk ordered. "Fetch Stern. We'll find out."

Ten minutes later, the confusion had been resolved. It was established, and Charley was at first a little disappointed, that the young man they had hauled out of the sea was not a prince or duke or anything like that. What he was, Charley realized, was something very close to what he himself was, the son of a responsible, respectable member of the middle class.

He wondered if his father had sensed this when he ordered Willi fed in the wardroom. Probably, Charley decided. His father was very good in seeing people for what they were.

"Stern," Charley ordered. "Ask Mr. *von* Kolbe if he would like a cup of tea with me in the wardroom."

It was not necessary for Stern to translate. Willi put his hand on his arm and stopped him.

"Tea?" he asked, and Charley nodded. "Me?" Willi asked, and when Charley nodded again, Willi said, "Thank you."

4

Within a few days, Willi had explored *The Eleanor* and come to understand something of the routine. There were three officers in addition to the captain, and each of them was in charge of the ship for four hours, followed by eight hours off duty. Charley Selkirk, for example, had what they called "the watch" from midnight until four in the morning, and then again from noon until four in the afternoon.

In a mixture of English, German, and wild gestures, Charley had explained that he was the junior officer, and therefore the least desirable watch was his. In the winter, it was coldest from midnight until four in the morning, and in the summer, the heat was worst from noon until four in the afternoon. With more gestures and mime, Charley explained why the first mate Mr. Porter's watch was the most desirable: it permitted him a full night's sleep, from midnight to a few minutes to eight. He had four hours' duty, whereupon it was time for lunch. Then he had his afternoon and early evening

341

through dinner free, and went back on from eight to midnight.

The officers' lives revolved between the quarterdeck and the wardroom. On his own first meal in the wardroom, Willi was pleased to find Mary Selkirk at the table. He had really grown quite fond of Mary. For a child, Willi thought she was remarkably competent and smart. And despite the jokes he shared with Charley Selkirk about sisters, the truth was that Mary was much nicer and far more interesting than his own sisters.

The quality of the food served at his first wardroom dinner surprised him. There was roast meat and potatoes and even a pitcher of milk set before Mary by the boy called Tony. When Mary saw him looking at the pitcher, she pushed it toward him. He was used to drinking milk at home, and really thirsty for some here. But no sooner had he raised the mug when he realized, from Charley's and Mr. Nelson's raised eyebrows, that men apparently didn't drink milk. He had apparently made a fool of himself, and was embarrassed.

But then Captain Selkirk said something to him, and when he looked at him in incomprehension, the captain had gestured for the milk and poured and drunk a mug full. He did that, Willi realized, to be kind to me. Captain Selkirk, obviously, was a good man, like his own father.

The quality of the food went down almost immediately, however, after the first meal as the fresh meat began to spoil, and it was necessary to turn to the salted and corned meat. The milk output of the cows decreased until there wasn't enough for the Sedge children, who had first call on it, and thus none for the officer's table.

Willi was surprised that the Sedges were not fed in the wardroom but rather in their crowded cabin. He thought it would be out of place for him to inquire why, since he now had a place at the table, that they didn't, so he didn't ask. And then he understood. Children should be seen and not heard, and there were eight Sedge children with whom Captain Selkirk did not wish to dine. Willi had been almost fourteen before he had been permitted to eat at table with his father. Before that, it had been the kitchen.

The more he saw of Captain Selkirk, the more he understood how much he and his father were alike. There was even chess. Baron von Kolbe had taught Willi chess when Willi was no more than eight or nine. The first time that Captain

342

Selkirk had asked with raised eyebrows if Willi played, and then, when Willi nodded, motioned him to sit down and play, Willi remembered how pleased his father had been the first time Willi had beat him.

He played Captain Selkirk to win, and won, and Captain Selkirk was visibly pleased, and thereafter the two of them spent long hours over the board, learning, to their mutual pleasure, that they were about equally matched. Willi took more than a little smug pleasure in knowing that he could beat Charley. And he thought it cute, as if she had adopted him as a brother, that Mary rooted for him to win when he played her father.

They were in the Mediterranean by then, and the weather was pleasant, warm without being hot, and the seas seemed to get smoother every day. He had the very odd thought one afternoon, two days out of Naples, that he was really going to miss these people when he was put ashore, the day after tomorrow.

That same afternoon, as he made his way to the cabin he was sharing with Charley Selkirk, Willi found the adjacent door open. He saw Stern in the cabin, cleaning and oiling firearms.

"Can you use some help?" Willi asked, not especially because he was anxious to clean guns but because it would give him a chance for some conversation. He was rapidly learning English, but he was nowhere close to being able to carry on a conversation in it.

"You know anything about guns?" Stern asked.

"Yes," Willi said. "Pistols and muskets. But I never saw anything like those muskets before."

"They're not muskets," Stern replied, motioning Willi into the cabin. "They're rifles. Pennsylvania rifles."

"They spin the ball?"

Stern nodded.

"My father has told me about them," he said. "And a friend." He had a sudden mental picture of Karl Lahrner, now dead and drowned, and quickly forced it from his mind. "I was going to London to learn all about them."

"You won't have to go all the way to London for that," Stern said. "I can teach you all you have to know right here."

He took a rifle from the rack and put it in Willi's hands. Compared to the muskets with which Willi was familiar, it was very slim, even delicate. Stern let him heft it in his

343

hands, watching him carefully as Willi cocked the hammer, and then let it down gently to avoid damaging the lockworks. That apparently satisfied Stern that Willi knew enough about firearms to be worthy of showing him how a rifle worked.

He took the weapon back from Willi, laid it on the table, and took the barrel from the stock. Then he put the barrel in a vise and unscrewed the breech plug. What was left was a four-foot length of steel, octagonal in shape, and with a hole drilled through its length.

He handed it to Willi, telling him to look through the hole. Willi looked out the port. For a moment, he saw nothing, and then he saw circling lines on the inside of the barrel, making one complete turn every twelve or fourteen inches.

He had expected deeper cuts, and said so.

"That's enough for the lead to grab," Stern told him. "What happens, I think, is that when the powder blows, it expands the base of the ball, like hitting it with a hammer, so that it fills the lands and grooves."

"And you can really hit what you aim at a hundred paces?"

"Two hundred, maybe more," Stern said. "If you're a good enough shot."

Willi looked doubtful.

"Help me oil these," Stern said. "And then we'll take a couple on deck, and I'll 'test' them."

Mr. Dillon had the watch when they went on deck, carrying two of the Pennsylvania rifles, and a supply of powder and ball. He showed no surprise when Stern announced he was going to test the rifles by firing them off the quarterdeck. Stern showed Willi how to charge the piece. He first poured in a measured amount of powder and told him that in a rifle, unlike a musket, the amount of powder loaded was critical, and for accuracy had to be precisely the same each time the piece was charged.

Stern took a circle of cotton cloth, centered it carefully over the muzzle, and then pushed a lead ball against the cloth with his thumb, shoving both down the muzzle. Finally, he took a ramrod from under the barrel and rammed powder, patch, and ball home.

He let Willi load the second rifle, and then threw a scrap of lumber, about five inches wide and twice as long, over the side. The lumber was painted solid white, and Willi reasoned hat their target had been prepared in advance, and that target practice was a standard thing aboard *The Eleanor*.

Stern waited until the white scrap was seventy-five paces or o behind *The Eleanor*, and then put the rifle to his shoulder. Ie took careful aim and fired. There was the crack as the rifle fired, then a puff of smoke, and then, not more than six nches from the piece of wood, a little eruption in the water. Stern swore, for he had intended to show off, and had missed. Ie took the second rifle from Willi and fired again. This time he piece of wood flew into two pieces. Stern looked pleased vith himself. He handed the rifle to Willi and then reloaded he first.

Mary Selkirk, who had heard the firing, appeared on the quarterdeck, followed a moment later by her brother. Willi, as a matter of courtesy, offered the rifle he had just loaded to Charley, and Charley, disappointing him, took it. Stern threw another wood target over the side. Charley threw the rifle to his shoulder and fired. There was an eruption in the water six inches from the target. Coming that close, Willi saw, pleased Charley.

"How'd you do?" Charley asked Willi. When Stern saw that Willi obviously didn't understand him, he told Charley that Willi had not yet fired one of the rifles. Charley took the rifle Stern had reloaded and handed it to Willi. He turned to Stern for another target, for the target he had missed by only six inches was now a good hundred paces away, and too difficult a target. Willi, not understanding what Charley said about throwing a new target, put the rifle to his shoulder, lined up the sights, and fired. The piece of wood flew in pieces.

Mary Selkirk yelped in pleasure and clapped her hands.

"I'll be damned," Charley said. "Talk about beginner's luck!"

The rifles were reloaded. Targets were again thrown overboard. Charley motioned for Willi to fire first. Willi gestured for Charley to fire first. Charley shrugged and fired and missed again by an inch or so. Willi fired again and again the piece of wood splintered.

Mary yelped with pleasure and clapped her hands again. Charley slapped Willi on the back. "Tell him," he said to Stern, "that he's all right."

Willi was pleased with himself. He had another quick mental image of Karl Lahrner, thinking that Lahrner would have

345

been proud of him. Then he forced that image from his mind, too.

Willi was pleased with himself at dinner that night, too, when Charley told his father and Mr. Porter what a "crack shot," whatever that meant, Willi was, and how Stern had reported that Willi knew all about such fine points of firearms as flint chipping and action stoning.

He was thus very surprised the next morning, when he tried to leave the cabin and found Stern in the companionway, blocking his passage.

"You're to stay in the cabin until further orders," Stern told him. "Captain's orders."

"Have I done something wrong?"

"We're about to make Naples," Stern replied.

"But I am to go ashore at Naples."

"It doesn't look that way, Willi," Stern said. "It looks as if you're going to stay aboard for a while." He shut the door in Willi's face.

Chapter Eighteen

1

board the Prinz Wilhelm
'est longitude 36°15', north latitude 51°35'
pril 16, 1770

Lady Caroline Watchbury had come to the conclusion that
ıe had become an experienced ocean traveler. The proof
as that she had sailed to India on an English man-of-war;
`om Tatta to London aboard an American merchantman;
ınd, more important, was now more than two weeks into the
ondon-Philadelphia voyage of the German merchantman
rinz Wilhelm, without once having been sick to her stom-
ch.

Of the three, she concluded as she leaned on the maindeck
ailing of the *Prinz Wilhelm*, looking at the endless rolling
`aters of the North Atlantic, *The Eleanor* had provided the
ıost comfortable and pleasing accommodation. She meant by
ıat, she told herself with a private naughty smile, the *actual*
ccommodations, not the presence in her bed during most of
ıe voyage of *The Eleanor*'s third officer.

Her cabin aboard *The Eleanor* had been twice the size of
ie cabin she had shared with Edgar on H.M.S. *Indomitable*,
ınd five or six times the size of the floating closet she occu-
ıied on *Prinz Wilhelm*. Her bed on *The Eleanor* had been
arger and far more comfortable (again, excluding the
ıresence of her bedmate) than her bed on either the *Prinz
Vilhelm* or H.M.S. *Indomitable*.

Aboard the *Indomitable* and *The Eleanor*, she had taken
ıer meals with the officers in the wardroom. Here she took
ıhem with twenty-five other passengers in a small, smelly,
`rowded cabin absurdly called the Grand Salon. The food,
ıoreover, was what she thought of as "heavy German,"

347

consisting mostly of sausage of one kind or another, potatoes
invariably boiled, and sauerkraut, sometimes with caraway
seeds and sometimes without. Breakfast was heavy rye bread
spread with pork fat, and tea. Sometimes she really missed
the ham and eggs that had been routine fare aboard *Th*
Eleanor.

There were no passengers, either, with whom she could be
come friendly. The half-dozen other females aboard wer
middle-class women, busy with their children. There were n
interesting men aboard. Four of the male passengers wer
Lutheran clergymen, three of them married and all of then
serving to cast a dull religious pall over the voyage. Betwee
them, they offered twice-daily prayer and hymn-singing serv
ices, and they had doubled their religious fervor on the tw
Sundays they had been at sea.

There was beer in kegs, but little wine, and no spirits what
ever, except what she had brought with her in her trunk, an
which she was reluctant to drink outside her cabin, where th
others could see and frown their disapproval.

Despite the fact that she had had a letter of introductio
from an officer of the Bank of England to *Prinz Wilhelm*'
master, that portly, pompous little man paid no more atten
tion to her than he did to any of the other passengers. Sh
had expected that she might at least be invited to dine onc
or twice in the wardroom, as a simple gesture of courtesy
but that had not happened.

Captain Beitermann was even more pompous and aware o
his own importance than the captain of H.M.S. *Indomitable*
whose name she could no longer recall. She had had anothe
private amusing thought: if Captain Paul Selkirk had some
how appeared on board, in that battered and sweaty tricor
nered hat of his, in his open-collared cotton shirt, bagg
pants, and scarred shoes, Captain Beitermann, in his perfect
immaculate uniform, complete to powdered wig and dres
sword, would not have acknowledged his presence, an
would, had he somehow learned the facts, have been aston
ished that a fellow master of an even larger ship—in fact, th
owner of a larger ship—could hardly be told from one of th
ordinary seamen.

She had noticed the difference in the seamen too. The dis
cipline exacted of the men aboard *Prinz Wilhelm* was eve
more rigid than that aboard H.M.S. *Indomitable*, and *Indom*
itable had been a *man-of-war*, not a merchantman. There wa

348

no comparison between *Prinz Wilhelm* and *The Eleanor*. None of the seamen aboard the Hanoverian would have dared engage the captain, or the ship's officers, in conversation as they regularly did on *The Eleanor*. When an officer approached one of them aboard this ship, they stood to attention and averted their eyes. It was apparently considered bad manners for them to look directly at their betters.

The only interesting thing aboard *Prinz Wilhelm* was the mystery passenger. He had been the last person to board the ship, and he had been carried aboard on a stretcher and put into one of the two most "desirable" cabins (Lady Caroline occupied the other; they were on the same deck, two decks below the quarterdeck, as the Grand Salon) and had not been seen since.

It was possible, Caroline thought, that by now the mystery had been explained, but there were only a few people who spoke English, and she spoke to them only rarely and briefly, and she had heard nothing.

She had just been thinking of the mystery passenger again when she turned from the railing to return to her cabin and saw him coming out of the door to the companionway to their cabins.

He was an enormous man, with a large and flowing mustache, in his forties, she judged, and then added, from the mustache and his erect stature, from a military background. He looked, too, pale and white, as if he were ill. Or had recently been ill and was now recuperating.

She saw him support himself on the doorjamb and look around the deck with curiosity. And then he saw her, and stared at her with frank curiosity, and, she had the oddest feeling, with recognition and surprise. She gave him a look of what she hoped was devastating hauteur, and then turned away from him, to walk forward and then circle back to the companionway door to avoid meeting him.

She failed, and then something else quite astonishing happened. He raised his tricorn to her, and in English (heavily German accented, to be sure, but English) said, "Good day, lady."

Caroline was so surprised that she smiled at him and said, "Good day," before walking past him to the companionway.

At dinner, Caroline considered herself lucky enough to find one of the tiny two-person tables mounted to the ship's bulk-

349

head vacant and sat down at it. With a little bit of luck, one of the Lutheran clergymen who spoke English would consider it Christian charity to sit with her (and perhaps to get away from his own wife and children) and she could have a little conversation over the inevitable sausage, potatoes, and sauerkraut.

But it was the sick, pale, enormous man who showed up at the side of her table.

"Good night, lady," he said.

"Good evening," she said, a little uncomfortable.

"I would salute the Herr Major," he said. For a moment, she had no idea what in the world he was talking about. And then she understood.

"You're speaking of Sir Edgar?" she asked.

"Yes, lady," he said. "You are the Herr Major's lady, nicht wahr?"

Everybody in the Grand Salon was looking at them in unabashed curiosity.

"Please sit down," Caroline said.

"I would not steal the Herr Major's place," the man said.

"Please sit down," Caroline repeated, and he took the chair (actually a sort of shelf, permanently attached, like the table itself to the bulkhead) and smiled at her.

"The Herr Major," he said, trying to suppress a tolerant smile about the Herr Major's weakness, and rather proud of his skill as a linguist, "has the *mal de mer*, nicht wahr, lady?"

"My husband," Lady Caroline said, hoping that she looked properly mournful, "has gone to his reward."

He obviously didn't understand what she meant.

"My husband," she said, speaking very slowly and carefully, "*Colonel Sir* Edgar Watchbury, is dead."

"Lady," he said, looking legitimately mournful, "I am sorry."

"Thank you," Caroline said.

"Right away, nicht wahr?" Karl Lahrner said, actually quite pleased at how well he was doing with his long unused command of the English language.

"I beg your pardon?"

"The Herr Colonel is dead right away, nicht wahr?" Lahrner said.

He means recently, Caroline decided.

350

"Actually, the colonel went to his reward in November," aroline said. Lahrner looked surprised and uncomfortable.

"I thought," Lahrner blurted, "that lady go home to father d momma to have baby."

And then a stricken look crossed his face, as he realized oth what he had said and what he had implied. He got to s feet, looked down at her, said, "Lady, please forgive," and early ran out of the Grand Salon.

It was the first time that Caroline had any idea that her regnancy was obvious. That was bad enough. But she had ist admitted to this enormous German—*and who the hell is e?*—that the child she carried had not been put there by the te Colonel Sir Edgar Watchbury.

With a massive effort, she suppressed the terrible urge to et to her feet and run out of the Grand Salon after the uge, pale, mustachioed German.

2

ast longitude 12°45', north latitude 38°29'
The Mediterranean Sea, off Capo San Vito, Sicily)

pril 29, 1771

Willi von Kolbe had not been let out of the cabin he had een sharing with Charley Selkirk while *The Eleanor* had een in Naples, and from the moment Willi had found Stern utside the door, Charley Selkirk had never returned to the abin. Willi could not ask why he had been made a prisoner ecause he saw no one except Stern and Mary. Stern brought is food to him, and Mary had come to his cabin a half ozen times to play chess with him.

As a gentleman, Willi knew that he could not ask questions f his status of a girl. Even if she understood his questions, nd he could not make himself understood to Mary as well as e could to Captain Selkirk or Charley.

The girl was actually astonishing. She was a better chess layer than her brother, almost as good as he himself was. Ie had had no idea that females even played chess.

That seemed to be a question he could, as a gentleman, ose and he did, and he thought he understood her reply to e that her mother had been taught to play by her father,

351

Mary's grandfather, and that she had taught her husband and both her children to play.

On its face, the idea of a woman (not even a woman, he had to keep reminding himself, *a young girl*) possessed of the mental logic to play chess, which was, after all, the science of war reduced to symbols of assets, and played on a symbolic map, was absurd. But the fact was that he had to work just about as hard to defeat her as he did to defeat his father.

Worse, she seemed to be getting better. The only explanation for that was that she was (as his father told him really good chess players did) studying his game and finding weaknesses in his processes of logic. He told himself that if she was a woman, he would have been humiliated. It was only that she was a young girl that he was not.

She had, moreover, a very disconcerting way of studying him when he was thinking over his moves. He'd glance up at her, and there would be those eyes of hers on him, one eyebrow raised in unabashed curiosity. It was like looking into a deep pool of water. And sometimes she leaned so close to him that he could see the whiteness of her scalp, and smell her hair.

But although Mary came often to see him, and he was served really good food now (as supplies from shore came aboard), and he actually had nothing to complain about, there was no question that he was a prisoner. His port had been nailed shut, and there was always a man outside his door. While not armed, the men outside had always been large enough to restrain him physically if that had been necessary.

Willi had debated trying to break open the sealed porthole and then to scream for help, but after considering it (there was no way he would be able to break through the porthole without being heard; the moment he tried to hammer at the port, the man, the *guard*, in the companionway would hear it and come into the cabin and stop him), he decided against it. He reasoned that if they meant him harm, he would already have been hurt. The thought of harm was absurd. If they meant him harm, Captain Selkirk would not have permitted Mary to visit him. He bided his time, for there was nothing else to do.

He knew they had left Naples when the ship's carpenter came into the cabin and unsealed the porthole. The guard

as gone from the door, too. But they continued to deliver
s meals to the cabin, and he didn't leave it.

A full day after the porthole had been opened, he was
ummoned from the cabin to the captain's cabin. He found
harley Selkirk waiting there with Captain Selkirk, and Stern,
ho would be the translator. Willi had come to believe that
e and Charley had become friends, and that the main reason
harley had not shown up in the cabin was that he was
hamed that "his friend" was being treated as a prisoner.

If Charley Selkirk was ashamed now, there was no sign of
on his smiling face.

"Guten tag, Willi," he said, cheerfully. His accent so bad
aat Willi had to smile, even though smiling was the last thing
e wanted to do.

"Good evening, Mr. Selkirk," Willi said, as icily correct as
e could manage. "Good evening, Captain Selkirk."

"Morning," Charley corrected him, pleasantly. *"Morgen."*

Willi managed to give him a dirty look.

Captain Selkirk said something to Stern, who translated it.
The captain says that Mr. Selkirk told him you were entitled
» an explanation, and this is what this is."

"Thank you," Willi said.

"We're an hour or so out of Trapani," Captain Selkirk
aid, through Stern. "Trapani is a small port on the northwest
>ast of Sicily. We're going to put you ashore there, *if* we
on't find an English or American ship in the harbor. We'll
ive you enough money to live on until a ship calls there that
ill carry you either back to Italy or to France or England.
Vherever you want to go. And money for your passage."

"Thank you," Willi said. "May I ask why I was not put
shore at Naples?"

"I wish neither to lose my ship nor spend seven years
hained in the hold of an English prison ship," Captain
elkirk said.

"I don't understand," Willi said, in English, not through
tern.

"You've seen the Sedges," Charley said, through Stern.
'illi nodded. "Sedge is a journeyman ironworker, bound by
»ntract to a steel mill in England for twenty-two years. He
risking seven years in prison for breaking his oath of serv-
e."

"I still don't understand," Willi said, this time in German.

"The English Parliament passed a law to protect the En-

353

glish steel makers," Charley said. "They made it illegal te build steel mills in the colonies. The idea is that the colonie will provide the raw materials, which the English will turn into finished products and sell back to the colonies. You un derstand?"

Willi nodded, even though he really didn't, and had n idea what any of this had to do with his having been hel prisoner and not being put ashore at Naples.

"To keep the colonies from making their own steel," Charley went on, "they have prohibited the colonies to im port either steel-making equipment or steel craftsmen, th men who have the secret of making crucible steel."

"And you are taking Sedge and his family against th law?" Willi asked.

"Yes," Charley said. "That's it."

"And steel-making equipment, too?" Willi asked.

Charley and Captain Sedge shrugged in reply to that, re fusing a more precise reply. There was no question whateve in Willi's mind that somewhere aboard *The Eleanor* wa contraband equipment. And then, all of a sudden, he under stood.

"And you thought *I* would tell the authorities?" Will asked, incredulously.

"There is a reward," Captain Selkirk said. "They sell th confiscated ship at auction, and the equipment, and the Ad miralty pays a reward to whoever was responsible for lettin H.M. Customs know."

"And you thought," Willi said, so surprised that the ange was only now starting to build, "that I would repay you fo saving my life by getting into trouble?"

"We didn't know," Captain Selkirk said.

"Well, Goddamn you, sir, you should have known," Will said. Stern was reluctant to translate that. He looked in hor ror at Willi and nervously at Captain Selkirk.

"What did he say?" Captain Selkirk, who had heard Willi' tone, asked.

Stern still hesitated.

"Tell him exactly what I said!" Willi said to Stern.

Stern examined his shoes as he made the translation.

Charley laughed, and put his arms around Willi's shoul ders.

"See, I told you!" he said to his father.

"I couldn't take the risk," his father said.

'Tell the captain I do not wish to be put ashore on some
ange island," Willi said to Stern.

'Tell him we're going to go straight to Philadelphia," Cap-
n Selkirk said. "If he doesn't get off here, he'll have to go
Philadelphia."

'Tell him I will go to Philadelphia, and since he obviously
es not regard me as a gentleman, I will work my way as a
man," Willi said, still angry. "As a gentleman whose honor
been questioned, I cannot accept his charity."

'Tell him," Captain Selkirk said, laughing, "that in Amer-
, when one gentleman says 'Goddamn you' to another
tleman, he's liable to get himself shot in a duel."

When the translation was made, the response from Willi
s not what anyone expected.

"While I would be reluctant to kill the man who saved my
," Willi said angrily, "if Captain Selkirk wishes to duel, I
ait his pleasure."

Stern reluctantly made the translation.

"Goddamned arrogant young pup!" Paul Selkirk said, and
rn translated that.

Willi and Captain Selkirk glowered at one another for
rty seconds. Then Captain Selkirk said, "Tell him that I do
t shoot boys who think they are gentlemen, but that since
son has talked me out of throwing him over the side, I
now turning him over to my son, who can, for all I care,
ign him to milking the cows all the way across the Atlan-
"

He stood up, and made an elaborate, sweeping, mocking
w. He started to walk out of the cabin.

Willi colored, realizing he had gone too far. His damned
per again.

"I'm sorry," he said. "Tell him that I am sorry and I apol-
ze."

Captain Selkirk looked at him a long moment.

"Tell him," he said, "that I accept his apology because I
ow he suffers from the same malady as this one." He
nted to Charley. "An uncontrolled mouth."

3

East longitude 3°0', north latitude 37°5'
(The Mediterranean Sea, off Point Pescade, Barbary Coas[t])

May 6, 1770

Mr. Dillon had the helm, and Captain Paul Selkirk was si[t]ting on the quarterdeck across a small table from Willi vo[n] Kolbe, bent over a chessboard, on which it appeared that [in] two moves von Kolbe would have him in checkmate.

"Willi's got you, Father," Mary said. "In two moves. Loo[k] at his queen's knight and the queen."

"I said you might watch," Captain Paul Selkirk said. "I d[id] not recall soliciting your opinion."

She chuckled and smiled at Willi, and then when their ey[es] met, she flushed and looked away. She had never known an[y]one with eyes quite like Willi's, pale blue and as deep as [a] well.

"Never teach a woman to play chess, Willi," Capta[in] Selkirk said.

"Excuse?" Willi asked.

"Women," Captain Selkirk said, "should not play chess[."] He made sufficient gestures so that Willi understood h[is] meaning. He smiled.

Then Captain Selkirk turned over his king. If you were g[o]ing to be whipped, you might as well get it over with. Prolon[g]ing it accomplished nothing. He got to his feet and looke[d] down at the board and shook his head. "Thank you for t[he] game," he said.

"Thank you," Willi repeated.

Mary sat down on the stool and started to reset the boar[d.] Captain Selkirk walked off the quarterdeck and made his wa[y] forward. He always made a point of visiting the fo'c'sl twi[ce] a day to check it for cleanliness and signs of disease and [to] inspect the food in the galley. He had once been on a shi[p] when he had first gone to sea, where the food served the m[en] had been unfit for human consumption. He had vowed th[en] that when he had his own ship he would see that the fo[od] served was not rotten, and he had kept the vow and learne[d] that it paid dividends beyond the satisfaction of doing the d[e]cent thing.

He had never had an epidemic on either *The Mary* or *The Eleanor*, and he lost far fewer seaman to illness at sea than any other master he had ever met. While it was true that you could get all the seamen you needed in fifteen minutes at any waterfront tavern, he preferred a ship where the men stayed aboard, and where you didn't have to go around with a pistol in your belt to guard yourself against a knife in the back.

Food didn't cost that much, and he was convinced that serving as good food as he did was actually a wise thing to do in a business sense. He was also equally convinced that the way to insure that good food was served was to check it personally and make Cookie eat anything that looked wormy or smelled rotten.

He had just entered the fo'c'sl when he heard the lookout call out the sighting of a sail three points off the starboard quarter. He didn't bother to look then, because no matter what it was, it wouldn't be close enough to look at for fifteen minutes. The odds were, too, that the sail would disappear from the sea before the ship ever got close enough to look at.

He set about examining the seamen's living quarters. It generally took the new seamen about two weeks before they really understood that it was easier to go ahead and bathe, and wash their clothing when it was dirty, than it was to try to hide dirty bodies and clothes from the captain.

He found nothing that really annoyed him to the point where he would mention it to Theo LaSalle. As bosun, Theo was responsible for insuring that the captain's policies regarding personal cleanliness were followed by the men. Theo did this by punching violators in the mouth. While Captain Selkirk, who had been a bosun himself, found nothing at all wrong with corporal punishment, up to and including the cat-of-nine-tails for serious offenses, he was not as ready to apply it as Theo was. He only reported violations to Theo that would have had, in his own days as bosun, seen him use his fists in the interests of good order and discipline.

When he went back on deck, he saw most of the watch gathered at the starboard rail, and when he looked in that direction, he saw the ship the lookout had spotted earlier. She was a three-masted merchantman about the size of *The Eleanor*, flying French colors, and, more than likely by coincidence, on a course which would intersect theirs.

Captain Selkirk looked aloft. *The Eleanor* was flying all her canvas, making about all the speed she could. It was more than likely that the two ships wouldn't come much closer together than they were now; by the time their paths intersected, *The Eleanor* would be several miles ahead of the Frenchman.

He continued his inspection of the ship, even going down into the holds to examine the cargo. When he came on deck again, the Frenchman was getting closer. He went to his cabin and looked out his starboard port. He couldn't tell if the other ship was getting any closer, or if it just looked that way, but she certainly wasn't falling much, if any, behind.

He went to the compartment under his bed and took out the enormous telescope they had pulled out of the English Channel with Willi von Kolbe. Without telling anyone (for it was none of anyone's business), he had often played with the telescope late at night. Once he'd learned to operate it (for some scientific reason he couldn't imagine, the eyepiece was arranged at right angles to the tube itself, and he had been embarrassed at how long it had taken him to figure that out), he had shown Mary how it worked and then asked her not to tell her brother, or anyone else ("If they know I'm using it, they'll want to, and I think I can get a better price for it if it looks new").

He rigged a mount for it by putting a feather pillow in the port and resting the tube on that. Then he rigged a harness for it with lengths of quarter-inch line. It was far too large to hold steady by hand.

It was so powerful, and its field of vision so narrow, that he had a good deal of difficulty focusing it on the Frenchman. He would have thought that sighting down the tube, as one sighted down a rifle barrel, would have aimed it, but he had learned that some peculiarity of the lenses made the device look some distance to the right, and some distance below, where it was apparently pointed.

Finally, however, he got the Frenchman's mainmast topgallant in view, and after that it was relatively simple to raise the rear end of the telescope and get the rest of the ship in his eyepiece.

The first thing he noticed, when his first adjustment of the lines dropped his view to her waterline, was that she was riding unusually high out of the water. She was empty, which explained her speed.

And then he got his eyepiece on the deck.

He didn't make any snap judgments. He looked at what he

358

saw for a full minute, then rested his eyes and looked for as long again. Then he pulled the telescope back into his cabin and stored it under his bed. Then he went to his chest, opened a locked drawer, and took out his pistols. He stuck them in his waistband and then took his cutlass from its hooks above the head of his bed.

Then he climbed the ladder to the quarterdeck and motioned for Tony to come to him.

Mr. Dillon still had the helm.

"Ask Mr. Porter and Mr. Selkirk to join me immediately, Tony," he said.

Willi von Kolbe trailed after Charley when Charley came quickly up to the quarterdeck. A moment later, Mr. Porter came up.

"That Frenchman's crew is Arab," Captain Selkirk said. "She's empty. And she's already run her cannon out her starboard side."

Mr. Porter's eyebrows went up.

"I had a good look at her through that great big German telescope," Captain Selkirk said.

"She's been gaining steady on us, Captain," Mr. Porter said.

"I'll have eight riflemen aloft," Captain Selkirk said. "One at a time, while we're readying the aft and port cannon. When she turns to rake us with her starboard cannon, we'll let her have our aft cannon as we turn, and then our port cannon. She won't be expecting that."

"Aye, aye, sir," Mr. Porter said.

"I want no unusual signs of activity," Captain Selkirk said. "Spread the word among the men, get the arms ready, but no wild running around. I don't want them to know we know who they are. Charley, you get the Sedges into their cabins, and your sister into mine. Tell them what's going on."

"Aye, aye, sir."

Willi von Kolbe sensed this was not the time to ask questions, and he asked none. He followed Charley back down the ladder to the main deck, while Mr. Porter used Captain Selkirk's private skylight ladder to get to the aft-mounted cannon.

Captain Selkirk went to Quartermaster Peter O'Keefe and told him to get two more men onto the quarterdeck. If nothing else, they could help the helmsmen turn the wheel more quickly when he gave the order to bring her around. And if the Barbary pirates, for that's what they obviously were, managed to sweep *The Eleanor*'s quarterdeck with grape shot, they would serve as emergency helmsmen.

Charley saw Stern as he headed toward Mistress Sedge, and went to him.

"Barbary Coast pirates," Charley said. It was the first time the term had been said aloud. Willi understood "pirates" and asked Stern for an explanation.

"You just go to the arms room," he said, "and start loading and priming the rifles. I'll get the marksmen. And I'll tell you then. Don't run!"

Charley started for Mistress Sedge but saw Sedge himself and went to him instead.

"Just to be sure," he said, "go to the arms room and get some pistols for your wife and children. In case something goes wrong."

"My wife has never held a pistol in her hand in her life, and neither have I. And for the children?"

And then he understood Charley's meaning, and went white.

"Oh, my God!"

"All the stories you've heard," Charley forced himself to add, "about what the Barbary Coast pirates do to women. They're true."

He didn't know that. But he'd heard his father and Mr. O'Keefe and Theo LaSalle talk about American prisoners in Barbary Coast dungeons—Tripoli was supposed to be worst—and he knew what they said to be true.

"Get pistols, Mr. Sedge," he said, and then he went looking for Mary. Mary had heard the tales Charley had heard, from the same people, and when he told her to get a brace of pistols and take them with her to the captain's cabin, she just nodded her head in acceptance.

4

Willi was impressed to see the planning that had been done for precisely what was happening now. One of the compartments in the arms room held a supply of long, narrow bags. Each bag was large enough to hold four of the long-barreled Pennsylvania rifles, plus two small bags each of premeasured powder in little silk bags, spare flints, and balls. Each bag was connected to a coiled length of line.

As Willi loaded the rifles, Stern told him that the marksmen were divided into two-man teams. One two-man team would climb the shrouds of the mizzenmain, and foremasts, to their tops. The coil of line would be attached to their belts as they climbed, so they could haul the rifle bags up after them.

One of the men on each team was the marksman. He would fire all eight rifles, while the other reloaded. If the marksman was hit, the second man would take over the firing. The fourth team would remain on deck to serve as replacements for anyone wounded aloft, or any of the rifles that didn't work or were destroyed.

The idea, Stern told Willi, was to locate and identify, and then kill, the officers of the attacking ship, and to make the crew lose control by shooting the enemy quartermaster, helmsmen, and the officers on the quarterdeck.

"There's not really enough of us to repel a boarding party," Stern said. "And we don't carry enough cannon to really do much good."

The marksmen were waiting in the companionway before Willi and Stern finished loading the rifles.

When they were all gone, Stern looked at Willi.

"There's no sense me staying here," he said. "You can load what's left as well as I can, and pass them out, and I can make myself useful on deck." He took three loaded rifles and hung them on slings around his shoulders, then took a fourth from the rack and, carrying it in his hand, went out of the cabin.

Willi spent the next twenty minutes passing out muskets and pistols to the crew. And when the crew had been armed, first to Mary and then Mr. Sedge.

If the ship was boarded, Willi decided, he would make his stand where he was, in the companionway leading to the cabins where Mary and the Sedges would wait out the fight. He carefully loaded four pistols and put them where he could get at them quickly.

Because the arms room was aft, below the aft-mounted cannon, there was nothing but open sea when Willi looked out the port.

He looked out the companionway. It was deserted. He knocked on Sedge's cabin door. Sedge opened it. He was, Willi saw, both terrified and determined. Willi nodded encouragingly at him, and Sedge managed a weak smile.

Willi closed the door again, and then knocked on Mary

Selkirk's door. There was no answer there, either. He trie◦
the captain's cabin door.

"Come in," Mary called.

Willi stepped inside. Mary was standing by a port. Sh◦
smiled when she saw him, and he was amused to recogniz◦
the smile. She was encouraging him, trying to tell him every◦
thing was all right. She nodded her head toward the aft por◦
and he went to look through it.

The pirate ship was out there, five or six hundred yards off◦
heading in approximately the same direction, still flying ◦
French flag from her flagstaff aft.

"It won't be long," Mary said, and Willi had learne◦
enough English to understand what she said.

"It won't be long," he repeated, and smiled at her. An◦
then he reached over and laid a hand on her shoulder an◦
patted her.

"I'm not a dog," she flared. He smiled at her, and, after ◦
moment, she smiled back.

He looked out the port again, and then wondered why th◦
captain hadn't stationed a rifleman here in his cabin. It wa◦
high off the water, and its ports offered firing points to th◦
rear and on both sides. Then the question answered it itself◦
Captain Selkirk's plan had been based on his available re◦
sources. His planning had not considered the presence aboar◦
of Wilhelm von Kolbe, son of Hauptmann Baron von Kolbe◦
Commander of the Landgrave of Hesse-Kassel's Squadron o◦
Cavalry, who had been around firearms all his life and who◦
the very first time he had fired a Pennsylvania rifle, had bee◦
as good a shot as Stern and Charley Selkirk.

Willi walked quickly out of the cabin and back down th◦
companionway to the arms room. He scooped up six of th◦
remaining dozen Pennsylvania rifles, a bag of measured pow◦
der bags, and a bag of balls and carried them back to Cap◦
tain Selkirk's cabin.

"What are you doing?" Mary demanded of him.

He laid the rifles on Captain Selkirk's bed, then picked on◦
up and gestured toward the ports.

"No," she said, frowning, shaking her head and waving he◦
hands in a "no" signal. "You have to wait!" She gesture◦
overhead.

He understood.

"Ja, naturlich," he said. "Yes. Wait."

She seemed relieved that he understood her. He went t◦

362

the ports and looked out again, and was surprised to see how close the other ship had come in so short a time. It was nearly abreast, no more than three hundred yards away.

There was almost no one visible on her decks. Willi looked at her rigging. There were only a few men in the rigging, and since none of them seemed either to have rifles, or to be in positions where they could fire rifles, Willi reasoned that Captain Selkirk had one advantage the enemy hadn't considered.

Then he corrected himself: *two* advantages. The riflemen aloft, probably pretending to be tending the sails, and his preparedness. The pirates were counting on surprise.

And then, suddenly, just as Willi noticed that the other ship was now a half length, maybe more, ahead of *The Eleanor*, it began to turn, ever more sharply, toward them. And then Willi felt *The Eleanor* begin to turn, in a sharper turn, in the same direction, away from the approaching ship.

Willi glanced at Mary, and saw the look of fear in her eyes. Aware that she had resented being patted on her shoulder like a dog, he decided that he would simply have to make do with a smile to reassure her. He grinned at her broadly. The smile must have been transparently artificial, for she shook her head and laughed at him with her eyes.

Then, all of a sudden, as if with a mind of his own, his arm went around her shoulders, and he hugged her against his side. It was the sort of hug he would have given one of his sisters. But all of a sudden, she was in his arms, rather than under it, and he was very much aware of the warm contours of her body against him, of how tight her arms were around his waist. He felt her warm breath, and then her lips themselves, as if she were kissing him, on his neck.

She's just a little girl, he told himself furiously. But another part of his mind at the same time told him that she was no longer a little girl, even with that child's face of hers. He fought down the shameful urge to kiss that face.

He looked out the port. The pirate ship was now directly behind *The Eleanor*, and her decks were full of sailors, many of them wearing only short pants.

There was a boom, and then another, and then two more, almost together, right below him. *The Eleanor*'s aft cannon had been fired. A moment later, there was a cloud of choking smoke in the cabin.

When it cleared, he had somehow let go of Mary and was standing at the port with a Pennsylvania rifle in his hands. He saw a cluster of men on the fo'c's'l deck of the pirate ship. One of them was obviously giving orders to the others. Willi judged the distance, lined up the sights of the Pennsylvania rifle on him, and pulled the trigger.

Willi had aimed at his midsection. The man's head exploded, and he seemed to have been flung backward by an invisible hand. I'm holding too high, Willi thought, and then he thought, *Oh, my God! I've just killed a man!* He looked away, for some reason wanting to look at Mary.

White-faced, she was looking at him. She looked as if she was going to be sick, but another of the rifles was in her hands, the hammer already cocked. She handed it to him, and he handed her the fired rifle and turned back to the port.

The pirate ship was passing them. *The Eleanor's* aft cannon fired again, but their shot splashed harmlessly into the sea. When the smoke cleared again, Willi could see the pirate ship's quarterdeck. He lined his sights up on what was obviously an officer and fired. And missed. He swore and put his hand out for another rifle. He got off a shot at a helmsman, and without knowing if he had hit him, leaned the rifle against the bulkhead and, taking another rifle from Mary en route, went quickly across the cabin to a starboard port.

He took aim again at a pirate officer on the quarterdeck, but before he could pull the trigger there came the sound of cannon firing, and another cloud of choking smoke swirled into the cabin. *The Eleanor* had fired her starboard cannon.

When the smoke cleared, the pirate ship had veered off, and Willi realized that *The Eleanor* was turning too. He couldn't see anyone on the quarterdeck of the pirate ship at all, but when he looked up in her rigging, he spotted a lookout, took careful aim at his midsection, and fired. This time he hit exactly where he had aimed. The man fell from the mizzenmast shroud and was caught by the shroud itself, hung there a moment, and crashed to the deck.

He fired once or twice at poor targets. Then when he turned to Mary, she said helplessly, "That's all, Willi!" and he understood that he had fired all the rifles he had loaded.

He quickly loaded one rifle, intending to fire it, but when he had rammed the ball home and primed the pan, Mary snatched the rifle from his hands and handed him another. He immediately decided she was right. It would make more sense to have several of the rifles available to him at once, rather than to fire one and then reload.

He loaded all of them as quickly as he could. Mary carried em to the ports while he did so, and always had another aiting for him to load. But when he was finished and went the port, the enemy ship was nowhere in sight. He couldn't e it even when he leaned as far as he dared out the star-ard porthole. She was probably dead ahead.

It was possible, he thought, that she'd had enough and was nning from the fight.

Mary asked him what was going on with her eyes. Willi rugged his shoulders. And then he grabbed a rifle and left e cabin and started on deck. There was a good deal of ac-vity on deck. He saw dead and wounded men, and part of he Eleanor's foremast was down. He hadn't seen the pirate ip fire its cannon, but obviously it had.

There was rifle fire from the rigging, and Willi looked up st in time to see one of the marksmen fire his rifle. Then he w Charley Selkirk on the quarterdeck and ran up the lad-r to it. Selkirk, a rifle in his hand, looked up to see who as coming onto the quarterdeck.

Willi was shocked at the anguish on Charley's face, and at e tears that ran unashamedly down his cheeks. Then he oked down at the deck. Captain Paul Selkirk, his chest and lly a bloody mess, was lying there, a look of surprise on his ce, quite obviously dead.

5

Willi became aware that the firing from the rigging of The eanor had died down and stopped. When he looked for the rate ship, it was no longer dead ahead of them, but to star-ard. Her fore and mainmasts were broken, the mainmast st above the mainmast topsail, and the foremast no more an six feet above the fo'c'sl deck. The Eleanor's cannon d done their work.

The Eleanor, except for the foremast, was relatively undam-ged. As the pirate ship slowed, The Eleanor, most of her ils intact, had continued to move through the water and as passing the pirate ship.

"Ahoy, aloft!" Mr. Porter called, putting Willi's question to words. "What's going on?"

"They've all gone below decks, sir," one of the men in the ging called down.

"If you see anyone moving, kill him!" Mr. Porter ordered.

Then he turned to Charley Selkirk. "What are we going to d
to her?"

Charley looked up from his father, searched the sea, and
found the pirate ship.

"Why have they stopped firing?" he asked. He had no
heard Mr. Porter's shout, or the reply.

"There's no one on deck on her," Mr. Porter replied.

"Bring her about," Charley said to Mr. O'Keefe. "Sta
about as far from her as you are."

"Aye, aye, sir."

Charley Selkirk saw Willi.

"How is my sister? And the Sedges?" Charley asked, in
strange, distant voice.

Willi understood the question, but couldn't find the word
in English to reply to it. He nodded and smiled, and Charle
took his meaning.

"I'll have to tell my sister what has happened," Charle
said. "Mr. Porter, would you organize a boarding party, an
ready the longboat?"

"Aye, aye, sir," Mr. Porter said. "You don't want to brin
us alongside her?"

"They'd be likely to try to blow us up with them," Charle
said. "What have they got to lose?"

"We could set her afire," Mr. Porter said.

Charley looked at him a moment.

"My father was a frugal man, Mr. Porter," he said. "We'l
do what he would have done. We'll rid that ship of vermi
and take her with us."

Porter nodded his agreement.

6

The riflemen in *The Eleanor*'s rigging kept the decks of th
pirate ship under constant fire, shooting at the bodies layin
on her decks, and at her hatches and deck openings and ca
non ports as the longboat made its way across the swells t
her.

It was only when Theo LaSalle gained her deck and raise
his arms, a cutlass in one hand, a pistol in the other, that th
firing stopped. The whistling of the bullets overhead ha
frightened Willi on the way over. He had impulsively sli
down a rope into the longboat at the last moment.

Charley Selkirk followed Theo up the cargo net the pirat

d put over the side of their ship in anticipation of boarding
e Eleanor, and Willi tried to follow him but was roughly
shed aside by two of The Eleanor's seamen.

When Willi finally made it aboard, Charley Selkirk was
ning against the rail of the ship, pale and obviously fight-
g nausea. His feet had slipped in a thick puddle of drying
ood from a headless corpse lying across the body of an-
her dead pirate, in an obscene embrace in death.

When he saw Willi, it seemed to shame him, and he
shed himself off the railing and walked forward toward
e fo'c'sl.

Willi walked after him, and Theo LaSalle stepped in front
them. As they approached the hatch to the fo'c'sl the door
vung open. Theo raised his cutlass over his head, Charley
inted his pistols at the open door, and called, "Watch it!"

Willi put the Pennsylvania rifle to his shoulder and won-
red what he would do to defend himself after he fired the
eapon. There had been no time for him to think of acquir-
g pistols or a cutlass when he slid down the rope into the
ngboat; and after he fired the rifle he would be weaponless.

A man, an Arab, a *pirate*, Willi realized, dressed in a filthy
ue robe, crawled out of the fo'c'sl door onto the deck. Like
snake, on his stomach, not on his hands and knees. Theo
aSalle jammed his pistol in his waist and put both hands on
e hilt of his cutlass. Willi realized with horror that he in-
nded to cut the man's head off.

"Hold, Theo!" Charley Selkirk said, in a croak.

LaSalle, the cutlass poised above his head, looked at him in
sbelief.

"Goddamn it, I said no," Charley Selkirk said. LaSalle
ery reluctantly lowered the cutlass halfway, so that he was
ill poised to slash the moaning man on the deck, if not with
e force necessary to slice his head off.

Charley Selkirk walked to the man and gestured with his
istol for him to move across the deck to the rail. The Arab,
is moans now wails, slithered across the deck. Another pi-
ate appeared, this one in a torn white robe, and without or-
ers, joined the first man.

"Let them all come out, don't kill them, Theo, and then
ok inside," Charley Selkirk said to Theo LaSalle. Then he
otioned to several of the seamen to follow him, and he
ade his way down the deck, stepping around the patches of
rying blood and the bodies, until he reached the ladder to

the quarterdeck. Willi followed him, having a hard time keep ing from retching. The sweet stench of death was alread overcoming the smell of burned gunpowder and burnir wood and canvas.

Willi saw the head that went with the decapitated body h had seen when he first came on deck.

The quarterdeck was slippery with blood and littered wit bodies, and several spokes of the wheel had been splintere by rifle balls.

"Take the helm, and bring the rudder amidships," Charle ordered one of the seamen. Then he climbed the mizzenma shroud and gestured toward *The Eleanor*. When there was a answering wave, he signaled to Mr. Porter to bring *Th Eleanor* alongside.

There was no access to the cabins below the quarterdec from the deck itself, as there was on *The Eleanor*. Charle led his party back to the main deck and then into the compar ionway. The cabins on either side of the companionway wer empty. But when they opened the door to the master's cabi a man was kneeling on the deck, his forehead touching th deck, waiting for them.

He showed no signs whatever of having been in a fight. H flowing white robe was spotless, as was the white cloth h had tied around his forehead. There was a curved sword wit a jeweled handle on the floor in front of him. After a mo ment, he raised his head and moved backward to squat on h heels. He smiled warmly, ingratiatingly, at both of them, an then, deciding that Charley was an officer, leaned forwar again and picked up the curved, jewel-handled sword in bot hands, and offered it to him.

Willi had a mental image of Captain Selkirk lying in th mess that had been his stomach and intestines on the quarte deck of *The Eleanor*. He felt a cold, dispassionate fury in hi own stomach. Without raising the rifle to his shoulder, ju holding it out in front of him with one hand, he shot the p rate captain in the center of his forehead.

Chapter Nineteen

1

board the Prinz Wilhelm
'est longitude 74°37', north latitude 42°11'
pril 17, 1770

The enormous man with the flowing mustache who had
·mehow known that Lady Caroline Watchbury was preg-
·nt, and to whom she had as much as confessed that she
·as carrying a bastard in her belly, was not, to her enormous
·lief, at breakfast the next morning. She would have hated
·face him.

But neither was he at the noon meal, and she then began
· wonder if he had fallen ill again. He wasn't at the evening
·eal, either, and by then, for reasons she couldn't under-
·and, she was quite concerned. Feeling more than a little the
·ol, she went to the man who seemed to be in charge of pas-
·nger concerns, and tried, and failed, to make him under-
·and she was making inquiries into the health of the large
·ntleman with the large mustache who occupied the other
·rge cabin.

The man seemed to be unable to comprehend what she
·anted of him, and impatiently and impulsively Lady Car-
·ine nodded at him, said "Danke schön," and went directly
·wn the companionway to the door of the other large cabin
·d knocked on it.

He opened it in a moment. He was wearing only his open-
·llared shirt, and in his free hand he held a stick of sausage.
·e was as surprised to see her as she was at his bulk; he real-
·towered over her.

"Lady?" he asked.

"I wondered if you were sick," she blurted.

369

He looked at her almost coldly for a long moment, and then seemed to make up his mind, favorably, about her.

"I have no sick," he said. "Come!" It sounded like an order, and he held his door open.

"Thank you, no," she said, flustered. She sensed that she had somehow hurt his feelings.

"I have French schnapps," the huge man said.

"I couldn't," she said lamely. He raised his bushy eyebrow in question. "What would people say?"

"Does matter?" he asked.

She glanced up and down the companionway, to see if anyone was in it, and then, surprising herself, she stepped inside his cabin. She saw that he had been served the evening meal in his cabin; there were plates and bowls on the table.

She had just time to glance quickly around his cabin, to wonder what had possessed her to enter it, when he thrust a glass with a dark fluid in it at her.

"Not much," he said. She raised her eyebrows in question. "Much not good for baby, lady," he said, kindly, gently.

What an extraordinary thing for him to say!

"Thank you," she said, and sipped at the glass. It was brandy. She felt its warmth almost immediately. "Thank you," she said again, and smiled at him.

"Not much," he said, and shook his head and wagged his finger at her. It wasn't quite fatherly, she thought, but it was kind and protective: like an uncle.

She smiled her understanding. He was concerned about her condition. What she didn't understand was how he knew about her condition. After his astonishing announcement the night before, when she returned to her cabin, she had stripped and examined her body. So far as she could tell, her belly wasn't swollen at all. Her breasts seemed slightly larger and her nipples seemed darker and more sensitive. But she was not "heavy with child."

The more important question was, *who is this man?*

"How do we know each other?" she asked.

He put his glass down on the table, came to attention, clicked his heels together, bobbed his head in a crisp bow and, in English, very carefully pronouncing each syllable, identified himself: "Chief Sergeant Lahrner, Cavalry Squadron, the Hessian Regiment of Light Foot."

"Hesse?" she said. "I have been to Hesse-Kassel."

"Yes, lady," Lahrner said.

370

And then she knew who he was. *Of course*, she knew him:
: had been the sergeant in charge of the escort from Kassel
Marburg.

She thought of Marburg, and then of Alexei, and put that
ought from her mind. Then she reminded herself that she
as the widow of a colonel, and that colonel's ladies do not
nverse with, much less share intimacies with, common ser-
ants. But that social taboo seemed to make absolutely no
nse here.

"What are you doing here?" she asked. "Why are you go-
g to Pennsylvania?"

He told her the story of escorting the telescope, and of
ing shipwrecked, and of watching "young von Kolbe, the
dy remembers the Baron von Kolbe?" being rescued.

"Yes, of course. The baron's son, you mean?"

"Willi," Lahrner said, nodding his head.

"And he was picked up at sea?"

"Yes, lady. And now I go get him."

"But how do you know where he is?"

"I see the name of the ship," Lahrner said. "And I have
und where the ship goes: to Philadelphia. I will be there
hen the ship, *The Eleanor*, comes home to Philadelphia."

He pronounced each syllable carefully, separately: "Ell-
-e-Ann-Ohr; Phil-Eye-Del-Phee-Ah." There was no mistak-
g what he said. Caroline felt a little dizzy.

"You're sure it was *The Eleanor*?" she asked, faintly.

"You know *The Ell-eee-ann-ohr*?" he asked, pleased.

She nodded, and incredibly, tears came.

He laid a huge, amazingly gentle hand on her shoulder.

"I say something wrong?" he asked. "I am very apologize."
e shook her head, and then it spilled out of her.

"The . . . uh . . . baby's father. The baby's father is an
ficer on *The Eleanor*."

"And now you go marry him?" Lahrner asked. He was
aming.

She thought, of course, instantly, *No! I'm not going to
arry him!*

She nodded her head, and looked at him.

He was really pleased.

"Good man?" he asked. She nodded. "Young man?" She
dded again.

*Oh, yes, he's a young man! He's nothing but a boy, to tell
e truth of it.*

371

The huge hand patted her shoulder approvingly.

It was going to be necessary for her, she understood, to te
this man everything before they reached Philadelphia. And a
preposterous as that was, the prospect almost immediately be
came comforting. She didn't feel nearly as alone an
frightened as she had felt when she knocked at his door.

"How could you tell?" she heard herself asking.

"Please?" he asked, not understanding her.

"That I am with child?" she asked, blushing furiously.

He smiled happily at her. His eyes lit up. He looke
around the cabin. There was a lantern on the table. H
picked it up, and removed the glass, and went to a candle
holder over his bunk. He took the candle and lit it from th
wick of the lantern, and then blew out the lantern. He hel
the candle in his hands, very gently.

In a moment, she understood.

He meant that she glowed.

She felt like crying again. Instead, she reached out an
touched his hand. He blew out the candle and laid his hug
hand on hers.

"Beautiful mama," Karl Lahrner said. "Beautiful baby."

2

East longitude 3°0', north latitude 37°5'
(The Mediterranean Sea, off Point Pescade, Barbary Coas

May 7, 1770

The Mediterranean was like a pleasant, endless lake. Ther
was just enough wind to ripple the surface of the wate
There were no seas, just a succession of gentle swells, n
more than a foot high. The sun was bright, turning a fe
high clouds brilliant white, and the sky beyond was dee
bright blue.

It was entirely too beautiful, Willi thought, for what ha
happened the day before, and what they were about to d
now.

Except for a dozen men, and Mr. Dillon, who were aboar
the pirate ship, standing guard over the prisoners in th
fo'c'sl, the crew and the passengers of *The Eleanor* wei
gathered on the deck. There were still some unpatched hol
in the sails, but the sails had been reefed, and the holes wei

not in sight. *The Eleanor* had been cleaned up. The blood and gore on her decks had been washed away, and then her decks had been stoned. Most of the damage to her rigging had been repaired. There had been relatively little damage to *The Eleanor*, except for the rigging and the railing and other furnishings of the quarterdeck, which had been raked with chain shot from the cannon on the pirate ship. One of the cows and several of the goats had been wounded and later destroyed. The remaining cow was mooing.

Laid neatly out on the deck, amidships, starboard, were eleven canvas bundles. Each bundle was about six feet long. Each bundle was tightly trussed with clean, new, white line. Each bundle contained the body of a crewman of *The Eleanor*, a penny on his eyelids, three thirty-pound cannon balls between his legs. One of the bundles rested on a board raised off the deck between two chests. It was covered with the English flag, the Cross of Saint George. That bundle contained the body of Captain Paul MacTavish Selkirk, Esquire, of Philadelphia, cut down in the forty-fourth year of his life, in the Year of our Lord 1770, by a length of rusty chain fired from a cannon on a ship in the hands of Barbary pirates.

Mr. Porter and Bosun Theo LaSalle, in clean uniforms, stood on the deck. Mr. Charles Selkirk, who had the helm, and Mistress Mary Selkirk stood on the quarterdeck rail with the German lad, the only one of the gentlemen who had the balls to give the bloody pirate master what he deserved, a rifle ball into his forehead, blowing his brains all over his cabin.

"Carry on, Mr. Porter," Mr. Selkirk ordered.

Mr. Porter put on his spectacles and opened the ship's Bible.

"In my father's house," he read, "there are many mansions. If it were not so, I would not tell you."

And the twenty-third Psalm.

Mistress Mary was white in the face, and although not crying, seemed dizzy and close to fainting. She leaned against the German lad, who had put his arm around her shoulder to steady her.

"Into the deep we commit the body of our brother departed, in the sure and certain knowledge of resurrection and life eternal," Mr. Porter read, and nodded at Theo LaSalle, who gestured to four seaman, who went to the bundle under the flag and pulled the corners of the flag from where they

373

had been tucked into the clean, new, white line with which the bundle was trussed, and then held the flag taut, six inches above the bundle.

Then Theo picked up the end of the board on which the long bundle rested and let it slide over the side into the smooth sea. They could all hear the soft splash it made.

Four cannon fired, one at a time, and a cloud of smoke rose up from the gunports and was blown over the deck.

When all the other bundles had gone over the side, the four cannon fired again.

Mr. Selkirk put his tricorn back on.

"You may dismiss the men, Mr. Porter," he called.

Mary Selkirk freed herself from Willi von Kolbe's arm and went to Tony the cabin boy and wrapped her arms around him. And then she cried with Tony.

"Theo," Mr. Selkirk ordered, "go relieve Mr. Dillon on the Frenchman, and ask him to come to the captain's cabin."

3

The meeting was actually held in the wardroom, rather than the captain's cabin as Charley Selkirk had originally intended. He explained the change by saying there would be more room in the wardroom, but actually it was because he was uncomfortable in his father's cabin when he first went there after the funeral service.

There were only three men present, the surviving officers of *The Eleanor*. Neither Charley Selkirk, now legally the owner, nor Mr. Porter, now the senior officer, sat in the empty captain's chair at the head of the table.

"We are four officers short," Charley began.

"Five," Mr. Porter corrected him, and named them. "A master and three mates for the Frenchman, and a master for *The Eleanor*."

The Frenchman, whose papers they had found aboard, even though her name plate had been removed, was the *Jeanne-Marie*, out of Marseilles. Her log was intact, but there was no one aboard *The Eleanor* who could read any of the French beyond the date of the entries. Mr. Porter theorized that the pirates had taken her, six weeks before, the date of the last entry in the log, unloaded her cargo somewhere on the Barbary Coast, and had been at sea looking for what they had found, a merchantman flying the British flag. They could capture her and scuttle the *Jeanne-Marie*, which would have given them a British ship, and save them from French wrath.

"We have to make up our minds about what to do with the Frenchman," Charley said. "One option is to take her to Marseilles, have the French hang the pirates, and offer to sell her back to her owners."

"She'll sail slow, with only one good mast," Mr. Porter said. "It would be a long voyage with her to Philadelphia."

"On the other hand," Charley went on, "if we take her to Marseilles, we know we'll have to deal with the British consul, which will damned well mean we'll have admiralty lawyers snooping around us, to 'protect our interests.' "

"We'll have that problem in Philadelphia, too," Mr. Porter countered. "There's no reason you and Dillon couldn't take *The Eleanor* home. That way I could take the Frenchman to Marseilles."

"I think it would be best if you took *The Eleanor* home," Charley said. "She's the most valuable ship, and should be in the hands of the most experienced officer."

"Then you think Dillon should sail the Frenchman to Marseilles?" Mr. Porter asked. Charley sensed that that solution was what Porter had wanted all along. He was also aware that Porter had not suggested that he take the Frenchman to Marseilles. Because, as owner, he would naturally want to be aboard *The Eleanor*? Or because he wasn't qualified to take the Frenchman by himself?

"With any kind of luck at all," Charley went on, "you could off-load the machinery and the Sedges in Philadelphia before the officials started snooping."

"If you want me to take *The Eleanor* home, Charley, I will, of course," Porter said.

"There's really no choice to make about that," Charley said. "I don't want to take the risk going to Marseilles with her would pose. *The Eleanor* goes home under you."

"That brings us back to your original question," Porter said. "What do we do for officers?"

"O'Keefe," Mr. Dillon said.

Charley and Mr. Porter nodded their agreement. Quartermaster O'Keefe was ripe for a promotion anyway.

"But then, who else?" Porter asked. "And who goes on which ship?"

"Theo," Mr. Dillon said. "He can serve as an officer on either."

375

Charley remembered what his father had said about Theo being the kind of man who never should be permitted to leave the fo'c'sl.

"You think Theo will make a good officer?" he asked.

"I've never known a better seaman," Porter said.

"That's two," Charley said, deciding that if other, better, names came up, he could raise his objections to Theo LaSalle then. "We'll need three more."

"Most of the good men were killed," Porter said. "We've got a crew of ordinary seamen who're going to have trouble moving up to fill the jobs they'll have to."

They went down the list of names on Mr. Porter's crew list. They moved men up, apprentice seamen to ordinary, ordinary to helmsmen and able-bodied, but there was trouble finding able-bodied seamen to move to the officer ranks.

"Maybe this would be easier if we knew which of you is going on the Frenchman," Mr. Porter said, looking at Charley and Mr. Dillon.

"If Mr. Dillon is willing to serve under me, I'll take him aboard the Frenchman as chief mate."

There was silence, and Charley understood that Dillon had believed, quite naturally, that as the next senior officer, he would take the next senior command, that of prize-master of the Frenchman.

After a moment's hesitation, Charley decided to offer an explanation. "I've been thinking," he said, "that it will be a good deal easier to claim my majority when we reach Philadelphia, and protect my interests in my father's property, if I sail into Philadelphia as a master."

"God, I forgot the captain got married!" Mr. Porter said. "Do you think there's going to be trouble with that woman, Charley?"

"I don't think there will be, but it never hurts to be careful."

"There's no reason, obviously, why you and Dillon couldn't take the Frenchman," Porter said.

"Mr. Dillon?" Charley asked.

"I'll sail under you, Charley," Dillon said. "You're your father's boy."

"Now that you've said that, Mr. Dillon," Charley said. "I'll tell you that it's in my mind, when all this has settled down, to make you chief mate of either the Frenchman, or *The Eleanor*, whichever you'd rather have."

There was a burst of quick laughter among the three of
them, and then they returned to their immediate problem of
manning the two ships.

"If we make Stern quartermaster," Charley said, "then
there's no reason we couldn't take von Kolbe with us on the
Frenchman."

"As what?" Porter asked.

"As sort of a third mate."

"You must be joking," Mr. Porter said. "This is the first
time he's been on a ship."

"He knows men," Charley said. "The men think of him as
a gentleman. They would take his orders because of that."

"Men won't take orders from an officer they don't respect
as a sailor."

"I don't think Theo's going to have an easy time of it, either," Charley said. "Men don't like to take orders from a
seaman they don't respect as an officer."

"I'm surprised to hear you say that about Theo," Mr. Porter said, "since he taught you about everything you know."

Charley remembered what his father had said about one
incident where correction was needed being passed and leading inevitably to a second, worse, insubordination, and he had
been expecting Mr. Porter to try to put him in his place as a
boy. He had dreaded the confrontation. But now that it had
come, it didn't seem to be much of a problem at all.

"No, that's not true," Charley said, rather coldly. "Theo
taught me to climb the rigging, and whip a line, and man an
oar. He taught me nothing about being an officer. I learned
what I know about that from my father. And from you and
Mr. Dillon."

Mr. Porter thought that over a moment, and then decided
to make a joke of it.

"With splendid teachers such as those you just named, you
can't fail to be a fine officer," he said.

"Aye, aye," Mr. Dillon laughed.

"So what's been decided, then," Charley said, "is that I'll
go aboard the Frenchman as prize-master."

"Right," Mr. Dillon said.

"And you, Captain Porter," Charley said, for the first time
using that title to address Porter, "will take *The Eleanor*
home." He was aware that his tone of voice was making what
he said an order, and wondered if he had consciously done
so.

Porter nodded.

"You can take O'Keefe and LaSalle with you, and anyor else you want, so long as it's not Stern," Charley went o. "Mr. Dillon and I will need him aboard the Frenchman we can talk to our third mate."

Porter laughed at that.

"You really think taking him as an officer is a good idea? he asked.

"You make the best of what you have," Charley said.

"That still leaves me shy one officer," Mr. Porter sai "Who do you have in mind for your second mate?"

"We'll do without," Charley said. "Mr. Dillon and I w take twelve-hour watches, and hope to get our sleep whenev we think we can leave Willi von Kolbe alone on the quarte deck for a couple of hours."

"Then at least let me leave Theo with you," Porter said.

"No," Charley said. "I don't want Theo serving under n as an officer."

"You're the owner," Porter said. "You can do what yo will."

"Yes, I can," Charley said, coldly.

"We are, of course, going to sail together?" Porter said.

"No," Charley said, immediately. "I've had some though about that, too."

"Oh?" Porter asked, not quite keeping the suspicion out his voice.

"I'm going to ask Sedge to come with me, him and h oldest two boys. Mistress Sedge and the other children wi sail with you. That'll break up the large English family th authorities may be looking for."

"All right," Porter said, somewhat less suspicious.

"We'll transfer the steel-making equipment to the Frencl man," Charley went on. "That way, if it's found, it'll b found aboard the Frenchman, and not *The Eleanor*, and w can try to talk our way out of that."

"Aye," Dillon said, agreeing out loud.

"You and *The Eleanor* will go ahead, and arrange to ge Mistress Sedge and her children settled in Chester."

"Good idea, Charley," Porter said.

Charley gave him a broad smile.

"Since I addressed you as 'Captain'," he said, and let th rest of the sentence hang.

"Aye, aye, Captain," Porter said, after a barely perceptible hesitation.

"Now, I suggest we muster the crew, and tell them what's going on," Charley said. "And see if I can recruit some volunteers to come aboard the Frenchman with me."

"You'll have no trouble there, Captain," Mr. Dillon said.

He did not.

4

Captain Charles Selkirk, prize-master of the Marseilles merchantman *Jeanne-Marie*, stepped onto the midships railing of *The Eleanor*, then down to the base of *The Eleanor*'s mizzenmast shrouds, and then jumped the five feet to the corresponding shroud base of the *Jeanne-Marie*. Then he climbed up on the *Jeanne-Marie*'s deck and made his way to the quarterdeck.

Tony was already there. He had begged to be allowed to go onto the *Jeanne-Marie* in any job, even though he had been told they might make port as much as a month after *The Eleanor* got home.

"I'll have all hands on deck," Charley said, from force of habit, and Tony shouted the order through the leather megaphone he had brought with him from *The Eleanor*. The first man on deck was Willi von Kolbe, now wearing, at Charley's insistence, a tricornered hat to signify his new status as an officer. He came up onto the quarterdeck and tipped it at Charley. That gave Charley a moment's time to consider that since Willi felt a little silly playing officer, perhaps this whole business, his demanding the owner's right to command, was nothing more on his part but a childish gesture.

Then he walked to the port railing and saw Theo LaSalle on the quarterdeck of *The Eleanor*. I guess I'm not the only one who likes to pretend I'm something I'm not, he thought.

He took the megaphone away from Tony.

"You're a helmsman now," he said. "Stand by your wheel." He walked to the quarterdeck railing, and cupped his hands over his mouth: "Stand by to let loose all lines!" he called, and when he saw the men step to the lines, he completed the order: "Let loose all lines, fore and aft!"

The lines were untied and then hauled aboard. For a long minute, nothing happened, and then the wind and the current

began to move the two ships slowly apart, inches at first, an
then feet.

He heard Theo LaSalle bellow orders on *The Eleanor*
There were very few seamen aboard either ship. *The Eleano*
would not now get smartly underway, with her canvas fallin,
almost at once from the yards of her three masts. There wer
only enough men to man one yard of one mast at a time.

Theo sent them aloft on her foremast main yards first, an
her foremast main dropped from its yard with a flapping flut
ter, and then filled with air. As soon as the sail was taut, th
seamen climbed quickly down the foremast shrouds, trotte
down the deck to the main mast shrouds, and began to climl
them.

The distance between the ships grew as *The Eleanor* bega
to move more quickly to port.

Charley called for the bosun. By the time they had se
down on paper the names of the available men against th
jobs that had to be filled, it was clear that Stern was thei
only choice for bosun. The quartermaster's job he was sup
posed to fill was now held by a man who had four days be
fore been an ordinary seaman.

"Send the men aloft," Charley called to Stern when he ap
peared on the deck below him.

"Where away, sir?" Stern asked.

"We have only one mast, Bosun," Charley called down
"Where else would they go?"

Stern ordered the men aloft, and Charley turned to th
quartermaster.

"Rudder amidship until we get underway," he ordered.

"Rudder amidship, aye, sir," the new quartermaster said
and then went and leaned over the stern railing to make sur
that the new helmsman had turned the wheel so as to put th
rudder where it was supposed to be.

Mary Selkirk appeared on the quarterdeck of *The Eleanor*
Charley knew that she was furious with him for insisting tha
she return to Philadelphia aboard *The Eleanor*, and eve
more furious when he refused to tell her why. He wasn't go
ing to tell anybody why he had made that decision. He had
given in to her only in so far as promising her that if she had
any trouble with his father's wife, she could go and ask Cap
tain and Mistress Ephraim Lewis if she could stay with them
until he returned. He had written a letter to Captain Lewis,
asking that he do them that service, and given it to Mary.

There were two reasons he had insisted that Mary return to Philadelphia aboard the relatively intact and thus faster *The Eleanor*. One was that *The Eleanor* was safer. There was in the back of Charley's mind the awareness that if the *Jeanne-Marie* were caught in a winter storm in the middle of the North Atlantic with but one mast and less than half a crew to handle her and man her pumps, he was going to be in trouble.

The second reason he was sending her home on *The Eleanor* stood beside him, uneasily wearing an officer's tricorn. Willi von Kolbe and Mary Selkirk were unaware, he was sure, that he had seen them locked in an embrace in the cabin he had shared aboard *The Eleanor* with Willi.

They hadn't been doing anything but holding each other. They had all their clothes on, and they weren't even kissing, but he was holding her and she was holding him.

It was entirely possible, Charley had decided, that all Willi was doing was again comforting Mary as he had comforted her during the funeral services, and that he truly thought of her, as he said he did, as one of his own sisters. On the other hand, it was possible, God knows she had grown curves like an overnight mushroom, that there was more to it than brother-sister affection. He didn't know what the situation was, and he had known that he wasn't going to be able to find out easily, and certainly not by asking them.

The solution was to separate them. A very simple solution to a problem that he was fully aware was more than he was equipped to handle.

He looked over his shoulder and saw Willi, leaning on the *Jeanne-Marie*'s quarterdeck railing, looking over at Mary on *The Eleanor*. She was holding her hand, with a handkerchief in it, above her head, but for some reason not waving her arm.

Charley had no way of knowing, of course, that Willi was just as confused and concerned about Mistress Mary Selkirk as he was.

Willi had felt shamed and indecent about having hugged Mary and having those nasty thoughts about kissing her innocent child's mouth, in the first place, in Captain Selkirk's cabin just before the battle with the pirates. He had really felt ashamed of himself during the funeral service, when Mary leaned against him in her hour of sorrow and loss, turning to him in innocence and trust, and the evil man in him had been so aware of the sweet smell of her, of the pressure of her hip (and her upper body) against his hip and arm, that he'd actually had the same reaction to her that he'd had when Trude, in the Golden Ram, had stuck her tongue in his ear.

It was a damned good thing, he thought at the time, that the trousers he'd gotten from Charley had been so large on him, or the whole crew would have known what a dirty and ungrateful bastard he was, getting a hard-on during funeral services for a man he admired (and even maybe loved) almost as much as he admired his own father, while he had a supposedly comforting arm around the man's orphan daughter.

And then there had been the final thing. Toward the end of the second long day they had been tied up beside *The Eleanor*, transferring cargo and stores, Charley had told him to take a man and go to their cabin and move everything he owned aboard the *Jeanne-Marie*.

Mary had come to the cabin when they were just about finished, and he hadn't even wanted her to get close, because he'd been working like a draught horse all day and was soaked with sweat and dirty bilge water, and he didn't want anyone as clean and dainty as Mary to smell him. And then all of a sudden, she was looking at him out of those damned eyes of hers, and he had his arms around her again, and this time he really was a dirty ungrateful bastard, and kissed that child's mouth of hers, and she was such a child that she didn't know what was going on, and before he knew it, her mouth tasted the same way Trude's mouth had tasted, sort of acid sour, when she had wanted him to do it to her, and Mary was pressing her body against his, and it was all he could do, it took *all* his will power, to take his mouth off hers and just hold her, and then to put his hands on her arms and sort of push them apart.

Just in time, too, for Charley had shown up in the cabin not two minutes later, and God only knows what would have happened if Charley had seen him doing what he'd been doing to his sweet and innocent sister. The absolute horror of that had been that he'd had the damned hard-on again, and Mary must have known about it, because she had been pressing so hard against him that he couldn't breathe. He could only pray that she didn't know what it was, and

382

thought maybe it was a knife, or a belaying pin, or something.

He was sure that was the case. If there was ever a sweet and innocent and pure young woman, it was Mary Selkirk. She didn't know how evil men's souls could be. She was just pure, period. The proof of that was the note he'd just found in his trousers pocket when he changed.

"Willi, I will pray God to keep you safe and bring you soon again to me. Your loving Mary."

If she knew the sinful thoughts he had had about her, she certainly wouldn't have written him a note like that.

She had been holding her hand over her head with a handkerchief in it, without moving. All of a sudden, she waved her arm back and forth. He waved back at her. Then the handkerchief flew from her hand into the sea.

Willi watched the distance between the *Jeanne-Marie* and *The Eleanor* increase, until he no longer could make Mary out on *The Eleanor*'s quarterdeck, and he kept watching until he couldn't see *The Eleanor* at all.

Chapter Twenty

1

Philadelphia, Pennsylvania
May 29, 1770

Lady Caroline Watchbury had come to the Pennsylvania colony planning to sell land. Instead, she almost immediately found herself writing a draft against her letter of credit on the Bank of England to buy some. Specifically, she purchased a forty-acre farm, with a small house and barn, on the banks of the Schuylkill River, near a small village called Germantown.

Karl Lahrner negotiated the sale for her with the owners, who were immigrants from Schleswig-Holstein and spoke little English, and buying the farm was his idea. She had confessed the truth to him, that what she really wanted to do was quietly have Charles Selkirk's baby, turn the infant over to the Selkirk family to raise, sell her lands in Pennsylvania, and return to England, probably to marry Captain Sir Richard Trentwood, but in any event to resume her proper station in life.

Lahrner seemed to accept, without condemnation, her solution to the problem as being the practical one. He had, she quickly learned, a very practical mind, a logical one, which saw problems for what they were, and could thus easily see their best solution.

He pointed out to her that she would have to be in Pennsylvania at least long enough to deliver the child and care for it until it was strong enough to be turned over to the Selkirks. She was going to have to stay someplace for that length of time, and a lady such as herself could not stay in an inn, nor, considering her condition, as a guest in the house of anyone whom she had letters of introduction who would feel obliged to offer their hospitality.

She could not, he pointed out to her, even use the letters of introduction she had. If she came to know people of her own class in the Pennsylvania colony, and they should come to England, they would remember that Lady Caroline Watchbury had been with child, and wonder aloud what had happened to it.

That made her feel like a fool, and even more dependent on the calm common sense of the huge German. She accepted without hesitation his solution to her problem of where to live until after the child was born: buy a farm on which she could live invisibly if she chose, and which, when he left Pennsylvania, she could discreetly turn over to the Selkirks for whatever purpose they wanted; to keep or to sell, with the proceeds applied to the support of the infant.

He would, he agreed, stay with her on the farm until *The Eleanor* and Wilhelm von Kolbe and the king of England's telescope arrived. The proprieties would be observed by staffing the house with a married couple, and by an announcement, with a slight change, of his purpose in Pennsylvania. It was her idea that he forget, so long as he was in Pennsylvania, that he was Chief Sergeant Karl Lahrner of the Cavalry Squadron of the Landgrave of Hesse-Kassel's Regiment of Light Foot, and that he identify himself as *Herr* Karl Lahrner, in the service of the landgrave, and dispatched to the colony to reclaim the son of Baron von Kolbe and the telescope.

Philadelphia was nothing more, really, than an overgrown village, and questions would be asked about them. That problem was solved by taking an advertisement, printed on the front page of the *Philadelphia Gazette*:

LADY WATCHBURY
River View Farm
Regrets Her Inability To Accept Invitations
Due to Her Observation of a Period of Deep Mourning
Following the Death of Her Beloved Husband
Colonel Sir Edgar Watchbury
Late of the Life Guards of Horse

The announcement, of course, resulted in a dozen caller
to River View Farm within a week of its publication, thos
Philadelphians who considered that their official position o
social status either permitted or required them to offer thei
support to an English aristocrat who for reasons they wer
dying to know was now on a farm outside Philadelphia, nea
Germantown.

Karl Lahrner was introduced to all of them as a gentlema
in the service of Lady Caroline's, and the late Sir Edgar's
dear friend the landgrave of Hesse-Kassel, who, having busi
ness of his own in Pennsylvania, had been so kind as t
offer his masculine protection to a widow who otherwis
would have been all alone on her inspection trip of her Penn
sylvania landholdings.

One of the carriages which rolled down the lane to Rive
View Farm was that of Captain Ephraim Lewis, harbormas
ter of the Port of Philadelphia, whose wife had insisted that i
was both his Christian and professional obligation to call o
the widow. The post of harbormaster was, after all, a roya
appointment, and unless Ephraim did what he was expecte
to do, the widow was liable to return to England and repor
to Buckingham Palace that she had been ignored by the har
bormaster of Philadelphia. He could not afford to ignore, o
fail to offer to help, the widow of a colonel of the Househol
Cavalry.

Captain Ephraim Lewis was delighted when the Germa
who was taking care of the widow asked about *The Eleanor*
in explaining his business in Pennsylvania.

"Let me assure you, sir," he said to Lahrner, "that if th
young man you seek was picked up by *The Eleanor*, he i
now in the hands of one of our finest mariners. I am privi
leged to claim Captain Paul Selkirk as one of my closes
friends."

"What Herr Lahrner was asking," Lady Caroline said
"was if you had word of the arrival date of *The Eleanor*.
already know what a fine man Captain Selkirk is. I returne
from India aboard *The Eleanor*."

"What an extraordinary coincidence," Mrs. Lewis said
"Then we seem to have mutual friends."

"Indeed," Lady Caroline said. "It is really at Captai
Selkirk's suggestion that I came here. I intend to sell m
holdings here, and he wisely suggested I would do better i
that regard if I came here."

386

"He's absolutely right, of course," Captain Lewis said.

"And I have been considering," Lady Caroline went on, the propriety, considering my state of mourning, of calling on Mistress Selkirk. I do not know the lady, of course, but am also privileged to call Captain Selkirk, and Mr. Charles Selkirk, and Mistress Mary, my friends."

She had about ten seconds to consider that she had just, very cleverly, arranged to meet Mistress Selkirk (and thus might be able to ally her on her side before Charley arrived home—She could, she was sure, paint herself as the wronged woman, rather than the shipboard trollop Captain Paul Selkirk more than likely thought her to be) when she saw by the pained look on Mistress Lewis's face that something was wrong.

"I have a closed marriage," Lady Caroline went on. "If I called upon Mistress Selkirk, it need not be public knowledge."

"It isn't that, Lady Caroline," Captain Lewis said, bluntly.

"I don't understand."

"I think, Ephraim," Mrs. Lewis said, "that we have imposed enough on Lady Caroline's time."

"Did I understand you to say, Lady Caroline," Captain Lewis went on, "that you consider yourself a friend to Captain Paul Selkirk?"

"Yes, I do."

"Then you are aware that Mistress Selkirk is Captain Selkirk's second wife, his first having tragically died?"

"No, I was not," Caroline admitted. Now that she thought of it, she had never heard any of them say anything about Selkirk's wife.

"We are simple people here in the colonies, Lady Caroline," Captain Lewis went on. "You will have to forgive my bluntness."

"Eph!" Mistress Lewis said, trying to shut him off.

"Captain Selkirk is one of my closest friends," Lewis plunged on. "The first Mistress Selkirk, likewise. Neither my wife nor I receive the present Mistress Selkirk, nor she us."

"I see," Lady Caroline said.

Oh, damn, she thought. *If Charley's mother is dead, and Captain Selkirk's wife is troublesome, what am I going to do with the baby?*

"I am sure, Lady Caroline," Mrs. Lewis said, "that you understand that what my husband said was in the strictest confidence."

Furious that his wife, who had gotten him out here in the first place against his wishes, was now treating him like a backward child, Captain Ephraim Lewis blurted, "What I was trying to do was spare Lady Caroline the embarrassment of being publicly associated with that Swedish harlot!"

"I very much appreciate your kindness in telling me this," Lady Caroline said.

"With your permission, Lady Caroline," Captain Ephraim Lewis said, "when *The Eleanor* makes port, I will get word to Paul Selkirk that you are here and that you would be willing to receive him."

"Not willing," Caroline replied. *"Very pleased."*

"I'll take care of it," Captain Lewis said.

"And, Lady Caroline," Mrs. Lewis said, "if I may be so forward, I would be pleased, when you're in the city, if you would feel free to just drop in on me."

"That's very kind of you," Caroline said politely. But her mind was full of this new, unexpected, and unpleasant development. *What was she to do now, marry Charley?*

He didn't want to marry her. His father would not want him to marry her. It was absurd that she could even consider marrying a colonial commoner, a mere boy. But what else was there?

With a feeling of enormous relief, she realized that she could talk it over with Karl Lahrner. He always seemed to know the right thing for her to do.

2

Philadelphia, Pennsylvania
June 19, 1770

Theo LaSalle, acting third mate, was the first man ashore from the merchantman *Eleanor* when she docked at the foot of Market Street. He was carrying a letter, written the night before, when they had been lying off Cape May.

Your Excellency,

· The Eleanor, *which docked this day, from Naples, was beset by pirates off the Barbary Coast, on the 6th May. Capt. Paul Selkirk, Esq., master, was killed in the engagement, together with many of our crew.*

The pirates were aboard the merchantman Jeanne-Marie, *of Marseilles, which was taken, together with twenty-four of her crew, and to which Capt. Charles Selkirk, who came into possession of* The Eleanor *upon the death of his late father, intends to lay claim as a prize on his making a port under the British flag.*

As owner, Capt. Selkirk directed Your Excellency's obdt. servant, undersigned, to bring The Eleanor *to Phila., and she lays now at the foot of Market Street, carrying aboard twenty-four Barbary pirates as prisoners.*

Capt. Charles Selkirk is aboard the Jeanne-Marie, *which is reduced to one mast, as prize-master, and is making for this port.*

Your Excellency is requested to take what steps are necessary vis relieving the undersigned of the prisoners, bringing them to trial, and so forth, and to bring the entire matter before His Majesty's Admiralty Court for the Pennsylvania colony.

For Your Excellency's information, Mistress Mary Selkirk, who was aboard The Eleanor *during the outrage, was unhurt and is aboard* The Eleanor.

I have the honor to sign myself, in anticipation of Your Excellency's prompt attention, Your most obdt. servant

> James Porter
> Acting Master, and late chief
> mate, *The Eleanor*

Capt. Ephraim Lewis, Esq.,
H.M. Harbormaster, Phila.,
Customs House

LaSalle, accompanied by Captain Lewis and Philadelphia High Constable Edward Kells, came back across *The Eleanor*'s gangplank thirty minutes later.

Porter was waiting for them on the main deck. After the first courtesies had been exchanged, he said, "I'm glad both of you are here together. I'd like to ask a personal kindness of you."

"Of course, Porter, anything within my power."

"We're carrying a woman and six children aboard, on her way to Baltimore. I'd like to have your permission to set her and the children ashore, right now. They have nothing but terrible memories of *The Eleanor*."

"I understand," Kells said, sympathetically. "As far as I'm concerned, she's free to disembark right now."

"Mr. LaSalle," Porter said, "would you take the widow and the children, and see them safely to Baltimore?"

"Aye, aye, sir," LaSalle said.

So much, Mr. Porter thought, somewhat smugly, for the problem of getting Janet Sedge and her children ashore without attracting the attention of the authorities.

Porter led Lewis and Kells to the master's cabin. Mary Selkirk, was waiting for them there. After a moment's hesitation, Captain Ephraim Lewis held his arms wide for her, and she ran into them.

"I'm so sorry, girl," Lewis said. "I've sent word for my wife to come here directly." And then, over her shoulder, he added, "I sent to the Regiment for a guard of soldiers. They should be along directly." Then, carefully, he asked, "What shape are the pirates in?"

"Better than they deserve," Porter said. "They either don't understand what they face, or if they do, they don't seem to care."

"You kept all of them?" Lewis asked.

"All that was alive but one when we boarded her."

Lewis raised his eyebrows.

"Her captain died," Porter said.

"Have you a German lad aboard?" Lewis asked. "Von Kirby? Something like that?"

"Why do you ask?" Porter replied, as Mary blurted, "It's von Kolbe, and he's with Charley as third mate." She freed herself from Lewis's gentle, if awkward, embrace.

"The same man?" Lewis asked. "I had the feeling he was a boy. The one I'm after, I mean."

"What do you mean, 'after'?" Mary asked.

"Some German prince sent a man after him," Lewis said. "A great hulk of a man named Lahrner. He's sort of looking after someone else you know."

"Who would that be?" Porter asked. He had caught Mary's eye and warned her to watch her mouth.

"Lady Caroline Watchbury," Captain Lewis said.

"She's *here*?" Mary asked, incredulously. Porter gave her another silencing look.

"She asked me to give you word that she would be pleased to receive you," Lewis said. "Despite her deep mourning."

"How gracious of her," Mary replied, with a thick sarcasm that was lost on Captain Lewis and High Constable Kells, but not on James Porter.

"Willi von Kolbe's on the *Jeanne-Marie* with young Selkirk," Porter said.

"And he's not a boy, Captain Lewis," Mary said, firmly. "He fought like a man in the engagement. And he himself killed the pirate captain. Blew his brains out with a rifle ball."

Captain Ephraim Lewis looked at her in astonishment. This was not the girl he had last seen.

"Well," he said lamely, "he would have been hung here, anyway." Then he thought of something else. "As soon as my wife gets here, Mary, she'll take you to your stepmother." He saw the look on her face. "If you'd like."

"I'm not leaving Philadelphia, and I'm not going to that woman," Mary said flatly. She very much reminded Captain Lewis, at that moment, of her father. The determination was that of a Selkirk.

"Well," he said. "You're welcome to stay with us, of course."

"Thank you," Mary said.

The arrival of Mrs. Lewis was announced, moments before she burst into the cabin, and wrapped Mary in her arms.

"Poor little lamb," Mrs. Lewis said.

Whatever Mistress Mary was, Ephraim Lewis thought, it was not a little lamb.

"Mary would stay with us," he said. "For the time being."

"Of course," Mrs. Lewis said. And then as if she were presenting Mary with a gift, she said. "And did you tell her who's been asking after her? Asking that she call?"

"I understand Lady Caroline is here," Mary said flatly.

"Take her with you," Ephraim Lewis said to his wife. "A

guard's coming to take the pirates off, and when that's done
we'll carry the sad tidings to the widow."

"You're going to Durham Furnace?" Mary asked.

"Your stepmother's living in your house on Arch Street
here," Captain Lewis said.

Mary frowned, but said nothing for a moment. Then Lewis
repeated his suggestion that his wife take Mary home with
her. They left. As soon as they were out of hearing, Captain
Lewis asked about Paul Selkirk.

"He was killed with chainshot no sooner the fight began,"
James Porter replied.

"And the girl saw it?" he asked.

"Why do you ask that?"

"She doesn't seem to be a little girl any more."

"She's turned into a young woman," Porter said. "A fine
one."

"Well, I'm glad about that at least," Captain Lewis said,
and when Porter's eyebrows wordlessly asked the question, he
told him what he had heard, and what he knew, for sure,
about Mistress Ingebord Johnson Selkirk and the Reverend
Ingmar Sooth.

3

"I don't believe the mistress is to home," the Irish maid
who greeted the three-man delegation of Porter, Lewis, and
Kells said. "If you're not expected."

"Would you tell Mistress Selkirk," Lewis said, "that The
Eleanor has this morning landed with word of Captain
Selkirk?"

"I'll tell her," the maid said, and shut the door in their
faces, and then returned a minute later to open it wide and
motion them inside.

Mistress Selkirk and the Reverend Ingmar Sooth were in
the living room.

"I believe you know the Pastor?" Ingebord Johnson Selkirk
said, and then, without waiting for a response, asked, "What
is the word of Captain Selkirk?"

"I'm afraid he's been taken from us," Captain Lewis said.

Mistress Selkirk and the Reverend Mr. Sooth looked at
each other.

"The Eleanor was attacked by pirates on the Barbary
Coast," Lewis went on.

392

"And the ship was lost?" the Reverend Mr. Sooth asked.

"She lies at the foot of Market Street," Captain Nelson said.

"But Captain Selkirk was killed?" Sooth asked.

"He was killed," Captain Lewis said.

"The Lord giveth and the Lord taketh away," Ingmar Sooth said. "And the Selkirk children?"

"Both safe, thank God," Captain Lewis said.

"Why aren't they here?" Ingebord Selkirk asked.

"Mary is with my wife, mistress," Lewis said.

"I'm not surprised," Ingebord Selkirk said. "She doesn't like me, and never did."

"But her place is now with you," Sooth said.

Ingebord looked at him, as if she didn't understand why he said that. Then she said, "I'll have her here, Captain Lewis, if you please."

"Mistress," Lewis said, "the girl is disturbed, quite naturally disturbed, by what has happened. And we've known her all her life. And my wife is more than happy to do what she can for her."

"Captain Lewis," the Reverend Ingmar Sooth said, pleasantly, "surely you understand that Mistress Selkirk, especially now that Captain Selkirk has been called to Heaven, has the legal responsibility for the children."

And through them, Lewis thought, angrily, she can have "legal responsibility" for their share of their father's property.

"Charles Selkirk is hardly a child," he said.

"He is *legally*, of course," Sooth said.

"Under the circumstances, Reverend," High Constable Kells said, "all he has to do is petition the governor for a certificate of majority."

"I'm sure Mistress Selkirk would oppose that," Sooth said, smoothly.

"Of course I would," Ingebord Selkirk readily agreed. "There's a lot of property and money involved. That should not be entrusted to a boy."

Ephraim Lewis made two decisions. One of them he kept to himself. He would not turn over the chest Paul Selkirk had given him for his children under any circumstances to this woman and her clergyman lover. The second decision he announced aloud. "I must tell you, mistress," he said, "that I will strongly recommend to the governor that he grant Charles his majority."

393

"And I, mistress, too," High Constable Kells said.

"Well," Sooth said, "we understand each other, then, don we?"

"Yes, Reverend, we do," Lewis said.

"Until, if indeed he does, the governor grants the Selkir boy his majority, of course, he is a minor under the contr of his stepmother," Sooth said.

"I'll have him here, High Constable Kells," Ingebord sai "Under my roof. Or I'll have him in the city gaol as an inco rigible youth."

"And would you gaol the girl, too, mistress?" Kells de manded, angrily.

"I am sure that you will have her sent to Mistress Selkirk, Ingmar Sooth said, "where, under the law, she belongs."

4

Karl Lahrner heard the dogs bark, and then the banging a the door. Thieves, he thought, after the chickens and mayb the young pigs. He took a pistol from his bedside table an primed the pan with powder, then cocked the hammer an got out of bed.

He could see nothing from the kitchen window, but then glow from in front of the farmhouse caught his eye, and h went carefully around the corner of the house. He saw a ca riage with lit lanterns on the road, and a man holding an other lantern standing in front of the door.

"What want you?" he demanded, leveling the pistol at him.

The man raised the lantern so it would illuminate his face It was Captain Ephraim Lewis.

"Who's that?" Lewis asked.

"Lahrner," Lahrner said, turning the pistol over and shak ing it to get rid of the priming charge before lowering th hammer carefully, so that it would not strike a spark on th flint.

"I would see Lady Caroline," Captain Lewis said.

"At this hour?" Lahrner said. "It's past midnight."

"It's important," Lewis said.

"Important or not, it'll have to wait," Lahrner said. "Th lady is in her bed."

"I said, man, this is important. More important than a hour's sleep."

"The lady is with child," Lahrner said. "I will not wake er."

They both looked at the house, as the glow from a candle lled the previously dark windows. They heard her call out, Karl? Karl?"

"All right," Lahrner said to Captain Lewis. And then he aised his voice, "All right, lady! Open door!"

The door opened.

"What's going on?" Caroline asked. Then she saw Captain ewis and said his name.

"I very much regret disturbing you, Lady Caroline," Lewis aid. "But I consider it important enough to do so."

"You talk in bed," Lahrner ordered her flatly.

"I . . . uh . . . felt a little out of sorts earlier in the eve-ing," Caroline said. "And Mr. Lahrner is more concerned nan . . ."

"I told him, lady," Lahrner said.

"*Why?*" Caroline asked, angry and anguished.

"Because everybody know soon anyway," Lahrner said, un-bashed. "And because Captain Lewis and his lady Christian eople." He paused, and then repeated, "You talk in bed," nd gestured toward her bedroom.

"You're very fortunate," Captain Lewis said, touched by oth the huge German's compliment to him and by Lahrner's oncern for Lady Caroline, "to have as caring a friend as Mr. .ahrner."

"Yes," she said, "I am. But that doesn't mean I have to go o bed, just because he thinks I should. Why are you here, :aptain Lewis?"

"You told me, Lady Caroline," he said, "that you regard ourself as a friend of Captain Paul Selkirk?"

"Yes, I do," she said. It was all that she could say, because he had made the terribly clever little speech when she'd first net him. Now she regretted it, for she disliked lying to this nan.

"Then I bear bad news," he said. "Very sad news."

"Oh?"

"*The Eleanor* was attacked by pirates off the Barbary Coast," Captain Lewis said. "I very much regret to tell you hat our friend Captain Paul Selkirk was killed in the engage-nent."

"Oh, my God!" Margaret said, and then she looked at him lesperately. "Charley? What happened to Charley?"

She had not, he noticed, inquired about Mary Selkirk.

"Charley's all right," Lewis said. "He . . . and the youn man you seek, Herr Lahrner, are making for Philadelph aboard the pirate ship, which they took."

"Charley is all right?" she asked, desperately demandin confirmation.

And then Ephraim Lewis, somehow, knew.

"And Mary?" Caroline finally asked.

"Mary landed with *The Eleanor* this morning," Lewis sai "She's all right." Caroline smiled her relief. Lewis made u his mind. "I was unaware of the degree of affection you fe for Charley."

"I am sure, sir, that I have no idea what you imply," Ca oline flared.

"Tell him, lady," Lahrner said. She looked between the tw of them and felt faint.

"Tell him, lady," Lahrner said, again. "He's Christian man She raised her eyes to meet those of Ephraim Lewis.

"The child I carry," she heard herself saying, "is Charl Selkirk's."

Captain Ephraim Lewis didn't seem surprised. He nodde his head, and then he said something which surprised her.

"Then, Lady Caroline, in this circumstance, I find myse less reluctant than I thought I would be to ask a service you."

"I don't understand you," she said.

"It's a long story," he said, "which I will relate in due tim I have Mary outside in the carriage. She needs your prote tion."

"Protection?"

"May I bring her in?"

"Yes, of course," Caroline said.

Mary came into the room and looked directly at Caroli and said nothing.

"I'm very sorry about your father, Mary," Caroline sai "And I will, of course, do anything within my power to he you in any way I can."

"If I had known where Captain Lewis was bringing me, would not have come," Mary said. "I don't want your help."

"At the moment, you're in no position to be either ind pendent or rude," Captain Lewis said, angrily. "Sometime mistress, there is too much of your father in you!"

"I will take your aid, and see to it that Charley pays yo

396

or it later," Mary said, but not in quite the same defiant tone of voice.

"Thank you," Caroline said, sarcastically.

"Mary, this is Mr. Lahrner," Captain Lewis said.

Lahrner, in the German manner, clicked his heels, bobbed his head, and said his last name.

"*Lahrner?*" Mary asked, in disbelief. "You're not *Sergeant* Lahrner?"

Lahrner popped to attention again. "Chief Sergeant Karl Lahrner, of the Cavalry Squadron, The Hessian Regiment of Light Foot," he announced proudly.

"But Willi told me you were dead!" Mary said.

"No, lady. I am so much alive," he said.

"Willi will be so happy!" Mary said, beaming.

"There is more good news, Mary," Captain Lewis said. She looked at him curiously. "Your brother and Lady Caroline are going to have a child," he said.

"There was no need to tell her!" Caroline snapped.

"I presumed, Lady Caroline," Captain Lewis said, "that it was your intention to marry Captain Selkirk."

Mary and Caroline looked at each other.

Finally, Mary spoke. "If it is a boy, I would be happy if you named him Paul, after his grandfather."

"Of course," Caroline said, and held open her arms. Mary hesitated, and then she went to Caroline. "And if it's a girl," Caroline said, her voice breaking, "she'll be named Mary."

5

Aboard the Jeanne-Marie
Delaware Bay, off Cape May Point
July 4, 1770

The officers on the quarterdeck of the *Jeanne-Marie* were bearded, and where there was no hair, badly sunburned, and dirty. They were down to three mugs of sweet water per man per day, and shaving and washing were out of the question. They were down to a few ounces of salt pork, and two hard biscuits at each of the two "meals" they took. Mr. Dillon, the chief mate, had been sick and unable to stand his watches for nearly a week.

But they'd made it, with their one mast, and even passed through a couple of spring storms.

"There's a sail to port, Captain," George Sedge said Captain Selkirk.

"Who cares?" the captain replied, and he and Third Ma Kolbe shared a delighted laugh at his wit.

Sedge shook his head at them and then pointed to the lar beyond.

"Pennsylvania?" he asked.

"No, that's still New Jersey," Selkirk said. "Pennsylvania over there." He pointed at the barely visible shore. "Oh, forgot. Permit me, gentlemen, to welcome you both to the New World."

Thirty minutes later, it appeared that the sail Sedge ha seen was making for them, and an hour later, there was r question about it.

Selkirk finally took a closer look at the approaching sh through his glasses.

"It's not a revenue cutter," he announced, and then he p the glass to his eye again. "By God, I think that's *The Mar* Goddamn it!"

"Why do you say that?" Willi von Kolbe asked him.

"It can't be good news," Charley said. "And it mean within goddamned sight of Pennsylvania, we'll have to hov to."

"Take it easy, Charley," Willi said, and laid his hand o Charley's arm.

"If I send men aloft to take in the sail," Charley said, ' don't think there's enough strength in them to get them alo again to let it fly."

"There will be men aboard the other ship," Willi said "They can bring us in."

"Goddamn you, you're right," Charley said. He looked Willi. "Take the helm, Mr. von Kolbe, and hove to. All of sudden, I don't feel too well."

Willi looked at him in time to see his eyeballs roll upward but he couldn't reach him before Charley slumped heavily the deck.

"Sedge!" Willi called. "Get up here!" he knelt ove Charley, and then ran to the nearly empty sweet water barre and got a mug full, and cursed as he saw it, and smelled it. was anything but sweet.

He knelt beside Charley, lifted his head, and tried to forc some of the near-putrid water past his cracked lips.

Chapter Twenty-One

1

Charley woke up in his cabin, with Captain Ephraim Lewis looking down at him.

"How are you, Charley?" Lewis asked, when he saw that Charley's eyes were open.

"I must have had a lady's vapors," Charley replied.

"You must have worked too hard, and too long, without either food or water or sleep," Lewis said. "You're as thin as a rail."

"It was not a pleasant crossing," Charley said. "When did we get to Philadelphia?"

"We're not in Philadelphia," Captain Lewis said. "We're at sea. *The Mary*'s got us under tow. We should make Norfolk by early tomorrow morning."

"Norfolk? Why Norfolk?"

"Because if you made Philadelphia, your father's wife has some of Edward Kells's constables waiting on the wharf to grab this ship, as she grabbed *The Eleanor*."

"You better tell me what you're talking about," Charley said, and forced himself into a sitting position. "How do you mean, 'she grabbed *The Eleanor*'?"

"I've got some beef broth for you," Captain Lewis said. "Take it, and it'll give you some strength."

Lewis handed it to him.

"Thank you," Charley said.

"There's milk, too, and some roast pork, if you think your stomach can handle it."

"Good God, no," Charley said. "I'll be lucky if I don't throw this up all over the deck."

399

Lewis watched him sip the beef broth.

"I haven't told you how sorry I am about your fathe Charley," he said.

"You didn't have to put it in words, Uncle Eph," Charle said.

"About the only thing I can say is that he went quick, Lewis said. "He would have wanted it that way."

"He went quick," Charley said. "He was near cut in ha' with a length of rusty chain."

"He lived to see his son a man," Lewis said. "He used t tell me that was all a man could expect, to see his childre grown."

"I had a chance to kill the man who killed him, the pira captain, I mean, and didn't take it."

"One of the tests of a Christian man, Charley, is that h doesn't give in to his animal impulses."

"Christian?" Charley snorted. "I guess I'm not a Christia for I envy the satisfaction the man, and he's a younger ma than I am, who did kill him has."

"You mean von Kolbe?"

"You've met him?"

"He had the helm when I came aboard," Lewis said. "I'v got things to tell you about him, too."

"Tell me what you meant about The Eleanor bein 'grabbed.' "

"You're sure you're strong enough to hear all this? I would be better if you could."

"Let's have it," Charley said.

"Under the law, as your father's widow, and with you no yet legally a man, she comes into her share of your father' property, and into yours and Mary's, as your stepmother."

"I wondered about that. I don't know the law."

"She went to the court the day The Eleanor made Philadel phia, and had her seized. Including the ship's strongbox. Sh paid off the crew and put her up for sale."

"Goddamn her!"

"Edward Kells did what he could," Lewis said. "But sh has the law on her side, and there wasn't much he could do."

"Where's Mary?"

"I took, my wife took, Mary to our house when Th Eleanor landed. When your father's widow demanded tha she come to the house on Arch Street, Mary ran away. You

400

ther's widow went to court and had a warrant sworn out
ainst her as a runaway girl," Lewis said.

"You don't seem very concerned about that," Charley said
arply.

"No."

"So you know where she is?"

"Aye, I know and Edward Kells knows, and where she is
the one place Kells's constables won't look."

"She's safe, then?"

"For the moment."

"You've really stuck your neck out for us, haven't you?"

"Your father would have done as much for me," Lewis
id.

"So what do I do now?" Charley asked.

"Unless we can get you granted your majority, Charley,
ur father's wife is going to get her share of this vessel, too,
d everything else you two would come into from your fa-
er."

"I took this vessel!" Charley said.

"Under the law, you're a child, so what you took is hers to
rotect'."

"The way she's protecting *The Eleanor*?"

"*The Eleanor* was sold at auction last week, Charley."

"*Sold*? God*damn* her!"

"Half the proceeds went to Mistress Selkirk," Lewis ex-
ained. "As your father's widow. She also got Mary's quar-
r-share, to 'protect'."

"But not mine?"

Captain Lewis shook his head, "no."

"Why not?"

"I went to the governor," Lewis said. "I couldn't get him to
ant you your majority, which is what I wanted. He has less
a backbone than I thought. But he would admit there was
me question. So the governor's holding your share of what
he Eleanor sold for, and your share of the contents of the
ongbox."

"Until when?" Charley asked. "I understand very little of
is."

"Until your status is clear."

"What does that mean?"

"Until you petition the governor for your majority, and a
cision is made."

"How do I do that?"

"I've talked to the governor," Lewis said. "I hoped, rea[d]
thought, he'd grant it on your being an officer, a master, b[ut]
he says not, he says that the widow could claim, in cou[rt]
that it was only an emergency, and that Dillon was really t[he]
master."

"What the hell does he want from me?"

"What the law requires is that you have self-sustaining e[m]
ployment, which you do, and that you be a married man."

"Married?"

"Married."

"I don't know anybody I would marry," Charley sai[d]
"Even if I was willing to get married."

"Not even Lady Caroline Watchbury?"

Charley, stunned, looked at him in absolute confusion.

"What has she got to do with this? How do you kno[w]
about her?"

"She came to Pennsylvania," Lewis said.

"To sell her lands," Charley said, thinking he understood.

"No," Lewis said. Charley looked at him and asked e[x]
planation with raised eyebrows.

"She came to bear your child, Charley," Ephraim Lew[is]
said. "Her plan was that she would turn it over to your fath[er]
and mother."

"Because I am but a boy, is that it?"

"That was the circumstance," Lewis said.

"And now she is willing to marry me?" Charley asked, b[it]
terly. "Now that she can't conveniently get rid of our basta[rd]
child?"

"I don't much care, Charley," Captain Lewis said, almo[st]
angrily, "about your relationship with the lady. But I am te[ll]
ing you I think you don't have much of a choice."

"What good will my marrying her do me, or Mary?"

"If you go to the governor as a married man," Lewis sai[d]
"he will not only grant you your majority, but award custo[dy]
of your sister to you."

"We're sure of that?"

"I know the Norfolk harbormaster," Lewis said. "Who [is,]
as I am, H.M. Admiralty Courts officer." Charley looked [at]
him for explanation. "If we make port in this vessel, claim[ed]
by you as prize, and you are accompanied by your wife, th[e]
Honorable Mrs. Charles Selkirk, he's not liable to as[k]
whether you're twenty or twenty-one. He'll be too impresse[d]
with you as the husband of a bona fide English aristocrat."

402

"So what?"

"So you arrive in Philadelphia a week or ten days from
[no]w, and you can't understand, *and neither can the governor,*
[wh]y there is a question of your majority. The agent of the
[go]vernor of the Virginia colony, the Norfolk harbormaster,
[an]d the officer of the H.M. Admiralty Court have already
[re]cognized you as a man. You don't award prizes to boys.
[An]d it would be insulting for the governor of Pennsylvania to
[in]sult the governor of Virginia colony by declaring a boy
[so]meone Virginia has recognized as a man."

"You apparently have everything figured out," Charley
[sa]id, after thinking it over. "Except getting me married to
[La]dy Caroline. How do you propose to do that, before we
[ma]ke Norfolk?"

"Lady Caroline's aboard."

"Aboard?" Charley asked, incredulously.

"Aboard *The Mary*," Lewis corrected himself. "When you
[fe]el up to it, we'll hove to and transfer you aboard *The
[M]ary.*"

"Why?"

"Masters have the crown's authority and the church's
[so]mewhat reluctant permission to marry people," Lewis said.
[B]ut not themselves, and only aboard their own ships."

"Good God!" Charley Selkirk said.

2

Lady Caroline Watchbury, who had once thought her sec-
[on]d marriage would take place in the Guards' Chapel, in a
[sm]all, discreet ceremony at which it was reasonable to expect
[th]at His Majesty would appear as a mark of respect to her
[lat]e husband, stood on the deck of the coaster *Mary* and
[wa]tched her bridegroom approach.

He was in a small longboat. He was wearing torn and tat-
[te]red clothing, was bearded and as gaunt as a cadaver. And
[wh]en he climbed up the ladder and stood on the deck, he em-
[br]aced not her but the Irish master of this stinking little
[ve]ssel, and it was a long time before he came to her.

"You look awful," she blurted. "Are you all right?"

"You're sure you want to go through with this?" he asked,
[ig]noring her question.

"Neither of us, apparently," she flared, "have much of a
[ch]oice."

"Right," he said. "Let's get it over with."

Captain Richard MacMullen, who was more than a littl[e] concerned that he was inviting everlasting damnation, as [a] good Roman Catholic, reading a Church of England weddin[g] service over two Protestants, had more than a little difficul[ty] getting through the ceremony. So did the groom, who twi[ce] staggered and appeared about to faint, and had to be held [up] by Captain Lewis and Willi von Kolbe.

It was only after she had ritualistically promised to lov[e,] honor, and obey Charles Selkirk, to keep herself only un[to] him, and to care for him in sickness and in health, that sh[e] learned that she was immediately expected to care for him [in] sickness.

"I thought you understood," Captain Lewis said. "We'[re] going to go ahead of you into Norfolk. It's very important [to] all this that the Norfolk harbormaster's records show th[at] when the *Jeanne-Marie* made port, with Charley as captai[n,] his wife was aboard."

In the boat carrying them back to the *Jeanne-Marie* fro[m] *The Mary*, Caroline was sick to her stomach again for t[he] first time in a month, and it came on her so suddenly that t[he] vomitus splattered all over her dress.

Charley was very weak, and it was all Willi von Kolb[e] could do to get him up the *Jeanne-Marie*'s ladder and on[to] her deck. By the time she made it up the ladder (and she w[as] terrified that she would faint and fall into the sea and drow[n] as she climbed it), *The Mary* had hoisted sail and was f[ar] away.

A man whom she had never seen before helped her on[to] the deck.

"Sedge, ma'am," he said.

"Could you help me with my things to the captai[n's] cabin?" she asked.

"I'm afraid not," he said. "With everybody sick, I've g[ot] the watch."

She knew enough about the layout of a ship to find t[he] captain's cabin, and she dragged her case across the deck a[nd] down the companionway to it. It smelled terrible. She sa[w] her husband lying naked, face down on his bed, and for [a] moment, she was furious to think that he had the gall to wa[nt] her now. Then she saw that he was asleep.

And then she wondered if the sleep was really sleep, or [...]

he had fainted. She went to the bed and laid her hand on his back. He was burning with fever.

Still wearing the dress reeking of her vomitus, she went on deck and asked Sedge for water. He pointed out four small kegs rolling loose on the deck.

"Since we're not supposed to have met at sea, they didn't bring much aboard," he said. "But you can have that, if you have to wash."

She didn't reply. She went to the kegs, picked one up with an awful effort, and staggered back to the master's cabin with it in her arms. Then she stripped off her foul dress, and in her chemise, spent the afternoon of her wedding day, and her wedding night, sponging her unconscious husband's feverish body.

3

Sometime very early in the morning she sat down for a moment in the chair by the table in the master's cabin, and closed her eyes for a moment.

She was startled into wakefulness by a terrifying rattle that seemed to come from directly under her feet. Then she heard the splash as the anchor met the water. She realized that they must be in Norfolk.

She looked at Charley, just in time to see him sit up, startled, in bed.

"God," he said. "Was that the anchor?"

"I think so," she said.

"You should have wakened me," he said petulantly, and swung his feet out of bed. There had been, she realized bitterly, a miraculous recovery. He didn't even know that he'd been unconscious with a fever, and would never be grateful to her for spending all night caring for him.

While he was still dressing, there came a knock at the cabin door.

"Come!" he ordered, automatically.

"No!" she shouted. She was wearing nothing but her chemise. She opened her case and found another dress, and hurriedly put it on.

"All right," Charley called, when he saw that she was dressed.

"Captain, the harbormaster is aboard," Willi von Kolbe announced.

405

"Ask him to come in," Charley said.

A tall, erect man in a powdered white wig stepped into the cabin, followed by Captain Ephraim Lewis.

He bowed to Margaret. "My lady," he said.

"Lady Caroline," Captain Lewis said, and bowed to her. "After your ordeal, you are as lovely as ever."

The man in the powdered wig bowed to Charley.

"Captain, I have just learned of your exploits in taking this vessel."

"Charles Selkirk, sir," Charley said. "If I correctly presume you to be the harbormaster, I herewith claim this vessel as a prize."

"Captain Eldon Waite, harbormaster of the Virginia Port of Norfolk, sir, at your service. There will be no trouble about your prize, sir, I am sure. But first things first. With your permission, sir, I will have Lady Caroline carried ashore. My wife awaits her with our carriage on the wharf. We all know what a terrible ordeal Lady Caroline has been through, and are anxious to do what we can for her."

"You are more than kind, sir," Charley said.

Caroline looked directly into Charley's eyes. "It *has* been a dreadful ordeal," she said, and then she gave her arm to Captain Waite, and permitted herself to be escorted from the cabin.

4

River View Farm
Near Germantown, Pennsylvania
July 18, 1770

Charley Selkirk had been accompanied to his audience with the governor by Captain Ephraim Lewis and Chief Constable Edward Kells. They were almost identically dressed for the formal occasion in powdered wigs, knee breeches, silk stockings, silver-buckled shoes, and dress swords.

Thirty minutes after walking into Government House, by virtue of an ornately calligraphed document to which had been affixed the seal of H.M. governor general of Pennsylvania, Charley walked back out, now legally Captain Charles

Selkirk, Esquire, adult and legal guardian of Mistress Mary Selkirk.

The governor had been most obliging. He told Charley that he was sure Charley understood that under the law his hands had been tied when *The Eleanor* had been sold, and that much as he would have liked otherwise, there simply had been no way he could block the sale. The Widow Selkirk (now Mistress Sooth) had been within her rights. If there was ever anything he could do, the governor said, for either Charley or Lady Caroline, he would be honored to oblige.

Charley took a glass of sherry with Captain and Mrs. Lewis at the Lewis home before getting back into the carriage and setting out for Germantown. He would have much preferred to ride to the audience astride, or if not that, then at least drive himself, but Caroline had told him that he had a certain role to play, and that having himself driven was part of that role.

A number of people were going to be waiting for him at River View Farm. He spent the hour's drive slumped back against the cushions of the carriage, his feet on a chest Captain Lewis had put into the carriage just as he left the Lewis home, his head sweating and itchy under the wig, dark sweat-soaked areas spreading under his arms and down his back, deciding how to deal with them.

He had to face Lahrner with a confession. There had been no opportunity to bring the damned telescope up with the governor, although he had promised Lahrner he would try. Captain Lewis and High Constable Kells had both assured him that the telescope Lahrner considered so important was in the same category as *The Eleanor*. It had been legally part of *The Eleanor*'s cargo, as salvage on the high seas. That Swedish bitch had every legal right to sell it, as she had sold *The Eleanor* herself, and Mr. Benjamin Franklin's title to it was unquestioned. He had been the high bidder, and paid the price, and it was now his.

Personally, Charley was glad Mr. Franklin had bought it. He had caused to be engraved upon it a legend Charley thought his father would have liked:

This German Telescope was rescued from
the sea by Captain Paul Selkirk, Master of *The
Eleanor* of Philadelphia, and purchased from

407

his estate and donated to the Philadelphia Public Library Company in his Memory by his friend Benjamin Franklin,
1770

To hell with the king, whose property Lahrner insisted the telescope was.

James Porter would be at River View. Now that he had a few pounds in the bank he could draw against, he was going to send Porter to Norfolk to take charge of refitting the *Jeanne-Marie*. Porter would be her captain. Charley owed him that. He would sail aboard her as owner and third mate. He had a thousand-stand of rifles to get manufactured and shipped to Tatta.

That was his only chance of ever making enough money to have his own ship of the quality and size of *The Eleanor*. Germans, he had learned, had bought *The Eleanor* with pounds sterling and taken her to sea within forty-eight hours. They had known what a good ship they had, and it was childish to consider getting her back.

His real chance for the future was getting the rifles to India.

And he was going to have to deal with Mary, too.

The arrogant little wench had announced, and she wasn't quite sixteen, that she was in love with Willi von Kolbe and was going to marry him and go where Willi was going, whether or not he liked it as brother *or* legal guardian.

He hadn't discussed that with Lahrner yet. And the two of them would be at River View Farm, too. And his wife, who had had a change of mind now that she was going to carry a legitimate child. Now she wanted to have it in England.

Goddamned nonsense. It was his baby, and it would be born here.

When he got to the farm, they were all sitting outside drinking cool tea, in the shade of a tree.

He got out of the carriage.

"You will all be doubtless delighted to hear that I am now officially a man," he said, and walked into the house and into the bedroom he now shared with Caroline, although there had not been time to face that question, either. There had never been any place since they'd been married where they could be together, alone.

The idiot woman married to the harbormaster in Norfolk

408

ad had plenty of room, but had put Caroline into a room
with a black nurse to watch over her, because of the "ordeal"
she'd been through.

And then they'd spent nights in post hotels along the Post
Road and the Baltimore Pike, ladies in some rooms, gentlemen in the other. And at the house Porter had bought for the
Hedges in Chester, God, with eight children, he had almost
found up on the floor. And last night, when they'd got here,
Mary had been in Caroline's bed and couldn't be disturbed,
so he had had to sleep crowded into a bed with Willi on one
side of him and Lahrner snoring on the other.

He took off his tricorn and powdered wig as one unit and
threw it onto the chest. He sat down on the bed and removed
his silver-buckled shoes, which had really hurt his feet. He
pulled off the silk stockings, and then the shirt, and only then
his sword belt. He remembered that goddamned woman had
even sold the sword, which had been his father's. Captain
Lewis had bought it for him.

He was going to have to find some way to repay Ephraim
Lewis, but he had no idea how.

Caroline came into the room.

Willi von Kolbe followed her, carrying the chest Lewis had
put in the carriage.

"Put it right there," she said, "thank you."

Willi left the room and Caroline closed the door behind
him. Charley finished taking off his trousers. His underclothes
were sweat-soaked, and he took them off, too.

"What is it?" he asked.

"You haven't looked in it?"

"No."

"You should have," she said.

"Why?"

"Because it's half-full of gold and jewels," she said.

He walked to the chest, dropped to his knees, and opened
. There were gold and jewels inside, and a letter addressed
to him in his father's hand.

He tore open the envelope.

"What does it say?"

His eyes teared.

"My father was a man of few words, you will recall," he
said, his voice breaking. "All he says in this letter is that he
left this with Captain Lewis for Mary and me, in case something should happen to him."

She started to say something, but changed her mind.

"There's enough here for you and Mary in London," ⌐ said. "If that's where you would go."

"Where would you have me go?" she asked.

"I would have you go wherever you would be happy," ⌐ said.

"That's not what I asked," she said.

"What do you want me to say, Caroline?"

"That now that you have money, and your majority, an⌐ need neither my position nor my money, that you still wa⌐ me as wife."

"I am a selfish man, Caroline," he said. "There is one thir⌐ I must have beside you. I'm not sure I can afford both."

"*The Eleanor*?" she asked.

"Now that I have the money," he said, "I am obliged ⌐ find out where she is, and buy her back. At twice what she⌐ worth, if that's what it costs."

"She's that important to you?"

"Can you understand that?"

"Your mother understood," she said. "Why do you think ⌐ don't?"

"You embarrass me," he said, looking at her. "I'm not use⌐ to having a woman love me."

"I would be happy here," she said. "If I knew you wante⌐ me."

"I want you," he said, "and our child, here. But you're n⌐ used to being poor, and until I complete the next voyage . . ⌐

"*The Eleanor* lays at Mystic," she said. "In Connecticut. ⌐ that far?"

"Not far. Up the coast apiece," he said. Then, "How d⌐ you know that?"

"I know."

"And do you think I can buy her back?"

"You won't have to buy her, Charley," Caroline said. "⌐ own her."

He looked at her in disbelief.

"Lahrner bought her for me at the auction," she said. "H⌐ showed me how I could borrow money against my land."

"Lahrner seems to be a very useful fellow," Charley said.

"He says that he thinks that if we have someone importar⌐ here write Willi's father a letter, saying he can learn the gu⌐ making business here, the landgrave will go along with it."

"Leaving Willi here with Mary?"

410

"That would be better than having her stow away on a ip bound for Germany," she said. "And I think I can keep em apart, that way, until they're a little older." She uckled. "We could get Willi, in exchange for permission to ay here, to give his word as a gentleman to stay out of her d. He's the only gentleman I ever met whose word I would ke."

"Oh, yes, Willi's a gentleman," Charley chuckled.

They looked at each other and smiled.

"That leaves us with only one major decision to make right w, then," he said.

"What's that?" she asked, confused.

"Whether I get dressed, or you take your clothes off."

"Right now?" she asked. "With all these people here?"

"To hell with them," he said. "We're married."

She turned her back on him. So that he wouldn't see how r fingers trembled as they worked the buttons of her dress.

About the Author

Eden Hughes was born on Philadelphia's Main Line to parents who trace their ancestry back to Pre-Revolutionary British colonists, and was educated privately and abroad in both England and Germany. THE WILTONS, Eden Hughes's first novel, is also available in a Signet edition.

A WORLD OF CONQUEST

From the crude cabins of the American colonies to the
jeweled palaces of India...from piracy on the
high seas to abduction in England...from the most
corrupt courts of Europe to the savage lower
depths of society...from seduction between silken
sheets to swordplay in brutal battle—Captain Paul
Selkirk of *The Eleanor* would take any risk
and flout any law to build an empire for himself...and
for his son, Charley, who matched him in
daring and desire...and for his daughter, Mary, whose
beauty was the one thing he would not sell at any price

This is the ultimate, stirring, full-blooded saga of
men and women living and lusting without limits in an
age of unsurpassed challenge and tumultuous
adventure. This is all the rich romance of our
American past.

THE SELKIRKS

ISBN 0-451-11506-6